THE
PERFECT
KILL

A. J. Quinnell

THE PERFECT KILL

CHAPMANS

Chapmans Publishers Ltd
141–143 Drury Lane
London WC2B 5TB

A CIP catalogue record for this book is available from the British Library

ISBN 1 85592 060 3

First published by Chapmans 1992

Photoset by Ace Filmsetting Ltd, Frome, Somerset

Printed and bound in Great Britain by Clays Ltd, St Ives plc

For Jane
forever

PROLOGUE

HE WAS NOT like the others. The doctor in the makeshift mortuary noticed that immediately. As he looked down at the two
bodies the man's face showed no expression. No grief. No tears.
He looked at the girl of four whose body was totally unmarked.
She lay on the table as though asleep. Even her long dark hair
had been combed. The man's passive face shifted to the body of
the woman. The sheet was drawn up to her neck. The man
reached down and pulled the sheet back. The body was naked
and terribly mangled.

The doctor murmured, 'It must have been very quick, sir, a
matter of seconds only.'

Later the doctor was to wonder why he had called the man
'sir'. He was not in the habit of doing so. A uniformed policeman
came forward, with a pad in his hand. He looked down at the
woman's body then he looked away. He handed the pad and a
pen to the man, and said, 'Would you mind, sir?'

The man signed his name on the pad, nodded at the doctor
and the policeman, and walked out past the long rows of other
bodies. The doctor and policeman watched him go. He was a
tall, bulky man, with cropped, grey hair. He had a curious walk;
with the outside of his feet making first contact with the ground.
Both men would always remember his face. Eyes, seemingly
without interest, set deep and wide into a square face. Heavy
lidded and narrow, as if to avoid cigarette smoke, even though he
was not smoking. He had a vertical scar over his right eye, and

7

another, deep and wide, from his right cheekbone to his chin, but the doctor knew that they were old scars. As he went through the door, the policeman said, 'He didn't show much.'

'No,' the doctor corrected him. 'He showed nothing, absolutely nothing.'

He pulled the sheet up over the woman's broken body.

Although a farmer all his life, and though long used to hardship, Foster Dodd was an emotional man. He ran sheep over a hundred and fifty acres of low hills near the small Scottish town of Lockerbie. When the Pan Am jumbo jet blew up at thirty thousand feet, many of the bodies fell onto his fields, among his sheep, together with the almost intact nose cone of the aircraft. And so began a night of horror that would stay with him for the rest of his life.

It was two days later when the man came to the farm. He was accompanied by a sad-faced young policeman. Like the men in the mortuary, Foster Dodd noticed that this one was different. The others, and there had been many others, had been in a state of shock and total grief. They had invariably wept, and Foster Dodd and his wife had wept with them.

The man did not weep.

The policeman introduced them and asked, 'Would you show him where you found the young girl? The one in the bright red jumpsuit?'

They walked half a mile across the fields. It was cold, with a north wind blowing, and the farmer and the policeman were warmly clothed under their raincoats. The man wore grey corduroy trousers, a woollen checked shirt and a denim jacket. They looked as though they had been slept in. In the distance, a long line of soldiers was walking ahead of them, each one scrutinising the ground.

They reached a small group of bushes. The farmer pointed.

'I found her here. In amongst the bushes. I spotted the red of her clothing.' His voice dropped a decibel. 'It must have been instantaneous. She must have felt nothing.'

The man was looking around the fields.

'It must have been a hell of a shock for your livestock,' he muttered.

That began a conversation which would live in Foster Dodd's mind forever. For ten minutes they chatted about sheep and farming. The man was knowledgeable. He spoke with a slight American accent, in a deep, measured voice. Several times the farmer glanced at him. The slate-grey, deep-set eyes never lifted their gaze from the clump of bushes. Suddenly, Foster Dodd saw again the splash of vivid red, remembered clawing his way through the bushes, and finding the girl. Since she had no marks on her and thinking she might be alive, he had picked her up and run stumbling through the fields to the farmhouse. It had only taken seconds for the waiting doctor to examine her and shake his head. The farmer would never forget the serenity of the child's face. The memory brought back tears to his eyes and his voice broke.

The man put a hand on his shoulder and gently turned him, and they walked slowly back to the farmhouse.

Later that night, lying in bed, Foster Dodd told his wife.

'He comforted me.'

'Who?' she asked.

'The father of the little girl in the red suit. He lost his child and his wife and he comforted me . . . and he said he was sorry about the sheep we had lost.'

Peter Fleming had set up a temporary office in an empty plant that belonged to a chemical company. He was the senior officer and as Pan Am Flight 103 had come down in his district he was the man in charge of the operation. Over the past two days he had managed to snatch only a few hours' sleep. His body was tired to its bones and his mind was numb. His district was normally quiet, with one of the lowest crime rates in Britain, but no policeman in that country had more determination or tenacity. Yet again his eyes were perusing lists; passenger manifests; next of kin; identifications – list after list. He looked up as the policeman brought the man to his desk and then stood up when

9

he was introduced. As he shook hands, he said, 'I'm terribly sorry. You will have been told that it must have been so sudden that they could not have known much at all.'

The man nodded.

'I guess not.'

Fleming gestured at a chair. The man sat down and the young policeman turned away.

'Any idea what happened?' the man asked.

Fleming shook his head. 'Far too early,' he replied. 'The wreckage was scattered over a vast area. We think at least two hundred square miles. It will take many weeks before we find everything and piece it together.'

The voice that came back at him over the desk was flat and cold.

'It was a bomb.'

It was not the statement that riveted Fleming's attention; it was the voice. Low, deep and vibrant. A voice of certainty. Fleming looked into the man's eyes and said, 'We cannot know that yet. And I can make no statement until we have all the facts.'

The man nodded and stood up.

'It was a bomb,' he said. 'That's what all the facts will eventually tell you.'

Fleming also stood up.

'If it was a bomb, it will be my job to find out who put it there and to bring them to justice.'

The two men looked at each other for a long moment, then Fleming said, 'I hope you'll be able to claim the bodies within forty-eight hours. Is there anything I can do in the meantime?'

'I'd like a list of all the passengers and the names and addresses of their next of kin.'

'I'm not sure I can do that.'

'Why not?'

The policeman shrugged.

'Procedures. This kind of thing has not happened in my district.'

'Let's hope it never happens again. Anyway, for insurance

purposes the next of kin will have to form an association – will have to be in touch with each other.'

The policeman nodded.

'I suppose you're right, I'll try and get it for you before you leave.'

They shook hands and the American turned and threaded his way through the desks towards the door.

Fleming noticed something strange. There were a dozen or more policemen and policewomen sitting at the desks and manning the radio centre. They had all stopped what they were doing and were watching the man. They only resumed their work when the door had closed behind him.

Fleming pulled another list of names in front of him. It was of the next of kin. He ran a finger down it until he found a name. Then he beckoned to an assistant, handed him the list and said, 'Call Jenkins at Special Branch. Ask him to check out that man.'

The assistant turned away. Peter Fleming remained standing, looking at the closed door. He shivered slightly. He would have to order some more heaters.

ONE

IT WAS DARK and the Dobermann bitch saw nothing, heard nothing and smelled nothing. But she felt something. A sharp, stinging pain in her side. She erupted to her feet with a puzzled growl, managed to move a few paces beside the swimming pool and then her legs collapsed and she rolled onto her side. For half a minute her body twitched and then she stilled.

Thirty yards away a black-clad figure slid down a rope from the top of the high garden wall.

For several minutes it crouched, watching and waiting. There was only a faint illumination from distant street lights. Finally the black figure moved, crossing to the swimming pool, pausing for a moment to check the dog, then moving on to the rear of the house, enfolded in darkness.

Miguel was watching television: an antique episode of 'I Love Lucy'. Miguel was fascinated by Desi Arnaz's Spanish accent and assumed it paralleled his own. He was half-way through a long chuckle when he heard the click of the door. He turned in surprise. The chuckle died. He saw a man in black. Saw a squat hand-gun rising. Heard a compressed phut; felt the sting in his chest. He pushed himself up, terror on his face, a hand groping at his chest. The man in black became hazy. Miguel heard a voice: low and vibrant.

'Don't worry. No harm. You are just going to sleep.'

Miguel crumpled. He was asleep before he hit the carpet.

The dinner was boring, but necessary. There was no way that

James S. Grainger, Senior Senator for the State of Colorado, could have decently avoided it. When the Governor gave a dinner for the Secretary of State for Defence his presence was expected.

As usual of late, the Senator had drunk too much. Too many whiskies before dinner, and too much wine with it. But he knew that none of the dozen people around the dinner-table would have noticed anything. Only Harriot would have noticed, but then she would have had thirty-five years of experience to draw upon.

James S. Grainger was an intelligent and practical man. He had been taciturn during the dinner. None of the guests had expected anything else.

He was the first to leave. None of the guests was surprised. The Governor saw him to the door. Taking him by the arm, he said, 'Jim, please reconsider. I'd like you to chair that finance committee.'

They stopped in the hall. The Senator said, 'Craig, give me a couple of days to think about it . . . it's a hell of a lot of work.'

The Governor looked at him with sympathy. These past months there had been sympathy in everybody's eyes.

'Jim, maybe a heavy work-load is the best therapy.'

The Senator shrugged, 'Maybe; give me a couple of days . . . listen, Craig, I took a little too much on board tonight. Could you have your guy call me a taxi? It wouldn't be good for this Senator to be stopped by the Highway Patrol.'

The Governor grinned and looked at his watch, 'It's no problem, my driver is waiting to take the Secretary to the airport and for sure he won't leave for at least an hour and four more brandies.'

The Senator let himself into his house, which could be called a palace. In his younger days he had made a fortune out of real estate, and although he himself had simple tastes, Harriot, for all her many virtues, had a taste for grandeur. As he walked down the marble hall he wondered yet again whether he should sell the place and get something infinitely smaller.

13

He instantly dismissed the thought. Harriot was somehow still in this house. She had worked with the architect and with the builders. It was her house. He would never live anywhere else. He opened the door to the drawing-room. The lights were on. Miguel had forgotten to switch them off. It was an elegant room in the European manner.

Crystal chandeliers, heavy, comfortable chairs and settees, and a Louis XIV bureau, which Harriot had never let him take up to his study. It was a large room and at the very end of it, after a major argument with Harriot, he had installed a mahogany bar, with four black, leather-topped barstools. A man was sitting on one of them. He was a big man, dressed in black slacks and a black polo neck shirt.

He had a drink in his hand. He had scars on his face. His hair was close-cropped. He was middle-aged.

The Senator's eyes swept the room. Nothing out of place. The edge of drunkenness left him. He was instantly alert. Before he could speak or move the man said, 'Senator, I'm sorry to intrude, I mean no harm. I just need ten minutes of your time and then I will leave.'

The Senator's eyes flicked to the telephone on the bureau. Apologetically the man said, 'I disconnected it.'

The man's voice carried a faint accent from the deep South. It was a low voice, reaching up from his belly.

'Who the fuck are you? Did Miguel let you in?'

The man shook his head.

'Miguel is comfortable in his room. He will sleep quietly until the morning.'

James S. Grainger was not immune to fear. He had fought in Korea and been wounded and much decorated. At first sight of the man he had felt fear, but now it washed away. As he walked to the bar, he asked, 'Why the hell didn't you make an appointment?'

The man said, 'I rang your secretary three days ago. She asked me to state my business. I said it was personal. She told me to leave my number, which I did. I rang again the next day, twice. I told her it was personal and urgent. I know that you are leaving for Washington in the morning.'

The Senator had reached the bar. He put an elbow on it. It was exactly the right height. He had designed it so. He was facing the man.

'What's your name?' he asked.

'I use the name Taylor.'

The Senator slowly nodded his head.

'I think I recall seeing the message, but I'm a busy man, Mr Taylor.'

'So am I.'

The Senator's voice went flat. 'State your business.'

'Pan Am 103.'

The two men stared at each other. The Senator was older by ten years, smaller and thinner, grey-haired but fit. He swam seventy lengths in his pool every morning. His pool was fifty feet long. Slowly, he went behind the bar. As he poured himself a large Scotch, he asked, 'How did you get in here?'

The man said, 'Senator, you have a highly sophisticated security system. Before I leave, I will tell you how to improve it.'

'What about the Dobermann?'

'She's out, by the pool.' He held up a hand. 'Don't worry. She's just sleeping.'

The Senator was looking at the man's glass. It was almost empty.

'What are you drinking?'

Taylor pointed with his chin at the shelves behind, 'Some of your excellent Stolichnaya.'

The Senator reached behind him for the bottle, poured a generous slug, took the top off the ice-bucket and filled the glass with ice. There was a half soda bottle on the bar. The man topped up the glass and lifted it. The Senator also raised his glass and said, 'What about Pan Am 103?'

'Your wife was on it.'

'So?'

'So was mine, and my daughter.'

There was a silence, then the Senator said, 'How old was your wife?'

'Twenty-nine.'

15

'And your daughter?'

'Four.'

For reasons he could not later understand, the Senator asked, 'What were their names?'

'Nadia and Julia.'

Another silence, then in a quiet voice, the Senator said, 'My wife was called Harriot. She was sixty-three. We never had children . . . couldn't have children . . . just the two of us.'

The man topped up the drinks and brought them over.

'Let's go outside,' he said. 'For some reason I think better near water.'

The Senator took his glass and slid open the French doors. They walked around the pool to the dog. The man bent down and put a hand under its chin. He held it there for half a minute, then straightened.

'She's fine,' he said. 'She'll wake up about dawn and be in quite a bad temper.'

'And how did you take Miguel out?'

'The same way, Senator . . . after all, we are all animals.'

They walked around the pool together. The man asked, 'What are you going to do about Harriot?'

They had made two circuits of the pool before the Senator replied.

'What are you going to do about Nadia and Julia?'

'I'm going to kill the bastards that did it.'

They did two more circuits in total silence, then the Senator said, 'Let's go inside.'

He gave a wry smile. 'I have exactly the same intention. I've already started the ball rolling.'

'How?'

The Senator was a very precise man. He glanced at the calendar window of his Rolex and said, 'Three weeks ago I hired a man . . . an expert.'

'An expert what?'

'An expert killer.'

'American?'

'Yes.'

'May I know his name?'

Slowly the Senator shook his head. 'Regretfully not, that was part of the conditions of contract.'

The man sighed. 'His background then, even part of it.'

'He was a mercenary.'

'Where?'

'The Congo, Biafra, and elsewhere.'

'Tell me, Senator, who is this killer going to kill?'

The Senator shrugged. 'Obviously the target is not yet fully identified, but with my connections I have access to the interim reports of the FBI and CIA. They are already sure that it's a Palestinian group, either the PFLP or the PFLP-General Command, or Abu Nidal's group, or even the Hizbollah. They expect to have identification in a matter of months.'

'So what's your killer doing right now?'

'Preparing an operation to infiltrate into either Lebanon or Syria, depending on who the final target is.'

'Has he had experience in the Middle East?'

'Yes, extensive.'

'How did you find him?'

'He found me.'

'You checked him out of course.'

The Senator smiled. 'I had the FBI pull his file from Interpol. They keep a central data bank on all known mercenaries. As a matter of fact, it's an interesting story. He told me the story before I called the FBI. He faked his own death about five years ago. The FBI confirmed that he had been killed. The guy was some character, one of the few Americans who had done time in the French Foreign Legion.'

Very softly the man asked, 'When was that?'

'I don't know exactly, but he fought for them during the Algerian War of Liberation.'

'Do you know what battalion?'

'Not precisely, but it was a parachute battalion.'

'How much did you pay him . . . how much up front?'

Again the Senator hesitated, then said, 'The full contract was for a million bucks, twenty-five per cent up front, twenty-five per

17

cent when the target is positively identified, and the balance when he makes the kill.'

There was a silence. Then gently the Senator asked, 'Were you going to make a similar proposition?'

The man shook his head. 'Not similar. I need you for help with your connections, and access to information. I checked the background and connections of every passenger on that plane. You fitted what I needed . . . money and power which gives you access to information via the CIA and FBI. I have money of my own, but not enough. Such an operation would cost out at around five hundred thousand bucks. I would put up half and want you to put up half.'

'I guess you're too late.'

The man shook his head. 'No, Senator. I'm not too late.'

'What do you mean?'

The man shrugged. He said, 'The person you describe did serve in a parachute battalion in the Foreign Legion. He was kicked out after the Generals' revolt and became a mercenary. He did fight in the wars you have described and others. He did fake his own death about five years ago.'

'So?'

'So he is not the man you talked to. He is not the man you gave a quarter of a million bucks to three weeks ago. You've been conned, Senator.'

The Senator felt his anger rising.

'What in hell are you talking about?'

'Senator, the man you described is sitting across this bar from you right now, drinking your fine vodka. I was the only American serving with the French Foreign Legion in a Para battalion during the Algerian War of Liberation.'

The Senator's jaw dropped. The man could see the gold fillings at the back of his mouth.

'What is your real name?' he finally asked.

'Creasy.'

The jaw snapped shut. 'You can prove that of course?'

'This man came to see you. Presumably he was able to get past your secretary more easily than I was. Describe him to me.'

'He was about your age, hair moderately long but neat, grey-ing at the temples; he had a moustache and a scar on his fore-head, a thinnish face, very tanned. He would be close to six feet and he was dressed in a business suit, I would say from a good tailor.'

'His accent?'

'Mid-west, but not very pronounced, blurred . . . a bit like yours, like he had been out of America for a long time.'

The man's smile was wry. He said, 'The guy who came to see you, Senator, was Joe Rawlings . . . a con man. After you gave him the money in cash or negotiable securities, where did he say he was going?'

The Senator's face was bleak. 'He said Brussels. He was gonna meet up with some guys and recruit a couple. He said that was the place to do it.'

'Has he been in contact?'

'No, he said he would phone in a month.' He looked at his watch again, 'That will be in one week.'

'Did he leave an address?'

The Senator grimaced, 'He left a poste restante number in Brussels, and another in Cannes in the South of France.'

The man said, 'You have indeed been conned, Senator. The con would have gone as follows. In a week Rawlings would have phoned you and told you that he was forwarding an interim report. That report would arrive listing his expenses . . . which would be heavy, plus the names of various mercenaries he had recruited and various expensive equipment he had so far pur-chased, together with receipts. Once the bombers of Pan Am 103 have been identified, you would notify him to both the poste restante numbers. He would then ask for the second instalment. You will receive proof of all this in a matter of days.'

He pointed at the empty glass in front of him. 'My finger prints are on that glass. Put it in your safe. In a matter of days you will receive another finger print, it will be of Joe Rawlings. Ask your friends at the FBI to verify them both. Some time later you will receive a letter from me. Tear off the blank piece at the bot-tom right-hand corner of the page. Send it to your friends at the

FBI. It will have my thumb print on it. Do the same with any communication you receive from me. If you ever receive a phone call from me, I will start with the word "Lockerbie" and the date ten days previous.'

He stretched his shoulders again, his face was tired. So was the Senator's.

Then the Senator straightened and said grimly, 'We're going after the bastards that caused the pain.' A thought struck him. 'Will you go alone, or recruit some of your old buddies?'

Creasy shook his head.

'No. This is personal. But I will add a new element, something I may need. I will add youth. A kind of youth that I will mould myself. In a way I'll try to clone something of my past onto someone young . . . and in doing so bind him to me. It will be a kind of insurance. We don't know how long it will take to identify the target . . . it might take months or years.'

Grainger smiled and shrugged. 'I wish I had your years and skills. I'd come with you. I wish to God I could come with you.'

'From this night you are with me. From this night you are not so lonely as you were . . . and that goes for me too. From this night I have a friend . . . we will live with our grief together.'

He held Grainger by the shoulders at arms' length for a brief moment, then said, 'Senator, I'll try to get some of your money back for you . . . if there's any left. Now I have to get moving. Let's have a quick look at your security system, and reconnect your phone.'

TWO

THE FOOTBALL PITCH was small and dusty. No grass grew on the Maltese island of Gozo, at least not the type for football pitches. The ages of the boys ranged from fourteen to seventeen. Five months had passed since Pan Am 103 came down on and around Lockerbie, and it was almost the end of the football season.

The man sat beside Father Manuel Zerafa on the church steps, watching the game. The priest was in charge of the local orphanage. They had known each other and had been friends for many years.

The ball was kicked wildly upfield. There was a mêlée around it, from which emerged a dark-skinned youth, with the ball at his feet. With startling acceleration, he rounded two defenders, and coolly flicked the ball past the goalkeeper into the net.

The priest leapt up, shouting wildly and clapping his hands. He was short and round and his wild enthusiasm seemed somehow out of place.

'It's the cushion we needed,' he said, sitting down. 'The orphanage hasn't beaten Sannat for the past seven seasons.' He looked at his watch. 'Only ten minutes more. They won't get two goals in ten minutes.' The priest pointed with his chin at a man sitting the other side of the pitch and grinned wickedly.

'Father Joseph will be mad as hell.'

'Who's the boy?' Creasy asked. 'The one who scored the goal.'

'Michael Said,' the priest answered warmly. 'The best player

21

we've had in the twenty years that I've run the orphanage. One day he'll play for Malta. Hamrun Spartans want him for their youth team next season. They've agreed to pay the orphanage three hundred pounds. Can you believe that, *Uomo*?'

Because there are so many common surnames on Gozo, everyone is given a nickname. Creasy's nickname was *Uomo*. It was Italian and meant simply 'Man'.

'How old is he?'

'Just seventeen last week.'

'How long has he been at the orphanage?'

'From birth.'

Creasy was watching the boy as he moved around the pitch, dominating the game. He was not tall, nor heavily built, but he covered the dusty ground with a combination of grace and determination and he tackled even the bigger boys with fierce concentration. Creasy had been watching the boy for the past half hour, ignoring the others.

'Tell me about him,' he said.

The priest glanced up at the big man beside him.

'Haven't you seen him before?'

'Yes, around the village but I never noticed him much . . . Father, tell me about him.'

His voice was quiet and intense and the priest glanced up at his face again, then shrugged.

'It's a common enough story. His mother was a prostitute in Gzira, in Malta. From his dark skin I guess his father was an Arab. There were and are a lot of them in Gzira. She didn't want the child, so he ended up with us.'

'Does he speak Arabic?'

The priest nodded somewhat bitterly.

'Yes, very well, or so I'm told by the Kuwaiti teacher we had seconded to us for two years. He was a good man that, for an Arab. A good footballer even. He trained the juniors at Qala. He took a special interest in Michael. When the new government came in they made Arabic optional in schools. But that's a joke because they sent all the Arabic teachers home.'

At that moment the boy split the defence with a perfect

through-ball. Another orphan sped onto it and hammered it past the goalkeeper. The priest erupted with joy.

'Three–nil!' he shouted. 'We've never ever beaten Sannat by three goals.' Laughing out loud, he made a rude gesture at the other, younger priest across the pitch and got a glare in return. He sat down chuckling.

Creasy asked, 'Is he intelligent?' Father Zerafa smiled and said, 'Between you and me, that priest is an idiot. I don't know how he got through the seminary, except that his second cousin is the bishop.'

Creasy smiled, 'I meant the boy.'

'Of course he is,' the priest answered. 'Anyone who can make a pass like that has to be intelligent. I tell you, he'll play for Malta.'

'What about other subjects, apart from Arabic and football?'

'Yes, consistently good.'

'In other sports?'

'He's the best table tennis player in the orphanage, and there are some good ones. Apart from football, that's about the only recreation they get.'

Creasy's eyes had never left the moving boy.

'And his character,' he asked. 'What about his character?'

The priest spread his hands. 'Difficult to fathom, he's a loner. We have sixty-eight boys in the orphanage, and most of them seem to form groups within their ages. But Michael never joined a group. He's got a couple of friends, but I couldn't say they were very close.'

There was a silence between them and the priest could sense Creasy's continuing curiosity.

He went on: 'Like all young boys he's sometimes naughty, but less than most, and now hardly ever at all.'

'Did he ask about his parents?'

'Yes, on his thirteenth birthday he came to see me, and he asked.'

'And what did you tell him?'

'The truth.'

'What did he say?'

23

'He said nothing. He thanked me for telling him and left the room. He has never mentioned the subject since.'

Another silence, and then Creasy asked quietly: 'Is he religious?'

Sadly the priest shook his head. 'I fear not.'

'But he attends Mass?'

'He has to. They all have to, but not with great enthusiasm.'

The referee blew the final whistle and the orphan players all hugged each other. Creasy and the priest stood up, the priest brushing the dust from his cassocked backside.

'Could you send him to see me?' Creasy asked.

Father Zerafa looked surprised. 'To see you? Up at the house?'

Creasy was looking across the pitch over the low village houses towards a long ridge. On its left, nestling below the highest point, was an old stone farmhouse, blending into the hill.

'Yes,' he said, 'at the house, at around six o'clock this evening.'

He turned to look at the priest.

'It was a good win, Father. Well done.' He punched the priest lightly on the shoulder and walked down the steps of the church to his jeep.

The priest watched him drive off and was then engulfed by his players.

The sun was dipping to the west as the boy walked up the dusty path to the house on the hill. The priest had been brief as usual. Back at the orphanage, he had simply taken him aside and said:

'Go up and see *Uomo* at his house at six o'clock.'

'What for?' the boy had asked.

The priest had shrugged, 'I don't know. Just be there.'

The boy knew all about *Uomo*, or at least what everyone else on the small island knew. Apart from his nickname, he was also known in Maltese as *Il Mejjet*: The Dead One. He knew that some years ago, *Uomo* had spent several months on the island and then disappeared. Knew that he had returned in the night some months later, and remembered that he and all the other boys had been told by Father Zerafa never to talk about him. He knew something else. Gozo was the most religious community on earth in that more than ninety-five per cent of the population attended church. He knew, on that same Sunday, every priest in every church on the island had included in their homilies a message to their congregation.

'Do not speak about the man known as *Uomo*, especially to strangers. He is one of us.'

Naturally, on a small island, everyone immediately talked of *Uomo*, but only among themselves and never to strangers, not even to Maltese. And so in that small community the rumours grew and multiplied. The boy knew that *Uomo* had returned on a police launch, in the middle of the night. He knew that for many months he had stayed without going out in the farmhouse of Paul Schembri and later had married his daughter Nadia, and they had had a baby girl. He knew that the wife and daughter had been killed in the Pan Am crash, over Lockerbie.

He knew something else. The boy was friendly with the son of Rita, who ran the village grocer shop. Her husband was a policeman and a member of the élite squad that was formed within the police force to act against any terrorist attacks that might take place against Malta. His friend had told him some years ago that Creasy had helped train that squad in weaponry and tactics. It was no coincidence that Paul Schembri, the farmer, had a nephew, who had been and still was the commanding officer of that squad.

He reached the farmhouse, sweating slightly and very curious. There was a rubble wall around the farmhouse which looked very old, but the boy knew it had been built only a few years ago. From the village, the boy had watched it being built and sometimes had walked across the ridge and watched the workers converting the farmhouse, using only old stone. The wall was five feet thick and about twelve feet high. Set into it was a wide wooden door, and beside that an old-fashioned metal bell handle.

The boy was wearing frayed jeans and a T-shirt. He tucked the

25

T-shirt tighter into the jeans and pulled the bell handle, curious and a little nervous. From inside he heard the bell tinkle, a minute later the door opened.

The man was wearing a brightly coloured swimsuit and nothing else. There were terrible scars down his left side and across his stomach and also from his right knee, disappearing under his swimsuit. The man held out his hand and said, 'Hello Michael, welcome.'

Michael shook his hand and noticed immediately that the little finger was missing. He also noticed the mottled scars on the back of the hand, on the backs of both hands. The man released his grip and stood aside. The boy passed through the door. In front of him was a wide expanse of limestone paving, surrounding a blue rectangular swimming pool. The pale limestone was relieved by splashes of colour. Palms, bougainvillaea and vines, spread up the walls of the house and over a wooden trellis work, extending out from the two wings. Under the shade of the trellis was a round stone table, surrounded by old, wooden chairs. The man gestured towards the table.

'Have a seat. What do you drink?'

The boy was stuck for an answer. The man said, 'It's quite a walk up here. Some cool wine or a cold beer?'

Pocket money from the orphanage was minimal, and the boy had only drunk alcohol during the village feast the year before.

'Could I have a lager?' he asked.

'Sure. I'll join you with the same.'

The man went into the house and the boy stood by the table, looking out at the vista of Gozo spread in front of him, and in the distance the small island of Comino, and beyond that the island of Malta. At that time of the year it was a vision of patchwork: green fields, deep blue sea and light blue sky. The house was set on the highest point of Gozo. He was looking down on the capital and the ancient Citadel. At that moment the boy decided that it was the most perfect spot in the only place he had ever known.

THREE

FATHER MANUEL ZERAFA was not a man to be surprised easily. He had been a priest for thirty-three years, the first ten of which had been spent in Somalia and northern Kenya. He was a man of the world and knew the world. He sat on the balcony of Gleneagles Bar in Mgarr, looking out over the small harbour and the brightly-coloured traditional fishing boats. Creasy sat next to him. Both had empty glasses in their hands. For several minutes the priest digested the words he had just heard. Then, without turning his head, he said in a sombre voice, 'You would have to marry again . . . It's the regulations, *Uomo* . . . only a married couple.'

Uomo nodded, 'I understand that.'

Now the priest turned his head sharply. Surprise showed in his eyes and also shock.

'You will marry again so soon?'

Again Creasy nodded, 'As you say, it's necessary.'

The priest shook his head. 'The people here would be shocked, even offended. They all loved Nadia. They all know how much you loved her . . . It's only been five months . . . The church was overflowing at the mass we said for her and Julia. It had never been so full.'

'It will be a marriage of convenience, Father, only to satisfy the authorities . . . your authorities.'

Again the priest was shaking his head.

'But whom will you marry?' he asked.

'I don't know.'

27

The priest's head snapped up in surprise.

'You don't know! You want to rush this adoption through in the shortest time and you don't know whom you are going to marry?' he snorted, almost in derision. 'She'll have to be acceptable to the panel who will interview you both to be sure you're suitable parents.'

Gruffly Creasy said, 'She will be acceptable.'

The priest sighed. 'But why the rush? Why not wait at least a year? It will be more acceptable to the panel and to the people here. Besides, you've only spoken to the boy once.'

'That was enough,' the American answered. Abruptly, he reached for the priest's empty glass and stood up. He walked into the cool, high-ceilinged bar and put the glasses in front of the balding bartender, 'Two more lagers, Tony, please.'

There was a group of fishermen playing cards in the corner, a local game called Bixkla, a game where it was necessary to cheat in collaboration with your partner. They excelled at it. Creasy watched them bluff and counter-bluff while Tony filled the glasses. One of the fishermen winked at him. He was the only foreigner who could ever hold his own at the game. He picked up the glasses and said, 'Have one yourself, Tony.'

The bartender shook his head, 'It's too early for me.'

Creasy waited patiently. After ten seconds the bartender grinned from ear to ear and said, 'Blue Label Beer.'

Creasy turned away. It was always like that. It was no coincidence that the bartender's nickname was 'Why Not'.

Back on the balcony, he handed the priest the glass.

It was early evening. A big, white ferry was pulling away from the jetty, taking the day-trippers back to Malta. The lowering sun was turning the limestone hills a coppery colour.

'You said, six to eight weeks.'

The priest sighed, 'Yes, but only with a lot of hustling and only because the bishop knows you and you have connections with the civil authorities.'

Creasy took a sip of his beer. 'Then I'll talk to the boy tomorrow, and the day after I'll leave. I'll be back within four weeks with a wife and all the legal documentation. How long will she have to stay?'

The priest turned to look at him, the puzzled look back in his eyes.

'What do you mean?'

'I mean how long will the wife have to stay in Gozo?'

Slowly, awareness came into the priest's eyes.

'So it's like that?'

The ferry was turning out of the harbour entrance. Quietly Creasy said, 'Yes, Father, it is exactly like that!'

The priest said, 'At least six months, otherwise it would be too obvious. It would make me look bad and the panel look even worse. She would have to stay in your house and cohabit with you and the boy, and live the part of his mother.' A note of sternness crept into his voice. 'Six months, *Uomo.*'

Creasy drained his glass and stood up, 'So be it,' he said. 'Six months. Will you talk to the bishop tomorrow and then to the boy? And then send him up to the house to see me at six o'clock . . . That's assuming that he wants to come.'

The priest made one last effort. Looking up at the man he said, 'Why not wait a few months . . . why not adopt a younger boy? I have several that would be suitable.'

Creasy shrugged, 'I'm sure you do, but I want Michael Said, and I want him within eight weeks.' He turned and went out.

At the orphanage, Michael Said sat in a corner of the courtyard, looking at a magazine without seeing it. His mind was in the house on the hill, and the evening before.

He had stayed for two hours at the table under the trellis, and during those two hours he had drunk three lagers. At one stage the big American had gone to the kitchen and returned with a large plate. On it were thin strips of dried beef.

He said, 'In America we call it "jerky" but I learned to make it in Rhodesia.' He glanced at the boy, 'Do you know what Rhodesia is called now?'

'Zimbabwe,' the boy replied instantly.

The man's head nodded in approval. He munched a strip of

beef and said, 'There they call it biltong, and there they make it from game, usually gazelle. It's heavily salted and then hung in the sun for several days. It keeps for years. A man can survive on ten pounds of biltong for several weeks.' He had pointed with his chin towards the village.

'I have to use beef, which I get from John the butcher. Try some.'

The boy picked up a piece of meat and put it in his mouth. It tasted like leather. He chewed vigorously. It tasted like salty leather.

He chewed some more and began to taste the meat. He decided it was delicious. Within fifteen minutes the plate had been cleared.

They had talked. The American had asked many questions. The boy realised now that he had been probing his mind. At the house he had not noticed it. He had answered the questions easily, without difficulty. After the second beer, he was relaxed enough to say the words he had been rehearsing all the way up the hill.

Looking straight into the big man's eyes, he asked, 'What do I call you?'

The man had smiled slightly. 'Creasy,' he said. 'Drop the "Mr"; or by my nickname. You know what that is?'

The boy had nodded and said very simply, '*Uomo*, I want to tell you how sorry I am about your wife and daughter. We are all sorry. She used to bring presents to the orphanage at Christmas and she used to bring special food sometimes. Good cuts of meat, I think from her father's farm, and lots of fruit. We all miss her.'

He was still looking into the man's eyes. They had showed no emotion. Heavy-lidded, almost drowsy, they had just stared back at the boy. Then he had nodded, stood up and gone into the kitchen to fetch two more lagers.

They had talked on as the sun dipped away behind them. The boy had felt relaxed enough to ask questions of his own. The first was, 'How did you get the scars, *Uomo*?'

The man shrugged. 'In several wars.'

30

'Where?'

'All over. Africa, North, South and West. Asia, the Middle East. All over.'

The boy felt emboldened.

'Were you a mercenary?' he asked.

'Anyone who works for money is a mercenary.'

'Have you killed many people?'

There was a long silence. The man was looking out, over the undulations and the villages of Gozo, across the blue waters, and over Comino and Malta.

Very quietly, he gave the standard reply, 'I can't remember.'

Then Creasy had stood up, saying, 'Can you swim?'

'Of course.'

'Let's go then.'

'But I didn't bring my trunks.'

The American had smiled, 'You don't need any, but if you're shy, swim in your underpants.'

The boy had taken off all his clothes. They swam together. The pool was forty feet long. At one point the man had said, 'I'll race you two lengths.'

The boy was a good swimmer and fast, but he lost by six feet. As he clung to the edge of the pool, he gasped, 'You are strong, *Uomo.*'

The man had smiled, 'I swim a hundred lengths every morning . . . It's the best exercise a man can get.'

When the boy was leaving, the man had said to him at the gate in a low and serious voice, 'I will talk to you again, Michael. In a couple of days. After that, you can come up here any time you want. Use the pool, help yourself to a lager . . . but you must always come alone.' The boy said nothing. Halfway down, he had stopped and looked back up at the house. He had stood there for many minutes, totally still, just looking. Then he had continued down to the village.

31

FOUR

FATHER MANUEL ZERAFA had not slept well. Just before he had gone to bed in his sparse, simple room, a thought had crept into his head. A thought that had troubled his sleep and woken him several times.

In the morning he had phoned the bishop's secretary and arranged an appointment for three o'clock in the afternoon. Then he rearranged his own day. At exactly one o'clock he was driving his battered twenty-year-old Hillman down the track to Paul Schembri's farmhouse on the slopes leading up to Nadur. He knew that, like all farmers, Paul Schembri would have come in from his fields at noon and by now would just have finished a hearty lunch.

His timing was perfect. As he brushed past the fly netting across the open door, the farmer and his son Joey were wiping up the last of the gravy from their plates with chunks of bread. Paul's wife Laura could be seen through the kitchen door, washing up. He had not seen them since the Mass for Nadia and Julia. Paul was small, dark and wiry, in his mid-fifties. His wife was younger and bigger. A tall, handsome woman. Their son Joey favoured his mother's looks: also tall, but wiry like his father and with a good-looking, open face. They looked up at the priest, a little surprised.

Immediately, Paul said, 'Joey, fetch some wine for Father Manuel.'

He gestured at a chair and the priest sat down.

'Have you eaten?'

32

'Yes, thank you.'

While the boy was in the kitchen, the priest said, 'Paul, I have to talk to you. Alone.'

'About what?'

'About Creasy.'

The farmer had known the priest for many years. He nodded, popped the last piece of bread in his mouth, stood up and called, 'Joey, bring the wine outside and two glasses.'

The priest and the farmer sat on the patio, looking out to sea, talking in quiet voices and consuming the large bottle of wine made by the farmer from his own grapes.

When they stood up the farmer said, 'I think you're right, Father. It can only be that. We both know what kind of man he is. He would never marry again so soon, if ever, unless it was for that reason.'

Both men looked sombre and the farmer said, 'Shall I talk to him? Tomorrow's Sunday. He always comes for lunch on Sunday and stays until evening. Shall I?'

Slowly the priest shook his head.

'No, Paul, thank you.'

He was not a man often to ask advice but he knew this farmer and his wisdom.

'Tell me, Paul, I see the bishop at three o'clock. Shall I mention this to him? I mean about what we think. I have to get his clearance for this adoption, even before it goes to the panel.'

The farmer thought for a long time and then smiled slightly.

'Father Manuel, the bishop is a good man and a holy man with many worries. After all, our thoughts are only speculation.'

The priest drained his glass, reached down and put it on the table.

'You make good wine, Paul . . . and strong.'

At four o'clock in the afternoon Father Manuel Zerafa arrived at the American's house. He refused the offer of a drink.

As he sat down under the trellis, the man asked, 'Have you talked to the bishop?'

The priest nodded, 'Yes, there are no problems, there will be no hold-ups.'

'Have you talked to the boy?'

The priest shook his head, 'No, I'll talk to him when I leave here, if I'm satisfied with what you tell me.'

The American was sitting opposite him, across the round table and looking at him steadily.

'But I talked to Paul Schembri today. He agrees with me.'

'Agrees with you?'

The priest sighed, 'That you are going to use the boy.'

'Use him how?'

The priest wiped a hand across his face.

'For vengeance!' he said.

The American stood up, walked to the pool and stood looking down. He was only wearing a swimsuit. His feet were bare. The priest straightened in his chair and looked at him. Looked at the scars. He sighed again. It was a day for sighs. He spoke softly to the scarred back, '*Uomo*, I know what you did those years ago in Italy. It was an ungodly act.'

The man did not turn. He remained standing, totally still, looking down at the pool. The priest went on.

'Vengeance belongs to God. Yes, they were evil men, but God gave you no licence to kill them.'

Now the man turned and looked at the priest.

'If there is a God', he said, 'then maybe, just maybe, he hands out a few licences, now and again.'

The priest raised his eyebrows.

'To the Godless?' he asked.

The man's smile did not reach his eyes.

'Who else?' he said. 'If your old car broke down, would you ensure that the mechanic who fixed it was a God-fearing man, or would you worry more that he was a good mechanic?'

The priest gritted his teeth. His old Hillman often broke down and Paulu Zarb was the best mechanic on Gozo. He always fixed it. Knew it like a child. Paulu Zarb was one of the few men on Gozo who never went to church or, if he could avoid it, near one. The American was well aware who fixed the priest's car.

The priest was slowly shaking his head.

'Creasy,' he said, his voice sad, 'nothing will bring Nadia and Julia back.'

The American moved to the table and sat down.

'Exactly. But Father Manuel, apart from believing in God, don't you believe in justice?'

'Vengeance is not justice.'

The man's voice was grim. 'It is in my book.'

The two men looked at each other across the table, then the priest said, 'You will use the boy as a weapon.'

'Only if I have to.'

'But he is only just seventeen . . . and are you no longer a weapon yourself?'

The scarred man shrugged.

'Yes, but this weapon is getting old. Yes the boy is only seventeen but if I need him it will not be next month or even maybe next year. Vengeance . . . even justice has patience! It will take time to identify the target.'

The priest drew hope from that last statement.

'Are you sure it will ever be identified?' he asked.

The American immediately sensed his own strategy.

'It's impossible to be sure,' he answered, shaking his head. 'This adoption is only a contingency. It might take several years.'

'He will have to know,' the priest said. 'I'll only go along with it if the boy knows.'

The man nodded. 'I understand your position, Father. You can tell him everything that we have talked of. He is intelligent as you know. He is almost a man. Let him make his own decision.'

The priest shook his head.

'No, *Uomo*, I will only tell him that you wish to adopt him and only on the condition that *you* will tell him exactly why you want to adopt him. Then let him make his decision.'

'You accept the word of a Godless man?'

The priest moved toward the gate saying, 'I will accept your word, *Uomo*. I will talk to the boy and if he wishes it, I will send him up to see you.'

At the gate the priest turned and looked at the American.

'There is something you should know, *Uomo*. When Michael Said was seven years old a couple from Malta wanted to adopt him. They were a very pleasant couple who could not have children. There's a system in our rules that if within one month either the parents or the boy wish to break the arrangement, then that is permissible. Within three days, they brought him back to the orphanage, and they would not or could not explain why. When I questioned him, he just shrugged. When he was thirteen, another couple wanted to adopt him. He was a wealthy Arab businessman, living in Rome. She was an Italian. They had adopted two other children, a boy from Vietnam and a girl from Cambodia. They were a fine couple. He talked to them for five minutes and then walked out of the room.'

'Thank you for telling me,' the American said.

Creasy worked in his study in the old part of the farmhouse. It was the only upstairs room and backed directly onto the rock-face of the ridge. Its ceiling was high and arched. Down the length of one wall was a long old refectory table. On it were piles of newspaper cuttings and magazines. Opposite, against the other wall, was a row of heavy steel filing cabinets. His desk was in front of a large arched doorway. From it, he could look down over the surrounding wall at the track which led up to the house. He was going through a batch of magazines and cuttings which had arrived that morning. He had clipping services in London, New York and Bonn. Anything that appeared in any newspaper or magazine which referred to Lockerbie was sent to him. The flow had slowed down a lot over the last three months but was still enough to keep him busy for two or three hours a day. He was reading an article in *Time* magazine, speculating about a connection between the bombing and Arab terrorist organisations in Germany and Scandinavia. Occasionally, he jotted a note on a pad beside him. More often, he lifted his head and looked down at the track leading up from the village. Each time he did that, he would then glance at his watch.

It was an hour after the priest had left when he saw the boy far down on the track, walking steadily upwards. He concentrated again on the article. He had left the gates of the house open.

Fifteen minutes later he heard the gates close. He stood up, moved round the desk and looked down. The boy was standing by the pool, wearing a Pink Floyd T-shirt and jeans.

'I'll be down in ten minutes,' he called. 'Help yourself to a drink and there's some biltong in the cupboard above the fridge.'

He went back behind the desk and concentrated on the article.

They walked around the pool, the boy on the outside. There was a faint south-westerly blowing, rustling the palms. They walked steadily for half an hour. When they finally stopped, they stood, looking at the house.

The American said, 'When I die, this house will be yours and enough money to maintain it.'

The boy looked at the house for a few minutes, then turned and for another minute looked out at the view of the islands, then back at the American. Almost imperceptibly he nodded his head.

They resumed walking.

'What happened with that first couple who wanted to adopt you?'

The boy spread his hands, 'I don't know. I suppose they just didn't like me.'

'Did you like them?'

'They were all right. The food was better than at the orphanage.'

Creasy looked down at the boy, 'And what about the second couple, when you were thirteen?'

Michael Said shrugged and said, 'He was an Arab.'

Creasy stopped walking. The boy walked on a few paces, then also stopped and turned. They looked at each other.

The boy smiled slightly and said in perfect Arabic, 'Yes, *Uomo*, you chose well.'

They started walking again. And talking in Arabic, a language he had learned during years in the Foreign Legion in Algeria, Creasy said, 'So why did you choose to come with me?'

This time it was the boy who stopped. He was looking at the house again and then at the vista sweeping beneath it.

Reverting to English he said simply, '*Uomo*, you will know that my mother was a whore.'

At the gate, Creasy reached into his pocket and handed the boy a bunch of keys, saying, 'I'll be leaving tomorrow and will be gone between two and four weeks. Use the house. You will have to sleep at the orphanage until the papers go through in about eight weeks. I will return with the woman.'

They shook hands and the boy walked down the track without looking back. The American stood by the open gate watching until he had disappeared into the village. Then he went back up to his study. He phoned the airport to make his booking and then spent two hours working through the stacks of magazines and cuttings.

FIVE

SHE WAS THE seventh out of the fourteen he had interviewed the previous day. This was the second interview, the one where he would tell her the full details of the job and the role.

They sat facing each other across the table in the drab interview room of the Agency office in London, just off Wardour Street in Soho. He had the open file in front of him. It contained a typical actress portfolio. He guessed that the photos had been taken some years ago. She retained a severe attractiveness and from the way she walked and held herself she had obviously kept herself fit. He looked again at the name at the top of the portfolio. Leonie Meckler. She was dressed in a smart, two-piece black suit, with a cream blouse.

He noted her age on the file, thirty-eight.

'When did you last work?' he asked.

'Eight months ago,' she answered. 'I had a small part in a TV serial.'

'And before that?'

'I did some fringe work at the Edinburgh Festival the year before.'

She had a sad look on her dark face. She smiled grimly, 'If I were in great demand, I wouldn't be sitting here.'

'Why are you sitting here?'

Again the grim smile.

'I have a flat in Pimlico, and with the interest rates what they are at the moment, I stand to lose it if I don't find work soon. It's all I own apart from my clapped-out Ford Fiesta.'

He looked down at the portfolio again. It had only scant personal details.

'Were you ever married?' he asked.

She nodded.

'Children?'

She nodded again. 'A son.'

'How old?'

'He was eight.'

She reached for her handbag and took out a packet of cigarettes.

'Do you mind?'

'No.'

She lit up and inhaled deeply. He noticed again the nicotine stains on her fingers.

She exhaled and said, with only a trace of bitterness, 'His father was a very heavy drinker . . . an alcoholic. He was driving him home from prep-school one afternoon, after a heavy liquid lunch. He hit the back of a container lorry on the motorway. My son died.'

'And the father?'

'He survived.'

'Where is he now?'

She shook her head. She had straight, black hair to her shoulders, 'I don't know. I divorced him very soon after.'

There was a silence, then Creasy asked, 'Do you have a drink problem?'

Again, she shook her head and said firmly, 'No, and I never have. I enjoy a glass or two of wine. That's all.'

He studied her face, then he pushed a pad and pen across the table to her and said, 'I'm going to tell you what the job is, precisely. It will be easier if you don't interrupt. Just make notes about any questions you want to ask at the end.'

He talked for fifteen minutes and when he finished she was looking down at an empty pad.

'Any questions?' he asked.

She lifted her head. 'Just two. First, can you give me a thumbnail sketch of the boy?'

He thought for a moment and replied, 'As I told you, he's just seventeen years old. He's intelligent but does not communicate too well ... perhaps chooses not to. He's been in an orphanage all his life. Although it's a caring one it tends to make a child mentally tough and withdrawn. I doubt that he will stir any maternal instincts.'

She smiled wryly and said, 'Second question, of course, is money. Harry said it would be good . . . how good?'

The American closed the portfolio, stood up and stretched.

'As I told you, it's essential that you stay the full six months, not a day less. In four days, I will phone and let you know if you have the job.' He stopped and looked at her. 'During those four days, I will be having you checked out . . . very thoroughly, and during those four days you can reconsider. If you check out and you accept the job we will go to a lawyer, of your choice, and draw up the contracts. At the same time we will post the banns at the Register Office. You will then receive three thousand pounds for expenses and I will give the lawyer a certified cheque for fifty thousand American dollars, which he will hold in escrow for you until he receives a declaration from a Gozitan notary confirming

40

that you have spent six consecutive months in cohabitation with me in Gozo. During those six months you will receive an allowance of one thousand American dollars a month. Of course I will pay all household expenses. You will have your own car.' He smiled slightly. 'Coincidentally, a not-so-clapped-out Ford Fiesta, but you will not have an independent social life.' He could see that she was calculating the sums in her head.

'Does it cover your mortgage?' he asked.

For the first time, her whole face smiled.

'Yes, it does, and more besides . . . I hope I check out OK.'

'So do I. I'll call you in four days, Ms Meckler.'

She wore a simple, white lace dress, slim-fitting to just above her knees. Tapered at the waist, it revealed her soft, long curves. She showed considerable beauty. He wore beige cotton trousers, teamed with a salmon-coloured polo shirt and brown suede brogues.

They stood in front of the registrar, who decided that they made a handsome couple. He also decided that this was a marriage of convenience. He had married thousands of couples and his judgement was honed. First the man had arrived without a ring. The registrar had pointed out, tartly, that although it was not a necessity, it was a nicety. The man had gone off down the King's Road to a jeweller's and come back with what must have been the cheapest ring in the shop. Also the registrar had to verify the various documents. The two birth certificates, her divorce papers, and his late wife's death certificate. He had noted the date on the latter document, 21 December 1988 – only six months previous. Yes, it was certainly a marriage of convenience, but the registrar couldn't fathom what the convenience might be. Usually, it was a would-be immigrant, marrying a British girl for permanent status.

They had not even brought the required two witnesses and so the registrar had drafted in a clerk and his secretary. When the brief ceremony was over they did not kiss, but they did shake hands with the registrar and the witnesses.

*

41

Back on the pavement of the King's Road, Creasy looked at his watch and said, 'I have to grab a cab and head for Heathrow.'

She nodded solemnly.

'When will you call?'

'In about a week.'

She noticed the impatience on his face but said stubbornly, 'When will we leave for Gozo? I need to know. If I can let my flat, it will help with the mortgage over the next six months.'

He answered, 'Between two and three weeks from now . . . I'll call you.'

He turned away and walked down the street.

She stood on the crowded pavement, watching him, with his strange walk, weave through the pedestrians. The sides of his feet seemed to come into contact with the ground first.

She looked down at her dress and her new shoes and felt somehow used. She looked up. He was walking back. He came close to her. 'How much remains on your mortgage?'

'Thirteen thousand four hundred and twenty pounds and fifty-seven pence.'

'How much interest do you pay?'

'Seventeen and a half per cent.'

For half a minute he calculated. Then he reached into his hip pocket and pulled out a thick roll of hundred dollar bills. He counted off several, put them in her hand and said, 'That will take care of the interest for the next six months . . . I'll call you.'

She stood, clutching the money, watching him walk away. He hailed a cab and ducked in. She turned and walked down the road, until she came to a wine bar. She went straight to the ladies' room, counted the money and made her own calculation. It was at least a hundred dollars more than she needed.

She checked her face in the mirror and walked out to the bar.

'What's the most expensive vintage champagne you have?'

'Dom Perignon, '59.'

'I'll have a bottle.'

He served her the bottle of champagne in an ice bucket at a table in the corner.

An hour later the bartender watched as she drained the last drop. Then she took a handkerchief from her handbag and wiped the tears from her cheeks.

Joe Rawlings had paid top money, and when he paid top money he expected the best, the very best. He was in a suite at the Carlton Hotel in Cannes. That was certainly the best, but the girl under him was not the best, and he had paid top money.

'Turn over,' he muttered. She turned over. He tried to force himself into her rectum. She muttered something in French, and pulled away.

'Dammit,' he snarled, 'I gave you five hundred bucks up front.'

'For that it's another five hundred,' she said flatly.

He cursed and then said, 'OK bitch.'

He tried again, and again she writhed away.

'Five hundred in my hand,' she said.

Another curse. He rolled off the bed and walked into the bathroom. A minute later he came out holding five hundred-dollar bills. She was lying on her stomach, her bottom raised, her left hand open. He put the bills into her hand. She pulled them in front of her face and studied them all carefully, just as she had the first five.

'All right,' she said. 'Go ahead.'

It was brutal, but it didn't last long. There was not a shred of gentleness in him. When it was over, he rolled off with a satisfied grunt.

Within seconds she had gathered her clothes and her large handbag and disappeared into the bathroom. Within five minutes she came back out fully dressed. She did not look at him, just walked out into the lounge and then into the corridor; the door slammed behind her.

'Bitch,' he thought, but then all his thoughts were frozen. The heavy maroon curtains opening onto the balcony had parted and a man was standing there.

Joe Rawlings always liked to have sex with the lights full on. He recognised the man instantly and his heart turned to ice.

The man, dressed in black trousers and a black long-sleeved

43

polo neck shirt, walked over and stood looking down at him.

'Hello Joe,' he said. 'Or should I say hello Creasy?'

The man held a black bag in his right hand, the kind of bag that doctors carry around. It was a full minute before Joe Rawlings moved. He edged himself up on the bed into a half sitting position.

'Go and get it, Joe.'

Joe Rawlings's eyes were those of a cornered snake looking into the eyes of a mongoose. His voice was a croak. 'Get what?'

'The money, Joe, what's left of it – go get the money – it's in the bathroom.'

Again a croak, 'What money?'

'The money Senator James S. Grainger gave you, Joe . . . the sodomy money, Joe. Go get it, and if you leave as much as a single dime, I'll cut your prick off . . . and Joe, if I do that the girl who just left would give me the whole damn thousand back.'

Joe Rawlings very slowly, very carefully rolled off the bed. He moved to the chair on which his clothes were draped.

'No, Joe. Go into that bathroom naked.'

Rawlings crept to the bathroom door. He had matted black hair on his back. As he reached the door the voice stopped him. The voice that was so soft, so gentle.

'Joe, also bring the gun, the little Beretta – the one you always leave with your stash. And Joe, when you come out of that bathroom door, you will be carrying the bucks in your right hand and holding the Beretta in your left – holding it by the end of the barrel between your thumb and forefinger.'

Rawlings was about to move, but the voice came again, as soft as silk, 'On the other hand, Joe, if you want to hold it by the butt you do just that.'

The snake moved into the bathroom. The mongoose dropped the black bag on the floor, spread his legs and slipped his right hand into his trouser pocket.

A minute later the snake came out of the bathroom. In his right hand he held a thick wad of hundred dollar bills. In his left, a small black gun. He held it by the end of the barrel, between his thumb and forefinger.

Creasy said, 'Toss them both onto the bed, Joe.'

The money and the gun thumped onto the bed.

Creasy reached down, picked up the black bag and gestured at the door to the lounge.

The left index finger came off easily, but then the instrument was a surgeon's saw, and Creasy was a powerful man. He had used only a heavy local anaesthetic, the rest of Joe Rawlings's hand and left arm would be numb and senseless for twenty-four hours. They sat side by side. On the table in front of them were the twelve inch square wooden block, the small silvery surgeon's saw, the syringe, the electric cauterising iron, the gauze and the bandages. Creasy worked swiftly and with great expertise. He laid the severed finger on the block, cauterised the bleeding stump, applied some ointment and gauze, and then bandaged the whole hand.

From the black bag he took out a small heavy metal box and opened it. A white vapour erupted. He placed the finger into the box pushing it down into the dry ice and closed it tight. As he packed everything away he continued in the same low silky voice.

'You ever use my name again, Joe, I know where to find you ... every hole, every pit, every sleazy little swamp, even if you are paying a thousand bucks a night for it.'

The snake sat totally immobile, looking down at his bandaged hand. He said, 'I thought you were dead ... everyone thought you were dead.'

'I am, Joe, and if anyone ever finds out differently you will be also.'

He walked into the bedroom and came back out carrying the wad of money. The snake had not moved a millimetre. Creasy counted off a hundred of the bills and laid them in front of Rawlings.

'Ten thousand bucks, Joe ... Tap City Money, Joe ... next time play in a different poker game.'

Creasy picked up the bag and let himself out into the corridor.

SIX

MICHAEL SAID EXPLORED the house. He roamed around it as though he owned it. It was a very special feeling. He knew that it had been designed by Creasy's wife Nadia and that for two years she had overseen the construction of the new wing and the reconstruction of the old part. All the rooms were large with high, arched ceilings. Creasy was a man who liked space.

Although the construction was in the old manner using huge limestone slabs cut from the local quarry, the windows were not usual. They were rectangular and very large and from every room a different vista opened up over the island.

He walked across a small patio into a bedroom. It had its own bathroom and from its windows he could see the lighthouse at Ghasri and out across the open sea. He knew that in about eight weeks it would be the place where he would sleep.

On the wall hung two portraits painted in oil. One was of Nadia, the other of Julia aged about two. Creasy had shown him the two paintings and had said, 'The woman who's coming only represents a practicality and a convenience. Nadia and Julia will be your family.'

He stood looking at the paintings for a long time, then he walked into the bathroom. It was also overly large; in one corner was a shower with a huge old copper showerhead. In another corner was a high wooden bathtub. The toilet was in a separate cubicle.

He remembered during one of his conversations with Creasy how the man had told him of his first visit to Japan. He had been

46

with a Japanese woman in a typical country inn. She had filled the wooden bathtub while he undressed. He had walked into the bathroom and climbed into the tub. The girl had been horrified. 'How come you wash in your own dirt?' she asked him. 'A tub is only for soaking afterwards,' and she had made him climb out and sit on a small wooden stool. She had emptied and refilled the tub, and while it filled she had poured small buckets of water over him and washed him as he sat on the stool and shampooed his hair. Then they had both climbed into the steaming tub and soaked for half an hour.

Creasy had explained that since this was the first house he had ever owned, all the three bathrooms would be Japanese style. First a shower, then a soak.

'Did Nadia used to wash you?' the boy had asked. Creasy had nodded sombrely, 'Yes, always. It was a ritual. And she used to shampoo my hair.'

The boy walked out to the front of the house and dived into the pool. Very steadily he swam for sixty lengths. At the end his muscles ached. But by the time the man came back, he would be swimming more than a hundred lengths. By then, he would beat him over two lengths or four lengths or over any distance.

Leonie Meckler spent some of her expense money. It had been many years since she had been on a shopping spree. She had checked out the climatic conditions of Gozo over the next six months. She knew that it would be mostly hot and bought a selection of brightly-coloured sarongs and swimsuits, and loose shorts and T-shirts for the day. For the night she chose long and flowing cotton dresses, mainly backless, but fitting only at the waist. She then went to her favourite French cosmetics counter, Lancôme, and bought face creams and make-up, choosing only natural colours, peaches and beiges.

SEVEN

WHEN IN WASHINGTON Senator James S. Grainger was always at his desk by eight a.m., and always worked steadily through the morning until one p.m. On this morning his direct private telephone rang at precisely nine a.m. He heard the crackle hum of an overseas call. The voice said, 'Lockerbie, May 15th.'

The Senator glanced at his Rolex. The date window showed May 25th.

'Go ahead,' he said.

'At ten o'clock a package will be delivered to your office by a DHL courier whose name is Harry White; he will insist on delivering it to you personally. The package is from me. Do not let that package go through the normal security checks. Open it when you're on your own. It contains the proof you asked for, and something else. I'll be in touch within a couple of weeks.'

The telephone went dead. The Senator called the head of security.

At four minutes past ten, his secretary rang through that a DHL courier was in the outer office with a package for him, accompanied by a security guard. He told her to show them through.

The courier was big and burly, the security guard small and puny. The Senator asked the smaller man, 'Did you check his identity?'

'Yes, Senator, he is Harry White – no middle initial.'

The courier held a heavy metal briefcase. He laid it on the broad desk in front of the Senator, and then placed a piece of paper on top of it. Both men left, and the Senator picked up the piece of paper. On it were written six numbers. The Senator glanced at the briefcase. It had two, three-digit combination locks. He pulled the briefcase towards him, set the numbers and opened it.

Inside were two very thick wads of hundred dollar bills held together with elastic bands, a small heavy metal box, and an open typewritten sheet of paper.

He picked up the piece of paper and read the words.

'I met up with Joe Rawlings and recovered one hundred and sixty thousand bucks of your money. I left him ten thousand dollars Tap City Money – if you don't know the expression, ask a serious poker player. I should have smeared the SOB, but that would have started an investigation which neither of us needs. I also enclose proof of his real identity. Have your pals at the FBI verify it and also verify my print on the glass in your safe. And the print on this note.'

There was no signature.

Apart from the money and the letter there was nothing else in the briefcase except the small heavy metal box. Set into the lock was a small key. The Senator picked the box up and then instantly dropped it. It was freezing cold. For a moment he contemplated calling Security, then he reached out and turned the lock and flipped up the lid. A white mist engulfed the briefcase and the Senator jerked back into his heavy chair. Slowly the mist cleared, only a few traces rising from the box itself. The Senator peered into the box. He saw a white piece of cloth, and on it a finger. There was blood on the cloth. He stared, mesmerised, for a few seconds, then flicked the lid closed and reached for the telephone.

The Senator's Washington apartment also reflected Harriot's taste for grandeur. Heavy European furniture, Persian carpets, and paintings by failed old great masters. He had decided a few days before that he would sell that particular abode, and buy something smaller.

Curtis Bennett, a Deputy Director of the FBI, arrived at exactly six p.m. He was an old friend and a precise one, tall and angular, and with a wry humorous look in his eyes. He carried a briefcase.

Without being asked the Senator poured him a dry Martini.

They sat down in front of the mock Tudor fireplace, with its mock coal flames.

'So tell, Curtis,' the Senator said.

Bennett took a sip of his drink and sucked his lips in appreciation, then picked up his briefcase and took out a folder.

'The prints from the glass were those of Creasy, the mercenary. The dead mercenary, Senator.'

He tapped the file.

'In here I have a faxed copy of the Death Certificate, issued by a very eminent professor named Giovanni Satta. I spoke to Professor Satta by phone this afternoon at the Cardarelli Hospital in Naples, Italy. He confirms the Death Certificate unreservedly. He personally attended the patient who died from terrible wounds received during a shoot-out in Palermo, Sicily, with a Mafia family several years ago.' He slid a glance at the Senator and said, 'Jim, eminent doctors are not given to telling lies.'

The Senator shrugged. Bennett looked down at the paper in front of him and said, 'So if this guy died five years ago, how come his prints are all over a glass which comes from a set that I gave you and Harriot for Christmas two years ago . . . and our guys at the lab tell me that they are recent prints . . . like within two weeks. What's going on, Jim?'

The Senator held up a hand.

'Hold your water, Curtis. What about the finger?'

Bennett's smile was brief. He tapped the file.

'First of all, the guys at the lab tell me that it was cut off a living man . . .'

'Whose finger is it?'

The FBI man lifted a page from a file.

'A guy called Joseph J. Rawlings, American citizen, born in Idaho, aged fifty-one. Been messing around mercenary circles for years, in Europe and Africa. Basically a con man, wanted in this country on three serious charges of felony by deception. Whereabouts unknown.'

He closed the file, dropped it back into the briefcase.

He picked up his Martini and took a large gulp, then gazed steadily at the Senator and asked again, 'So what's going on, Jim?'

The Senator stood up, his back to the mock flames. He looked down at his friend.

'Don't ask, Curtis. Not yet. In time I'll tell you whatever I know.'

The FBI man sighed, reached down and tapped the briefcase.

'Jim, I gave you all this stuff because of who you are, and because we're friends. I even approved it with the Director, which was a bit of a gamble, but he went along with it ... but Jim, he's asking questions – what do I tell him?'

The Senator smiled.

'Tell the SOB that I appreciate it. Tell him again when the FBI budget vote comes up in committee.'

Now Bennett smiled.

'OK, but can't you tell me anything on a personal basis?'

The Senator shook his head.

'Be patient with me, Curtis, I'll tell you when I can.'

Bennett also stood and handed him the empty glass.

'Then at least give me another Martini. The two things you do best in life, Jim, are make Martinis and keep your mouth shut.'

The Senator grinned. As he mixed the Martini and a Chivas and water for himself, Bennett asked him, 'It's to do with Harriot, isn't it?'

The Senator looked at him but said nothing.

Bennett sighed.

'Jim, I know how much you loved her. Love is a word that cannot even express what you felt. I know George Bush made a public statement that when we know for sure who did it, the United States of America will bring them to justice. We also know that that is rhetoric. Whoever planted that bomb, and we're getting close to finding out, will almost certainly be holding American hostages in the Lebanon. So bringing them to justice is gonna be near impossible.'

The Senator handed the glass to Bennett and he said nothing, just sipped at his whisky.

51

Bennett sighed again.

'Jim, I have to guess. I have to make an assumption that you are doing something on your own. I just hope you're not doing something stupid.'

'Am I a stupid man, Curtis?'

The FBI man shook his head slowly.

'No, Jim, you are not, but great grief can do strange things to a man.'

The Senator nodded gravely.

'That's true, and I did something stupid a few weeks back.'

Then he touched his friend on the shoulder.

'But Curtis, I'm not doing anything stupid now . . . tell me, how's the investigation going?'

The FBI man said, 'I think it will work out. I had a chat with Buck Revell, who's handling liaison with the Scottish police. The guy in charge over there is a Peter Fleming. Apparently he's doing a hell of a job. He's dogged, determined and simply a damn good detective. We already know that the bomb was placed on the plane in Frankfurt or routed through that city, we know the possibilities, even the probabilities. I think in a matter of months this guy will come up with the name of the terrorist group and have the proof to back it up.'

'And then our President will send in the Marines.'

The FBI man's shrug was eloquent. He finished his drink, picked up the briefcase and said, 'I gotta be going.'

Grainger said, 'Wait a minute, Curtis. You're a keen poker player. Have you ever heard the expression "Tap City Money"?'

Bennett looked surprised.

'Sure,' he said. 'But it's only used by pro poker players. They go into a game with a fixed stake, all they have except the clothes on their back. They all have the same stake. It could be hundreds or many thousands. If they lose their stake they're out of the game. They call it being "tapped out". Means they're flat broke. Then, the players left in the game will contribute some cash so the guy can eat. That's "Tap City Money" . . . You taking up poker, Jim?'

Grainger smiled and answered, 'Maybe I am. Thanks for everything, Curtis. It's appreciated.'

Bennett said, 'You're damn welcome and you know it.'

He looked the Senator up and down and said, 'You're losing weight, Jim. You're not eating enough. We'll fix a date for next week, come by the house and Mary will make all your favourite things.'

'I'll do that . . . wait a second, Curtis.'

Bennett turned. The Senator was deep in thought. Finally he said, 'This man Creasy . . . if he is alive, how would you quantify him?'

Bennett's response was also thoughtful.

'Since you first asked for an input on the guy I've taken a very personal interest. I've got reports in from the French Sûreté on his time in the Legion. I've got reports from the Belgians and the British on his time in Africa. I've got a report from the CIA on his time in Vietnam, Laos and Cambodia. I'll be getting a report from Italian security shortly on what he was doing in Italy, when according to the good Professor Satta he ended up dead . . . Jim, I'll send you the reports, and maybe soon you'll send me something back, like a little info . . . like so I don't have to feel like a messenger boy . . . See you next week. I'll phone.'

He had his hand on the doorknob when the Senator's voice stopped him again.

'Curtis, if he is alive . . . sum him up for me in a sentence.'

Bennett was looking at the doorknob. He remained looking at it for half a minute, then he opened the door, turned and said, 'I told you I studied the man's files and all reports. He doesn't exactly fit the mould. Sure he's been a mercenary most of his life. Sure he's the perfect killing machine. But I have a gut feeling that although he was a mercenary, money was never his only motive.'

The Senator said again, 'Curtis, sum him up for me in a sentence.'

The FBI man shrugged.

'If he's alive . . . and if he has a motive . . . that man is death on a cold night.'

He went through the door and closed it behind him.

EIGHT

PETER FLEMING TOOK two days away from Lockerbie. It was not to be a holiday, although he needed one. First he drove down to London, leaving early in the morning. After a quick lunch he was at New Scotland Yard, conferring with half a dozen very senior policemen and two civilians. One from MI5, the other from MI6. The meeting lasted for two hours. He then drove to Fort Halstead in Kent, which housed perhaps the finest criminal laboratory in the world. The two forensic experts from the FBI were waiting for him. He asked whether they were getting full co-operation and they assured him that they were.

The briefing lasted for an hour and he noted with satisfaction that the British scientists and their American counterparts got on well together. It had not always been so, but somehow, the scale of the Lockerbie tragedy had blotted out national rivalry. He was shown the tiny fragments of plastic, metal and cloth and how they had narrowed it down, over weeks of meticulous work, to a single suitcase stored in a particular cargo bay.

They asked him to stay on and have dinner at a nearby restaurant but being tired, and wishing to be alone, he declined.

About ten miles from Fort Halstead, he found a small country hotel, set well back from the road. It had a three-star RAC rating and fully lived up to it. His room was old-fashioned but comfortable. The food was good and imaginative; the service, efficient and unobtrusive. Afterwards, he had a Cognac in the bar and went to bed.

He woke, refreshed, at seven o'clock and had a full English

breakfast with all the trimmings, before setting off for the Defence Armaments Depot, near the village of Longtown.

It was there, in a giant hangar, that technicians from the British Air Accident Investigations Board were reassembling the Pan Am 747. It was named 'Maid of the Seas'.

When he was shown into the hangar, he pulled up abruptly in surprise. He had never seen such a cavernous building before in his whole life. Some of the technicians were even using bicycles to get from one end to the other. In the middle of it, they were literally reassembling the 'Maid of the Seas'. They had placed the almost intact nosecone at one end and parts of the tail at the other end. Bits of wing were laid out each side. Dozens of overalled and white-coated men were working on it.

'It's like a giant jigsaw puzzle,' the Chief Technician explained after they had been introduced.

'Your people up there are doing a wonderful job.' He pointed to rows of metal shelves, laden with pieces of metal, wires, bits of seats and other items.

'In a few weeks, we'll have it pretty well reassembled, apart from the bits that we'll never find.'

'It's amazing,' Fleming said. 'Show me where cargo bay 14L would have been situated.'

The Chief Technician pointed and said, 'There, not far behind the cockpit. It's why the crew didn't even have time to reach for the microphone and issue a Mayday. That plane disintegrated within seconds.'

He looked at the policeman and asked, 'Are we getting close to finding out who did it?'

Peter Fleming was studying the restructured wreckage.

He nodded and said in a hard voice, 'Yes. We're getting close to finding out who the bastards are.'

Leonie Creasy, née Meckler, had never been to the Maltese Islands before and her first impressions were not good. Malta itself looked like a building site, with apartment blocks and hotels sprawling all over the coastline, and limestone dust drifting through the hot air.

But once on the ferry her mood changed. It was late afternoon, and as they passed the small island of Comino, she could see Gozo ahead. It was greener than Malta, and much smaller, with a series of undulating hills, each capped by a village, and each village capped by the spires or domes of a church. She stood at the rail watching it, and then turned to Creasy.

'It looks beautiful.'

'It is.'

He had been reticent on the flight, hardly speaking a word, and also in the taxi to the ferry. Obviously he had been deep in thought.

As the ferry turned into the entrance of Mgarr harbour, he started talking.

'Leonie, you're a good actress. I dug up some videos of some of the TV series that you've been in. On the face of it the role you're going to be playing in the next six months looks easy, but in reality it's going to be very difficult.'

'Why?'

He gestured at the island.

'Gozitan people are among the friendliest and most hospitable in the world. They lead simple lives, are deeply religious, and have big families. The men drink a lot and love shooting at every bird or rabbit that moves. They don't work very hard, except at their hobbies. Most of the foreigners that come here usually fall in love with the place, and come back time and again. Some come back forever. The problem for you is that you're going to hate the place.'

'Why?'

'Because the Gozitans are going to hate you.' He sighed. 'And the moment we step off this ferry, they're going to dislike me.'

Again she asked, 'Why?'

'I've been living here for years, I married a Gozitan girl. Most of my friends are Gozitan. I live in their style, I've been totally accepted ... but therefore I'm expected to respect their ways. If a Gozitan loses a wife or husband they go into mourning for at least a year. Some up to five years. The same thing happens when they lose a parent, even an uncle or aunt. The women wear black

56

and don't go out. It's changing slowly, but very slowly. The idea of a Gozitan marrying again five months after his wife died is unthinkable. You will be bitterly resented. When you go to the shops, when we go out to the cinema or to a restaurant or a bar, you will meet blank faces.'

He pointed to a building on the waterfront, with a long balcony jutting out.

'That's Gleneagles bar. That and the restaurant below is run by two brothers, Tony and Salvu. They are very close friends. I spend a lot of time with them, get my mail there. In their way they both loved Nadia. We will go in there now and you will find out what I mean.'

The ferry was warped in against the quay, and the ramp dropped with a great clang. Creasy picked up her new Samsonite suitcase and his battered old canvas bag and they followed the crowd off.

'My jeep will be parked behind Gleneagles,' he said as they walked up the hill.

'When will I meet Michael?' she asked.

'He'll be waiting at the house; I left word.'

There was a ramp leading up to the bar. The jeep was parked near the entrance. He dropped the suitcase and the bag into the back of it, then took her hand and said, 'You start acting from now, and you keep it up for six months no matter what. In public you show me the normal affection of a new wife, but don't overdo it.'

They walked into the bar. Some fishermen were playing Bixkla in the corner. There were several men bellied up against the bar. Salvu was behind it, younger than Tony and with more hair.

Creasy waved at the card players. They looked up only briefly.

He nodded to the men at the bar.

They nodded back. Salvu was looking at Leonie. Creasy was still holding her hand. He said, 'Salvu, this is Leonie, my wife.'

With a face showing no expression, Salvu held out his hand across the bar. She shook it. It was a very brief handshake. His voice was as flat as a piece of paper.

'Welcome to Gozo, Leonie.'

'Thank you,' she smiled at him. 'I'm so glad to be here.'

Creasy gestured at the men at the bar and introduced them by their nicknames. 'Shriek, Bajlo, Bazoot, Wistin.'

Four more brief handshakes, a few muttered words. Salvu handed some packages and envelopes across the bar. Creasy took them and said, 'Thanks, can you book me a table for two tomorrow night at the restaurant?'

'Sure.'

There was a silence, and then Creasy said to Leonie, 'Come on, honey, let's go, I'll show you the house.'

He took her hand again and they walked out.

They drove in silence towards the centre of the island, and then she said, 'You were bloody right. It was like walking into a deep freeze.'

'It won't get any easier.'

He pointed to his left, at the massive dome of a church.

'That's the village of Xewkija. That dome is the third largest in the world. The church can hold five times more people than live in the entire village.'

'Why?' she asked.

He shrugged. 'Competition. The villages compete with each other. They compete in football matches, they compete in the amount of fireworks they have in their village feasts, they compete in everything. Even the priests in the different villages compete with each other. Up to a couple of decades ago it would have been a great scandal if a boy from one village married a girl from another. Even the accents between the villages are different.'

They drove through Rabat, the island's capital, and he pointed out various shops and buildings. Five minutes later he pulled the car into the side of the road and pointed up to a high ridge. She could see the house nestling under its brow.

'That's where you'll be living for the next six months.'

'It's beautiful,' she said, 'but when I walk in there will I also be walking into a deep freeze?'

He shook his head. 'No, that house will be your refuge. There

58

you can relax and stop acting. Apart from the boy there will be few, if any, visitors, except a woman from the village who will come in two mornings a week to clean.'

'Did the woman know Nadia?'

'Of course.'

'Then I will do the cleaning.'

Again he shook his head. 'No, the woman is a widow and needs the money.'

'I will pay her from my allowance.'

'Without doing the work she will not accept it; they are proud people. It's only a couple of hours twice a week. While she's there you can always go down to the beach.'

He put the jeep into gear and moved up the hill.

NINE

THE BOY WAS in the swimming pool, half-way down at a steady crawl. He did not hear the gate open. He did not see them come in. Creasy put down the bag and the suitcase, took the woman by the arm and led her towards the pool. The boy did a racing turn and moved back down the pool. They stood looking down at him. At the other end he did another racing turn, but now he was tiring. Half-way back he noticed them, but did not break his stroke.

He reached the end beneath their feet and rested his elbows on the side, his chest heaving.

'How many?' Creasy asked.

The boy looked up at him: black hair, dark eyes, dark face.

'A hundred and twenty,' he said. 'And tomorrow I'll beat you over two lengths, five lengths or a hundred lengths.'

The woman turned and looked at Creasy's face. For the first time she saw him smile.

'Make me a bet,' he said.

The boy grinned back.

'I was looking in the cave, under your study, where all the wine is. The French and Italian wine. I made a note of all the labels. Father Manuel is an expert. I showed him the list. He said they were all good, but he said the best was the Château Margaux. He asked what year it was and I had to check the next day. When I told him it was seventy-one, his eyes gleamed and he licked his lips . . . so the bet is a bottle of Château Margaux seventy-one.'

'You will drink it yourself?'

The boy grinned again, 'I'll give it to Father Manuel but if he doesn't share it with me, I'll not talk to him again.'

Creasy nodded and gestured at the woman.

'This is Leonie . . . my wife.'

The boy pulled himself, dripping, out of the pool and held out his hand.

She took it and murmured, 'Hello, Michael, did you really do a hundred and twenty lengths?'

He looked straight into her eyes and said, 'Yes, I don't tell lies.'

Creasy glanced at her and saw the confusion in her face.

He gestured at the suitcase and bag by the gate.

'Michael, would you put the bags in my bedroom while I show Leonie around the house.'

He took her by the arm and led her away.

It was only after the boy had gone down the hill, and they were sitting under the trellis, that she spoke.

'You were right,' she said, 'about two things. This house will be a refuge for six months. I love it. Your wife had wonderful taste. In a strange way I feel safe here. I don't care what people on the island think about me. They can think what they like.'

She was drinking a gin and tonic and he had a glass of lager in front of him.

'And you're right about Michael . . . he certainly won't arouse any maternal instincts in me . . . or for that matter any other woman.' She smiled, but it was a sad smile, 'He's about as cold as you are.'

Creasy sipped his drink and said nothing. She went on: 'Is it necessary that I sleep in that huge bed with you?'

Creasy nodded, 'If you don't, the woman who cleans will know. She'll look for hairs on the pillow, she'll note how your clothes are arranged in the room . . . She'll have an instinct about it. If she knows, everybody will know. After the panel approves the adoption and after a few weeks have passed you can sleep in another bedroom.'

He took a sip and then went on. 'As I told you before, you need have no worries . . . I'm many things, but I'm not a rapist.'

She had to ask the question.

'Don't you find me attractive?'

He shrugged and said, 'I find you a good actress. By the way, can you cook?'

She lifted her head and laughed out loud but it was not an amusing sound.

'Yes, Creasy, I can cook. I'm told I cook well but I suppose that depends on who's eating it. What are your favourite things?'

'I eat simply.' He gestured at a large stone barbecue, set into the garden wall. 'I like steaks and chops . . . grilled things. I also like roasts . . . especially beef. I pointed out the butcher shop in the village. Tell him, if he doesn't give you the best beef on the island I'll go down there and cut his goolies off and barbecue them.'

'I guess he knows that already.'

On the Sunday, Creasy went as usual to the Schembri farmhouse to have lunch with Paul and Laura and Joey.

He had entered the house with an unusual feeling of trepidation. The Schembris held a special place for him. It was not that they were Nadia's family. It was not that they had twice nursed him back to health. He held them in total respect.

They spoke their minds, especially Laura, and he liked their minds. He knew that by bringing a wife back within five months, he would have hurt them deeply. Knew that their friends would have expressed sympathy to them. They were strong people and would not have liked to have answered to sympathy.

But it seemed as though nothing had changed. They talked about the early tomato crop and the policies of the new government towards agriculture. No mention was made of his new wife or the pending adoption. It was as though nothing had happened.

After the late lunch, he sat on the patio with Paul and Joey. He looked on the young man as more of a son than a brother-in-law. He teased him gently about his girlfriend, whom he had been seeing for almost a year. In traditional Gozitan society, a boy will see a girl for many months. If he brings her home or goes to her home it becomes a very serious matter. Many months later they will become engaged and that is an extremely serious matter. Engagements in Gozo are not broken. They last at least a year and then comes the monumental wedding feast.

'How's Maria?' Creasy asked.

The young man shrugged. 'She's fine.'

'I saw her parents yesterday, in Rabat . . . I had a drink with her dad . . . good people . . . good family.'

Joey shrugged again, saying nothing.

'They have a damn fine house. You've seen the house, Joey?'

'Of course.'

'You've been inside?'

Joey squirmed a little on his chair.

'No.'

Paul was smiling slightly. Creasy poured more wine into his glass and into Joey's and said reflectively:

'Damn fine house . . . good-looking girl too. I saw her on Friday in Gleneagles, with her friends. That policeman, Mario, was trying to chat her up. You know Mario, don't you? . . . The tall one, good-looking with the black moustache.'

Joey grunted, picked up the empty wine jug and went through into the kitchen.

Paul laughed softly.

'If I'd said that, he'd have gone off in a sulk for days.'

'She is a fine girl, Paul, and from a good family. The trouble with Joey is that he keeps thinking of the coming summer and dancing with the blonde tourist girls in the discos.'

The farmer nodded.

'You're right. We hardly see him in July and August and Maria's father won't let her out after ten o'clock at night. Any suggestions?'

Creasy thought for a while and then said, 'That old ruined farmhouse down the edge of your land, the one your uncle used to have, tell Joey to start fixing it up . . . He's good with stone and like me, he enjoys working with his hands. Tell him you're thinking of selling it. Prices for old farmhouses are shooting up, with foreigners buying them. Once it's fixed up, you'll get thirty thousand or more for it. I'll come and help him. It'll be like the old days when he and I used to work together, rebuilding the rubble walls on this farm.'

The farmer smiled back.

'And then he thinks about a family.'

The American nodded and said quietly, 'Paul, it's time that you and Laura had grandchildren again.'

After Creasy had left with Joey, to have a drink at Gleneagles, Laura walked out onto the patio, sat down with her husband and had her first glass of wine.

'She's a good cook, Paul.'

The farmer glanced at her with an enquiring look.

Laura said, 'Normally, he'd have eaten twice as much. She's been feeding him well.'

'I suppose that's something,' the farmer said.

'Yes,' Laura said firmly. 'That is something.'

TEN

HE DID NOT look like a ruthless leader of a highly successful terrorist unit. He looked more like a successful salesman or an upmarket con man.

Ahmed Jibril sat in his well furnished, massively defended office in the heart of Damascus. He was small, plump and sleek, and dressed in neat grey trousers, a double-breasted blue blazer with silver buttons, a cream shirt and a maroon tie.

He had been born in 1937 in the village of Yazur, near Jaffa, in the then state of Palestine. His whole life had been devoted to returning to that village in the new state of Israel. At nineteen, he joined the Syrian Army and, with his driving ambition and determination, rapidly rose through the ranks to become Captain in the Engineering Corps. Perhaps not coincidentally, he was obsessed with explosives, and became a demolition expert.

During the mid-nineteen sixties, when Syria began to mount incursions into Israel, they sponsored the formation of several terrorist organisations. Many Palestinian officers in the Syrian Army were assigned to them, including Ahmed Jibril. For a while, he spent time with George Habash in the Popular Front for the Liberation of Palestine, but later he broke away to form his own group, which he called the Popular Front for the Liberation of Palestine General Command. By now he had a wife called Samira, who became head of the group's women's committee. They had two sons, Jihab and Khaled, who held senior positions in the organisation.

With strong financial backing from Syria and others, Jibril quickly built up a reputation for spectacular action. PFLP–GC became the best trained terrorist group in the Middle East and the most highly motivated.

It was responsible for the bombing of Swissair Flight 330, en route from Zurich to Tel-Aviv. They were also able to plant a bomb on an Austrian Airline flight from Frankfurt to Vienna, but the pilot made an emergency landing. The bombing of civilian aircraft in flight became Ahmed Jibril's trademark. In 1986, he proudly informed a press conference that there would be no safety for any traveller on US or Israeli airlines.

During the mid-eighties, Jibril established several cells in European cities, including Rome, Frankfurt and in Malta. He also recruited a Jordanian national called Merwan Kreashat, who happened to be one of the world's great bomb makers.

He was leafing through various magazine and newspaper articles when the red scrambled telephone on his desk rang. He reached for it and heard the voice of Colonel Jomah, his direct contact with President Assad. Jomah was brief.

'Our embassy in Paris has had a contact which claims to have information of benefit to you.'

'What information?'

'He didn't say, but he mentioned the word "Lockerbie". Then he said, if you were interested, you should insert a message in the personal column of the *International Herald Tribune* within seven days. The message should read, "Helen Woods call home soonest".'

Jibril thought for a moment and then said, 'What do you think?'

The voice at the other end of the phone sounded slightly sarcastic.

'I think, Ahmed, that such a message would only cost a few dollars . . . do you want me to have it placed?'

'I would be grateful,' Jibril replied in silky tones.

'Very well. I'll get back to you if anything develops.'

The line went dead. Jibril cradled the phone and for several minutes sat gazing at the small crystal jar on his desk. It contained a reddish brown grainy substance. It was soil, taken from a field in the village of Yazur, near Jaffa, brought reverently to him two years earlier by one of his own fighters.

ELEVEN

LEONIE PLAYED HER part perfectly.

The panel comprised the bishop, Father Manuel Zerafa, another elderly priest and a Maltese woman from the social services department. They sat behind a long table in an office in the Curia. Creasy and Leonie sat in front of them. The panel had already examined all the relevant documents including proof of Creasy's financial means.

During the questioning the bishop had gently referred to Leonie's dead son and asked whether Michael Said would be an emotional substitute. She had thought for a moment and then opened her handbag and taken out a tissue and wiped the tears from her eyes. At that moment, Creasy knew that the adoption would go through but he did not know whether the tears were genuine. Later, as they left the Curia, he decided not to ask her.

They had settled into a routine. The boy would come up every morning at seven and swim and exercise with Creasy while she cooked them breakfast. It was always the same. Lightly scrambled eggs, grilled bacon, grilled tomato and a rack of almost burnt toast, together with freshly squeezed orange juice, percolated coffee for the man and lemon tea for the boy. She would eat her own breakfast an hour later and then drive into Rabat and do the shopping. For the rest of the morning, Creasy would be in his study working. She would lie by the pool reading and sometimes swimming. In Creasy's study there were thousands of books, covering a wide range of topics both fact and fiction.

She would make him a light lunch of salad and cold meat at twelve o'clock. After lunch, he would go off for two or three hours wearing old jeans and a denim shirt. He had told her that he was helping a friend build a house. On his return, he would strip off the clothes and go under the shower set into the wall by the pool and then swim a few lengths.

The boy would arrive at about five o'clock and he and Creasy would talk for an hour or two. Sometimes sitting under the trellis drinking lager, but more often making endless circuits of the pool. The man did most of the talking. During this time she would sit apart, out of earshot, or work in the kitchen, or watch a film on the video. Often she would tune the television in to broadcasts from Italy. To help pass the time, she had decided to learn Italian. She had spent holidays in Italy and already knew a little. She had also bought a Linguaphone course. She was determined that by the time the six months were up, she would speak the language well.

Two or three times a week, Creasy took her out to dinner. The restaurants were varied. A small bistro in Xaghra one night, with simple local food, the restaurant under Gleneagles, where Salvu cooked in the open kitchen, and at the ludicrously named 'Pink Panther', which was a simulation of an English pub, but which had a lovely alfresco dining-room at the back.

At night they slept in the huge bed, but they did not sleep together. The bed was seven feet wide and as the weeks passed, during all the nights, he had not once touched her, not even involuntarily.

After seven weeks, the adoption papers came through and the routine changed. She had driven with Creasy in the jeep to the orphanage to pick him up. There had been no ceremony. Michael had been waiting at the entrance, with Father Zerafa. At his feet was a small sports bag containing his possessions.

She acted her part kissing him on both cheeks and giving him a hug.

She had also kissed the priest on both cheeks and murmured,

'Father, thank you for looking after him so well. Now I will look after him.'

The priest's face had held no expression. Then the boy had tossed his bag into the back of the jeep and climbed in after it.

She had watched him walk into his bedroom, the one with the portraits of Nadia and Julia, watched through the open door, watched as he tossed the bag onto the bed, watched as he surveyed the room, watched as he moved slowly to the portraits and watched as he gazed at them.

Creasy had immediately taken the boy out of school and had begun to educate him personally.

After the exercises and swimming in the morning, and after the usual breakfast, they would disappear into Creasy's study and not emerge until lunchtime. After lunch they would both leave the house and go to work on the house his friend was building, except two afternoons a week, when Creasy would go alone and when an elderly courteous Arab would arrive and give the boy lessons in Arabic. They were not written lessons, only verbal. The Arab had given his name as Yussuf Oader. All Leonie had learnt about the man was that he was retired in Malta but had originally come from a mountain village in the Lebanon.

She noted that the boy respected the old man and was attentive to his lessons.

She also noted something else, that an edge of competitiveness had developed between Creasy and the boy. It had started the day after she had arrived. The boy had come up in the afternoon and said to Creasy, 'What about that race then?'

'How many lengths?' Creasy asked.

The boy had thought, then answered.

'Let's make it ten.'

She had sat at the table under the trellis and watched. By the end of the first length the boy was ahead by two feet. By the end of the second, by five feet. By the end of the fifth length, by ten feet. She had decided that Creasy was going to take a hiding and wondered how his pride would accept that, but on the sixth length the boy began to slow. Creasy had been swimming with a steady rhythmic crawl, never changing his pace. He passed the

68

boy on the eighth length. He had finished the ten lengths about eight feet ahead of the boy. He pulled himself up and out of the pool and sat with his legs in the water. He reached down and pulled the boy out next to him. They had sat there for several minutes, talking. Mostly Creasy talked. He spoke in a low voice but Leonie could hear it.

'What was your mistake?'

The boy's chest was heaving.

'I started too fast,' he answered.

Creasy had shaken his head.

'That was your second mistake. Your first was in making a challenge that you were not sure of winning. Don't ever do that, not in a race, not in life. Don't ever strike a man if you're not positive you can win the fight. Don't ever battle, unless you know damn well you're going to win the war. Don't ever chase a woman unless you know you'll get her.'

There had been a silence while the boy had digested that, then Creasy asked, 'Have you ever been with a woman?'

The boy had answered with a trace of bitterness in his voice.

'No. The local girls here are practical and orphans have few prospects.'

'But there are plenty of tourists in the summer.'

'Yes, and I see the girls down at Ramla beach and in the streets at Rabat but my pocket money is fifty cents a week. I'm told that the price of one drink at La Grotta Disco is fifty cents, and the entrance price is seventy-five cents.'

There had been a silence, then Creasy said, 'The day the adoption papers go through . . . the day you move into this house, your pocket money will cease. Your allowance will be twenty-seven pounds a week, which is the minimum wage in Gozo . . . but you will earn it, Michael, because you will be working like you've never worked before.'

She had watched the boy turn his head and look up at the man and nod his head.

'I will earn it, *Uomo*.'

'You know my brother-in-law, Joey Schembri?'

'I've seen him around. He brought me and some other boys at

the orphanage drinks at the last feast . . . I spoke a few words with him. He used to play football for Ghainselum, but injured his knee a couple of years ago. He was a good striker.'

'OK, the Saturday after you move into this house Joey will take you down to La Grotta. Don't be ashamed of being led by him, both in that or anything else, but don't ever get smart with him. Don't ever try and pull one of his girls. He's got a wicked right hand. I've seen him in action.'

The Saturday after the boy had moved into the house, Creasy drove him into Rabat to meet Joey. He had then taken Leonie out to dinner at Ta Frenc. They had returned at one o'clock in the morning and the boy was not home.

She had heard him come back at four o'clock. Heard him smash into his bedroom door. Heard the thump, as he hit the floor. She had started to get out of bed, but Creasy's hand had stopped her, gripping her by the arm. It had been the first time he had ever touched her in that bed.

'Leave him,' he had said.

In the morning she had found him sprawled across his bed, fully clothed, snoring against the pillow.

In spite of a monumental hangover, Creasy had made him do a hundred lengths of the pool before breakfast.

It was now July, glorious long summer days and evenings. She spent most of her waking hours outside. All meals were now eaten outside. Many evenings Creasy would barbecue. He was an expert, always marinating the meat overnight in his own special marinade. She would make her salads. He taught the boy the art of how to do a good barbecue, of the way to cook different kinds of meat and the fish he would bring back from his fishermen friends at Gleneagles. He asked her to teach the boy how to make salads and prepare vegetables. The boy was quick to learn and she noticed that he enjoyed cooking.

Once she had asked him how the orphanage was and he had grimaced and said, 'They filled us up like putting petrol into a car and it tasted the same.'

With the sun and the setting, the days and nights should have been idyllic for Leonie but as each day passed she slipped into an ever deepening depression. It was not just that the people of the island continued to treat her as though she had a communicable disease, nor because, as the man and the boy drew mentally closer day by day, she felt increasingly isolated.

She was an intelligent, experienced woman. She was also sensitive. Apart from cooking, shopping and teaching the boy how to cook, she made no contribution whatsoever. She was never asked a question or an opinion. As the days moved through July, she dreaded waking up in the mornings and then it got worse, because she found herself unable to sleep. She spent hour after hour lying on the huge bed near the man, hearing his breathing, occasionally a muttered sound, as he talked in a dream.

Her only thoughts centred on her mortgage and her clapped-out Fiesta.

It was three o'clock in the afternoon. Laura Schembri stood on the patio of her farmhouse and watched in the distance as her son and Creasy worked on a wall of the old farmhouse. That morning she had been shopping in Victoria. Her cousin was a gossip. She had told Laura that the woman living with Creasy – she had not called her his wife – shopped in the supermarket almost every day; told her with relish how she and everybody else had frozen her out.

'I never talk to her,' she had smiled. 'Not a single word. Not since the day she first walked in.'

At the greengrocer's, the woman behind the counter had said similar things with the same relish. Laura looked at the two men working in the distance. Her son was on the wall itself. Creasy was passing up old limestone blocks to him. Her eyes swept across the fields, to where her husband was ploughing with a small tractor.

She looked at her watch and made a decision.

She went into the house and picked up her handbag and the keys to the Land-Rover, and wrote a note to Paul.

Leonie was lying on a lounger by the pool when the old-fashioned doorbell rang. She glanced at her watch. It was too early for Creasy to be returning. Michael and his Arab teacher were under the trellis, deep in conversation. As she walked to the door, the thought crossed her mind that, as well as everything else, Creasy might teach the boy some manners.

She opened the door and found herself looking at a woman, tall, well-built, almost statuesque. She had a handsome face, with ebony-coloured hair.

The woman said, 'Hello, you must be Leonie. I'm Laura Schembri.'

For a moment, Leonie's mind was blank and then the woman said, 'Nadia's mother.'

The blankness in Leonie's mind turned to confusion. She could not find any words. The woman smiled. A warm, pleasant smile. She held out her hand.

'I'm pleased to meet you finally.'

Leonie took the hand and said, 'Please come in.'

The woman shook her head.

'Another time. It's Thursday afternoon and on Thursdays they play Bingo at the Astra Band Club. I wondered if you'd like to come along? It's quite a social occasion,' she said. 'A lot of the local women will be there . . . hundreds of them. We have a few drinks during and after, and we all get acquainted with the week's gossip.'

She looked at Leonie steadily and the younger woman gazed back at her, then nodded her head firmly and said, 'Thank you. I'd love to join you.'

Laura Schembri had not played Bingo for twenty years but as they walked into the cavernous room, and as her eyes swept across the scores of tables and the hundreds of women, she recognised almost all of them and almost all of them recognised her. She was known for her forceful personality and short temper, her direct talking and her integrity. She was known as a woman who had lost both her daughters, one in a car crash in Naples and one in a plane crash in Scotland. She was known to go to Mass every Sunday. Her youngest daughter had died only eight months before but she was walking into the Astra Band Club, not wearing black, but wearing a brightly-coloured, red and blue dress and she was walking in with the woman who had recently married her dead daughter's husband.

At the far end of the room, a man sat on a high podium. In front of him was a huge transparent plastic bowl, containing ping-pong balls with numbers on them. He held a ping-pong ball in his hand and called out into the microphone, 'Eleven, legs eleven!'

But nobody was listening. Heads were turning, looking towards the entrance. A hush fell over the room and then a rolling murmur of whispers.

Laura took Leonie's arm, smiled and said, 'Let's get a drink at the bar first, and then I'll introduce you to some people.'

Leonie smiled back and said, 'I think I know some of them already.'

Laura shook her head.

'You don't, but you will.'

TWELVE

ON SATURDAY EVENING, Joey Schembri passed by the house to pick up Michael and take him to the disco. Michael was still in the bedroom getting dressed, in his faded new frayed jeans with holes at the knees, and his new Chris Rea T-shirt. Leonie was in the kitchen, preparing dinner. Creasy brought a couple of lagers out to the table under the trellis and chatted to Joey about the house they were working on. All week they had been building a new wing, which was to be the dining-room and kitchen. They couldn't decide whether to use arches or wooden beams for the roof. In fact they had had a couple of arguments over it.

Joey drained half his glass, gave Creasy a very severe look and said, 'I've decided, *Uomo*, and I don't want any more fucking arguments.'

'Decided what?'

'It's going to be arches instead of beams.'

'Why?'

'Because I like arches, it's more traditional.'

Creasy shrugged, non-committally.

'Yes, but you have to think of the market. After all, most of these farmhouses are bought by English people, or lately, Germans. They like the old wooden beams, think they're more rustic. Let's face it, Joey, you're not going to be living in the place . . . are you?'

Joey gave him a narrow-eyed look. He drained his glass and stood up, walked across the patio and shouted through the wide-arched door in Maltese.

'Michael, if you're not ready in two minutes, I'm leaving without you, and that Swedish girl will be heart-broken.'

A voice shouted back, 'Coming, Joey, coming!'

Joey walked back to the table and grinned down at Creasy.

'I've got a feeling that later on tonight he just might be. That girl is crazy about him.'

'Don't let the young bastard drink too much!'

Joey shrugged.

'The deal is I take him there and bring him home. Anyway, I wouldn't worry. Last week was just his first real night out and he went over the top. I did the same thing.'

'You went over the top more times than I like to remember.'

Joey grinned again and then as he heard the clattering of the pans in the kitchen, the grin faded. He looked down at Creasy and said, 'By the way, I have a message from my mother.'

'Tell me.'

'Tomorrow's Sunday. She said don't bother coming to lunch unless you bring your wife with you.'

Creasy grimaced.

'Your mother can be a pain in the ass. When was the last time she played Bingo?'

Joey spread his hands.

'I didn't even know she'd ever played and you're right, she can be a pain in the ass.'

Michael walked out under the trellis and Joey whistled and said, 'Holy shit, man. What a knockout! Where did you get that T-shirt?'

The boy grinned and said, 'I had it flown in yesterday from London. You haven't got a chance tonight!'

Creasy made his announcement on Monday night over dinner. In the morning he had picked up a number of letters from Gleneagles. One of them was post-marked Washington.

In the afternoon, he had not gone to work with Joey on the farmhouse. He had stayed in his study and made a series of overseas phone calls and some local ones.

'I'll be leaving tomorrow,' he said. 'I'll be away a couple of weeks.'

'Where are you going?' Michael asked.

'Here and there. I've got things to do.'

He looked at the boy steadily and said, 'You know a man called George Zammit . . . He's Paul Schembri's nephew, Joey's cousin?'

Michael nodded.

'You know what he does?'

Again Michael nodded.

'OK. Well I talked to him early this afternoon on the phone and made some arrangements. Starting tomorrow, and thereafter every Tuesday and Thursday, you'll catch the seven o'clock ferry in the morning and then the bus to Valetta. From the terminal, you'll walk down to Fort St Elmo. George will be there.'

'What will I do?'

Creasy thought for a while and then glanced at Leonie.

'Further your education,' he said in a flat voice.

To Leonie he said, 'It's very early, but I'd prefer your driving him to the ferry, while I'm away.'

'Of course.'

75

THIRTEEN

FIRST HE WENT to Luxembourg and spent an hour in an office of a small private bank. Then he went to London and checked into the Gore Hotel in Queensgate, a small, comfortable family-run hotel. They knew him there as Mr Stuart. The concierge arranged a single ticket for him for *Phantom of the Opera* that night.

When he returned to the hotel it was after midnight. The night porter let him in and told him that there was a man waiting for him in the bar. The bartender had been long gone but the night porter made them drinks and then left them alone.

The man was short and slightly plump with sandy hair. He was in his late fifties.

'They've been asking about you,' he told Creasy.

'Who has?'

The walls of the bar were covered with paintings, all done by one man, a friend of the owners of the hotel. They were all for sale but in the years that Creasy had been coming to the hotel he had never known one of them to be sold. The sandy-haired man was looking at one.

He said, 'I don't like these paintings, Creasy, they're too bizarre, what do you think?'

Creasy shrugged and said, 'You get used to them. Who's been asking?'

'First of all Peter Fleming. He's in charge of the Lockerbie investigation. He asked Special Branch, who asked us. It landed on my desk.'

'And so?'

'And so I gave him the one-sheet hand-out, the one that ends up with you dead in Naples. A week later I had a query on it.'

'And so?'

The small man smiled. 'And so I told the man at Special Branch that's all we had . . . and what with all that's happening around Eastern Europe these days, I had enough on my plate not to waste time on a one-time mercenary who died five years ago.'

'Thanks.'

The small man took a sip of his whisky.

'That's OK, Creasy, but then we had a G1 request from the FBI from high up.'

'How high?'

'A man called Bennett. He's a Deputy Director.'

Creasy leaned over the bar, took the top off the ice bucket and dropped some cubes into his glass.

'Was he specific?' he asked.

'Yes, very. He came through the DG personally.'

The small man's voice became apologetic.

'I had to push all the buttons on my little console and give them everything we have.'

Creasy was swirling the ice in his glass and looking down at it reflectively.

'And what was the bottom line?'

The small man's voice was still apologetic.

'The bottom line, Creasy, was that we had three reported sightings of you over the past five years, during the years that you're supposed to have been dead. The last only two months ago at Heathrow Airport . . . A man from the SB anti-terrorist squad . . . a watcher . . . you should have had plastic surgery, Creasy.'

'It was expected, especially from the FBI. I set it up myself.'

The small man looked surprised.

'Why?'

'I needed someone to know. Now he knows. How's the investigation going?'

77

The small man smiled grimly.

'Like all such investigations, very slowly. The last memo I saw was a week ago. That man Fleming is tenacious, but he's having problems with the German police. He thinks there's a cover-up or a foul-up. The Germans are determined to prove that the bomb didn't originate in Frankfurt. They're trying to pin it on Heathrow. Naturally, Security at Heathrow are trying to pin it on Frankfurt. It's got bitter enough to go to Foreign Office level.'

Creasy turned on his stool.

'George, give us another one.'

The night porter came into the bar. He had a very pronounced limp. Silently he refilled their glasses, then limped out.

'What's your view?' Creasy asked.

'It's got to be Abu Nidal or Ahmed Jibril, paid for by the Iranians, probably using other groups to front for them. Fleming will find out, I'm sure of that.'

'A simple policeman?'

The small man shook his head.

'Not simple, Creasy. Very bright and very tenacious and apart from the Germans he's getting very good co-operation. From the FBI, the CIA and us. We've got a whole team on it, eight people. Four of them in the field.'

'How long?'

'I'd guess within a year. Less, if the Germans start co-operating.'

'But you think it's Nidal or Jibril?'

The small man drained his glass and stood up. Creasy also stood up.

'That will be the bottom line, Creasy . . . and both very hard to get to. Mossad have been trying for years.'

Creasy shook his head.

'You're wrong. Mossad only say they've been trying . . . lip service to the Americans. Mossad just love those two bastards. Every time they kill an innocent, they hurt the Palestinian cause.'

He took a sip of his drink. He was looking at one of the bizarre paintings. It depicted a bunch of West Indians, working in a field. Their features were distorted.

78

Wryly he said, 'It wouldn't even surprise me if Mossad were funding those two bastards.'

He held out a hand and the smaller man shook it.

'Thanks, I owe you one.'

The small man shook his head and very quietly said, 'You'll never owe me one, Creasy. Not in a million years. Not since the night you came through that door and pulled me out. We were a bit younger then.'

Creasy grinned.

'We sure were and perhaps a little wiser.'

The small man nodded.

'If anything breaks, I'll be in touch. Walk on water, Creasy.'

Michael finished the last of the chicken casserole, glanced at his watch and stood up, saying, 'I'd better get changed. Joey will be picking me up in five minutes.'

He had almost reached the door when Leonie's voice stopped him. It was a low voice but very determined.

'Michael, come back here and sit down.'

Slowly the boy walked back and sat down, glancing at his watch again.

'Did you enjoy your meal, Michael?'

He looked puzzled.

'Yes, it was very good. I ate everything.'

'And you enjoyed your lunch and your breakfast and the roast lamb I made last night and the rabbit stew I made the night before?'

'Yes . . . the rabbit stew is my favourite. You make it like a Gozitan.'

She nodded slowly, her eyes never leaving his face.

'Yes, you ate enough for two men. Laura gave me the recipe . . . Michael, what is my name?'

He was no longer puzzled. He was looking down at the table. Very quietly he said, 'Your name is Leonie.'

'Good. I thought you had forgotten, now go and get changed, Michael.'

The boy stood up and walked to the door, then he turned and

looked at her. He said nothing, just looked at her for about half a minute, then turned away.

Two hours later he was standing at the bar in La Grotta, drinking a Heineken and surveying the dance floor.

Joey said, 'Michael, next week, you'll be on your own.'

The boy turned in surprise.

'What do you mean?'

Joey's smile was rueful, almost embarrassed.

'Tonight before I picked you up, I stopped by in Nadur, to see Maria.'

'So?'

'I stopped off to see her at the house. I went in. Had a drink with her parents.'

The boy whistled softly and then muttered, 'So it's like that, Joey?'

Joey was looking at the dance floor. There were scores of people dancing. The girls' ages ranged from sixteen to thirty. Almost all of them were tourists, mostly Scandinavians, Germans and English.

He watched them, then sighed and said, 'You know what it means, Michael. If I'm down here next week I'll be with Maria and I'll have to take her home at midnight and after that, go home myself.'

'You're lucky,' the boy replied immediately. 'She's a great girl.'

'She is,' Joey agreed. 'But what about you?'

'It's no problem. I can walk down to Rabat and hitch a lift.'

Joey smiled. 'That's not what I meant.'

'What did you mean?'

Joey gestured with his chin at the dance floor.

'There are two girls dancing. Both of them fancy you like hell. Have done for the past week. Now you and I know you're a virgin and it's time you ceased to be one. I'm not going to be around next week. I know you're as nervous as hell but tonight has got to be the night. You've got to make your mind up and go and do it.'

Michael looked at him, then turned to look at the dance floor. He heard Joey's whispered voice.

'But which one, Michael, the English or the Swedish one?'

'I don't know.'

'I do. I remember the first time for me. I was a bit younger than you and even more nervous. It was a disaster because the girl was as young as me and also nervous. The Swedish girl is beautiful but she is only seventeen. The English one is a woman of about twenty-five; you go for her.'

'But how do I do it?'

Joey laughed out loud. 'You don't know?'

'I mean how do I go about getting her?'

Joey watched the woman dancing. She was tall, small-boned with very typical English features, soft, milky-white complexion like a cameo, and slightly flushed cheeks. Thick fair tresses waved down her back. She wore a khaki, three-quarter-length skirt with a black lycra top, cut low and tight to reveal her small breasts.

As she danced, she tossed her hair from her face and smiled at the young Gozitan boy dancing in front of her. He moved in, mistaking her smile for mutual attraction. He was mistaken. She was looking at Michael.

Without turning his head and speaking almost in a whisper, Joey said, 'When she finishes dancing she'll come to the bar and order a drink. She'll come very near to you to order it. She always does. What does she drink, Michael?'

Michael whispered back, 'Scotch and soda water . . . Johnny Walker Black Label.'

'Right.'

Joey gestured at the bartender.

'Vince has been chatting her up all week. Without success. You've heard his questions and her replies?'

Michael muttered, 'Yes, I have.' His eyes were still on the woman.

'What's her name?'

'Saffron.'

'Where does she live?'

'A place called Devon.'

'Where does she stay here?'

'In a flat in Marsalforn, with her girlfriend.'

81

'What work does she do?'

'She works in a bank, she's taking a management course.'

'When is she leaving?'

Michael sighed. 'Tomorrow afternoon.'

'You know enough,' Joey whispered. 'It's got to be tonight. You also know that half the guys in here have been chasing her every night and getting nowhere. You also know that she fancies you . . . so what are you going to do, Michael?'

'Tell me.'

Joey had a half smile on his face.

'What you do, Michael, is that you change gear half-way through. First, you're going to be ultra cool, then you're going to be very uncool. You've got to throw them, Michael. In the last two weeks she'll have listened to the pulling words of dozens of smooth operators.' He gestured with his chin at the dance floor. 'Those guys out there. Some of them have been around a long time. Sammy over there has had more girls than you've had hot breakfasts and he hasn't got a hair on his head. Now listen.' He leaned closer. 'First you order a large Black Label Scotch and soda and keep it next to you. Tell Vince it's for Saffron and when you do that give him a hard look in the eye. He knows he's shot his bolt. When she's stopped dancing, which I guess will be the end of this track, she'll come next to you and order a drink. Vince will point to the drink already on the bar and tell her you bought it. She'll be a little confused or pretend to be. Immediately, you'll say, "Saffron, can I talk to you?" Don't forget to use her name. Then slowly and without looking at her, you walk over there.' He gestured to the other side of the dance floor at some tables and chairs, in subdued lighting under some trees. 'You do not look back, you just go over there and sit down. If she follows you, you're half-way there.'

'And if she doesn't?'

'If she doesn't you're going to look and feel like an idiot.' Joey laughed. 'Order that drink now, and be ready.'

'And what if she does follow me?'

'If she follows you and sits down you don't say a word, you just look at her with those eyes, straight into her face, into her eyes. Don't say a word. Make her start the conversation. She will say something like, "What do you want to talk about?" You will sigh and say, "It's a bit embarrassing . . . a bit difficult to talk about." At that moment you will look at her again. If her face shows any sign of concern or if she says something like "Tell me about it, Michael" then you are three-quarters of the way there.'

The boy was intrigued. 'And then what do I say?'

'You tell her that you're a virgin.'

'What!'

Joey smiled. 'Exactly that. She will laugh and ask you how old you are. You will lie a little. You look eighteen or nineteen. You tell her that you'll be nineteen next month, on the twenty-fifth.'

'And then what?'

'You say that you know tonight is her last night. And then, Michael, you don't say one more word, not a single word.'

'What if she asks me a question?'

Joey's voice was emphatic.

'You say nothing. Not a word. You just look at her. Straight into her eyes. Either she will get up and walk away or take you down to the flat in Marsalforn.'

She walked off the dance floor, came straight to the bar and Joey edged away from Michael. She moved into the gap between them. Joey turned his back to her.

She called out to the bartender, 'Vince, give me the usual, please.'

Vince pointed to the full glass in front of her and then at Michael. She turned her head, looking slightly puzzled. From behind him, Joey heard Michael say, 'Saffron, can I talk to you a moment?'

Joey waited for a while then turned. Michael was walking behind the dance floor to the table under the trees and the woman was following him.

Five minutes later, Joey watched them walk up the long sweep of stairs to the entrance. He turned his attention back to the dance floor, to the Swedish girl. After all, it was going to be his last week of freedom.

*

83

'Is it really true?'

'Yes, it is.'

They were on the balcony of a flat in Marsalforn, looking across the bay at the reflected lights. It was after midnight. Michael made a decision.

'It is true,' he said, 'but I lied to you about something else.'

'About what?'

'I'm not nineteen next month. I'm seventeen.'

She laughed and poured the last few drops of the duty-free Black Label into the two glasses.

'The first time for me was awful,' she said. 'It was in the back of a car, a small one. It was messy. I was drunk.'

They were lying on the bed and she was looking down at him. She stroked the black hair from his forehead and smiled.

'For you, Michael, it will not be awful . . . it will be beautiful.'

FOURTEEN

THEY MET FOR dinner at a restaurant four blocks from Capitol Hill. They sat at a secluded table at the back of the room. The Senator ordered a peppered steak, with a Caesar salad on the side. Creasy ordered *coq au vin*, with new potatoes and cauliflower.

After the waitress had left, the sommelier came with the wine list, a very fat one.

'Do you like wine?' the Senator asked.

'Yes.'

The Senator passed him the wine list.

84

'Order anything, as long as it costs less than a hundred and ten thousand bucks.'

'You mean that?'

'Sure.'

Creasy studied the wine list for several minutes.

The sommelier had the appearance that befitted his business: tall, sleek, and with a thin pencil moustache. He looked over Creasy's shoulder at the pointing finger.

Creasy closed the wine list and handed it to him.

'Let's have the Rothschild '49.'

The sommelier's pleasure showed on his face.

'Would you like me to decant it for you, sir?'

'Please do.'

Creasy looked across the table and said, 'Senator, that has made a dent in the hundred and ten thousand bucks.'

Grainger grinned.

'I hope so. I don't know a lot about wine myself. Did you pick up the expertise in the Legion?'

Creasy nodded.

'That's where it started. People don't know much about the Legion. They have this romantic thing about Beau Geste and the desert. It's not like that. It's a highly modern Corps. It's also unique in that a Legionnaire never has to leave if he doesn't want to . . . for many it's like an orphanage. The Legion has its own vineyards in France and makes its own wine. When a Legionnaire retires he can go and work in the vineyards or in the handicraft workshops they also have. The food is the best of any army in the world, not just for the officers but for everybody.'

'But you were pushed out?' the Senator said quietly.

'Yes, I was in the second REP. We had a Colonel we all worshipped. He was the bravest man I have ever known. He also worshipped his men.'

The Senator could see the memory in Creasy's eyes. The man went on:

'The Colonel decided to join the Generals' Putsch. We even got ready to parachute into Paris itself.' He smiled at the memory.

'After the Putsch failed we blew up our barracks and marched out singing Edith Piaf's song about having no regrets . . . *Je ne regrette rien* . . . The officers went into hiding or faced court martial, the NCOs were kicked out and the Legionnaires dispersed into other units.'

Quietly the Senator said, 'Yes, I read of it in your file. You were an NCO . . . would you have stayed on, if they hadn't kicked you out?'

Creasy thought for a moment, then nodded.

'I guess so, but I wouldn't be fighting now, I'd be on a vineyard north of Marseilles, picking grapes and making wine.' He smiled. 'But not quite like the wine we're going to drink in a while.'

The sommelier brought the wine, holding the bottle like a nurse holds a new-born baby. Very carefully he placed it on a trolley. Then he extracted the cork and rolled it between his fingers before holding it beneath his nostrils.

He nodded with satisfaction and said to Creasy, 'I think it's good, sir. It has lasted.'

The sommelier put the cork on the plate in front of Creasy and said, 'Senator, in all these years, you've never ordered a bottle of wine like this.'

As the sommelier had done, Creasy rolled the cork in his fingers and then sniffed it. He nodded and said, 'Perhaps you'd tell the chef to hold our order for half an hour to give the wine time to breathe.'

The sommelier walked away with the air of a surgeon who has just completed a complicated but successful operation.

Creasy was wearing a sober grey suit with a faint pin-stripe, cream shirt and a maroon tie. He reached into an inside pocket, took out a small business card and passed it across.

'Senator, that's the name of a bank in Luxembourg. On the back of it is the account number. I'd like you to transfer the quarter mill to that account within the next seven days. Unlike with Rawlings, you won't get any lists of expenses. At the end, whichever way it goes you'll get back any balance due to you. My quarter mill is already in that account. If you want to check that you call the man whose card that is and you give him the code, "East is East and West is West". He'll tell you anything you want to know about that account.'

The Senator looked at the card and said quietly, 'Creasy, since you sent me that finger, I've decided not to ask any more personal questions. Naturally, we'll stay in touch and pass back and forth whatever we know. Of course I want to know how things are going and also if there's anything I can do to help.'

'Later on you might be able to,' Creasy said. 'By the way, has your friend Curtis Bennett come up with any new information?'

'How do you know Curtis?'

'He's been asking questions about me.'

'How do you know?'

'That I have to keep to myself, Senator.'

Grainger nodded thoughtfully.

'I understand that. By the way "Senator" is a mite formal. Call me Jim; my friends do.'

'OK.'

'What do I call you?'

Creasy smiled slightly.

'Just Creasy.'

'You don't have a first name . . . yes you do, I saw it on your file.'

Creasy's smile widened.

'My father must have had a sense of humour. Creasy will do just fine. Now what has Bennett been able to give you?'

'Seems like it's narrowing down to two Palestinian groups, Abu Nidal's bunch or the PFLP–GC, headed by a guy called Ahmed Jibril. It might be some months before they prove which one.'

'I have the same info.'

He was looking over the Senator's shoulder. Very quietly he said, 'Jim, don't look round now. There's a woman sitting alone at the table behind you. Either she's interested in me physically or she's working for somebody. In a couple of minutes, go to the john and get a look at her.'

When the Senator returned from the toilet, he nodded

pleasantly at the woman as he passed the table. She smiled back.

He sat down and said, 'Nothing sinister. I know her. She works as a researcher for the House Committee on Justice . . . very bright. I've seen her in here quite a few times.'

'House researchers can afford this kind of place?' Creasy asked.

The Senator shook his head.

'No, not on their salaries. She comes from a wealthy family out in Maryland.'

Creasy looked at the woman. She was in her mid-thirties, tall with short black hair and a very graceful neck. The intelligence showed in her face. She was just on the right side of being not too pretty. She glanced up at him yet again and their eyes met. She looked away.

The food arrived and with it the sommelier. He picked up Creasy's wine glass and poured an inch of wine into it.

Creasy took a sip and his eyes narrowed as he savoured it. The sommelier nodded with great dignity and poured the wine into the Senator's glass and then into Creasy's.

'Fetch another glass,' Creasy said to him.

The sommelier did so. Creasy took the decanter, half filled the glass and passed it to the sommelier.

They all drank. The sommelier sighed in satisfaction and said, 'Thank you, sir, enjoy your meal.'

Then still holding his glass he walked away to the kitchen. Creasy guessed that he would be giving the chef a taste.

The Senator left first. It was still only ten o'clock. He apologised saying that he had a breakfast meeting at the House, and needed an early night.

'I'll stay on a while,' Creasy said, 'and have another coffee, maybe a Cognac.'

The Senator winked.

'I wish you luck, Creasy, she's a fine looking woman.'

Creasy shook his head.

'It's not that, Jim . . . it's just that I'm interested in researching justice.'

He decided to have his Cognac in the bar. The Senator had told him the woman's name. As he passed her table, he stopped, leaned down and said, 'Miss Parkes, if you feel like an after dinner drink, I'll be in the bar.'

Without giving her a chance to reply, he walked away.

The bar was all mahogany, dim lights with maroon tasselled lampshades and deep banquettes. Creasy went to a banquette in the corner and ordered a Cognac. When the waiter brought the drink, Creasy reached into his jacket pocket for money. The waiter shook his head.

'With the compliments of Mr Henry, sir . . . the sommelier.'

'Please send my thanks to Mr Henry.'

The woman timed it to perfection. Ten minutes passed. Creasy glanced at his watch and decided that if she didn't turn up in the next two minutes, she wasn't going to. She walked into the bar, two and a half minutes later.

She was taller than he expected, about five feet ten, and as she walked, the knitted woollen dress swirled around her calves. Black suede Bally shoes with stiletto heels matched her black suede purse. She moved to the banquette with a long-legged graceful walk and sat down. Not next to him, but across from him about five feet away. They looked at each other as the waiter approached.

She ordered a Drambuie and then said to Creasy, 'You must be important.'

'How so?'

'Senator Grainger counts his time carefully . . . he doesn't waste it.'

Creasy smiled.

The waiter brought her Drambuie and again waved away Creasy's offer of money. The woman took a sip of her drink and said, 'Did the Senator tell you my first name?'

'Yes . . . Tracey.'

She had a low voice, almost throaty. She lifted her hand and pulled her hair away from her eyes, stroked her hand down it, moved slightly on the banquette. Body language.

'And yours?' she asked.

'Creasy.'

'Is that the first or second?'

'It's the only name I answer to.'

She smiled again.

'Are you in politics?'

'No, and I never was. I'm retired.'

'What were you in?'

'I was a mercenary.'

She looked at him steadily and then asked the inevitable question.

'You've killed people?'

'I don't remember.'

He told her that he was staying at the Hyatt Hotel. She told him that she had an apartment around the block. They went to her apartment.

In the bedroom she took off her dress. He took off his suit with the faint pin-stripe. She looked at the scars on his body and then at the scars on his face and into his eyes.

'You should know now,' he said, 'and know it for sure. I'm not a sadist, not even slightly.'

She smiled; her eyes almost closed.

'I'm not a masochist,' she said. 'But I like it hard . . . Not rough but hard.'

She was high-breasted, and long-flanked.

When he entered her, hard, it was eleven o'clock.

With the time difference, it was four o'clock in the morning in Gozo and Michael was making love to a woman for the second time in his life. This time he was in control. The first time, which was three hours before, she had been in control. She had explained things to him in a soft whisper.

She had taught him how to kiss and been astonished when he told her that he had never kissed a girl before; never touched a girl's breast. She had laughed; not at him but with him. She had made him laugh. She had kissed him all over. She had taken him in her mouth but only briefly.

90

Then she had slid up his body and slid him inside her.

It had been brief but beautiful. He had clung to her, pulled her so tight as to cause the breath to pump out of her.

Eventually, as they lay side by side, he asked into the darkness, 'Is it always like that . . . so quick?'

She had laughed.

'For some men, yes, but not for you, Michael. The next time will be longer.'

He had kissed her breasts and fallen into a deep sleep and she had let him sleep for three hours before waking him with a kiss.

In the apartment in Washington, on the huge antique four-poster bed, Creasy watched the woman's face and increased his rhythm. The room was bright. She had wanted it that way. He squeezed her breasts and with his thumbs pushed her nipples deep into them. She arched her back and murmured, way down in her throat. He watched her eyes close tight, watched her mouth open. He kissed the open mouth pushing his tongue into it. He felt the shudders start, the spasms. Felt her long, elegant fingers digging into his back.

He knew when to stop. Knew when the pleasure would turn to discomfort. He left himself inside her, still hard, but eased his weight from her, still looking down at her face. She opened her eyes and smiled up at him. Her elegant fingers were now strok-ing his back like butterflies. She moved one of them and ran it down the scar on his cheek. Her body moved very slightly, savouring the aftermath. Savouring the feel of him.

'It didn't happen for you,' she murmured.

'It will . . . just keep moving like that . . . no more than that.'

He felt the muscles inside her contract, grip him. He did not move at all. For the next few minutes they looked at each other, their faces inches apart.

She saw the pupils of his eyes dilate, felt his chest expand against her breasts and then felt the liquid going up into her body. Apart from his chest and his eyes, nothing else had moved.

In the apartment in Marsalforn, the woman looked up at

Michael and said, 'Think of something you don't like . . . something you hate.'

His face showed surprise. He was moving smoothly, in and out of her. She was pushing up at him, breathing rapidly.

'Why?'

He was also breathing rapidly. His penis felt like a ticking bomb.

'Something you hate,' she murmured again, 'quickly.'

She had one arm wrapped around him like a vice, her other hand gripped his buttocks, pulling him into her.

He thought of spinach. He hated spinach with a passion. At the orphanage he had been forced to eat it more times than he could remember. Otherwise he got no dessert.

Thinking of the spinach only gave him three more minutes but it was enough. He felt it happening to her, felt the ripples of her belly, felt her long legs come around him and squeeze, felt her hands tighten on him. Then it was happening to him.

'That's the way it should be,' she said later.

In the four-poster bed in Washington the woman was watching Creasy get dressed.

'We should do this again,' she said.

He was buttoning his shirt. He looked at his watch.

'I leave Washington in five hours,' he said, 'and the country three hours later.'

'But you'll be back?'

'Maybe. But maybe not for a long time.'

'You'll call me if you do.'

It was a statement, not a question.

He was knotting his tie.

'Count on it.'

She smiled, but then her face turned serious. She rolled across the bed to be closer to him. She looked up and said, 'Creasy, physically it was great. It was a sensation. Somehow you got to every single nerve ending in my body . . . but I didn't get much feeling of emotion.'

He had finished tying his tie. He looked down at her. Hooded

92

eyes in a scarred face. Very quietly he said, 'We both used each other tonight and it was good. It will happen again and it will be good. But Tracey, don't look for emotion. In my life, I loved one woman. She died some months ago. My emotions died with her. If you want your nerve endings stimulated, I'm your man. If you want emotion, you'll have to look elsewhere.'

She reached out and put her hands behind his knee, squeezing it. She was looking at him pensively. 'Where do mercenaries live?'

He smiled at her. It was a warm smile. He liked her.

'Mercenaries live in holes, Tracey. They're like rodents or reptiles.'

'I'll give you my number,' she said.

He was putting on his jacket.

'I don't need it . . . if I return, I'll find you.'

The woman drove Michael back to the farmhouse. She had a yellow rented Suzuki jeep and they bounced around.

'Will you come back next summer?' he asked.

She was a fast driver and a good one, spinning the jeep through the narrow streets of Rabat.

'No,' she answered, 'next year I'm going to Hong Kong.'

'Won't you ever come back?'

She turned her head to smile at him.

'Maybe one day. I never plan more than a year ahead.'

She followed his directions through Kercem and then through the country lanes winding up to the ridge. They parked behind and above the farmhouse, looking out over it. It was dawn; the sun was rising, the whole island bathed in red.

'What a view,' she said in awe. 'What a beautiful house.'

Then she leaned across and kissed him lightly on the lips and put a hand on his cheek.

'Goodbye, Michael,' she murmured. 'Good luck.'

She had driven twenty yards down the track when she heard him call her name urgently. She stopped the open-topped jeep and looked back. He was smiling.

'Thank you,' he shouted.

She grinned and shouted back, 'You're welcome.'

In her bed, Leonie had woken at the sound of the jeep. She heard the exchange through the open window. She looked at the alarm clock. It was just after six. The clock was set to go off at seven, when normally she would get up and make Michael breakfast. She thought about whether she should let him lie in on this morning and then decided against it. Creasy would have got him up and made him do his hundred lengths, no matter what. She turned over, pounded her pillow and drifted back to sleep.

The alarm went off at seven. Thirty seconds later, she heard a tap on the door and Michael's voice.

'Leonie, are you awake?'

'Yes,' she called.

'Can I come in?'

'Yes.'

The door opened and he came in carrying a tray. He put the tray down on the bedside table. On it was a mug of tea and a plate with two buttered slices of toast and a jar of marmalade. It was all she ever ate for breakfast.

'What's all this?' she asked in astonishment.

'Isn't that what you eat in the morning?' he asked.

'Yes, but . . .'

He smiled down at her and said, 'Leonie. In future, I make breakfast.'

FIFTEEN

CREASY HAD TAKEN an overnight flight from New York to Brussels and after checking through Immigration and Customs he carried his single canvas bag to a row of pay phones and dialled the number of a bar. Although it was only seven a.m. he knew the bar would be open. It was almost unique in that it stayed open twenty-four hours a day. The floors got cleaned around the customers' legs.

A voice answered. Creasy recognised the voice but disguised his own.

'A message for the Corkscrew. Tell him that C called. Tell him ten o'clock tonight.'

He hung up, walked out of the terminal and climbed into the back of a taxi.

'The Pappagal,' he said to the taxi driver. 'You know where it is?'

'Sure,' the driver answered, 'but you won't get any action there this time of day. Unless you catch one coming out.'

'I can wait.'

It took forty-five minutes to reach the discreet brothel in a side-street near the EC headquarters. The heavy wooden door was opened by an old cleaning woman.

'We're closed,' she said. 'Come back tonight after eight.'

'Tell Blondie that Creasy is here.'

She looked up into his eyes and stood aside.

'I'll be in the kitchen,' he said.

He walked down the corridor on a thick pile carpet. Half-way

95

down he glanced through an open door into a room. It was very plush. Deep settees, thick, heavy curtains, chandeliers and a small bar. It was full of furniture but empty of people. He continued down the corridor to a door on his left.

He was making coffee when the door opened ten minutes later. It was Blondie, wearing a formal nightdress. Her jet black hair was in curlers. Her sixty-five-year-old face devoid of its normal caked make-up. She had an expression of rank suspicion. She had behind her, towering over her, a tall, dark-faced man. Creasy could see his right hand inside his open jacket. His eyes were black buttons. Eyes without expression.

The woman made a sign of the cross over her ample breasts and muttered a few words of prayer in Italian. Then in French she said, 'I'd heard you were dead.'

Creasy smiled. It was a smile of affection.

'Blondie,' he said, 'I'm sorry I couldn't let you know otherwise. It was necessary.'

Over her shoulder, she said to the man behind her, 'You can go now. It's OK. Close the door behind you.'

As it closed, she moved to Creasy, put her arms around him and hugged him for a long time. Then she slapped him very hard. So hard that his head rocked back.

'Don't ever do that again,' she hissed. 'I went to church. I prayed for your soul, just in case you had one. I lit candles for you . . . I cried for you.'

She was crying again now. He pulled her head against his chest and whispered into the curlers, 'I'm sorry, Blondie. It was necessary.'

She pulled her head back, wiped her sleeve across her eyes and said, 'I suppose it must have been . . . what do you want?'

'First a cup of coffee, then something to eat, then a good sleep.'

'How long are you staying?'

'Two, maybe three days.'

She started bustling around the kitchen; an instant mother.

'Go to your usual room. I'll bring the food and coffee up. Don't tell me what you like for breakfast, I know.'

She turned and gave him a severe look.

'Before you go to sleep, you will tell me everything . . . you will make up for my prayers, the candles and my tears.'

'I will,' he said solemnly.

He walked into the bar at nine forty-five in the evening and recognised several faces. Nobody recognised him. Blondie was a mistress of disguise. She had spent an hour changing the shape of his face, enlarging his eyebrows, fixing a moustache.

It was a large room with a long bar at the end. Everything very plain and utilitarian. Sawdust on the floor.

At the bar he ordered a beer, noting that Wensa, the bartender, had hardly seemed to age in the intervening years. He carried his drink over to an isolated table in the far corner. It was understood, in this bar, that when people wanted to talk business they went to that table or the one in the other corner.

The bar was a sort of brokerage house of the nether world. Information was asked for and given. Deals were made. Contracts given out.

The Corkscrew came in at exactly ten o'clock. He looked to be in his early sixties. Creasy knew he was much older. He had a man with him, a younger man. The Corkscrew's eyes swept the room and settled on Creasy. All of Blondie's skills would never fool the Corkscrew. He said something to the younger man, who moved to the bar.

The old man approached the table and said, 'It's only happened once before.'

'What?' Creasy asked.

The Corkscrew's smile was gap-toothed. He was called the Corkscrew because he could worm his way into anything and then pull out.

'Arising from the dead,' he said.

Creasy didn't offer him a drink. The Corkscrew only drank water and never in bars. He was also a man of very few words.

'What is it?' he asked.

'A job,' Creasy said. 'A complicated one . . . but it pays well.'

'How well?'

'Three hundred thousand.'

He did not have to specify the currency. The deals done in this bar were always done in Swiss francs.

'It will be intermittent,' he continued. 'Over the next year or two. No more than four or five days each month.'

'Where?'

'I need two holes. One in Damascus and one in Algiers. They must be secure. Small apartments in busy areas, preferably somewhere near the souks. They would have to be lived in and visited for a few days every month, so as not to attract any comment. You would need good cover and to be well documented, probably as a trader. Also, I would need you to get some machinery into Damascus and Algiers and stash it for me in the holes.'

'Heavy machinery?' the Corkscrew asked.

Creasy shook his head.

'Medium to light. A couple of RPG7s, a couple of submachine-guns, Uzis preferably, a couple of heavy hand guns, Colt 1911s would be good. Also two sniper rifles with night scopes and silencers. Finally, some grenades . . . a couple of dozen, fragmentation and phosphorescent. Plus the ammunition. Four rockets each for the RPG7s, eight mags each for the Uzis and the same for the Colts. I want everything in place within sixty days, although it might be up to two years before I use them. In each hole I also need a very complete medical kit. Can do?'

The Corkscrew shook his head.

'No.'

'You're busy?'

Another shake of the head. 'No, I'm retired. I was seventy last year.'

Creasy sighed in exasperation.

'So why the hell did you sit there and let me lower my pants. Why not tell me in the first place?'

The Corkscrew gestured at the bar. The man he had come in with walked over and sat down. He was about forty years old. So thin as to be almost skeletal. His hair was receding half-way across his head and he wore thick rimless spectacles. He had no other distinguishing features. No one would ever look at him twice.

'My son,' the Corkscrew said to Creasy. 'He will do the job.'

Questions arose in Creasy's mind. He was about to ask them and then stopped. The Corkscrew would not present his son if he was not totally capable. He would have trained him himself to do the family business.

'What are you known as?' he asked the younger man.

He got a very straight-faced answer.

'Corkscrew Two.'

'Are you married?'

'Yes, and I have two sons, Corkscrew Three and Four.'

Creasy asked the older man, 'Do I brief him now?'

The Corkscrew shook his head.

'No. I'll do it. Just a couple of questions. First, should the holes be rented or purchased?'

'Purchased. I don't need any luxury but they should be compatible with a man engaged in a modest business.'

'Funding?'

'Do you still have the same account in Luxembourg?'

'Yes.'

'A hundred thousand will be in it by close of business tomorrow. That will be for expenses, for the holes and the machinery. It should be enough. If you need more let me know. The three hundred for the job will be spaced at thirty thousand a month and paid up in full if the job ends early.'

He took the card from his inside pocket and passed it across to the Corkscrew.

'Keep me informed at that address. In an emergency call me at that number. If I'm not there, leave word with Michael Creasy.'

For the first time the Corkscrew's face showed expression.

'You have no brothers or sons,' he said. It was a statement.

'I have a son,' Creasy answered. He gestured at the younger man but was looking at the Corkscrew. 'Like you I continue the family business.'

*

Creasy got back to the Pappagal just after midnight. The door was opened by Blondie herself.

'I have a problem,' she said briskly. 'Raoul got sick and I had to send him home. The guy I usually use for backup is on holiday.'

'No sweat,' Creasy said. 'I'll fill in.' He followed her down the corridor. As he passed the open door on his right, he saw several business-suited men sitting at the bar. The girls were lounging on the settees watching them. Waiting. They were all dressed elegantly. They were all young and very beautiful. Blondie ran a very high-class house. Sometimes things could go wrong, especially with diplomats from the Third World. Sometimes, they became over-confident because of their diplomatic immunity.

He followed Blondie into the kitchen. The shoulder holster was lying on the table, the black butt of the pistol jutting out. He took off his jacket and slipped the harness on, then he pulled out the Beretta and checked the magazine. It was empty. He then pulled back the breech. It was empty. He put the gun back into the holster. It was an understanding that Blondie had with the police. The gun was always empty. It was only ever shown as a threat. He put his jacket on and left the kitchen.

'I'll bring you some coffee,' Blondie said.

The Pappagal had twelve rooms, eleven of them were used by the girls and one by Raoul or his stand-in. The girls' rooms were opulent, with many mirrors. Raoul's room was spartan. A single bed, a table, two chairs and a colour television to relieve the boredom. Above the television was a row of eleven light bulbs, each with a number underneath. If a girl had a problem with a client, she would press a recessed button in the headboard of her bed and the relevant bulb would light up in Raoul's room. Creasy turned on the television and tuned into Cable News Network. Five minutes later Blondie bustled in with a tray holding a large percolator of coffee, a cup, and a half-full Cognac glass. Creasy knew it would be Hennessy Extra. She put it on the table, asking, 'Are you hungry?'

He shook his head.

'I've eaten. Go about your business.'

'There's only one possible problem,' she said. 'He's coming at one o'clock. He's the military attaché at the Chilean Embassy. Macho type. Occasionally gets a bit heavy. He's booked Nicole for one o'clock. She's in room seven.'

She bustled out.

Creasy drank his coffee, sipped at his Cognac and watched the world's death and mayhem unfold on the television. Beirut. The West Bank. Kashmir. Ethiopia. Sri Lanka. It came into that spartan room from all corners of the earth.

At one thirty, it came from room seven. The bulb lit up. It took him six seconds to get there. As he opened the door, he heard a muffled scream. Nicole was lying on her belly, her face being pushed into the pillow. The man was straddling her.

Creasy closed the door behind him and said, 'Cut it!'

The man turned. Lust was stamped on his face. It turned to anger. He was a big man and very hirsute. Black hair covered his back, chest, legs and arms. Creasy's hand slipped into the side of his jacket and stayed there.

'Get off of her,' he said. 'Get dressed, then get out.'

The man swore at him in Spanish. Creasy answered in the same language.

'You don't have diplomatic immunity with me.'

He pulled out the Beretta.

The man swore again and rolled off the girl. She turned over, long legs, long body, long black hair. Hatred in her eyes as she looked at the man.

'What happened?' Creasy asked.

'He wanted to give me a bonus,' she answered. 'Just to hurt me a little. A thousand francs. I refused. He hurt me anyway. The bastard's leaving tomorrow and won't be back. He knew that.'

The man was getting dressed. He called her names. His language was totally vile. He spoke in French and Spanish. She started to come off the bed in a rage. Creasy's voice stopped her.

'Stay still. Exactly where you are.'

His voice carried authority and she froze.

The man finished knotting his tie and put on his jacket. He was in his late thirties and looked very fit.

101

He moved closer to Creasy, looked into his eyes and snarled. 'Listen, pimp, without that gun, I'd pull your arms off.'

Creasy opened the door, tossed the Beretta out onto the carpet in the corridor, closed the door again and held his arms out.

'Be my guest.'

The man smiled.

'You're no chicken,' he said.

Creasy smiled back.

'And you're no cockerel.'

He watched the hatred come into the man's eyes, watched him edge closer. The man started talking again. A soft voice.

'OK. I don't want trouble. She's not worth it. Not a slut like that.' He smiled and held up his hands, palms outwards. 'Peace, OK?'

'Whatever you want.'

Creasy saw the man's right hand curl into a fist. Watched the man's hips pivot. Creasy swayed back and to the left, and the fist swung past his face. The momentum carried the man forward into the upthrust jab of Creasy's stiff-fingered right hand. He dropped to the floor in a heap. Creasy kicked him in the face. The man rolled onto his back unconscious, blood oozing from his nose and mouth. Creasy knelt down, took his left arm, held it by the wrist and placed it over his right knee. The edge of his right hand slashed against it.

The girl on the bed heard the crack as the bone snapped. Five seconds later, she heard the crack again as the man's right arm was broken.

Creasy looked up. Her face was as white as alabaster. She crossed herself and muttered something under her breath.

'Go and fetch Blondie,' he said. 'Tell her we have a "baggage" job.'

The girl put on a red velvet dressing gown. She stepped over the man to the door, then turned and looked down at him. She leaned over and spat on his face. Then she looked at Creasy, smiled and said, 'He won't be going home tomorrow.'

Creasy finally got to bed at three o'clock. The tap on his door came at three fifteen. Nicole came in still wearing her red dressing gown. She sat on the edge of the bed and looked at him. The room was well heated and the sheet only came to his naked chest. She ran a hand across it. Across his scars. Then she stood and took off the dressing gown.

She looked down at him and murmured, 'Blondie told me not to waste my time. That you don't make love to whores.' He looked at her steadily, then pulled aside the sheet and patted the bed beside him. She lay down and he turned off the light. A few minutes later she was asleep, an arm across his chest; her head resting against his shoulder. Blondie had been right; but she was at peace. The ultimate intimacy . . . to sleep together and not to make love.

SIXTEEN

NORMALLY COLONEL JOMAH would have summoned Ahmed Jibril to his office at Syrian Airforce Intelligence. On this occasion, however, he decided to visit Jibril at his base. He phoned and told him he was coming.

As his black, unmarked Mercedes approached the entrance, he noticed the security on the street, both his own and that of the PFLP–GC. About a dozen men. He knew that in two rooms on the second floor of the building opposite the entrance there would be two more men with heavy submachine-guns.

The Mercedes pulled up at the entrance to the courtyard. Two men carrying submachine-guns came out, peered into the back, instantly recognised the Colonel and waved the car through. There were more men in the courtyard itself, all heavily armed.

Jibril himself came down the steps of the entrance dressed in an Italian-made business suit. He embraced the Colonel warmly and, taking him by the hand, led him up the steps and through the door.

As soon as they were seated in Jibril's office the Colonel said, 'I have had another communication from my man at the Embassy in Paris.'

Jibril noticed the bad manners. Normally an Arab would never state his business without going through the normal courtesies.

But he did not let the irritation show. He could not afford to offend the Colonel. Instead he gestured to an aide at the door to bring coffee.

'He has more information?' he asked the Colonel.

'Yes, he has the name of the would-be informant.'

'And that name is?'

'Joseph Rawlings.'

Ahmed Jibril had a renowned memory. He closed his eyes for a minute and thought. Then shook his head.

'It means nothing to me.'

The Colonel shrugged.

'It meant nothing to me either, but we have an informant in the French SDECE. He pulled out a file on the man, a very slim file. He's been a mercenary or has mercenary contacts. He's American, based mainly in Europe. Now our man at the Embassy set up a meeting with this Rawlings.'

At this moment the aide came back with a tray and the coffee. The Colonel waited until he had served them and left the room, then went on. 'He turned out to be a man of about fifty. Very sure of himself. He said he has the name of a man, a very danger-ous man, who has been hired to kill the organiser of the bomb that was planted on Pan Am 103.'

Jibril smiled.

'Colonel, you mean the genius who planted that bomb.'

The Colonel also smiled and dipped his head in acknowledge-ment.

'It was a work of art.'

'What else did the man say?' Jibril asked.

'He said that the project was being financed by a very wealthy American whose wife was on Pan Am 103. This wealthy American hired a man who Rawlings claims is one of the most dangerous individuals on earth.'

'Did he give a name?'

'No. For the name, and for the name of the American financier, he wants one hundred thousand American dollars.'

Jibril thought, then smiled again and said, 'But no one can put the finger on me for that bomb.'

'Not yet,' the Colonel agreed. 'But we know from our source in SDECE that they have narrowed it down either to you or Abu Nidal.'

The Colonel spread his hands in an eloquent gesture.

'We can assume that this man Rawlings has also approached Abu Nidal through the Algerian Embassy in Paris with the same offer. I expect confirmation of that within a few days.'

Jibril pondered again and asked, 'So what do we do?'

The Colonel's answer came in silky tones.

'Well, Ahmed, you got five million dollars for that job. I suppose you haven't spent it all yet?'

'Not yet.' He grinned. 'I only gave these idiot Libyans fifty thousand each. And they took the risk.'

'So you have two options. Either pay the money or arrange for your organisation or what's left of it in Europe, to snatch the man in Paris and force the name out of him. I can't help you there. We're keeping a low profile at the moment. Incidentally, my man at the Paris Embassy has arranged a meeting with Rawlings in four days' time to pass on your reply. Naturally we can be a conduit for the money if you decide to pay.'

'I wonder what Abu Nidal would do,' Jibril mused. 'If he did get the same offer.'

The Colonel shook his head.

'Nidal would not pay. First because he knows that you arranged it, secondly because he's out of favour now and therefore short of cash, and third because of his temper. He would not like to be shaken down like that.'

His voice went silky again. 'But you are not like that, Ahmed. You are smarter than Nidal, and lately more successful, and therefore richer.'

Jibril was a vain man. His smile was complacent.

'Colonel,' he said, 'I would be grateful if, at the next meeting, your man at the Embassy in Paris would make the deal. I will arrange the funds immediately. Yet again, I'm in your debt.'

The phone in the house in Gozo rang at three o'clock in the afternoon on a Tuesday. Leonie answered it on an extension in the kitchen.

'Is everything all right?' he asked.

'Yes, everything is fine.'

'And Michael?'

'He's fine. Right now he's in Malta. I pick him up from the six o'clock ferry.'

'Is he behaving himself?'

'He certainly is,' Leonie answered. 'He brings me tea and toast every morning, washes up the dishes after every meal and studies hard. He's reading all the books you told him to read. He also does his hundred lengths every morning, even when he's been out late to the disco.'

There was silence on the other end of the line. Then Creasy's amused voice came over.

'Maybe he lost his virginity.'

She laughed.

'I think he did. Two weeks ago he was driven home at six in the morning by an English girl.'

'What was she like?'

'I don't know. I didn't see her, I only heard her.'

Creasy's voice turned hard.

'He brought her into the house?'

'No. As she drove away, I heard him shout thank you. She shouted back, "You're welcome".'

'That sounds conclusive.'

Leonie smiled and said, 'He could have been thanking her for the lift home.'

106

'I doubt it.'

'By the way,' she said, 'he has to go to the disco on his own now.'

'He doesn't go with Joey?'

'No, a couple of weeks ago, Joey visited Maria's house in Nadur and had a drink with her parents. He says get back here quickly and help him finish the house.'

She heard a rarity, Creasy's laugh.

'Tell him it will be five or six days,' he said, 'tell him he can have arches instead of beams. Did anyone phone?'

'Yes, a man called Bob Dines. He phoned this morning. Said if you rang to get in touch.'

'Good.'

She went back to preparing the rabbit stew for dinner, humming to herself. She was no longer counting the days until she could leave. She was beginning to enjoy life in Gozo. A few days earlier, she had gone into the supermarket to buy provisions. There were trays of eggs by the checkout counter. As she was helping herself to a dozen, the checkout girl had called to her.

'No, not those, take them from that one over there.' She pointed and winked. 'They just came in and they're fresher.'

Later at the grocer's, the woman had fussed over her, making sure she got the right vegetables, even bringing potatoes from the back room, which she said were kept for her special customers.

On the Sundays that Creasy had been away she had gone to the Schembris for lunch with Michael. Laura had become a good friend. On the first Sunday, Joey had brought his girlfriend Maria. It was the first time she had been in the Schembri house and she was shy and nervous. So was Joey. She had noticed how Paul and Laura had put her at ease. Paul had told her some of the escapades he and her father had got up to in their youth. He was a good raconteur and soon she was laughing.

Afterwards, he had brought a bible from the bedroom and made her solemnly swear on it that she would not tell her father.

On the second Sunday, after lunch, she and Laura had walked

down to the farmhouse which Joey and Creasy were rebuilding. They had looked around the place and chatted. Laura had talked about her two daughters. The elder one, Julia, who had married Creasy's Italian friend, and had died in a car crash, and Nadia who had died on Pan Am 103.

She had talked easily and without visible emotion but when Leonie had asked her a question about Creasy, Laura had shaken her head and said, 'Whatever you want to know about Creasy, you must ask him yourself.' She had smiled to take any offence out of the words. 'He has a very private shell and it's very hard to break through . . . who knows . . . maybe . . .'

SEVENTEEN

CREASY TOOK A late flight from Luxembourg to London and checked into the Gore Hotel just before midnight. There was a message waiting to inform him that Bob Dines would be in the bar at twelve thirty. He took his bag up to his room, tuned the television to Cable News Network, turned the volume high and took a shower while he listened to the news. Twenty minutes later he was in the bar.

The small, sandy-haired man arrived five minutes early. He was always five minutes early. He carried a briefcase.

There was a young couple sitting in the corner, holding hands and working hard at being in love. Bob Dines studied them for a moment, and then, content that they were not watchers, said to Creasy, 'I'll have a large whisky and soda . . . it's been one of those days and nights.'

Creasy ordered the drink and a Remy Martin for himself.

When the night porter had limped away, Dines said very quietly, 'A couple of things may have broken on the Lockerbie case.'

'Like what?' Creasy asked.

'Well, I told you that the policeman Peter Fleming is a damn good detective . . . and very tenacious. Also the forensic boys, who are working on the reconstruction of Pan Am 103 and its contents, are probably the best in the world and the most meticulous. They've now found out which suitcase the bomb was in, and where it was located in the baggage hold. They've done that from tiny fragments. The FBI, who have their own experts, were massively impressed. They were able to identify some of the clothes that were in the suitcase. Peter Fleming was able to trace them all the way back to the source, which turned out to be Malta. They were manufactured in a factory in Malta. He even managed to trace the shop from which they were sold. A place in Sliema called Mary's House. The shopkeeper remembers selling the clothes to an Arab some weeks before the Lockerbie bombing.'

'Malta,' Creasy muttered. 'That's close to home.'

'Yes,' Dines replied. 'And it's significant because we have known, and the BND have known, for some time that the PFLP–GC have had a cell there for years. Under Mintoff, Malta was very friendly with Libya. Libyans don't even need a visa to visit Malta. So it's been a natural staging post for groups like the PFLP–GC. They get help from the Libyan cells there.'

'Do they still have a cell there?' Creasy asked.

'Yes, a passive one and we think we know where the Front is.' He tapped his briefcase, 'I have a report in here. Read it later and then destroy it. The thing is that it points more and more to the PFLP–GC and Ahmed Jibril.'

'Yes it does,' Creasy said thoughtfully. 'You said you had a couple of things.'

The small man nodded.

'Yes, the other thing concerns the Syrian Airforce Intelligence. They're the most powerful arm of the Syrian Intelligence Community. Very closely linked to President Assad himself. We know they work closely with the PFLP–GC in Europe. Use them for their dirty work. Several of their agents have been identified by ourselves, the BND and the SDECE. They generally work out of the Syrian Embassies. They're all under round-the-clock surveillance. The one in Paris, the trade attaché by the name of Merwad Kwikas, has recently had two meetings in a Paris bistro with an American. The first meeting was six days ago. It was only a conversation. The second meeting was four days later, when Kwikas gave the American a package and then the American gave Kwikas an envelope.'

'Do you know who the American is?'

'Yes,' Dines replied, 'and so do you. We were able to photograph the first meeting but not the second.'

He spun the combination locks on his briefcase, opened it and took out a photograph. He passed it to Creasy, who looked at it and then muttered:

'Joe Rawlings. I gave that bastard Tap City Money. Do you know where he is now?'

'Yes, from the first meeting he's been under surveillance. Between the first meeting and the second meeting, he was staying in a seedy hotel at the wrong end of Montparnasse. Immediately after the second meeting, he checked out and moved into the Plaza Athénée.'

'Yes, the bastard would,' Creasy said bitterly. 'Is he still under surveillance?'

'Yes.'

'Is there any way to pull it off for a few hours, perhaps tomorrow night?'

Bob Dines shook his head.

'It's being handled by our Paris station. I can't interfere, especially if, while the surveillance was called off, Joseph Rawlings happens to sadly die.'

Creasy went up to his room and phoned Brussels; the call was answered by Raoul.

'Put Blondie on the phone.'

'Is that you?'

'It's me.'

'Thanks for the arms you did, that prick needed it.'

'It made my day.'

A minute after, Blondie was on the line.

'Now I need Nicole,' Creasy said. 'I need her in Paris and I need her tomorrow.'

'It got that serious?' Blondie said in wonderment.

'No. Nothing gets that serious. I need her to pull a man. She should have clothes with her that give her elegance, in which she could walk into any hotel or restaurant in Paris and be thought of as Society. She should be prepared to take a risk. Tell her that.'

'And where should she go?'

'She will be booked into a hotel called the Plaza Athénée. She is to check in with a false name and a false passport. The Corkscrew will supply the latter. She should have a booking early the next morning on Iberian Airlines 422 to Barcelona. She should lie low there for three days before flying back to Brussels. She will take a taxi from Paris airport, check in and wait for me in her room. Order what she needs from room service and just wait. I will contact her tomorrow evening. Please arrange the airline tickets and give her three thousand dollars in cash. I'll settle with you later.'

'She'll be there.'

Joe Rawlings walked into the bar at the Plaza Athénée at eight o'clock. He was a man who understood luxury and enjoyed it when he could. His programme for the evening was mapped out. He would have a couple of drinks in the bar first, then have dinner at La Poupoule, then move on to the Crazy Horse for the late show, to raise the stimulation, then go on to Babette's and select the most delectable whore in the place.

The bar was busy, and the clientele smartly dressed; a mixture of wealthy locals and wealthy tourists. His eyes immediately picked out the woman sitting alone at the end of the bar. Remembering the line from *My Fair Lady*, he made his approach; 'oozing charm from every pore, he oiled his way across the floor' like a lizard, and slid onto the barstool beside her.

From the bartender he ordered a twenty-five-year-old Macallan Scotch. He guessed instantly from her clothes and jewellery, that she was from the upper class. Her dress was mid-night blue silk. Soft and clinging. Rawlings knew something about precious stones. He knew that the jade pendant at her neck, nestling between her high breasts, was worth a small fortune. He knew that the diamond bracelet on her left wrist contained genuine, flawless blue-white diamonds. At least ten carats. At least fifty thousand dollars.

He changed gear into overdrive, his mind working rapidly. He decided not to waste time.

'Are you alone,' he asked her . . . 'or waiting for somebody?'

'I'm waiting for my husband,' she answered coolly. 'But unfortunately he doesn't arrive until tomorrow.'

He noted the accent and asked, 'Are you French?'

'Belgian.'

'Staying in the hotel?'

'Yes, we normally stay at the Ritz but it's booked up. Full of Arabs.'

It took Joe Rawlings half an hour to make the pick-up. Or at least he thought it did. Following her query, he told her that he was a top international lawyer, at the moment on assignment for IBM, on a patents case. Then in an aside he said, 'Normally when I travel on business, I like to dine alone. I follow Gulbenkian's adage that the perfect number for dinner is two. Myself and a damn good head waiter.'

She smiled and said half-sadly, 'I hate to dine alone.'

They had dinner together at La Poupoule. During the meal he touched her from time to time, on her arm or her hand. Occasionally, his leg brushed hers under the table. By the time the coffee came he felt he was onto a winner. He had learned that her husband was the vice-president of a large steel corpora-tion and that he was twenty-five years her senior. He felt the eroticism that was growing and decided to wind it up.

'I had planned to see the late show at the Crazy Horse,' he

said, touching her hand . . . 'but would that be too risqué for you?'

She smiled and shook her head.

'I would not go there alone . . . but I like things risqué.'

After taking in the immaculate show at the Crazy Horse, and absorbing the beauty of the showgirls, Joe Rawlings was in a mood to be led anywhere. He was led to her room at the Plaza Athénée. She preferred it that way. In the lobby she had told him in a soft voice that after she had made love she preferred not to get out of bed.

She opened the door and ushered him in, saying with her soft, lilting voice, 'You thought you were going to get fucked tonight. You are, but not the way you imagined.'

The door closed behind him. He was looking at the large double bed, looking at Creasy sitting on it, looking at the silenced pistol pointing at him.

The words crossed the room, slow and deadly.

'I gave you Tap City Money, Joe . . . and you did that?'

Joe Rawlings's voice was strangled, his fear palpable.

'Did what, Creasy?'

Creasy tossed an eight by ten photograph at him. It hit him on the knee and dropped beside him on the floor. He looked down at it. It was the photograph of himself and Merwad Kwikas, sitting in a restaurant.

He knew he was dead.

'Easy or hard, Joe? I've got all night.'

Joe Rawlings tried to say something but could not. His eyes were fixed on the gun.

'You gave them my name?' Creasy asked.

Rawlings nodded.

'You gave them Grainger's name?'

Rawlings nodded.

'You approached Abu Nidal?'

Rawlings nodded.

'Did he pay?'

Rawlings shook his head.

The voice was musing.

113

'So you gave them all you know, and I got what I needed to know. Jibril paid. I guess it's in the bathroom.'

Rawlings nodded. He was mesmerised by the gun and by the eyes.

The gun exploded with a soft plop. The bullet went into his brain between his eyes.

Creasy opened the door. Nicole was standing across the corridor. He gestured and she walked into the room, looked at the body on the floor. Creasy hung the 'Do Not Disturb' sign on the outside handle and closed the door.

He said, 'Do you have his key?'

'It's in his pocket.'

He reached down, rummaged in the pockets and found the key. He handed it to her, saying, 'Go to his room and search the bathroom. You'll find a wad of money, probably behind the toilet system. Bring it here.'

She was back in five minutes, holding a thick envelope. The body had been covered by a long, white towel, which had a red stain at one end. Creasy counted out the money. It came to seventy-eight thousand dollars in used fifty-dollar bills. From that pile he counted out twenty thousand, put it back in the envelope and handed it to her.

EIGHTEEN

SENATOR JAMES GRAINGER walked into the same restaurant in Washington and saw Creasy at a banquette in a corner with another man. He walked over and sat down. Creasy introduced the other man.

'Frank Miller,' he said.

The Senator studied the man. He was in his mid-forties and totally bald. He had a small head and a big body. His face was round and plump, almost cherubic, his eyes nestling between a low forehead and fat cheeks. He was dressed in a dark suit, crisp white shirt and deep blue tie. He looked like everybody's favourite uncle. They ordered dinner and the Senator told Henry the sommelier to bring the same wine as before.

The Senator had received a phone call the night before telling him that events had changed. The dinner meeting had been set up.

'What events have changed?' the Senator asked Creasy, with a wary glance at the other man.

Creasy noticed the glance.

'We can talk in front of Frank,' he said. 'I've known him a long time . . . Jim, I made a mistake. I hope that's the last one. I should have taken Joe Rawlings out in Cannes but instead I gave him Tap City Money . . . thought that would buy his silence . . . it did not. He worked things out and sold my name and yours to Ahmed Jibril from the PFLP–GC. The fact that Jibril paid him confirms, to me at least, that Jibril planted the bomb. Now Jibril knows I'm coming after him. He knows what I'm capable of. He will not know where to find me. But Jim, he will know where to find you . . . you cannot hide yourself. It's almost certain that the PFLP–GC has a cell in the USA. It's almost certain they will try to get to you . . . abduct you and force information out of you.'

He gestured at Miller.

'I've brought this man over to make sure they don't do that.'

The Senator glanced at Miller and said, 'I have adequate security. All Senators do.'

Creasy shook his head.

'Adequate is not enough . . . Jim, you're going to have to live with this man, and his two partners, until the matter is over. Not just for your sake, but also for mine. You'll have to live with them for twenty-four hours a day . . . they'll be within yards of you, even when you take a shit . . . twenty-four hours a day, Jim. That's the way it has to be . . . until the operation's over, and that could be months or even a year or more.'

115

As though Frank Miller did not exist, the Senator asked, 'Who is he?'

Creasy replied, also as if Frank Miller was not sitting between them.

'He was a mercenary,' he answered. 'An Australian. Since mercenary work became scarce, he went into the protection business. Spent some years in Germany and Italy, looking after industrialists who were targets of terrorist groups . . . the Red Brigade and so on . . . he's the best. He never lost a client.'

The Senator looked at the Australian.

'And he needs two other people to help him?'

Creasy gestured.

'He has to sleep . . . occasionally he has to find a woman . . . or have you find one for him.' A half-smile formed on Creasy's lips. 'Don't worry, Jim, they're house-trained. Do what they tell you . . . in everything. It's your life and it's mine.'

The Senator said, 'He and his partners must be expensive.'

'Yes. The best always are. But it's ironic. A bit like the Irangate affair. Jibril is paying their wages.'

The Senator straightened in his chair, surprise on his face. Creasy said, 'Jibril paid Rawlings a lot of money for our names. I recovered some of it. For a few months, it will pay for Frank and his boys.'

The food came and Henry decanted the wine. He treated Creasy like a prodigal son.

The Senator noted that the Australian did not drink any wine. Only mineral water. He noted that he did not talk much, that his eyes constantly swept the room, watching every arrival and every departure. Over coffee the Australian said something to Creasy in French. Creasy answered in the same language and then said to the Senator, 'Jim, we both noted that there's a "watcher" in here. He's by himself, over in the corner. Don't look round but I guess he's a Fed. Is your friend Bennett watching over you?'

'It's possible,' the Senator conceded. 'He may be questioning what I'm up to. Maybe he's worried about me.'

'Can you call him off and keep him off? It's important.'

'It's very important,' the Australian added. 'I don't want extraneous people hanging around.'

The Senator lifted a finger and within seconds, the *maître d'* was by his side.

'Bring me a phone,' the Senator said curtly.

A minute later the Senator was punching the number into a portable phone. It was answered. Into the phone the Senator said, 'Curtis, if you know where I'm dining, you're having me watched. If so I want it stopped immediately. If not, I get heavy.' He handed the phone back to the hovering *maître d'*.

Three minutes later a man walked into the restaurant. He went to the man in the corner, dining alone, and whispered into his ear. The man dining alone called for his bill and paid it. Both men left, without a glance at the Senator.

'It's better that way,' the Australian said. 'Now, if anyone's watching you, I'll know who they are.'

'You're sure it's Jibril?' the Senator asked Creasy.

'He wouldn't pay good money for nothing . . . he's my target.'

'When will you move?'

'I'm moving.'

'How long?'

Creasy shrugged and took a sip of his wine.

'I move slowly and very carefully. The bad thing is that Jibril knows I'm coming. Damascus is not an easy city. He has immense protection. Both his own people and the Syrian Intelligence.' He took another sip of his wine and then looked into the Senator's eyes. 'But Jibril is the living dead. I need a little time to hone my weapon . . . a little time to let him sweat and wait. I make you a promise, Jim, when he dies, the last words that will enter his ears will be Harriot, Nadia and Julia. He will know why he died.'

The Senator drained his glass and said quietly, 'I never hated anyone before. Disliked, yes . . . many. But never really hated. I hate Jibril from my soul and I hate Joe Rawlings. That man conned me and then sold me.'

Creasy shook his head.

'Don't hate Rawlings. It's pointless to hate the dead.'
The Senator looked up at him.
'You took him out?'
'Between the eyes.'

The Senator had another breakfast meeting. 'The worst invention ever in America,' he said before leaving. As he stood up Frank Miller said, 'Wait.'

The Australian stood; went to the door of the restaurant and went out into the street. He came back two minutes later and nodded towards the table.

'He's careful,' the Senator commented to Creasy.

'He's your mother and father, Jim,' said Creasy, and then smiled. 'Introduce him to your Dobermann, they'll get on well. Also, be straight with him. If you break away from him, you break away from me. Keep something in your mind. Jibril has maybe a hundred bodyguards. All heavily armed. He'd be safer with Frank Miller alone.'

They shook hands and the Senator left with the Australian as his shadow. Henry brought a large goblet of Hennessy Extra and put it in front of Creasy.

'Come back at least four more times,' he said with a smile. 'I only have four more bottles of the '49 Rothschild left.'

Creasy nodded in acknowledgement, smiled and asked for a phone.

From memory, he dialled the number. When a voice answered he said, 'I'll be there in twenty minutes, Tracey. Be naked.'

The voice answered, 'I am naked.'

It's best to judge a woman's beauty when she sleeps. Artifice is lost. Pretence also sleeps. If wine brings out the truth then sleep brings out beauty.

It was early morning. He had been to the bathroom and then opened the curtains. Sunlight lit the room, reflecting off the pale walls onto her face. He sat on the edge of the bed and watched her face. Watched it like a predator not knowing what it was

118

hunting. She was in a very deep sleep. A sated sleep. The curves of her face were those of a child. He thought of his own child, of Julia. He thought of his life, and the waste.

He thought of what he was doing, and why. He had done it all before. He felt for a moment like he was on a treadmill, walking on into nothing. Thought of the boy's past life and his future, tried to analyse what he thought about the boy, but could not. He thought about Senator James Grainger, Frank Miller, the Corkscrew and Corkscrew Two. About what he was doing and why.

There was no why.

Only a heat inside of him, not in his brain but deep down. His brain was cold. Made cold by the image of the well-dressed Arab. He thought of Nadia the woman and Julia the child. He moved across the bed and placed his hand on the cheek of the child-woman.

The woman woke up and he made love to her.

NINETEEN

THIS TIME JIBRIL went to see the Colonel. He was not even offered a coffee. The Colonel simply handed him a piece of paper. On it were two names.

'That's what you got for your hundred thousand.'

'What do we know about them?' Jibril asked.

'They both had relatives on Pan Am 103,' the Colonel answered. 'Grainger is a United States Senator for Colorado and a very wealthy man. The other one, Creasy, is also American, an ex-mercenary. The strange thing is he's supposed to have been killed five years ago in Italy. It's documented.'

Bitterly, Jibril said, 'So that bastard sold me the name of a dead man?'

The Colonel stood up and stretched, walked to the window and looked down at the traffic.

'I think not,' he said. 'Two nights ago, Joseph Rawlings was found dead in a Paris hotel. He had a single bullet in the brain. Maybe he was compromised by meeting my man in Paris. Maybe the meetings were observed. Maybe this man Creasy is alive.'

He turned and looked at Jibril and smiled slightly.

'If he is, you have a problem, Ahmed . . . a serious one.'

'A problem from one man?'

The Colonel moved back to his desk and picked up a folder. He handed it to Jibril.

'One man, but a special man. Interpol keep a register of all known mercenaries. This morning I requested information on this man Creasy. In that file is the information they sent me through our police force. Read it, Ahmed.'

The Colonel moved back to the window and stood there for fifteen minutes, looking down at the traffic.

When he turned, Ahmed Jibril was reading the faxed papers in the file for the second time.

The Colonel moved back to his desk, sat down and said affably, 'You have very good security, Ahmed. So do I. But I tell you, I would not like to have that man coming for me. Not with the motive he has. Or with the kind of money behind him that Grainger can supply.'

His words were spoken with the faint pleasure of one man informing another of his possible impending doom.

Jibril clamped down on his irritation and asked, 'Is there any information on their location?'

The Colonel shrugged and said, 'Grainger is easy. He has homes in Washington DC and Denver, Colorado. He commutes between the two. As for Creasy, the last information anyone has is that he died of gunshot wounds in a Naples hospital five years ago. That's the last information, Ahmed . . . it's on the file. No one knows where he is.' His half smile came back again. 'But personally, I suspect that two nights ago he was in Paris.'

TWENTY

CREASY ARRIVED AT Luqa Airport in Malta just after noon. He was met by George Zammit who drove him to Cirkewwa to catch the Gozo ferry. On the way Creasy asked, 'How's he doing?'

'He's more than just a natural,' George answered. 'He drives himself. He's like a sponge, he soaks up everything he's told.'

'Weapons?' Creasy asked.

'It's only been three weeks but already he's achieved a three inch cluster at twenty metres with a Colt 1911. Yesterday he fired four magazines. Not one was outside of a six inch cluster.'

The policeman turned and looked at his passenger, smiled and said, 'That's almost at your level, Creasy, and three weeks ago he'd never held a hand-gun.'

'And the other weapons?' Creasy asked.

'Again, more than a natural. With the submachine-gun he has a total affinity. It's as though he carried it out of his mother's womb.'

'Maybe he did,' Creasy said thoughtfully, as though talking to himself. 'What about the sniper rifle?'

'A little too impatient as yet,' George answered. 'As you know, a sniper needs infinite patience. The best snipers are older and more mature. Michael is young and reacts instantly. He will be very good but it will take time.'

121

'Unarmed combat?'

'Wenzu says that he's going to be more of a street fighter. Sure he'll learn all the tricks but his nature is to be a street fighter and he'll be a dangerous one.'

'Good.'

'Incidentally, he's got a lot of guts. Last week I took the squad to a disused quarry. They practised rappelling down a sheer rock-face. It's damn frightening the first time. Most of the squad were reluctant to trust themselves to a thin rope against a hundred metre drop. Michael was over the edge without a murmur. How did you find him?'

'I saw him score a goal in a soccer match.'

George Zammit glanced at him and then he concentrated again on the traffic. Quietly he asked, 'What are you going to do with him?'

'Maybe nothing. Maybe one day he'll watch my back . . . maybe one day I'll aim him at somebody.'

George drove on in silence to Cirkewwa. Before Creasy got out of the car, the policeman said, 'I know what you have in mind, Creasy, and I want a promise from you.'

'What's that?'

'You know my position here as head of security. Don't do anything in Malta without letting me know first.'

'It's a promise,' Creasy replied.

'I want a second promise,' George said.

'It's all promises today, George. What is it?'

'If the boy survives, he's to join the police force . . . join my squad.'

'I promise to influence him in that direction. But the final decision will be his.'

As Creasy got out of the car the policeman called, 'Another promise.'

Creasy turned in exasperation.

'What now?'

'Next Wednesday is Stella's fortieth birthday. I'm throwing a party for her at the house. Be there.'

'OK.'

'Be there with Michael.'

'OK.'

'Be there with your wife.'

Creasy muttered something inaudible and strode away.

He carried his bag up to Gleneagles and ordered a lager. He also ordered drinks for Shriek and Baglu, who as usual were propping up the bar. Then he said to Tony, 'Have one yourself.'

'Too early for me,' Tony replied.

They all waited patiently, then after a couple of minutes Tony said, 'Why not,' and helped himself to a beer.

God was in His Heaven and everything in Gozo was normal.

After a couple more drinks, he phoned Leonie and asked her to pick him up. On the short drive home, she said, 'I left Gleneagles as a forwarding address for my agent. I got a letter yesterday.'

He glanced at her and said curtly, 'Don't tell me he's got you a part. Don't tell me you're gonna break our contract.'

She shook her head.

'No, I wouldn't do that. It's just my friend Geraldine . . . my best friend . . . perhaps my only friend; she thinks that I'm working on a TV series in Malta and she's coming out on Friday and staying at the Suncrest Hotel for a week. Can I see her and if so, what do I tell her?'

'I prefer that you don't,' Creasy answered. 'That was in the contract if you remember. No visitors.'

They drove on in silence. As they got out of the car Creasy noticed the look on her face and said again, 'It was in the contract, Leonie.'

'I know,' she answered. 'Forget about it.' She started to walk away.

He pulled his bag from the back seat and called after her. 'Wait.'

She turned and watched him.

Finally he said, 'OK, maybe you need a break. It's been tough on you here, with the people and all. The manager of the Suncrest is a friend of mine. He'll give you a very good rate on a room for a week. I've stayed at the hotel myself, it's a bit touristy but very good. They have an excellent restaurant called Coral Reef. Spend the time with your friend, have a holiday.'

'What do I tell her?' Leonie asked.

He shrugged.

'Tell her that the funding for the series has been held up . . . it usually is. Tell her that you're being paid, but you're sitting around on your butt. Tell her nothing about Gozo, me or Michael. Make a promise on that.'

She smiled. It lit up her face.

'I promise.'

'By the way, next Wednesday, you're going to have to get away from your friend for the night. Tell her that you have to have dinner with the producer or something.'

'What's happening?'

'We're going to a birthday party in Malta. A friend's wife. I'll pick you up from the Suncrest at eight.'

'OK. What about food while I'm away? Shall I cook some things and put them in the freezer?'

He shook his head.

'No, while you're away, Michael and I will be away.'

'Where are you going?'

His voice was curt.

'Somewhere to further his education.'

TWENTY-ONE

JOEY'S MOOD WAS black enough for Creasy to notice. They were working on the farmhouse together. It was a Thursday and Michael was in Malta at Fort St Elmo. They were building a dry-stone wall, to terrace a small garden.

'What's your problem?' Creasy asked curtly.

Joey lifted a stone for the wall and turned to look at him. Both were shirtless in the hot sun, both sweating.

'Why not me?' Joey asked.

'Why not me what?'

The younger man heaved another stone up on the wall and said, 'Why not train me for the job?'

'What job?'

'You know fucking well what job. I'm not stupid, Creasy. I know why you remarried so soon. I know how much you loved Nadia . . . I just hope I can love Maria that way . . . I've known since I was a boy. I know what you did in Italy . . . how your mind works. There's no way you're going to let them get away with killing Nadia and Julia. You're getting on a bit, so you're training Michael to help you. He goes to Malta twice a week to Fort St Elmo.'

'He told you that?'

Joey shook his head.

'He didn't have to. I have a friend in George Zammit's unit. He told me. Besides, George Zammit's my cousin.'

'He told you as well?'

'No. But when I asked him, he didn't deny it. Just refused to talk about it.'

They both lifted up stones for the wall, and with great bitterness Joey asked, 'Why not me? Why Michael? I'm young and fit and I have a better motive. Nadia was my sister and Julia my niece. I loved them as much as you did in a different way . . . why not me?'

He reached down to pick up another stone at his feet, a very heavy stone. Creasy moved over, picked it up and heaved it up onto the wall. He turned and grinned at the younger man.

'So I'm getting old am I?'

Joey did not smile back. Grim-faced he persisted.

'Why not me?'

Creasy answered.

'It's true that you're not stupid, so use your goddamn brains for a change instead of your prick and you'll know why.'

125

He used his arm to wipe the sweat from his forehead and went back to building the wall.

They both worked in silence for five minutes. Joey's face was still sullen.

Finally Creasy said quietly, 'Your parents had two daughters and a son, and they had a granddaughter. They lost both daughters and their granddaughter. They've only got you left. All their love is centred on you and beginning to centre on Maria.'

He heaved another stone up and said sternly, 'Now listen to me, you prick, we're gonna finish this house in about two months. Since I've gone against Gozitan tradition and thanks to your mother got away with it, you're going to get engaged to Maria next week. You're going to marry her a month later. She's going to have a baby nine months after that.'

With a grunt he lifted up a heavy stone. 'If not,' he said, 'I'll personally pull your prick off.'

They worked on in silence for a few minutes and then Creasy muttered, 'You know what I think of your parents. I never had much family and what I had is all gone. Paul and Laura are the only family I've got left . . . and I suppose you.'

Joey smiled slightly and asked, 'And what about Michael? He's your son now.'

Creasy's answer was abrupt.

'He's a weapon. Or he will be in about six months.'

'That's all?'

'That's all.'

The young man turned to look at him and asked, 'You have no feelings for him at all?'

'None.'

'And for Leonie?'

'None. She's just a necessity.'

They carried on working in silence and then Joey mused, 'You stitched me up with this house. You knew damn well that having rebuilt it I'd want to live in it. You gave me all that shit about arches and beams and all the arguments about where the kitchen and the main bedroom should go. You made me argue. You

126

made me get involved. You knew fucking well what you were doing.'

Creasy wiped more sweat from his face and grinned.

'Are you unhappy about it?' he asked. 'After all, she's a damn fine girl. Too good for you I'd say. She'd have done better with Mario the policeman. He's better looking and he's got a steady job.'

'He's a prick,' Joey answered and then smiled. 'No, I'm not unhappy, and I'll do what you say. A week next Saturday we'll get engaged and a month later we'll get married. Tonight I'll go and see her parents and make the arrangements.'

'Are you sure she'll accept you?' Creasy asked seriously.

Joey just grinned and lifted up another stone.

A few minutes later Creasy said, 'I won't be able to help you down here next week. Leonie's going to Malta to visit a friend and I'm taking Michael to Comino.'

'You're staying at the hotel?' Joey asked in surprise.

Creasy shook his head.

'No, we'll be staying on the other side of the island.'

'But there's nothing there. It's totally barren.'

'Exactly,' Creasy answered. 'I'll teach him how to live off the land and from the sea. What plants are edible and what plants are poisonous. How to survive in the open with nothing but a couple of fishing lines and a knife.'

'But there are hardly any plants there,' Joey said. 'It's just rocks and limestone . . . garigue.'

'There are plenty of plants there,' Creasy said. 'You just never noticed them, and there's the sea and there are fish in the sea. A man who knows how could live there to old age. Don't forget, Joey, that there's also animal life over there. Rabbits, mice, rats, snakes and even grasshoppers.'

Joey's face showed astonishment.

'You'd eat rats, mice, snakes and grasshoppers?'

Creasy nodded.

'If necessary. I've done it before. In some African countries, a barbecued rat is considered a delicacy and roasted grasshopper is a tasty dish.'

Joey was intrigued.

'You mean you're going over there with nothing except a couple of fishing lines and a knife?'

'That's right.'

'Nothing else at all?'

'Nothing. Just the clothes we're wearing.'

'What about water? The only drinking water on the island comes out of a bottle in the bar at the Comino Hotel.'

'We'll find water.'

Joey laughed.

'The government has been trying to find water over there for years. The hotel had to build its own desalination plant. You'll both die of thirst in a few days.'

Very seriously Creasy asked, 'You're a farmer, Joey, where would the plants on Comino get their water?'

'From the ground,' Joey answered. 'During the rainy season; then they store it for the dry season.' He looked up at the clear blue sky. 'And Creasy, the rainy season is over. It's unlikely to rain now until September or October.'

'Where do rabbits get their water from, Joey? . . . there are rabbits on Comino. Where do rats, mice, snakes and grasshoppers get their water?'

Joey thought about that and then asked, 'Where?'

'From the plants that store the water. They know very well which plants store the water best and how to get at it; besides, there are ways of drinking sea-water if you know how.'

Joey lifted up another stone and positioned it carefully on the wall. Building a dry-stone wall is like constructing a jigsaw puzzle. Every stone has to fit exactly. He looked over the wall at the island of Comino, two miles away.

'Can I come with you?' he asked.

Creasy glanced at him and then said, 'If you're getting engaged a week on Saturday you're going to be damn busy. Besides, Paul needs you here.'

Joey said, 'Creasy, you should know that engagement parties and weddings here are arranged one hundred per cent by the couples' mothers. If I even tried to interfere I'd get a clout from

128

both of them. As for the farm, I'll get a friend in to help Dad. He's out of work. I'll give him the meagre pittance that Dad gives me for slaving away twelve hours a day.'

'Meagre pittance? You've got two horses that you race at the feasts, a Honda 250 motorbike and that Toyota which you bought a couple of months ago.' He gestured at the almost finished farmhouse. 'And no doubt a few days after you get engaged, Paul will sign this place over to you. It's worth at least thirty grand. Don't give me that shit about a pittance.'

Joey grinned and then his face turned serious again.

'Can I come with you, Creasy?' he asked again.

Creasy realised the young man wanted to show his commitment. He chose his words carefully, put his hand on Joey's shoulder and said, 'Yes, you can come. Michael would like that . . . and so would I. Joey, when this business starts in earnest you can definitely be of help. When Michael and I leave, and that could be many months away, I want you to move into my house and set up a sort of operational base. There will be messages coming and going from different parts of the world. While we're in Comino, I'll bring you up to date on the situation and tell you all I know. Then I'll keep you up to date as it unfolds. I'll take you totally into my confidence.'

He moved his hand from the young man's shoulder and gently slapped his face.

'You'll be part of it, Joey. The Gozo part. A very important part . . . even a vital part. There might even be some danger. The people who put that bomb on Pan Am 103 know that I'm coming after them. They don't know where I am or where I live. If they find out, my house will become a target. You'll have to take precautions.'

'Who are they?' Joey asked, the anger showing in his eyes.

'I'll brief you on Comino,' Creasy answered, 'and also about the precautions you'll take. Now this friend of yours who's in George Zammit's squad, what did he tell you about Michael?'

'That he's damn good,' Joey replied. 'He gets a lot of personal attention from George and the other instructors.'

'What's your own opinion about Michael?'

129

The young man concentrated and then answered, 'I like him. He doesn't make friends easily, and neither do I, but I think we're going to become good friends. He's smart and something of a loner.' He smiled. 'A bit like you. Does he know what he's getting into?'

Creasy nodded.

'He knows exactly what he might be getting into. It's possible he might get into nothing. It's possible that I can do the job myself. I'm not that old yet.'

Joey smiled and asked, 'Will you be my best man?'

Creasy nodded solemnly.

'I'll be honoured and I'll kick your ass if you don't make me godfather to your first child.'

'It's a deal,' Joey answered, 'and I'll ask Michael to be a witness at the wedding . . . you'll have to buy him a suit . . . by the way, he lost his virginity.'

'I guessed that . . .'

The young man was looking across at Comino again.

'It's going to be an interesting week,' he muttered.

'It is,' Creasy agreed. 'And don't get any ideas about sneaking off in the night to the hotel bar.'

TWENTY-TWO

TWO NIGHTS LATER, Leonie was eating fresh lobster with her friend Geraldine in the luxury of the Coral Reef.

Creasy, Michael and Joey were eating black snake on the eastern cliffs of Comino.

It was not essential that they ate snake, because during the

130

afternoon, they had caught two dozen Rozetta fish in the bay of Santa Maria. Rozetta is a great delicacy, resembling a sole but much smaller. It is not fished commercially and so is a rarity. Both young men were looking forward to the evening meal but on the way back to the campsite in the early evening, Creasy had spotted the black snake away to his left. He had sent Joey and Michael off in two arcs to get behind it and to drive it towards him. It had slipped down a crevice in the limestone rock. They gathered some dry pieces of wood and Creasy lit a fire, very close to the crevice. He then put some dry moss on the fire, which created a lot of smoke. He positioned himself over the crevice and had Michael fan the smoke into the crevice. Within half a minute, the snake shot out and Creasy had grabbed it just behind the head. Its three feet of length coiled itself around his arm. He brought its head to his mouth and bit it behind its eyes. The two young men watched in awed fascination. They knew the snake was not poisonous. It was the only variety found in the Maltese Islands and legend has it that when Saint Paul was shipwrecked on Malta, he was bitten by such a snake, which at that time was very poisonous. The legend goes that Saint Paul did not die, because he extracted the poison from the snake and placed it on the tongues of Maltese women. Maltese women are notorious gossips.

After the snake was dead, they moved back to the camp on the cliffs.

The camp was a simple shelter, open to the sky. Because of the season, they needed no protection from rain, but still Creasy instructed them how to build shelters for different climatic conditions. He taught them about water run-off and prevailing winds. He taught them how to retain body heat and how little food and water a man needs to live on. He taught them how to make a fire without using matches, just the friction of heat between two pieces of dry wood.

'What if it was really cold?' Michael asked ... 'and there wasn't enough wood to keep a fire going all night?'

'Do you remember a US rock group called "Three Dog Night"?' Creasy asked.

Both young men nodded.

'You know how they got their name?'

The young men shook their heads.

'Well,' Creasy said, 'on a cold night in the outback, a shepherd would sleep with a sheep-dog hugged close to him, to get warmth from its body. On a very cold night, he would sleep with two dogs, one on each side. On a freezing night, he would sleep with three dogs. One on each side and one on top. Hence the expression, "It's as cold as a three dog night".'

'But we don't have any dogs,' Michael said.

'No, but we'd use each other,' Creasy answered.

He gestured at the ground.

'We would dig out a depression, about two feet deep, and then line it with leaves and moss. We would sleep in it, side by side, after having pulled the loose earth over our bodies. It would be very cold at first, but after half an hour or so, our natural body heat would create a warmth.' He smiled. 'It would be a three dog night, but if it ever has to happen, I'd prefer to be stuck with a couple of good-looking girls, and not two bums like you ... fact is I'd even settle for a couple of good-looking sheep-dogs.'

He had showed them how to skin the snake and take out its innards. He then chopped it up and tossed the pieces into the fire. From the twigs of wood, he then devised three sets of chop-sticks. He taught them how to use them and then said, 'Don't let it cook too long, or it loses its nutritional value.'

After a minute, he reached with his chop-sticks into the embers of the fire, selected a piece of snake, popped it into his mouth and chewed contentedly. The two young men were look-ing at the fire with great distaste.

'Imagine you're eating eel,' Creasy said, 'because that's exactly what it is. An eel that lives on land.'

First Michael then Joey reached forward and picked up a piece of snake. After munching for a few seconds Joey gagged and spat it out. Michael kept munching and then swallowed.

He said, 'I never tasted eel, but this tastes better than some of the stuff I've eaten at the orphanage.'

He smiled a secret smile, 'And it tastes better than spinach.'

Creasy was looking at Joey, who was looking at the two rows of Rozetta laid out by the fire. The young man sighed and shook his head and then reached for another piece of snake. This time he managed to swallow it.

Creasy relented.

'Put the Rozetta on the fire, Joey,' he said. 'Tomorrow the first course will be roasted grasshoppers, followed, hopefully, by rabbit. At dawn I'll show you how to track and then trap rabbits.'

TWENTY-THREE

STELLA ZAMMIT'S FORTIETH birthday was a watershed. Creasy was very fond of her and George, and as a present had bought her a beautiful ceramic pot which he had found in an antique shop in Rabat. Leonie had noticed that he seemed more relaxed than at any time since she had first met him.

As they drove to Sliema, he asked, 'Are you having a good time?'

She smiled, 'Geraldine's great fun ... she makes me laugh. Last night we even went to a disco.'

'Did you meet anyone interesting?'

'Not really. But it was fun. Geraldine met a very nice Maltese chap. She's having dinner with him tonight. I think he's a bit of a playboy, but she's a bit of a playgirl.'

'What's his name?'

'Joe Borg,' she answered. 'I was slightly worried because he has business interests in Gozo . . . but I've never met him and he doesn't know of my connection with you.'

'I know him,' Creasy answered. 'He's a good guy.'

133

They drove in silence for a while and then she asked, 'And how was your week?'

'It was good,' he answered. He glanced at her and then went on, 'We went to Comino. Me, Michael and Joey.'

'To the hotel?' she asked.

He shook his head. 'No, to the other side of the island. We roughed it for a few days. Just took some fishing lines and a knife each. Lived off the land and the sea. They took it well. I was surprised how quickly they adapted. Hell, at the end they didn't even want to come back to Gozo.' His voice took on a musing tone. 'It does you good, you know, to go back to that kind of situation. It did me good to show a couple of young men how to live off their own land.'

'Has it been a long time?' she asked softly.

'Since what?' he asked.

'Since you lived off the land?'

He thought about that and said, 'Yes and no. I guess in a way I always lived off the land.'

She digested that and asked, 'Will I know anyone at the party?'

'Yes. Paul and Laura and Joey will be there and they're bringing Michael. You'll like George and Stella. It's her birthday. There'll be mountains of food and rivers of drink.'

She did enjoy the party, a very family affair. At one point she found herself at a makeshift bar next to Michael.

'I hear you've been roughing it on Comino,' she said.

His eyes lit up. 'It was fantastic. We even ate snake.'

'Snake!'

'Yes, and grasshoppers. We trapped rabbits and caught lots of fish.' He grinned. 'I caught the most.'

She smiled back at him and said, 'It sounds better than my cooking.'

He shook his head earnestly.

'No, Leonie, your cooking is great . . . but it was different.'

He seemed somehow to be older and younger at the same time.

She was slightly drunk by the time Creasy drove her, with Michael, back to the hotel. As she got out of the car, Creasy told her that he would be leaving the next day for about ten days.

'What about Michael?' she asked. 'I wasn't due back until Friday. Do you want me to return tomorrow?'

Michael had climbed out of the back seat. He kissed her on the cheek and said, 'Don't worry, I can look after myself for a day and night. I'll cook you a rabbit on Friday night. But it has to be a wild one. I'll try to trap it tomorrow. I'll cook it on the barbecue.'

She kissed him on the cheek and said, 'I'll be on the five o'clock ferry.'

She waved at Creasy and went into the hotel.

At reception, she noted that Geraldine's key was still in the slot. She decided to go to the bar for a nightcap.

It was almost deserted, with only one elderly couple sitting at the end of the bar. She slid onto a barstool and ordered a champagne cocktail. Something had happened, she decided. At the party, she had covertly watched Creasy. She had never seen him so relaxed, smile so easily. Perhaps, she decided, she had seen a tiny piece of the man inside the shell.

TWENTY-FOUR

CORKSCREW TWO WALKED into the bar just before midnight. Unlike his father, he drank occasionally. He ordered a Cognac and carried it over to the corner table and sat opposite Creasy. However, like his father he was all business.

'I've acquired all the machinery,' he said, 'except for the Uzis. They should be arriving early next week.'

'Cancel the hole in Algiers,' Creasy answered. 'I'm satisfied the target area is Damascus.'

'You're lucky,' Corkscrew Two answered. 'I was going to Algiers on Wednesday to sign a contract and arrange to stash the machinery . . . you've saved some expenses.'

'What about Damascus?'

'I was going on there from Algiers. I've located a one bedroom apartment just off Jamhuriya Avenue, near the souk.'

'Good. Now since I have the target area, I want a back-up hole nearby. Lattakia, on the coast, would be ideal. It's a busy port and a good bolt-hole, with lots of strangers coming and going. The machinery that you were going to send to Algiers should be sent there.'

Corkscrew Two's smile was like the edge of a razorblade. 'It's convenient,' he said. 'The machinery for Damascus was going in through Lattakia anyway.'

'How long?' Creasy asked.

'Three or four weeks . . . Everything will be in place. I'll have a trading licence and make several small export and import transactions. Stationery will be printed. You will be Vice-President of the company, under the name of Henry Vessage. Your French is fluent enough to pass as a Frenchman of indeterminate origin.'

'I don't like the name much,' Creasy said.

Corkscrew Two shrugged and the razor smile came again.

'Too bad. I have a genuine French passport in that name, with a genuine history. I'll need some passport photographs tomorrow, at which time I'll give you your history.'

'I'm going to need another passport, for a nineteen-year-old male of Palestinian origin. He will be a student of archaeology at the Sorbonne. Ostensibly, a resident of Beirut.'

'It will have to be a forgery,' Corkscrew Two said.

'But a good one?'

'Of course . . . the best . . . but expensive . . . around thirty thousand.'

Creasy nodded and stood up. They did not shake hands.

'I'll be in touch in three weeks,' Creasy said. 'Meanwhile if anything comes up, contact me through Blondie.'

Leonie received the phone call just after two o'clock on Tuesday afternoon. It was George Zammit.

'There's been an accident,' he said curtly, 'with Michael.'

'An accident?'

'Yes, a serious one. He's in St Luke's Hospital, in intensive care.'

'What happened?'

There was a silence at the other end of the phone then George said, 'I think you better get over here as soon as possible, you can catch the three o'clock ferry. There'll be a police car waiting for you at Cirkewwa. It will bring you straight to St Luke's. I'll be waiting. Bring some clothes. You can stay with Stella and me.'

'But what happened?'

'Just be on the three o'clock ferry,' he answered.

She heard a click and the line went dead.

Quickly, she ran to the bedroom and put some clothes into a bag, then looked at her watch. She had plenty of time to catch the ferry. She felt a rising frustration at not being able to get there sooner, at not knowing what had happened.

Just then the phone rang. She ran to the kitchen. It was Laura. Good, practical Laura.

'I've just heard,' she said. 'Do you want me to come and pick you up and take you to the ferry?'

'What have you heard?'

'Only that Michael's had an accident and he's in St Luke's, and that you're catching the three o'clock ferry.'

'Nothing else? What kind of accident?'

Laura's voice was calming.

'I don't know, Leonie. George would not tell me. He just said that there was an accident and you may need some support. Shall I pick you up?'

'Yes please . . . thank you.'

She reached the hospital just after four o'clock and one minute later lost her temper for the first time in many years. Lost it completely. George Zammit met her at the entrance and told his driver to take her bag on to his house.

137

'What happened?' she asked immediately.

His face was doleful. 'It was an accident,' he said. 'He's still in the operating theatre.'

'What sort of accident?'

He shrugged. 'I'm sorry, Leonie, a very serious one . . . he has a fifty-fifty chance.'

The hospital was Victorian, almost Dickensian in its structure. They were standing in the vast entrance hall.

'What sort of accident?' she insisted.

He shrugged again and said apologetically, 'It's a police matter, Leonie. I'm afraid it's confidential.'

She looked at him incredulously for several seconds, then her temper snapped.

'Confidential!' she screamed at him. 'He's my son . . . if not by birth, at least legally . . . and you talk about confidential.'

He glanced around at the many people criss-crossing the hall, then he took her arm and said, 'We have a police office upstairs. Let's go there and wait for the results of the operation. They tell me it will be about half an hour . . . I'll get some tea for you.'

Angrily she shook off his hand.

'I'm not going anywhere,' she snapped. 'Not until you tell me what happened.'

'I'll try to explain as much as I can but only in private . . . it's a police matter, Leonie.'

She shook her head. 'Not to a mother it isn't. Either you tell me everything or I'll go straight into Valetta and find a lawyer.'

He had only met her briefly at his wife's birthday party and he knew her role. But he saw the determination in her eyes and decided that he might have underestimated her. He took a decision.

'Come upstairs,' he said gently, 'and I'll tell you what happened.'

First he arranged for a cup of tea. They sat in a spartan office while she sipped at it.

'Do you know when Creasy will be back?'

'In about a week.'

'Will he phone?'

'Yes, he phones every two or three days. He phoned last night. Maybe he'll call again Thursday or Friday.'

'I'll arrange for a policeman to stay at the house twenty-four hours a day. If Creasy phones, he'll be told to phone me.' He shook his head morosely. 'He's going to kill me.'

Leonie's temper had abated but her anxiety remained.

'What happened, George?' she asked.

The policeman sighed, stood up and started pacing the room.

'Do you know what my job is?' he asked.

'Only that you're a policeman,' she answered. 'A senior one. Superintendent, isn't it?'

'Yes, but more than that. I'm in charge of security for the islands and I'm head of our anti-terrorist squad. We have training facilities at Fort St Elmo. Underground shooting ranges, gymnasiums and so on.'

She took another sip of tea, not tasting it at all and watching him pacing, four paces one way and then four paces the other.

He stopped, looked at her and then asked, 'Do you know what Michael has been doing over here every Tuesday and Thursday?'

She shook her head. 'I only know that he goes to Fort St Elmo . . . that he goes to you.'

George started pacing again.

'Yes,' he answered, 'he's been training with my anti-terrorist squad . . . weapons, unarmed combat and that kind of thing.'

'Why?'

'It was a special request from Creasy.'

'But why?' she asked again.

The policeman said, 'I will tell you about the accident, but I cannot answer your last question . . . only Creasy can answer that.'

'So tell me about the accident.'

George Zammit sighed and shook his head.

'There's always a risk in that kind of training. It has to be real life training. We had another accident about two years ago. It's not a bad percentage over six years since the squad was formed.'

'Just tell me what happened,' she said, impatience back in her voice.

'It was on the shooting range,' he answered. 'Michael and two others were practising with 9mm pistols. One of the others got a jammed magazine. Instead of moving away as he should have done, he tried to unjam it on the range. There was still a round in the breech. He was a new recruit and inexperienced. Michael moved to help him. The round went off and hit Michael in the chest . . . in or very close to the heart. That happened just after one o'clock. He was in the operating theatre here by one forty.' He glanced at his watch. 'He's still alive now. If he survives the operation, he'll be in the intensive care unit in about fifteen or twenty minutes.' He stopped pacing and looked at her, shrugged again and said, 'Then it's a question for God and for waiting.'

TWENTY-FIVE

THEY LET HER stay by his bed in a room in the intensive care unit. She sat in a chair and watched him all night. He was on a respirator, with an oxygen mask over his mouth and nose. Clear plastic tubes snaked down from inverted bottles into both his wrists. The whole bed was covered by a clear plastic tent. A nurse sat at a desk in the corner, reading a romantic novel. Every few minutes she would glance up at the array of monitor screens in front of her.

Early in the evening, Leonie had asked her what would happen if there was an emergency. The nurse had pointed to a button on the desk and said, 'I hit that button and they will be here within seconds.'

During the long night, the nurse had hit the button four times. Each time, Leonie had retreated to a corner, while the doctors worked over Michael. They were swift and efficient, talking to each other in quiet tones.

Early in the morning the surgeon had arrived. Again she retired to a corner, while he read all the data sheets, conferred with the doctors and then examined Michael. After lowering the plastic tent back into place he walked over to Leonie.

He had a naturally pessimistic face. Perhaps surgeons acquire such a look as part of their training, but he had a very faint smile on his lips.

'He's young and very fit,' he said, 'otherwise he'd never have made it through the night . . . he's still in very great danger but if he gets through today and tonight, he should recover.'

She felt tears forming in her eyes and her voice quivered slightly as she asked, 'Will he be disabled in any way?'

The surgeon shook his head.

'No. If he makes it through the next twenty-four hours, he should go on to make a complete recovery . . . but it will take many weeks, of course.' He looked at her critically, 'Did you manage to sleep at all?'

She shook her head.

'Then you should,' he said. 'George Zammit will be here soon with his wife. She can stay with him while you get a few hours' sleep.'

Again she shook her head.

'I won't leave him during the next twenty-four hours.'

The surgeon studied her face, shrugged and said something to the nurse in Maltese. She picked up the phone on her desk. To Leonie the surgeon said, 'I'll be out of the operating theatre by noon and I'll look in on him. Meanwhile, he'll be well looked after.' He turned, looked at Michael and said, 'He's very lucky. If the bullet had been even three or four millimetres to the right he would have died within minutes.'

He left the room and five minutes later the door opened and a porter wheeled in a narrow bed and placed it alongside the broad bed on which Michael lay. He was young and cheerful.

'Would you like tea or coffee?' he asked Leonie.

'Tea please.'

141

'Something to eat?'

'No, thank you.'

She drank the tea sitting on the small bed looking down at Michael's face through the clear plastic. Normally, he looked a couple of years older than his age, but now she decided that he looked very young indeed. Just a small boy. She fancied he looked about the same age as her own son when he had died.

Tears formed in her eyes again and she remembered her words to Creasy all those weeks ago.

'He certainly won't raise any maternal instincts in me.'

George and Stella arrived half an hour later. They both gave her a hug and Stella said, 'I understand you're going to stay here for the next twenty-four hours. I'll bring you a change of clothes and a dressing gown and some food. I'm afraid the food here is not very good.'

'I'm not at all hungry,' Leonie answered, 'but thank you.'

Stella's voice was very firm. 'You must keep your strength up . . . you must eat.'

George was looking down at Michael from the foot of the bed.

'Did Creasy phone?' Leonie asked him.

'Not yet,' he answered. He turned to look at her. 'Leonie, you are sure you can't remember any address or phone number where we might find him?'

'No. He never mentioned anything.'

George sighed.

'Yes, when that man wants to disappear, he damn well disappears.'

Stella returned at noon with a bag and a wicker basket covered by a cloth.

'How is he?' was her first question.

Leonie had been lying on the bed, but not asleep. She swung her feet to the ground and answered, 'No change but the doctor says that's good.'

Stella put the bag and the basket on the bed and tapped the bag.

142

'Your clothes and toiletries,' she said.

She pulled the cloth off the basket and Leonie immediately smelt the aroma of fresh cooking.

'Fish pie,' Stella said with a smile. 'I took it out of the oven twenty minutes ago. It's still warm. It's a Lampuki pie. First of the season.'

Immediately, Leonie felt hungry.

As she ate, Stella chatted on in a low voice.

'George is sorry, but he can't come up until this evening. The internal enquiry has started and he's up to his ears in reports and interviews. It's always like that with a gunshot wound. This enquiry is very complicated, because Michael is not even in the police force and strictly speaking should never have been in Fort St Elmo.'

'Will George get into trouble?' Leonie asked.

'I don't think so. He's very close to the Commissioner, whom you met at my birthday party. So is Creasy.'

'Did Creasy phone yet?' Leonie asked.

Stella shook her head.

'Not yet, but George has a man sleeping right by the phone in your kitchen. We'll know as soon as he calls.'

TWENTY-SIX

MICHAEL SURVIVED THE twenty-four hours.

At eight o'clock in the morning the surgeon examined him, studied the data, conferred with the two young doctors in charge of the unit, and then nodded in satisfaction.

He walked over to Leonie and said, 'Of course, I cannot be

143

certain. Complications can always set in, but as I said, he's fit and young . . . it looks like he's going to make it.'

She didn't say anything. She was looking at the young man on the bed and was unable to speak. The surgeon noted that and said gently, 'The nurse told me you hardly slept at all in the night. Try to get some sleep now. Later in the afternoon we'll take him off the respirator and the oxygen and move him to a normal recovery room.'

She found her voice.

'When will he become conscious?'

The surgeon thought for a moment and said, 'Probably this evening or during the night. Once he's in the recovery room, we'll take him off the drug that's been keeping him asleep.'

'I want to be there when he wakes up.'

The doctor nodded and smiled. 'Yes. I doubt that we'd be able to prise you away with a crow-bar.'

Michael opened his eyes at two o'clock the next morning.

He focused on the ceiling, then closed his eyes and kept them closed for about half a minute. When he opened them again, he could not see the ceiling, he could only see Leonie's face above his. His eyes focused on the face and its anxious eyes. He felt her hand holding his and heard her voice.

'Michael, it's me, Leonie . . . can you hear me?' She heard his voice croak, 'Yes, Leonie.'

She felt his hand squeeze hers faintly.

Moments later, he felt her tears dropping onto his face.

Creasy had phoned the night before. Being the height of the tourist season, all flights for the next few days were fully booked. George Zammit had phoned the chairman of Air Malta and arranged to get him on the ten a.m. flight.

George picked him up from the airport. As they drove the fifteen minutes to St Luke's, he brought him up to date. Creasy listened in silence, then as they drove through the hospital gates, he asked a single question.

'How long before he's on his feet and fully mobile?'

'The doctors say he'll have to stay in hospital for at least two weeks, and then recover at home for several more weeks . . . but recover he will. Fully.'

They pulled up at the entrance and as Creasy was about to get out of the car the policeman's hand gripped him by the arm. In a low voice, he said simply, 'I'm sorry.'

'It's not your fault,' Creasy answered. 'You can't be everywhere. Will you have problems over this?'

'No, we've kept the lid on it. The press got nothing. The Commissioner told the Minister that I'd cleared it with him to have Michael at St Elmo . . . it was a friendly lie.'

'Did the Commissioner bollock you?'

George's smile was rueful. 'Just a little, but I told him that one day Michael would be the best man in my squad.'

'He's a good guy that,' Creasy muttered and climbed out of the car.

TWENTY-SEVEN

TWO WEEKS LATER, Creasy crossed over from Gozo with the jeep and drove to the hospital to pick Michael up.

For the last ten days Michael had been in a general ward on the third floor. Creasy had to ask directions to find it. He had not been to see his adopted son during the entire two weeks. He found the ward and went in. There were a dozen beds in it, all occupied except one. Michael was sitting in a wheelchair next to it. He was dressed in jeans and a T-shirt. There was a small plastic bag at his feet. Creasy walked over and asked, 'Are you OK?'

Michael smiled.

'Yes, I'm ready to get out of here. The people are nice but the food is lousy . . . I'd rather eat black snake every day.'

Creasy did not return the smile. Curtly, he said, 'Let's go then.'

Michael reached out above the bed to press a button saying, 'They told me to ring for a porter when you arrived.'

'You can't walk?' Creasy asked.

'Yes, but . . .'

'But what?'

'But they told me to ring for a porter to take me down to the car.'

Creasy leaned forward and said in a low, hard voice, 'Listen to me. They carried you in here on a stretcher because you were dumb enough to get in front of a loaded gun. Now when you leave this place, you walk out of here. Not like some fucking cripple in a wheelchair. Otherwise stay here until you can walk.'

Michael looked up at him and then dropping his hand from the bell, he pushed himself to his feet, picked up his bag and walked out the door.

Creasy followed him.

On the drive back to Cirkewwa they were both silent until they reached St Paul's Bay. Then Michael glanced at the older man and said, 'You're mad at me.'

'I'm not mad at you.'

'Yes you are. That's not fair.'

Creasy was staring straight ahead at the road.

'I told you back at the hospital,' he said. 'It's dumb to get in front of a loaded gun.'

They drove out of St Paul's Bay in silence, then Michael said, 'So you must have been dumb quite a few times yourself.'

Another silence until they had reached Melieha and then Michael said with bitterness, 'You didn't come to see me. Not once. You didn't let Leonie come. She wanted to come every day to bring me food. You didn't let Stella Zammit come to see me. She came once, just after they put me onto solid foods. She said she would bring me a Lampuki pie, and later on, rabbit stew . . .

but she never came. It's not difficult to guess you told her not to. Why?'

Creasy pulled the jeep over into a lay-by. He switched off the ignition and sat with his hands on the steering-wheel. He sat for a long while without saying a word. Finally Michael said, 'The food at the hospital was worse than at the orphanage.'

'But you survived.'

'Yes, but I was sick. I damn nearly died. Why was it necessary?'

'Why was it necessary for us to go to Comino and eat off the land when we could have walked a mile to the hotel and eaten great food in a Swiss-run restaurant?'

Michael's face showed his surprise.

'But I was sick,' he insisted. 'The doctor told me it was a miracle I lived through it.'

Creasy shook his head.

'There's no such things as miracles . . . and it's when you're sick, when you're down at your lowest point, that you have to learn to survive.'

Michael digested that and then said, still with bitterness in his voice, 'So it was just another lesson . . . I suppose you're going to tell me that all life is a lesson.'

Creasy shook his head.

'No, but I'm going to tell you that death is the final lesson.'

He switched on the ignition, glanced into the rear mirror and pulled out into the traffic.

TWENTY-EIGHT

'HOW COME YOU'RE all so old?'

Frank Miller swallowed a piece of steak. 'Old?' he asked.

The Senator waved a fork at him. 'Yes, anyway relatively old. How old are you?'

Frank Miller was looking puzzled. They were sitting in the elegant dining room of the Senator's Denver house.

'Forty-four,' Miller answered, 'but what's that got to do with anything?'

'And Maxie and Rene?' Grainger persisted.

Maxie MacDonald was an ex-member of the élite Selous Scouts of the Rhodesian army and subsequently a mercenary. Rene Callard was a Belgian who had spent fifteen years in the Foreign Legion, before leaving to make some real money as a personal bodyguard. Together with Miller, they kept a twenty-four hour body watch on Senator James Grainger. All three were intelligent, amiable men, as well as being unobtrusive in a difficult situation. They talked when the Senator wanted to talk. They were silent when he wished to be silent. It had now been three weeks and it had suddenly struck the Senator during this dinner with Miller that they appeared to be a bit old for the job.

'How old are Maxie and Rene?' he asked again.

Miller shrugged and said, 'I guess about the same age as me ... why?'

The Senator smiled to take away any offence.

'It just seems like a young man's job,' he said. 'I mean all the

Secret Service bodyguards I know are in their late twenties or very early thirties.'

Miller's smile was sardonic. 'Sure,' he said, 'and no doubt they're all karate black belts, can run a hundred metres in under ten seconds and can shoot the eye of a fly at fifty paces.'

The Senator nodded. 'Something like that.'

Miller chewed on a succulent piece of fillet, swallowed, murmured in approval, looked at the Senator and said, 'And yet those guys let a gunman get to within a few feet of President Reagan and fire several shots. He's lucky to be alive.'

Grainger was curious. 'I agree,' he said, 'but what makes you guys better?'

Miller noted that the Senator's wineglass was empty. He reached forward, picked up the bottle of claret and refilled it.

'Thank you, Frank,' the Senator said courteously. 'Now answer the question.'

Miller was drinking mineral water. He took a sip and asked, 'Senator, how long have you been in Congress?'

'Three terms . . . that's eighteen years.'

'During the first term, were you as good at handling a situation as you were in your second term?'

The Senator smiled and shook his head. 'Obviously not,' he answered. 'A Senator learns by experience, like anyone else.'

'Exactly,' the bodyguard answered, and popped the last piece of steak into his mouth.

Miguel appeared as if by magic and cleared away the plates.

'You want dessert?' the Senator asked.

'No thank you, Senator.'

'Coffee?'

'Thank you, yes.'

The Senator nodded to Miguel who went out with the tray.

The Senator continued the conversation.

'But certain jobs need a different expertise. I would think that in your job, expertise is everything.'

Miller shook his head. 'Not everything, Senator . . . far from it.' He thought for a moment and then said, 'Being a bodyguard, with a target under constant threat, is like being in a state of constant combat. Now any general will tell you that no matter how well a soldier is trained for no matter how many years, the first time he ever comes under fire he gets confused. It's only when he's been under fire that he knows what he's doing. No simulated training can replace a real battlefield. That's one of the reasons why you people lost the Vietnam War. Rotating too many novices in and out for too short a period. By the time they were battle-hardened, they were out and another bunch of well-trained novices were in. Now the whole point, Senator, is that bodyguards in the Secret Service are brilliantly trained, but none of them have been on the battlefield except the guys who were around Reagan . . . and he got shot.'

'That's true,' Grainger agreed, 'but then they don't have much chance to be on the battlefield. When it happens, it just happens.'

'Exactly,' Miller said. 'By their very nature, they have to be novices.'

Miguel brought a tray with the coffee. After he had left the Senator asked, 'And you are not?'

'Not what?'

'A novice.'

Miller shook his head. 'No, I've been on the battlefield most of my adult life, so have Maxie and Rene.'

'Have you killed a lot of people?'

Immediately Miller answered, 'I can't remember.'

The Senator smiled. 'That's what Creasy said. Do all you guys say that?'

Miller shook his head. 'Only the non-bullshitters.'

'Have you known Creasy long?' the Senator asked.

Miller's eyes narrowed in thought. Finally, he said, 'About eighteen years.'

The Senator leaned forward and asked quietly, 'Is he as good as I hear?'

'What do you hear?'

'That he's death on a cold night.'

'Senator, that about sums it up.' He looked at his watch and then drained the last of his coffee. He said, 'Maxie will relieve me

150

in five minutes. Now listen to me, all this stuff about age. Are you worried about your situation?'

The Senator smiled and shook his head. 'No, Frank, not at all.'

'Then you should be.'

His blunt Australian accent forced the Senator's head up.

'You have to understand,' Miller went on. 'I don't know all the details, but Creasy told me that Ahmed Jibril wants to either talk to you or have someone talk to you. That would be unpleasant and ultimately fatal. I know a great deal about Ahmed Jibril. He's ruthless and he has a great deal of money behind him. Enough money to hire people in this country . . . top people, to try to snatch you. So, you should be worried.'

'Even with you and your two side-kicks to protect me?'

The Australian nodded firmly. 'Yes. You yourself have to be totally aware and observant. You're a highly intelligent man, Senator. If you see or hear anything out of the ordinary you must let me know immediately, or Maxie, or Rene. Creasy would not have put us on this job if he wasn't pretty sure that something will happen. The only thing in our favour is that Jibril wants to talk to you, not just kill you. If he wanted to kill you, it would be ten times harder to protect you. In fact you'd have to go into total hiding until Creasy has done what he's going to do.'

'Do you know what he's going to do?'

Miller shook his head. 'No, but it's not too difficult to guess, and if my guess is right, I wouldn't want to be Ahmed Jibril on a cold night, a hot night, or any damned night at all.'

He stood up and walked to the door, opened it a crack and peered through. Then he opened it fully. Maxie MacDonald walked into the room, nodded at Grainger and said, 'Good evening, Senator.'

'Hi, Maxie. Do you feel like some coffee?'

'No thanks, Senator, I just had some in the kitchen.'

He turned to Miller. 'Frank, during the last two hours, a blue Pontiac has twice passed outside at cruising speed. Two men in it.'

'Did you get the plans?'

'Yes, we checked them out through Curtis Bennett's office. It

151

was rented from Denver airport this morning for just two days in the name of a company in Los Angeles. Paid in cash. The company is not registered.'

'It could be the first recce,' Miller muttered, deep in thought. He turned to Grainger. 'What time do we leave for Washington tomorrow?'

'I figure early evening,' Grainger answered. 'I have to be on Capitol Hill early the next morning and I want to get some work done first.'

'It's obvious that you're a wealthy man,' the Australian said. 'Can you tell me how wealthy?'

In the strangely open way that Americans have when discussing personal money, the Senator answered simply, 'About a hundred and twenty million.'

Miller's face showed no expression. 'In that case, Senator, when we fly between Denver and Washington or anywhere else, we do so by private jet, always using different charter companies on a random basis and at short notice.'

The Senator stood up, his face serious. 'I'll arrange it,' he said.

'But not through your offices either here or in Washington,' Miller said. 'You must have lots of friends in business here in Denver.'

'Plenty,' the Senator answered. 'And not just in Denver.'

'Good. Then arrange the charters through them, always a different one. Your name's not to be mentioned. I'm going to bed now. Goodnight, Senator.'

'Goodnight, Frank.'

Grainger moved round the table, saying to Maxie, with a smile, 'I'm going to have a Cognac in the bar, Maxie. Will you join me for one of your usual high-octane orange juices?'

Maxie smiled back and said, 'It will be more than a pleasure, Senator.'

TWENTY-NINE

THE ROW ERUPTED the morning after Michael returned from hospital. It was short but very bitter. Leonie had served the two men breakfast. When they finished, Creasy looked at Michael and said, 'Go and put your swimsuit on and get in the pool.'

Leonie was washing the dishes. She turned in astonishment. 'What!'

Creasy was still looking at Michael. He said evenly, 'Don't dive in, go down the steps. Just do four lengths slowly, but then stay in the water for half an hour. Sit on the steps with the water up to your neck.'

Leonie was walking to the table, her hands dripping wet. 'Are you mad?'

'Go ahead,' Creasy said to Michael. 'I'll join you in a minute.'

The young man stood up and left the kitchen.

Leonie stood in front of Creasy, her wet hands on her hips and her eyes radiating a mixture of disbelief and anger.

'Are you mad?' she repeated.

Creasy sighed and looked up at her face.

'Are you a doctor?' he asked.

'No.'

'A trained nurse?'

'No.'

'Ever had any experience of gunshot wounds?'

'No, I have not,' she snapped. 'But I spoke to Dr Grech on the phone yesterday, after you left the hospital. He said that Michael was to have complete rest and not to exert himself.'

153

Creasy shrugged. 'He's a very good doctor, but he's had almost no experience of gunshot wounds.'

'Oh,' she said scornfully. 'So you know better than a doctor?'

'In this case, maybe I do,' he answered calmly.

Her voice was emphatic. 'Well I'm not going to let it happen.' She turned and walked to the kitchen door.

Later she was to remember how fast he had been. She had not taken two strides before his hand gripped her arm above the elbow tight enough to hurt.

'You will not interfere.' He turned her to face him, his voice still quiet. 'If you interfere, you will leave this house and the island immediately and not come back. You know what that means? You will carry no letter with you from the Notary ... you know the terms of our contract?'

For a long time she looked up into his face, her eyes full of hatred. Then she spat the words out.

'You're a bloody bastard, an inhuman bastard. Why are you doing this to him?'

Without any sign of emotion, he answered, 'It's for his own good. In every way.' He gestured with his free hand. 'That pool is filled with sea-water and sea-water is good for wounds, makes them heal faster. The exercise is very gentle. I'll make sure he swims very slowly. Each day, he'll do just a little more and within a month he'll be fully fit. Believe me, I know these things.'

'Why the hurry?' she snapped. 'Why not let him take his time?'

He sighed. 'Because a gunshot wound is not like any other wound. It's mental as well as physical. If he lies around doing nothing, it will prey on his mind.'

'Why are you doing all this anyway?' she asked bitterly. 'Why are you training him with guns and things? He's only a boy after all.'

His voice rose in anger. 'He's not a boy! But he will be again, if he's mollycoddled after what he's been through.'

She laughed derisively.

'Mollycoddled! For God's sake, you wouldn't even let me go and see him in hospital, or anybody else. What the hell have you got in store for that boy?'

'He's a man,' he snapped back. 'And remember the contract. No questions.'

'You're a bastard,' she said. 'And you're hurting my arm.'

He released his grip and stood back, saying, 'Make up your mind, either go along with it or leave now.'

'I won't leave,' she answered fiercely, 'but I will move into the spare bedroom. I can hardly stand to be in the same room as you, let alone the same bed, even though you never touch me.'

She turned and strode out of the kitchen.

After she had moved her clothes into the spare bedroom she came out onto the patio. Michael was sitting in the pool with the water up to his neck. Creasy was sitting close to him, at the edge, with his legs in the water. They were talking quietly.

She walked over and said curtly, 'I'm going out. I'll be back in time to make lunch.'

Michael looked up and smiled at her and said, 'Don't worry, I did four lengths and I feel fine.'

Creasy said nothing, he just looked down at the water.

Laura was mopping the tiled floor of the lounge when Leonie came in, brushing aside the fly net.

Laura saw the look on her face and immediately asked, 'What happened?'

'I hate the bastard,' Leonie said. 'I'm sorry, Laura, but you're the only person on this bloody island I can talk to.' Then she burst into tears.

Five minutes later they were sitting on the patio. Laura was pouring coffee and Leonie pouring out her heart.

The Gozitan woman listened in silence. She heard how it had all come about. The Theatrical Agency, the marriage contract, which stipulated just six months and the registry wedding. Also the total lack of any physical contact between Creasy and Leonie.

'He'll end up killing the boy,' she finished bitterly. 'That bastard has no heart . . . none at all.'

'He does have a heart,' Laura answered gently. 'It's just that most times he locks it away in cold storage.'

Leonie snorted and said, 'Well as far as I'm concerned, the keys have been thrown away. I'd leave today, if it wasn't for Michael. Even if it did mean losing my flat in London. What on earth has he got planned for that boy?'

'I don't know,' Laura answered, 'but in some ways, Michael's very much like Creasy.' She shrugged and said, 'Before the accident I didn't see you show any emotion towards Michael. Obviously that's changed or you wouldn't be here now. You'd better ask yourself what your feelings really are for him.'

That produced a silence. Leonie looked out over Comino, then gave a short, mirthless laugh. 'Maternal,' she muttered. 'I don't believe it but my thoughts are bloody maternal.'

Laura smiled and poured more coffee. 'That's natural,' she said. 'You sat up for two nights and watched a boy who you thought was going to die. Did you cry when you knew he was going to live?'

'Yes.'

'Did you sit by his bed, hour after hour, holding his hand, after he became conscious?'

'Yes.'

'So it's natural. You look on him as a boy, perhaps a replacement for your own son, and Creasy looks on him as a man. That's why you hate him.'

'What am I going to do?' Leonie asked mournfully.

Laura's voice became brisk. 'You're going to see out your six month contract. You're not going to interfere with Creasy's physical treatment of Michael. Believe me, on that score he does know best. Twice in his life I've nursed him back from the edge of death. In this very house. Perhaps nursed is too strong a word, but I cooked him good and healthy food and watched him put himself back together again. He knows what the human body can and cannot take.'

'It's going to be hell living in that house,' Leonie said.

Laura shook her head. 'Only if you make it so. I know Creasy. He will act as though the argument never happened. Life will

156

continue in the same way as before the accident but only if you make it so.'

'If only I knew something about the man,' Leonie said resentfully, 'it might make it easier, but he never talks about himself and neither does anybody else. He's just a bloody robot.'

Laura patted Leonie on the shoulder and said reassuringly, 'It's not a long time. Do not tell Creasy that you talked to me about the marriage arrangement.' She smiled. 'But if he asks, tell him that you told me he's a bastard. He'll understand that.'

Leonie's returned smile was wan. 'Your daughter must have loved him very much,' she said. 'Or else she had more patience than anyone else I've ever met.'

'Oh, she did love him, very much,' Laura answered. 'And believe me, she had no more patience than I do.' She smiled, 'And as everyone knows, I have very little. The fact is that he loved her in the same way and whatever Creasy does, it's always one hundred per cent.'

She stood up and said, 'I have to get back to the bloody housework now, on this island it's still a man's world.'

Leonie rose, kissed her on the cheek and said warmly, 'Thanks, Laura, I'll try to follow your advice.'

Laura walked her through the house to the front door.

'See you Saturday night.'

'Saturday night?'

Laura smiled. 'Yes, it's Joey's engagement party up at Maria's parents' house in Nadur. It will be a good party.'

THIRTY

THERE WERE VERY few things that had caused Creasy trepidation in all his years. Laura Schembri in a temper could be included among them. It was three days after Michael had returned from hospital. After lunch, Creasy had left him and Leonie sunning themselves by the pool, and gone to help Joey work on the farmhouse.

After two hours, while they sweated in the hot sun, Laura had walked down the path, carrying a bucket containing ice and four bottles of beer. Creasy had been working on a wall, and watched her approach. His mind went back five years. Instead of Laura, he saw Nadia. It was only a few days after he first met her. He had been rebuilding a limestone wall with Paul, and Nadia had walked down the same path carrying the same bucket, with cold beers in it. It had been the start of everything.

But his memories were washed away as soon as Laura reached them. She put down the bucket and said to Joey curtly, 'Go and take a swim, Joey . . . make it a long one.'

The young man looked at his mother's face and turned away without a word. Creasy jumped down from the wall and said bluntly, 'Laura, don't start on at me about Michael. I've had enough of that shit already from Leonie. I know what I'm doing. You should realise that.'

She gave him a look that would have turned a pot of boiling water into instant ice.

The tirade started with the words, 'You're not just an unfeeling, stupid, mindless, thick-skinned, thick-headed bastard, but

158

also you happen to be my son-in-law. Now just keep your mouth shut and listen.'

He listened for the next ten minutes, leaning back against the wall, his eyes looking at her feet.

She ended by saying, 'Don't you have any feelings at all?'

Slowly, he lifted his head, looked at her eyes and said, 'No. My feelings were shattered together with Nadia and Julia on Pan Am 103. The only thing left is hatred.'

'You hate everybody?'

'No. Just the ones who did it.'

'So, you have no feelings of affection for anybody?' she persisted.

'I don't understand what you mean,' he answered flatly. 'The word doesn't come into my vocabulary.'

Her expression turned from anger to great sadness. She asked, 'What about me, and Paul and Joey?'

'You're my family,' he said simply.

'What does that mean?'

His eyes were looking down at her feet again. Very softly, he said, 'It means I love you . . . listen, you know I'm not good with words.'

He was almost quivering with embarrassment. She moved forward and put her arms around him. She was almost as tall as he was. She put her cheek against his, and said very quietly, 'Creasy, we love you too. I know what you're doing and from my heart I hope you succeed, because I know that if you don't those evil men will never be brought to justice. Now listen to me, and I don't want you to get upset. I said some terrible things just now. I was angry, but in a way I meant them. Now I'm going to tell you one more terrible thing . . . and I mean it. If Nadia were alive and saw the cold-blooded way you treat that woman, she would feel ashamed. Not for herself but for you.'

They both remained still, like a frozen tableau against the wall, and slowly she pulled her head back and looked into his eyes. She saw the pain. Fathomless pain. Again she laid her cheek against his. After a while his arms enclosed her and she felt tears on her cheek. They were not her tears.

THIRTY-ONE

THE CHANGE WAS subtle, and at first Leonie did not notice. It only became apparent at Joey's engagement party.

She had not wanted to go, feeling that she would be an outsider at a family gathering. She told Creasy, 'Why don't you and Michael go on your own?'

He had shaken his head. 'No. Joey will be upset if you don't come.'

'Upset?' she had said in surprise.

'Yes, and so will Laura. It will be a good party.' He smiled slightly and said, 'There's another reason. It's obligatory that I get drunk tonight. Joey will make sure of that and Pepe, Maria's father. The party may go on late and Michael may get tired. My plan is that we take both cars. If necessary you can bring him home early. Would you mind?'

So they went and it was a good party; ages ranged from babies to grandmothers.

Engagement parties, in Gozo, are more like weddings anywhere else in the world. Rings are exchanged and the priest gives the couple his blessing. Presents covered several tables. It was a large house, with a large garden.

After admiring the presents everyone spilled out into the garden. A bar had been set up on one side and a couple of Joey's friends manned it.

Laura was busy with Maria's family and Michael was chatting with the younger men.

Leonie stood off to one side and had just begun to feel out of it

160

all, when Creasy loomed up beside her, took her by the arm and said, 'Come, I want you to meet somebody.' Holding her gently, he guided her through the crowd to a priest. 'This is Father Louis,' he said. 'We first met twenty years ago in what was then Rhodesia.'

He grinned at the priest and said, 'Father Louis was a missionary. He used to convert the natives to alcohol.'

The priest grinned back and answered, 'And this godless creature was my right hand man.'

He turned to Leonie and said, 'I could tell you a few stories about that time.'

Then came the surprise. Cheerfully, Creasy said to the priest, 'Why don't you do that. I've got to go and find Paulu Zarb. The bastard promised to fix the radio on my jeep two weeks ago and I haven't seen him since.'

He moved through the crowd and Leonie was left with the priest.

She decided to ask a question.

'How did you happen to run into Creasy?' she asked.

Then came the second surprise. The priest answered her question.

'I was running a small Mission up in the Eastern Highlands near Mozambique. At that time, the war of independence was nearing its climax. The Mission was in a dangerous and remote area. We had a unit of the Selous Scouts camped close by. They had two functions. One to guard the Mission and the other to raid rebel camps across the border. Creasy commanded that unit.'

'Selous Scouts?'

'Yes, they were a crack unit in the Rhodesian army.'

She looked puzzled. 'But Creasy is American.'

The priest nodded. 'Yes, but at that time, the Rhodesian army recruited other nationals. They were in a desperate situation.'

She thought about that and then asked, 'So Creasy was a mercenary?'

'Yes,' he answered. 'There were many mercenaries there at the

161

time. You could say it was the last real war in which mercenaries played a part . . . thank God.'

She thought again, then said, 'And yet you became a friend of his.'

The priest smiled. 'Oh, yes. A good friend.'

She warmed to him.

'Was it very dangerous?' she asked.

He nodded soberly and then said simply, 'Yes. I owe my life to your husband, which is why if he gets drunk tonight, I will drive him home.' He smiled again. 'And he will get drunk tonight. It's rumoured that he engineered Joey into this engagement. Joey will exact his revenge.' He looked across the garden, where the table had been set up with elaborate flower arrangements, a large pink cake and several bottles of champagne. Joey and Maria were moving towards it.

'I have to go to work now,' the priest said, and with a mournful expression shook his head. 'It's a hard life. If I don't drink at least half a bottle of champagne, both families will be mortally offended.'

The two families gathered behind the table with Joey and Maria in the middle, and the priest between them. She noticed Creasy standing with Paul and Laura. She watched as he beckoned to Michael, who was standing with a group of young men in front of the table. He moved around the table and stood beside Creasy. Leonie began to feel out of it again but then she got her third surprise. Creasy bent over and whispered something to Michael, who nodded and smiled. He came round the table, walked across the garden to her, took her hand and led her into the Schembri family circle.

Father Louis blessed the rings and they were put onto Joey and Maria's fingers. The cake was cut, champagne corks popped and flash bulbs lit up the occasion.

She was standing next to Creasy and in an awed tone she said, 'So you are a mercenary?'

He shook his head. 'An ex-mercenary. I quit that business quite a few years ago.'

'Why?' she asked, and promptly received her fourth surprise.

'I don't like talking about those years,' he answered, 'but Laura knows most of it. If you ask her, she'll tell you.'

'I don't think so. I once asked a question about you and she wouldn't answer it.'

'Laura will answer your question.'

Then she got her fifth surprise. She heard him use a word she would not have believed possible.

'I apologise,' he said. 'You've had a rough time. It wasn't necessary.'

Before she could even think of a reply, Paul came up and said, 'I noticed that Michael already had two glasses of champagne. Maybe that's enough.'

'It is,' Creasy said. 'He's still on medication.'

His eyes were searching the crowd for Michael. Leonie put a hand on his arm and said, 'I'll find him and keep an eye on him. Let me know when you want me to take him home.'

Then she got her sixth surprise.

'You decide when he's ready,' Creasy answered.

THIRTY-TWO

THE SIGNAL REACHED Ahmed Jibril via Colonel Jomah. It had originated from Jomah's man at the Syrian Embassy in Washington DC. The signal informed him that the attempt to abduct Senator James S. Grainger would take place in about three weeks. It also informed him that because of the importance of the target, the price for the abduction would be five hundred thousand US dollars over and above the seventy-five thousand dollars he had already paid for one month's recce of the target.

He cursed and then read on. He was to have his interrogator in Denver within five days. A safe house would be arranged. If he wished for the Senator to be eliminated after interrogation, then the price would be increased by a further one hundred thousand dollars. If he wished the Senator to be merely held prisoner, the cost would be fifty thousand dollars a week. An immediate answer was required.

Jibril summoned his chief of staff, Dalkamouni, and they discussed the signal.

They finally agreed that they would wait until after the results of the interrogation before deciding whether to have the Senator eliminated or merely held for a few weeks in the nature of a hostage.

'They're expensive,' Dalkamouni said. 'Maybe we should have tried to send in our own people.'

Jibril shook his head. 'We only had one good man in America. To send in more would have taken many months. It took us years to establish our cells in Europe.' He tapped the signal. 'These people are rated the best in America.'

'They're just criminals,' Dalkamouni remarked. 'Their only motive is money.'

'True,' Jibril conceded. 'But they're very successful criminals, with a good organisation . . . anyway, money is always a good motive, as we both know.'

Two days later, Curtis Bennett was shown into Senator James Grainger's office. Rene Callard, the Belgian, opened the door for him, then closed it behind him and resumed his seat next to the door.

The Senator was seated at a large walnut desk, studying a brief. He looked up and smiled warmly.

'Hi, Curtis. Grab a chair, I'll be with you in a second.'

He finished the page, jotted some notes on a yellow legal pad, and asked, 'So what's the panic?' He glanced at his watch. 'Make it fast, Curtis, I've got a committee meeting in ten minutes.'

'I'll make it very fast,' Bennett said tersely. 'The CIA has managed to partly break the code used in signals between the Syrian

Foreign Ministry and their Embassies world-wide. You will know that the Syrians actively support several Palestinian and other terrorist organisations. The main one being PFLP–GC which is based in Damascus. They extend help through their own intelligence organisation. The main one is the Syrian Airforce Intelligence Unit, run by Colonel Jomah, who is very close to President Assad. The CIA has been able to identify those signals sent by Colonel Jomah, and also those received by him. His code name is HAWK. He sends a lot of signals to European Syrian Embassies, particularly Bonn, London, Stockholm and Rome. We know that the PFLP–GC has cells in all those cities.' He lit a cigarette and continued. 'Suddenly, last week, a flurry of signals went from the HAWK to the Syrian Embassy here in Washington. That was very unusual. The CIA was working on the signals, we put a watch team on all suspect personnel at the Libyan Embassy here. Four days ago, one of them, coincidentally their airforce attaché, had a meeting with a man in Lafayette Park. Some photos were achieved and computer enhanced. This morning we identified the man as one Joe Moretti, from Chicago. He and two other brothers operate the Moretti family specialists in contract killings and abductions. In the past, they've worked mainly for South or Central American dictatorships who want to take out embarrassing defectors in this country.' He took a drag on his cigarette, gave the Senator a hard look and said, 'Now, Jim, also this morning, the CIA gave us a prelim report on the batch of signals to and from the HAWK. Analysis indicates that the Morettis have been contracted to kill or abduct an important person in this country.'

'Very interesting,' the Senator remarked enigmatically.

Bennett leaned forward, mashed out his cigarette and then said quietly, 'Yes it is ... because I think that important person is you.'

'Why?'

The FBI man sighed. 'Jim, I'm not stupid. First, Harriot is killed on Pan Am 103. The leading suspect for that outrage is considered to be the PFLP–GC, which is closely linked to Syrian Airforce Intelligence and the HAWK. In the meantime, you've been messing around with strange people. First a con man on the fringe of the mercenary world and then a dead or alive mercenary who is or was considered one of the most perfect killing machines ever born.'

Bennett sighed again and lit another cigarette. He was obviously agitated, which was certainly not normal. He went on, 'Then you hire three bodyguards and ask me to pull off all normal security on you. Naturally, I checked out the three bodyguards.' Apologetically, he said, 'That's my duty, Jim. Both in my job and as your friend.'

The Senator nodded in acquiescence.

Bennett went on. 'Now those three guys all turned out to be ex-mercenaries . . . very hard men indeed . . . I presume they're all armed?'

The Senator nodded. 'Yes, they are, Curtis . . . and licensed to be so . . . as no doubt you would also have checked out.'

The FBI man's voice took on a hard note. 'Yes, I did check. Now hear this. The Moretti family is no ordinary mob family. They are not a huge organisation, like some of the others, but they do have about a dozen "soldiers" and they're all highly competent. We know what they do but we've never been able to get a grip on them. Not even a slippery one. Now as I read it, you unwittingly hired this con man Joe Rawlings, in an attempt to avenge Harriot's death.' He smiled grimly. 'Coincidentally, Joe Rawlings was found shot dead late last month in a Paris hotel room. A single bullet in the brain. The French police have no clue at all as to who did it. You hire this dead or alive Creasy and since I doubt you will be conned twice in a month, and since the print on the glass I gave you for a present was definitely authentic, my total assumption is that the man is alive and targeted by you at the PFLP–GC. My next assumption is that the PFLP–GC somehow found out about that and now you are their target, via the Moretti family, and that represents a very great threat indeed.'

The Senator looked at him quizzically and then glanced at his watch.

Bennett sighed in exasperation, then stood up, placed his

166

palms on the desk and leaned forward. Harshly, he said, 'Jim, face up to it. The threat is very serious. So you have three hard type bodyguards, but three is not enough . . . also they're in their mid-forties and that seems a bit old to me.'

The Senator smiled slightly and said, 'I'm very satisfied with them.'

Bennett leaned forward even further, and said, 'Well, frankly, I'm not. Just before I came here I reported my thesis to the Director. He's ordered that you have a full team, twenty-four hour cover. That's twelve highly trained men. Young men. They're already on assignment. It'll be a nuisance, Jim, but it has to be.'

Grainger shook his head.

'I appreciate your concern, Curtis, but I definitely don't want them. Tell the Director to pull them off.'

Bennett shook his head. 'I can't do that. I told him you'd object and he told me to tell you that it's his sworn duty to protect every congressman in this country. So that's it, Jim.' He straightened up and looked at his watch. 'You have two minutes to make that meeting, in your usual punctual way.'

The Senator looked up at him, then reached forward and punched a button on his phone console.

'June,' he said, 'get me the White House. I'd like to speak to the President, if he's available. If not I'll speak to his Personal Secretary.'

A minute later, he was arranging a meeting with the President for later that evening. Bennett looked on incredulously.

'You think he'll intervene?' he said.

'I know he will,' the Senator replied. He smiled slightly. 'He needs me.'

Curtis Bennett opened the door and walked out in disgust and frustration. At the door to the outer office he turned and looked at the man sitting beside the Senator's door. The man looked back, an unblinking stare.

Bennett went out, closing the door behind him, not exactly slamming it but closing it hard.

In his office, the Senator punched a button on his phone console again.

'June,' he said. 'Please phone the committee room and tell them I'm going to be late. About ten or fifteen minutes. Apologise for me. And please ask the gentleman sitting outside my door to come in.'

Callard entered the room and closed the door behind him. His eyes swept the room twice and then centred on the Senator's face.

'Where's Frank?' the Senator asked.

'Nearby.'

'Can you find him?'

The Belgian reached into his jacket pocket, took out a small black metal box and pressed a button on it twice. Five seconds later, it gave an answering bleep.

'He'll be here in a couple of minutes at the most,' Callard said.

Frank Miller was there in less than a minute. His eyes swept the room. His right hand hovered near the opening of his loosely fitted jacket.

'What is it, Mr Grainger?'

The Senator gestured at the chairs in front of his desk.

'Sit down, both of you. Something's come up.'

Miller shook his head and spoke in French to the Belgian, who immediately left the room.

As he sat down, he said to the Senator, 'If one of us is inside, one of us must always be outside. What's happened?'

Grainger quickly briefed him on Bennett's information. The Australian listened intently and then said, 'Good.'

'Good!'

'Yes, in a situation like this all information is good. The more information we have the better we can prepare.'

Grainger did not look anxious, but he did look thoughtful. Finally he said, 'Bennett told me they have about twelve "soldiers". You only have three.'

Frank smiled and shook his head.

'No, we are five, Senator. Two more arrived late last week.'

The Senator looked surprised. 'But I haven't seen them.'

'No, and you won't. They're outside men . . . weapons men.'

Grainger asked, 'Creasy sent them?'

168

'Yes, and they're both bloody good.' He smiled. 'And you'll be pleased to hear that both of them are in their mid-thirties.'

Grainger smiled back and asked, 'Does this change the routine?'

'No. Are you sure you can get the Fed cover pulled off?'

'Pretty sure. I'm seeing the President at seven o'clock . . . I'll let you know.'

The Australian was thinking. 'As a matter of fact, there are a couple of things your friend Curtis Bennett can do to help. I know a lot about the Mafia in Italy, a hell of a lot, but not in this country. It would help if Bennett could pull the file on this Moretti family. Everything the FBI has got, especially photos of the Morettis themselves and as many of the "soldiers" as possible.'

The Senator made a note on his pad. 'And the second thing?' he asked.

'Well, since he's got so many agents to squander, he could send a few to Detroit and monitor the movements of the Moretti "soldiers". I'm sure the FBI's already doing that but they could intensify it. Not too much because we don't want them to know that we're waiting for them. But it would be useful to know if any significant number of them suddenly leave Detroit. They would use at least ten men for the snatch.'

The Senator made another note, looked at his watch and said, 'Will do. Now I have to get to a meeting.'

THIRTY-THREE

MICHAEL'S RECOVERY HAD been very swift. After three weeks, Creasy took him to the hospital in Malta for a final check-up. Dr Grech was faintly astonished by the young man's progress. Afterwards, Creasy took Michael down to Fort St Elmo to resume his training.

While they were away, Leonie took Laura to lunch in the garden restaurant of the Ta Cenc Hotel. They sat at a table under a huge carob tree and ate Italian food and drank a bottle of Italian wine. After the main course Leonie began to ask questions and Laura answered them. She told the younger woman what she knew of Creasy but explained that the only person who really knew him well was her son-in-law Guido who had been with him in the Legion and fought with him in various wars around the world before Guido had married her eldest daughter Julia and they had gone off to live in Naples and run a *pensione* until Julia had been killed in a car crash. Guido still ran the *pensione* and visited Gozo frequently. After Lockerbie he had come to Gozo to stay with Creasy. He and Creasy hardly seemed to talk, but they had such a mental empathy that Laura believed no two men could be closer.

Leonie learned that Creasy had met Nadia after coming to Gozo to recover from gunshot wounds he had received while trying to defend a young Italian girl from kidnappers.

The girl had been killed by the kidnappers. After recovering Creasy had gone back to Italy and wiped out the entire Mafia family responsible on a road of vengeance that stretched from Milan in the north to Palermo in Sicily.

Again he arrived back in Gozo, this time secretly. Again he had been terribly wounded and Laura and Nadia had nursed him back to health while Nadia grew pregnant.

'He must have loved her very much,' Leonie said wistfully.

'I'm sure he did,' Laura answered. 'But he never showed much or said much.'

'But she knew he loved her?'

Laura nodded. 'Oh yes. He would have died for her.' She looked up at the younger woman and said very quietly, 'And maybe he will.'

Creasy stood beside George Zammit, on a raised platform behind the animated firing range in the bowels of Fort St Elmo. Several members of the anti-terrorist squad were standing on either side of them. They were all watching Michael below. He held an Uzi submachine-gun in his right hand. He raised his left hand. George reached behind and pressed a button on the wall. Immediately, targets in the form of male figures in camouflage uniform began to appear on the sides of the walls and rising from the floor. Occasionally the figure of a woman or a child appeared. Creasy did not look at the targets. His gaze was intent upon Michael, who had dropped to one knee and was firing short bursts. He watched as one magazine was emptied and a second one quickly inserted. When that magazine was empty, Michael took it out, checked the breech, then turned to look at the green monitor at the back right hand corner. Creasy, George and all the other men were also watching it. In digital figures, it showed sixty-five per cent.

'Not bad,' George remarked. 'It will take him two or three weeks to get back to his previous best, which was seventy-three.'

Michael laid the SMG and the two empty magazines on a metal table and walked up the stairs to them. He looked at Creasy who said, 'That was very good, Michael.'

The young man shook his head woefully. 'I've done much better. Also I hit one woman. I just lost my rhythm.'

171

'You were very good,' Creasy said again. 'But you need to work on your magazine change. It needs to be much faster. It's the time when you're most exposed.'

A member of the squad grinned and said, 'I've heard those words before.'

Creasy smiled at him and said, 'Shut up, Grazio. The only thing you know how to change in a hurry is a condom.'

They all laughed and Michael asked Creasy, 'Have you ever used this range?'

George said, 'He designed it, Michael, five years ago, and taught us how to use it and much else as well.'

He turned to Creasy. 'You want to have a go?'

'Yes,' Creasy answered. 'And later I'd like to have a session on the hand-gun range.'

He went down the steps to the range. All the young men moved forward to the rail and watched as he picked up the Uzi, stripped it down and reassembled it. All in a matter of seconds. He inserted a magazine and put a spare into the left hand pocket of his jeans. It protruded to his waist. He walked over to the black cross painted on the floor and raised his left hand. George punched the button.

Michael was to recall later that what followed was like a ballet dance. The targets appeared for only two seconds. Creasy dropped into a crouch. Michael never even saw the magazine change. He saw the used one bounce off the concrete floor, but the flow of fire was almost uninterrupted. Creasy walked back to the metal table, unsnapping the second magazine. He laid it on the table, checked the SMG and turned to look at the monitor. The digital figures showed ninety-six per cent. There was total silence on the platform. Targets were still moving in and out and up and down on the range. One of the newer recruits muttered, 'I don't believe it.'

'Believe it,' Grazio said. 'I've seen him hit ninety-eight.'

THIRTY-FOUR

SENATOR GRAINGER AND Frank Miller were just finishing dinner when the phone rang. Miguel was pouring coffee. The Senator asked him to answer the call and said, 'If it's Bob Holden, I'm not here.'

Miguel went to the sideboard and picked up the phone. He listened for a moment and then started talking rapidly in Spanish.

It was a language that Grainger understood well. He cocked an ear, listened and then stood up. Miguel put the phone down and turned, his face very agitated.

'It's my mother,' he said. 'She's had a heart attack. Her condition is not good. That was my brother.'

Immediately, the Senator went to the telephone, picked it up and punched a number. After a pause he said into it, 'Francis, Jim. I want a seat on the first available plane to Mexico City . . . no, not for me, it's for Miguel. His mother had a heart attack . . . yes I'll wait.' He cupped the mouthpiece of the phone and said to Miguel, 'You'll be at your mother's bedside in a matter of hours . . . even if I have to charter a plane.'

Miguel wiped a hand over his face and muttered, 'Thank you, sir. But what about you?'

'Don't worry about it,' the Senator said. 'I'll get someone temporary from the agency. Stay as long as you need to.'

Miguel started to say something. The Senator held up his hand and said, 'Wait a minute.' He listened into the phone and then looked at his watch and said, 'He'll be there, with a few

173

minutes to spare but make sure that plane doesn't leave without him. Phone Harry Robson if you need to and use my name. Get five thousand dollars from the safe in my office and give it to Miguel at the airport.'

He cradled the phone and said to Miguel, 'Go and pack, there's a flight to Dallas in forty-five minutes which connects with a flight to Mexico City. You'll be there within four to five hours.'

Miguel started to mutter his thanks. The Senator waved them aside and said, 'Get going.'

Miguel hurriedly left the room and Grainger asked Miller, 'Can one of your guys run him to the airport?'

Miller shook his head. 'Not possible. Rene is sleeping and needs his sleep, Maxie is back-up to me.'

'What about the other two guys I've never seen?'

Miller waved his hand. 'They're outside somewhere, and they stay out there.'

Grainger picked up the phone again and punched in a number. When it was answered, he said, 'Hi Gloria, it's Jim. I've got an emergency. Miguel just had a call from Mexico City that his mother had a heart attack. I've booked him on a flight which leaves in about forty minutes. I can't take him myself and a taxi will take too long to get here. Are any of your kids around?' He listened for a moment and then said, 'Good, thanks. He'll be ready in ten minutes . . . Francis will be waiting for him at the airport.'

He cradled the phone and said to Miller, 'Sometimes it's useful to have good neighbours.'

After Miguel left in the passenger seat of a Mercedes 500, the Senator went into the kitchen to brew more coffee. Miller followed him, as always.

'I feel like a Siamese twin,' the Senator remarked.

'You are,' Miller answered.

A thought struck the Senator. 'You know we could have all taken him to the airport. You, me and Maxie.'

Miller shook his head. He held a finger to his lips. There was a notepad and a pencil hanging on the wall next to the fridge.

174

Miller went over, took it off the wall and gestured at a chair by the kitchen table. Puzzled, the Senator sat down. Miller sat opposite him. He wrote rapidly on the pad and then pushed it across the table. The Senator read: 'It may be a set-up. They could be waiting between here and the airport.'

The Senator looked up in astonishment and drew a breath to say something. Again Miller put a finger to his lips and pointed to the pad. Angrily, Grainger tore the top sheet off, picked up the pencil and scribbled something. He pushed it across to the Australian, who read: 'Miguel has been with me and my wife for eight years. I would trust him with my life.'

Miller picked up the pencil and wrote one line underneath that. He pushed it over and the Senator read: 'I would not. Let's go and talk in the garden.'

They walked out by the pool and Grainger said sarcastically, 'Can I talk now?'

Quietly Miller answered, 'Yes, Senator, but in a low voice please.'

'What the hell is all this about?'

Miller was standing close to him. He said, 'I don't like unexpected things to happen. If the Morettis have been keeping a watch over you, and it's a good bet they have, they will know that you only have one servant and don't keep a permanent driver in the evenings. They will know that you have three body-guards and that you always move with two of them while the other one rests. They could also have found out the fastest way to get from Denver to Mexico City including the timing of the flights and so that telephone call could have been timed exactly so that you might decide personally to rush him to the airport . . . Senator, when it comes to planning an ambush the timing is everything. Their timing would have been accurate to within five minutes.'

'But it was his brother who phoned him.'

'That's what he told you.'

Grainger thought that over and said, 'You think his mother might not have had a heart attack?'

'It's possible,' Miller answered. 'And I have to check out every

175

possibility . . . now if it was a set-up, it's certain that Miguel would have planted bugs in the house. That's why we're talking in the garden. When we go back inside we just hold a normal conversation. If we find any bugs, we don't remove them, otherwise they'll be alerted.'

He took a small black metal box from his pocket and pressed a button on it twice. Maxie loomed out of the clump of trees at the bottom of the garden. The Dobermann was at his heels. Miller walked forward and held a whispered conversation. Maxie nodded. They both walked back to the Senator. Miller said to him, 'I assume you have Miguel's address in Mexico City?'

'Of course.'

Miller jerked a thumb towards the Rhodesian and said, 'Maxie has a Spanish friend, an ex-mercenary who married a Mexican woman and retired there. He lives in a small town about fifty miles outside Mexico City. They keep in touch. Maxie will phone him from outside the house and give him Miguel's address and whatever other details you have. By tomorrow evening, we'll know whether Miguel's mother had a heart attack.'

It took Miller and Maxie three hours to uncover all the bugs. The two mainline telephones and the six in the extensions were easy. It was the back-up bugs that proved more elusive. Each was hidden within three metres of all the phones and would have picked up conversations in any of the main rooms, together with one side of a telephone conversation, if the bugs in the phone had been neutralised.

They were out by the pool again just after midnight. Callard joined them.

'I can't believe Miguel could have planted those bugs,' the Senator said in a quiet voice.

'He didn't,' Miller answered. 'They were set by an expert, but someone had to let the expert in, while we were away in Washington. It could only have been Miguel.'

'Maybe they broke in,' Grainger persisted.

Again Miller shook his head. 'They would have had to kill the

176

Dobermann for a start and that would have left evidence. Also, your alarm system is damn good, internally and externally.'

'It is,' Grainger admitted ruefully. 'I had it upgraded after I came back one night and found Creasy sitting at my bar having a drink.'

Miller smiled and asked, 'What did he do about the Dobermann and Miguel?'

'He put them both to sleep with darts.'

Maxie grinned. 'He learnt that in Rhodesia,' he said. 'That technique was perfected when they built the Kariba Dam and flooded a huge area of the Zambezi valley. They rescued tens of thousands of stranded animals by darting them. Creasy used to go and help the Game Rangers, when he was on leave from the army.'

'So what do we do about it?' Grainger asked.

'Nothing at all,' Miller answered. 'We'll leave them in place, but just be careful what you say in the house or on the phone. It gives us a major advantage.'

'How so?'

Miller picked his words carefully.

'An ambush or a "snatch" is a war situation. There are the attackers and the defenders. There are two critical factors as far as the defenders are concerned. To know where it's going to happen and when it's going to happen.'

'But how will we know?' the Senator asked.

'Because now we'll have a good chance of setting the place and the time.'

The Senator was intrigued.

'How will we do that?'

All three bodyguards were smiling. Rene answered the question.

'Because in two or three days from now, Senator, you will make a phone call from inside the house. It will be a phone call to a young lady, to arrange a rendezvous . . . a rendezvous unencumbered by bodyguards.'

The Senator looked at the three faces and also smiled.

177

THIRTY-FIVE

'I WANT YOU to grow a moustache.'

Michael turned his head and looked at Creasy in surprise.

'Why?'

'Because it's a statistical fact that more than fifty per cent of young Palestinian males have moustaches.' He smiled. 'Quite a few Palestinian females have them too. Besides, it will make you look about twenty.'

They were sitting side by side at the edge of the pool, their feet in the water.

Turning serious, Creasy said, 'In about four months you'll be ready. Then we go.' He calculated in his mind and then went on, 'Leonie will be leaving in five weeks. After that all your training will be here in the house. I'll set up a pistol range in the cave and I'll borrow a silenced sniper rifle from George. We can practise up on the cliffs past Ta Cenc.'

'George says that's my weakest point in weapons,' Michael said.

'It's the weakest part of every member of George's squad, including himself. There's a reason for it.'

'What's that?'

'Temperament,' Creasy answered. 'Mediterranean temperament. You might call it impatience. That's fine with a hand-gun or an SMG. I can tell you that you're perfectly suited to an SMG. You have the rhythm. Within four months, you're going to be damned good.'

'As good as you?'

Creasy shook his head. 'No, but better than me at your age. When it comes to sniping, though, you have to be able to change your mentality. You have to cultivate patience and concentration. You have to learn to lie in cover for hours on end without moving. The best snipers in the world are Gurkhas.'

'Gurkhas?'

'Yes, they're from Nepal. To this day, they serve as mercenaries in the British and Indian armies. They're very small men but they make the best soldiers I've ever seen . . . and the best snipers. One of them will be coming here after Leonie has gone. He's sixty years old and retired but probably still the best sniper on earth. He will teach you.'

'Are you a good sniper?' Michael asked.

'Yes,' Creasy stated flatly. 'But I don't come close to Rambahadur Rai. He can freeze his body in total stillness for forty-eight hours and then take the top off a beer bottle at four hundred metres. He will arrive as soon as Leonie leaves and stay about a month.'

'I don't think Leonie wants to leave,' Michael said quietly.

'She has to,' Creasy answered. 'It's in her contract. You know about that contract.'

The young man kicked his feet, splashing water across the pool. 'You seem to be getting on much better,' he said. 'And I'll miss her cooking . . . so will you.'

Creasy shrugged and said, 'She's a good cook and a fine woman and I admit that I treated her badly during the first three months . . . but in five weeks she has to go.'

As if on cue, Leonie came out of the kitchen carrying a tray. She put it on the table under the trellis and called out, 'Lunch.'

There were plates of cold meats and salads and cheeses and a chilled bottle of Soave. As they ate, Michael looked up at Leonie and said, 'I want to go to La Grotta tonight . . . do you mind?'

Without looking at Creasy, she shook her head and said, 'No, I don't mind. As long as you promise me you won't drink more than four bottles of beer. You're still on medication for another week.'

'I promise,' Michael said solemnly.

179

'Why don't we all go?' Creasy said.

Leonie looked at him, startled. 'All of us . . . to a disco?'

'Sure. Why not? It's a good disco and they make damn fine pizzas.'

'It sounds fun . . . will you dance with me?'

'Sure.'

'And I'll dance with you too,' Michael said enthusiastically.

They were interrupted by the ringing of the telephone. Michael went into the kitchen. When he came back out he said, 'It's for you, Creasy. Overseas. He wouldn't give his name, just said, "Tell him it's the Aussie."'

Creasy came back ten minutes later. As he sat down, he said, 'Let's make it a good night tonight. I have to leave in the morning. I'll be away about a week to ten days.'

THIRTY-SIX

'NICOLE, HONEY, I miss you like hell.'

In his deep Australian accent Frank Miller answered, 'Sweetheart, I miss you too.'

Senator James S. Grainger burst into raucous laughter. They were sitting at a table at the far end of the swimming pool. Both held a sheet of paper in their hands. Very sternly, Miller said, 'Senator, you have to get this right. It's important. You have to make that call tonight and it's vital that you sound totally natural.'

Grainger grinned. 'You mean I must sound like I'm chatting up my mistress?'

'Exactly. Now let's start again from the top.'

The Senator took a sip of his whisky, looked down at the paper and repeated, 'Nicole, honey, I miss you like hell.'

'Sweetheart, I miss you too.'

The Senator burst out laughing again and the Australian sighed in exasperation.

Grainger said, 'Frank, tell me about this girl, like, how old is she?'

'I'd guess about twenty-seven or twenty-eight.'

'Is she beautiful?'

'Yes, very.'

The Senator spread his hands in an expansive gesture and said, 'Well if she was sitting across the table from me, instead of some hairy male antipodean, I might be able to get through this without cracking up.'

The Australian glared at him.

'So, I have to go out and buy a wig and get silicone injections?'

At that moment, they were interrupted by Maxie MacDonald coming out of the house.

He walked over and said, 'Senator, I have some unpleasant news for you. I just got back from phoning Mexico. Miguel's mother is fit and well. So well, in fact, that this morning she was able to go to a jewellery shop with her newly returned, obviously wealthy son. He bought her a very expensive bracelet.'

Suddenly there was no humour on Grainger's face. He looked down at the table and muttered, 'That bastard . . . we treated him so well.'

The two bodyguards remained silent and then Maxie said quietly, 'Do you want anything done about it?'

'Like what?'

Maxie shrugged. 'Well my friend down there is officially retired, but for a modest fee, probably less than the cost of the bracelet, he'll be quite happy to blow Miguel's head off . . . or any other part of his anatomy.'

Frank Miller watched the Senator's face, watched him think about it. Finally, Grainger shook his head.

'Thanks, Maxie, but no. Let's leave that kind of thing to the Morettis.'

Maxie shrugged again. 'Whatever you say.'

'Pull your chair next to the Senator,' Frank said. 'And if he starts laughing, hit him hard.' To Grainger, he said, 'Now let's get on with it.'

Grainger picked up the piece of paper and said, 'OK. Let's go. Nicole, honey, I miss you like hell.'

'Jim, sweetheart, I miss you too.'

Maxie MacDonald burst out laughing.

Miller snarled, 'Go and do something useful.'

The Rhodesian walked away, still laughing.

'Don't get upset,' Grainger said placatingly. 'I know it's important. I'll concentrate now and don't worry, Frank, at college I was in the theatre group and a damned good actor.' He smiled disarmingly. 'Any good politician has to be a good actor.'

So they got on with it and this time it went well. Grainger's voice was heavy with sincerity.

'Nicole, honey, I miss you like hell.'

'Jim, sweetheart, I miss you too.'

'There's no way this can go on. I've got to see you.'

'But how, sweetheart? If you've got bodyguards draped on each arm, day and night?'

Grainger sighed and said with exasperation, 'Honey, if it was just for a few days or even a couple of weeks, I could handle it. But this could go on for months . . . I'm gonna make an arrangement.'

'What kind of arrangement, Jim?'

'Honey, I'm gonna rent an apartment and find a way to sneak off for a couple of hours at a time.'

'But how, Jim?'

'Leave it to me, honey. As soon as I've found a place I'll mail you the key. Then I'll phone you later to set up a time.'

'I can't wait, sweetheart . . . I've been very lonely.'

'Me too, honey. What with work and all this bodyguard shit. I need a bit of relaxation.'

Miller tried a girlish chuckle and said, 'Just leave it to me, sweetheart.'

Grainger grinned, but kept his voice serious.

182

'I sure will, honey. Listen, I've got to run now. I'll get back to you. Ciao.'

'Ciao,' Miller answered, then looked up and nodded in approval. 'That was good, Senator, very good. We'll run through it a couple more times, and then make the call tonight.'

'Now, I have a question,' the Senator said sternly.

'Go ahead.'

'When are you and your two side-kicks gonna stop calling me Senator and start calling me Jim?'

The Australian said seriously, 'When we stop working for you, Senator . . . we prefer it that way . . . it won't be long. Within a week it will be over.' He picked up a pen and flicked over his piece of paper. 'Now I need the names and addresses of the restaurants here that you regularly eat at.'

'OK,' Grainger answered. 'But first sketch me in on the plan.'

'The plan,' Miller answered, 'is simple. All good plans are. We check out all the restaurants you give me and select one which gives you the opportunity to sneak out the back way. We then find and rent an apartment within five minutes' drive from that restaurant. You set up a dinner with a couple of male friends. In the meantime, you'll have mailed a key and the apartment number to Nicole. It's necessary that the apartment building has several empty apartments. In the afternoon before the dinner you phone her up. You will of course have mentioned the name of the building on the phone, but not the apartment number. You'll tell her that you'll phone her at the rented apartment and tell her you don't know when you'll arrive exactly, but that you have to leave her at eleven p.m. sharp. Maxie will accompany you to the dinner and sit with you at the table. Rene will be outside the restaurant as normal. I'll be in the apartment with Nicole. After the first course you will go to the men's room and then sneak out the back. There'll be a car waiting for you there, placed earlier. You'll drive to the apartment. That's one of the two exposure areas, but I'll come to that later.' He reached forward and took a sip of his mineral water.

'Now the Morettis would have picked all that up from the bug. They'll know the apartment building, but not the number.

They'll know your exact time of departure but not your time of arrival. If they have any brains, and they do, they'll be ready to make the "snatch" outside the entrance to the building, when you emerge.'

'Why not inside?'

'Because over the next two or three days we'll rent several apartments in that building under false names, so if they manage to get at the letting records, they won't know which one Nicole is in.'

Grainger nodded and then said, 'But as soon as I give her the name of the building they'll have it under observation.'

'Sure, but during the afternoon or early evening they will see several young attractive women, who could all be a Senator's mistress, entering the building. Nicole will already be in the apartment, apart from which, they don't know what she looks like.'

Grainger thought that over and then asked, 'When is the second moment of exposure?'

'When you emerge from the building at eleven o'clock. I'll be right behind you but for a few seconds you'll be exposed to sniper fire. After those few seconds, you'll be back in the building until it's over, which won't take longer than half a minute.' He looked the Senator in the eyes and said, 'I'm only allowing that exposure because we're ninety-five per cent sure they're planning a "snatch" and not an immediate kill.'

'But there is a risk?' the Senator asked.

'Sure,' Miller answered. 'In this business, there always is. Have you been under fire before?'

'Yes, I was in Korea. Wounded there.'

'Well, this is another kind of war, Senator, but just as risky . . . Strangely enough, thanks to that shit Miguel, we have the advantage. We choose the place and time.' He looked at his watch. 'Now, I think it's time to visit your good neighbour Gloria.'

'For what?'

'So we can phone Curtis Bennett. I need to talk to him.'

'About what?'

'About the surveillance on the Morettis' "soldiers". If within a day of your first phone call to Nicole a substantial number of them leave Detroit, then we know that they've taken the bait. I'll give him some code sentences so he can phone here. If he does, I'll be listening on an extension.'

The Senator stood and stretched his frame.

'OK,' he said. 'By the way, where did you find this Nicole woman?'

'I didn't,' Miller answered. 'She came via Creasy.'

'She's a girlfriend of his?'

'I didn't ask.'

THIRTY-SEVEN

IT WAS MARY BENNETT who phoned at eight o'clock the next night. Grainger was sitting at his bar with Miller. He picked up the phone.

'Jim,' she said. 'It's Mary, how are you?'

'Fine, honey.' He gestured to Miller, who slipped off his stool, moved quickly into the kitchen and picked up the extension.

'Jim,' she said. 'Are you going to be in Washington on the 5th of next month?'

'Sure, honey, I'm coming up around the end of the month and I'll be there about three weeks. I plan to buy a smaller apartment. Maybe you could give me a hand with the furniture and decorating . . . I'm hopeless at that.'

'It'll be a real pleasure, but I don't have Harriot's tastes.'

'You have fine taste, Mary. We'll keep it simple . . . what's happening on the 5th?'

'It's Sunday and we're having a barbecue. Not big, just about a dozen people, but fun people. Will you come?'

'Wild horses won't keep me away,' he said. 'Maybe we can discuss the apartment then. About what time?'

'Oh, about one o'clock. It might go on a bit late though. You know what Curtis is like. Don't make any plans until after six o'clock. Anyway, you'll enjoy it. It's quite a diverse bunch of people.'

He laughed. 'Yes, you do have the strangest friends. I look forward to it. 'Bye, honey.'

Miller came out of the kitchen, holding a piece of paper, on which he had jotted down the conversation. He put it on the bar and the two men leaned close and studied it.

With a pencil, Miller underlined several sentences.

Then he gestured and they carried their drinks out into the garden.

'So they took the bait,' Miller said with great satisfaction. 'Between one o'clock and six o'clock today six of the Morettis' "soldiers" left Detroit airport for diverse destinations.' He smiled. He was obviously enjoying himself.

He glanced at the Senator and said, 'Naturally, they wouldn't all pile on one plane and fly straight to Denver. That would have been obvious, but still, since they all left within five hours, it means they haven't tumbled to the extra FBI surveillance, otherwise they'd have spread it over two or three days.' He looked down at the paper in his hand and said, 'Senator, you'll have your fling with Nicole four nights from tonight.'

'Why wait that long?' Grainger asked. 'I'd like to get the damn thing over and get back to normal life.'

'Because I'm waiting for reinforcements,' Miller answered. 'They're bound to have two or three people here already, which makes a total of around nine or ten.'

'How many reinforcements?'

'Just one.'

The Senator glanced at him and remarked, 'So it's going to be six against nine or ten? Not very good odds, Frank.'

The Australian was still smiling. 'Beautiful odds,' he said. 'Just beautiful.'

THIRTY-EIGHT

JAMES S. GRAINGER found himself tense but not frightened. He was into his first exposure. Two minutes earlier, he had slipped out of the restaurant, through the back door via the kitchen, nodding pleasantly to the surprised chef. He found himself in a wide alley. The blue Ford was parked exactly where Miller said it would be. Miller had told him he would not be exposed until he pulled out into the street. Up to that point, he would be covered. He pulled on the white cotton gloves that Frank had given him.

Now he was tense. He was in the street amongst the traffic, his eyes watching the other cars and, when he stopped at traffic lights, watching the pedestrians.

It took him only three minutes to reach the apartment building, which was on a quiet, tree-lined avenue. As instructed he parked fifty yards past it. He felt the tension rising further. He looked around. Across the avenue, an old woman was walking an elaborately coiffured toy poodle. Further down a young couple came towards him, holding hands. He waited until they were alongside the car, swiftly got out, locked the door and followed them. They passed the building and he quickly moved to the door.

The apartment building operated on an entry phone system. He placed himself in front of it, shielding it from observation, and pushed number 204. Instantly, Nicole's voice answered. As instructed, he said into the speaker, 'It's Jim. 505.' The door clicked open.

With a surge of relief, he went in, closing it behind him.

In front of him was the elevator. The stairs were to his right. As instructed, he climbed the stairs to the second floor. Miller was standing in the open doorway of apartment 204, his pistol held high in his right hand, pointing at the ceiling. He stood aside to let Grainger in but remained at the open door for another two minutes, listening. The woman was sitting on the settee. She was indeed beautiful: long, dark, straight hair, high cheekbones and a wide, red mouth. But she was not dressed like an important man's mistress. She was wearing a denim shirt tucked into denim jeans.

She did not get up from the sofa. Grainger walked over and was about to say something when she held a finger to her red lips. He turned and watched Miller listening at the open door. He was wearing a knee-length black raincoat which bulged at the front and sides. Finally satisfied, Miller closed the door, walked over to the dining table, laid the pistol on it and took his raincoat off. Underneath, a webbed harness covered his chest. Clipped to it, on his left side, was a shotgun, with its barrels sawn off very short. It was an over and under shotgun but with a difference. It had two barrels on top, and two below. On his right side hung a very small submachine-gun with a folded butt. Next to it three spare magazines protruded from a pouch. He unclipped the weapons and laid them on the table. Then he picked up a pistol and slid it into a shoulder holster under his left armpit. He smiled and said, 'So far, so good.'

The woman stood up and as though he was running a dating agency, Miller said, 'Jim, this is Nicole. Nicole, this is Jim.'

She held out a hand and very formally, the Senator shook it. He found himself a bit lost for words, which for a politician is highly unusual. She smiled and withdrew her hand and walked to a cabinet in the corner saying, 'I'm told you drink whisky and soda, Jim.'

She turned to look at Miller who said, 'Nothing for me.'

He looked at the Senator and said, 'Drink it slowly, Senator, you're only to have three over the next two hours.'

She walked over and handed him the drink, sat down on the

188

settee, picked up a woman's magazine from the coffee table and started reading.

The Senator carried his drink over to Miller and asked, 'What happens now?'

'We wait,' Miller answered. 'We wait to find out if the hook has sunk in deep.'

'How will we know?'

The Australian pointed at the table. Next to the weapons was a small black metal box that he and the other two bodyguards always carried. Next to the box was a notepad and pencil.

'When that thing starts bleeping, we'll know.'

Back at the restaurant, Maxie MacDonald had acted out the charade of checking out the men's room and even the ladies' room. He questioned the chef and then hurriedly went out the back door. Rene was waiting for him in a rented car.

THIRTY-NINE

GRAINGER NOTED THAT both Nicole and Miller wore the same white cotton gloves. He was on his second drink when the little black box emitted its first beep. It went on beeping for several minutes, while Miller made notes on the pad. When it stopped, he hit the button five times at varying intervals. Then he turned and smiled at Grainger.

'The hook has sunk deep.'

The Senator walked over and looked down at the pad. There were just rows of letters, haphazardly arranged.

'Morse code?' he asked.

'No,' Miller answered. 'It's our own code.'

'What does it mean?'

Miller stood up, stretched his frame and adjusted his shoulder holster. 'It means,' he said, 'that the Moretti family have got two cars in position. One in the avenue with three men in it, including a Moretti brother. He was recognised from file photographs that Curtis Bennett gave us. They must be getting paid a hell of a lot of money, to risk inside family . . . a hell of a lot.' He walked to the window which fronted the avenue, opened the curtains a crack, and peered through. Over his left shoulder, he said, 'Can't see anything from here, but it's about forty yards to the left. A black Pontiac. I can't see it because of the trees. The back-up car is on the corner with one man in it. A spare car in case the other malfunctions. Very thorough.'

'What will their plan be?' Grainger asked.

Miller turned from the window and walked back to the table.

'It will be one of three things,' he said. 'The car in the avenue will be parked close to yours. They could wait until you get to your car and make the "snatch" there. Or as you come out of the entrance, the car will move in on you, come up onto the kerb and spill out the men.' He smiled. Grainger had the distinct impression that he was enjoying himself. Miller went on, 'But we think it will almost certainly be the third way.'

'Which is?'

'About ten or fifteen minutes before eleven o'clock, when you're scheduled to come out of the building, a man will be hanging around within a few yards of the front door. It could be a drunk or a well-dressed businessman looking for an address. It could be anyone, but definitely someone young and fit. When you walk out of the building he'll approach you with a question. It could be a request for directions or the drunk begging a buck for another drink . . . anything. He'll try to get very close to you. He'll then either grab you and hold you physically, or hold a gun on you, until the car pulls alongside and you're dragged in.'

'So, what do I do?' Grainger asked.

'What you do,' Miller replied, 'is not let that man get within four yards of you. As soon as he's that close you turn and head straight back for the door, which will be wedged slightly open.'

'What if he pulls a gun and shoots me in the back?'

The Australian shook his head.

'He won't. A second after you turn he'll be dead, and then there'll be a short sharp war. You will stay in the hall until you hear this signal on the door.' He bent down and with his knuckles rapped on the table three times, paused, and then rapped three times again. 'After that you come out fast.'

He started pacing up and down, always standing near the table and the weapons. 'But we're missing two or three men,' he went on.

'We are? But we only had six.'

Miller shook his head. 'No, we are missing two or three of their "soldiers". There are four in the two cars below, and the one who will be hanging about at the entrance. That makes five. We know they have maybe three or four more. One of them will certainly be manning their base, wherever it is, but the other two or three will be elsewhere.'

'Where might that be?' Grainger asked.

Miller stopped pacing and said to him, 'Because of their known expertise, we think they'll have a back-up team some- where. The logical place would be on the road leading to your house.' He looked at his watch. 'They'll probably not move into place until about twenty minutes to eleven. It's a quiet area and they wouldn't want to be seen hanging about too long. All the residents' cars in the area are parked off the road. We'll be look- ing for a vehicle parked beside the road. Anyway, we're now cer- tain of one thing. It's one hundred per cent positive that they've set up a "snatch" and not a "kill".'

He turned to look at Nicole and asked her, 'Would you mind making some coffee? How about you, Senator?'

'Yes. Thanks.'

She put the magazine on the coffee table and walked into the kitchen.

'How can you be totally certain?' Grainger asked.

Miller waved at the window.

191

'Because of the set-up out there. If it was a "kill" they'd only use up to three men. One to make the hit, one for a back-up and one to drive the car . . . believe me it's definitely a "snatch".' He looked at his watch. 'It's quarter past ten, so try to relax a bit. Have a last whisky.'

'I'll put it in my coffee,' Grainger answered.

Suddenly the little black box gave off a series of beeps. Quickly, Miller hurried forward, listened and made a brief note on his pad. Then he hit the button twice and straightened up. 'Just routine,' he said to Grainger. 'Nothing's changed. They'll check in now, every ten minutes, unless something happens.'

Nicole came in carrying a tray and served them coffee. Grainger took his over to the drinks cabinet and poured a slug of Scotch into it. Then he carried it back to the table and looked down at the two weapons.

'Quite a bit of fire power,' he said.

'Yes,' Miller agreed. He tapped the sawn-off shotgun. 'Probably the best close range weapon ever invented.'

'What's the submachine-gun?' Grainger asked.

'It's an Ingram Model 10. Its main advantage is its size. It's easy to conceal, but its rate of fire is too high. I'd have preferred an Uzi, but for this job, it's too bulky.'

They chatted about weapons and Grainger told him about his days in the army and about Korea. Then the little black box beeped again. Miller merely listened and then hit the button twice in acknowledgement.

'Routine again,' Miller said and looked at his watch. 'Half an hour to go.' He started pacing again.

FORTY

THE BLACK BOX beeped again ten minutes later, but again it was routine. But when it beeped five minutes afterwards, it continued doing so for a couple of minutes while Miller made notes. Then he punched out the acknowledgement, turned with a grin and said, 'They've located the back-up team.'

'Where?'

'About a mile from your home. They're in a small white truck. At least two of them and probably two more in the back.'

'How do you know it's them?'

'Because two of them got out, opened the hood and started fiddling with the engine. One of them was the youngest Moretti brother.'

'What are you going to do about it?'

'They'll be taken care of,' Miller answered flatly.

He looked at his watch, then glanced at Nicole and said, 'Fifteen minutes to go.' She nodded, got up and went to the bedroom. Two minutes later, she came out wearing a navy blue coat and holding a small bag. She put the bag by the door and went back to the settee. One minute later, the black box beeped and went on beeping. When it finally stopped, Miller hit the button five times in sequence, and then turned to face Grainger.

'It's a cop,' he said.

'What is?'

'The man we expected to turn up and hang about, near the entrance.'

'A cop!' Grainger said incredulously.

'Well, one of the Morettis' "soldiers" dressed as a cop.'

'How do you know?'

'It's an old trick,' Miller answered. 'It's been used by the Red Brigades in Italy and by right-wing hit squads all over Central and South America. People don't suspect a cop.'

'But you can't be sure?'

Again Miller shrugged. 'He's lurking next to a tree, ten yards from the entrance, in the shadows. Real cops don't lurk in the shadows. He's there in case a real cop car cruises past. He can move behind the tree. Don't worry, he's a Moretti "soldier".' He picked up the sawn-off shotgun and clipped it to his harness, its four blunt barrels pointing downwards. Then he clipped on the SMG in the same way. He slipped on the raincoat but didn't button it. It hung over the weapons, concealing them.

'Let's go over it again,' he said to Grainger. 'You walk out of the door and move three short paces forward, then stop and take in the night breeze. The cop will move towards you, saying something. Close your ears to what he says. When he gets to about four yards from you, you say loudly, "Damn, I've forgotten something." You turn and then very rapidly you come back through the door. You stay in there with Nicole until you hear the signal.' Again, he rapped on the table three times, paused, and rapped again three times.

'She's coming with us?' Grainger asked.

'Only part of the way. You can say your goodbyes in the hall.' His eyes swept the room to make sure nothing had been left behind. Then he looked at his watch and put his finger on the button of the little black box. He held it there for five seconds, then picked up the box and slipped it into his raincoat pocket. He looked at Grainger and said, 'Let's do it.'

FORTY-ONE

IN THE HALL Miller motioned to Nicole. She moved to one side and put her bag at her feet. She looked tense. So did Grainger.

Miller opened his raincoat, unclipped the sawn-off shotgun and held it in his left hand. He moved next to the door, turned, leaned against the wall and looked at Grainger.

'Are you ready?' he asked.

Grainger took a deep breath and nodded.

Miller gestured with the shotgun barrels at the door and said lightly, 'Let's go then. Don't hurry on your way out. Make it natural.'

Grainger took another breath, filling his lungs, then he moved to the door, opened it and walked out. Quickly he glanced to his left, saw the car parked about forty yards away. His own car was just beyond it. As he turned his head back he heard the engine start up and rev. The cop came out of the shadows to his right. He was tall, young and dark.

'Evening,' he called out. 'Do you happen to be a resident of that building?' He was walking slowly forward, a pleasant expression on his face.

Grainger said nothing, just watched him and measured the distance. Eight yards.

'There's been a bit of trouble in there,' the cop was saying.

Six yards.

'That's why I'm patrolling out here.'

Four yards.

'Damn, I've forgotten something,' Grainger said and spun on

his heel. He had only taken one stride before he heard the dull thwack behind him. He heard the screeching of tyres, and then was pushing the door open. He turned, glanced swiftly back and saw the cop spreadeagled on the sidewalk. His legs were moving, twitching.

Then Grainger was in the hall and Miller was moving through the door in a crouch, shouting.

'Shut it!'

The black car was screeching to a halt and two men were bursting out. One from the front and one from the back.

Miller fired all four barrels. The one in the back was slammed against the side of the car. The one in the front was blasted on top of the hood. Miller let the shotgun drop and hang from the harness. In half a second he was holding the submachine-gun. He fired two bursts as the car's engine revved. Both bursts were aimed at the tyres, and both were on target. The car moved about ten yards and then slewed sideways. The driver leapt out and started to run. Miller turned to look the other way, towards the sound of shooting at the corner of the avenue to his right.

The driver only got fifteen yards before he was cut down by a hail of bullets from across the avenue.

From a building further up a woman screamed, then there was silence. Miller's eyes swept the avenue. Then he reached into his raincoat pocket and pressed the button of the black metal box three times rapidly.

There was a single answering bleep and four seconds later a white Lincoln Continental turned the corner and moved sedately towards the building. Miller turned to the door.

Inside, Grainger heard the three sharp raps on the door and then three more. He opened the door.

He saw the dead cop on the sidewalk, two bodies on the street in front, further down, the disabled car and beyond that another body. The white Lincoln pulled up. Maxie MacDonald was in the driving seat. He reached behind and opened the back door. Miller was holding the SMG in his right hand. His eyes were still sweeping the avenue.

'You two get in the back seat,' he said tersely.

They crossed the sidewalk at a run. Nicole tossed her bag in and then dived after it. Grainger followed, pulling the door shut behind him.

Three seconds later, Miller was in the front passenger seat and the Lincoln pulled smoothly away.

No one spoke until they were three blocks away. Then Grainger asked, 'What about the guy in their back-up car at the corner?'

Maxie answered.

'Rene took him out.'

They could hear the wailing of sirens behind them. Miller was pressing the button on his black box and getting a series of answering bleeps.

Two blocks later, they pulled into an open parking lot. It was empty except for two cars, parked side by side. One was a green Datsun and the other a black Ford. There was a man in the driving seat of the Datsun.

'We change cars,' Miller explained, 'and say goodbye to Nicole.'

They all climbed out of the Ford and she quickly kissed the three men on their cheeks and got into the front passenger seat of the Datsun. It immediately pulled away.

Still bemused, Grainger called after it, 'Thank you.'

Miller said, 'Get into the back, Senator. It's not quite over yet.'

He did so and Maxie got behind the wheel, with Miller next to him. They drove off in the direction of the Senator's house.

After about a mile they pulled into the kerb and stopped. Maxie switched off the lights and looked at his watch. It was precisely twelve minutes past eleven. They sat silently until the Senator asked, 'What are we waiting for?'

Maxie held up a hand.

'Just wait, Senator. We'll only be a couple of minutes.'

They waited in silence again until a vehicle pulled up behind them. Grainger turned to look. It was an open, battered jeep, with one man in it, whom Grainger had never seen. The jeep's lights flicked on and off twice. Maxie turned on his lights and pulled out into the sparse traffic. The jeep followed closely behind.

What had happened during the past minutes would stay in Grainger's mind for ever. What was to follow would be embedded in it.

About a mile and a half from his house was a turnoff with a sharp bend. Two hundred yards before the turnoff the black box in Miller's pocket bleeped. Maxie pulled over slightly and slowed down. The jeep roared past them. Maxie speeded up again and kept the Ford about seventy yards behind the jeep.

'Watch this,' he said to Grainger over his shoulder.

The Senator leaned forward between the two men and peered through the windscreen. As they rounded the bend, he saw the white truck parked on the verge. One man was standing beside it, looking down the street at the two approaching cars. When it was fifty yards from the truck the jeep slowed and veered across the road. From the back seat, a figure rose, dressed in black. It held a fat tube about four and a half feet long across one shoulder. The front of the tube was mushroom shaped. Grainger watched as a gout of yellow-white flame erupted from the back of the tube. He saw the mushroom shape detach itself as if in slow motion and then suddenly pick up speed and hurtle across the street. It slammed into the truck, only inches from the standing man's left shoulder.

The truck reared up on its side, then Grainger felt the concussion in his ears from the explosion. Maxie had slowed the Ford down to a crawl. They watched as the truck burst into a fireball and then rolled over onto its roof. The man who had been standing beside it was lying on the grass. He was not moving but then suddenly he was jerking. The Senator switched his gaze across the street. The man in the back of the jeep, which was stationary, was now holding a submachine-gun. Grainger could see the muzzle flashes as he fired a magazine into the body of the man on the grass, then he ducked out of sight and the jeep accelerated away.

Grainger slumped back into his seat and muttered, 'I need a Scotch.'

Maxie laughed and said, 'You've earned it, Jim.'

They passed the burning wreck and drove at a sedate pace to the Senator's house.

In the few minutes that it took, Miller said, 'You did damn well, Jim. Now as soon as we get to the house, you phone your friend Curtis Bennet and tell him to put normal security cover on you . . . just normal. The Moretti family is finished and after what happened, nobody else is going to take a contract on you.'

'What about the other brother in Detroit?' Grainger asked. 'He might take revenge.'

Both men in front laughed and Maxie said, 'He's the eldest . . . Gino. And right now Gino Moretti is a walking corpse and in three or four days he'll be a dead one, like his brothers.'

'You're going to get him?' Grainger asked.

'No, Creasy is.'

'Creasy!'

'Yes. He's on his way now.'

'He's in the country?'

Miller said, 'He sure is. That was him in the back of the jeep just now. He handles an RPG7 like silk on a girl's thigh. Like Maxie said, Gino Moretti is a walking corpse.'

Rene Callard was waiting at the house. He was standing inside the front gates, with three black bags lined up next to him.

As they got out of the car, he asked Miller, 'The back-up team?'

'A bonfire,' Miller answered with a grin. 'Did you pull out the bugs?'

'It's done,' the Belgian replied.

Miller turned to the Senator and said, 'We won't hang about, Jim. It's been a pleasure working for you . . . and with you.'

'It sure has been enlightening,' Grainger answered. 'Now what do I tell Curtis Bennett? He's gonna have a million questions.'

Miller shrugged. 'Tell him the truth. You sneaked away from your cover to meet a woman and got in the middle of a mob war.'

'He won't believe me.'

Maxie had loaded the three bags into the trunk of the Ford. He came over, grinned and said, 'But it is the truth, Jim. That's

199

exactly what happened. It will be in the papers in the morning. "Mob warfare in Denver City".'

'I hope my name doesn't get into it,' Grainger muttered.

The three men were standing opposite.

'It won't,' Rene said. 'The only people who know you were there are either stone dead or on their way out of the country. You have nothing to worry about, Jim.'

Abruptly Grainger realised that during the past few minutes they had all been calling him by his first name.

'So, it's all over?' he muttered.

'Yes,' Miller said. 'Now go and pour yourself a stiff whisky and phone Bennett.'

Then came the strange ritual. Grainger was to conclude later that it must have been something from their old mercenary days. One by one, they came forward and shook his hand. They laid their left hand against his right cheek, pulled his face towards them, then kissed him hard and long on the left cheek, close to his mouth. They then climbed into the Ford and drove away.

It was in the papers the next day, complete with pictures of dead bodies and burnt out and bullet-riddled vehicles. But the Senator's name was mentioned nowhere.

Four days later there was another article, concerning the Moretti family. Gino Moretti was burying his two brothers. There had been a big mob turn-out, scores of long black limousines, and mounds of expensive wreaths. At the graveside, the two coffins had just been lowered, side by side. Gino Moretti moved forward, holding a large wreath. He looked down at the coffins and was about to drop the wreath onto them when he was struck by a mercury-tipped 8mm bullet in the centre of his spine. It exploded inside him and he was dead before his body was punched into the wide grave.

The police speculated it had been fired from the roof of the nearest tall building, which was three hundred and fifty yards away. It could only have been placed by an expert sniper.

FORTY-TWO

CREASY HAD SPENT two days in Brussels, conferring with the taciturn Corkscrew Two. He had concluded that the man was going to be as good as his father. Both safe houses in Syria were set up and the machinery was in place. Creasy had told him that he would probably start to move in about three months.

Now it was midnight and the American lay in his bed in his usual room at Blondie's, watching the late news on CNN. In the morning he would fly back to Gozo.

For the first time since the 21st of December 1988, his brain was taking a rest. He felt that he had passed a major hurdle by making Grainger secure. His set-up in Syria was in place and any suspicion it might arouse would diminish over the coming weeks. Both Jibril and the Syrian Intelligence would be expecting an operation to be mounted rapidly. When it did not happen they would lose their edge of concentration.

He stretched contentedly, feeling the rare experience of drowsiness and the anticipation of a sound night's sleep. He had just reached for the remote control to turn off the television when a tap came on the door. He switched off the television, reached for the pistol on the bedside table and called, 'Come in.'

The door opened. It was Nicole, dressed in street clothes. He smiled at her and put the pistol back in its place. She closed the door, walked over, sat at the end of the bed and smiled back at him.

'When did you get back?' he asked.

'About two hours ago.'

'So, you took that little holiday I recommended?'

She nodded enthusiastically.

'Yes. Four days. I . . . well, we went to Florida.'

'We?'

'Yes, "we". Maxie drove me to the airport. On the spur of the moment, he decided to come with me. We took separate planes, of course.'

Creasy grinned at her.

'On the spur of the moment?' he asked.

She looked a little embarrassed. 'Yes . . . well, in the few days of the build-up, we'd become sort of friendly.'

Creasy grinned again. 'And where is he now?'

'He gets back here tomorrow evening.'

'And then?'

She grimaced and said, 'That's what I want to talk to you about. I phoned Blondie from the airport and she said you were leaving early in the morning . . . so I came over.' She was agitated. He saw her glance at the side table in the corner. On it were a bottle of Scotch, a bottle of vodka, a bucket of ice and two glasses.

'Go ahead,' he said abruptly. 'I'll have a small Scotch and ice.'

She moved to the table and poured the two Scotches. She brought his over and then moved back to the end of the bed and remained standing there. He could sense the tension in her.

Quietly, he said, 'Sit down, Nicole. You can talk to me about any single thing in the world.'

She sat down and said hesitantly, 'Well, it's about me and Maxie.'

'I guessed that.'

She smiled and said, 'Yes . . . You see when we were in Florida we talked a lot.'

'Just talked?'

Her smile widened. 'Most of the time,' she said. 'He's decided he wants to get out of the business and do something else. I've decided I want to do the same. He's saved quite a bit of money and so have I . . . what with the money you've given me over the past weeks.'

202

'I gave you nothing,' he said sternly. 'You earned every cent. So what are you planning?'

Her mood lightened and so did her voice. 'We thought we'd open a small bistro and bar. He would run the bar and I'd look after the bistro. Do the cooking and so on.'

His eyes widened.

'Cooking!'

She said defiantly, 'I'm a very good cook. I learned from my grandmother.'

He raised a placating hand. 'OK . . . where?'

'Here in Brussels. I know a place for sale near the market . . . it's ideal. The old couple who own it are retiring.'

'So what's the problem?'

She sighed and said, 'There are two, you and Blondie.'

'How so?'

'Well with you it's to do with Maxie. He says he's going to quit completely and he means it. But I know that if you ever call on him, he'll come.' She had been looking down at the blanket. Now, she raised her head and looked him in the eye. 'I know that. He worships you.'

Thoughtfully Creasy said, 'It's not a problem, Nicole.' He smiled at her. 'The only time you or he will ever see me again is when I eat and drink at your bistro . . . what are you going to call it?'

Her face brightened. 'Maxie's,' she answered. 'But he told me that he thinks this operation that you're on is not finished yet.'

'That's true,' Creasy conceded. 'But his involvement is. Now what's the problem with Blondie?'

Her face went sombre again. 'That's my problem,' she muttered. 'When Blondie takes on a girl, it's understood at the start that she stays for at least a year . . . I've only been here five months. Blondie is very powerful in this city and I wouldn't want to start out with her as an enemy.'

'And you want me to talk to her?' Creasy asked.

She nodded glumly.

'I'll talk to her,' he said.

'It will be all right?'

203

'That's a promise,' he answered. 'Now go away and let me sleep.'

She drained the last of her Scotch, stood up and looked down at him.

'Do you want me to get into bed with you?' she asked. 'It would be the last time.'

Equally seriously he replied, 'Nicole, I've done one or two stupid things in my life but going to bed with Maxie Mac-Donald's woman never was and never will be one of them.'

'I'll tell him you said that.'

'You don't have to.'

FORTY-THREE

THE FIRST RAIN came to Gozo in late October and within two weeks the seemingly barren island was carpeted in green.

The beauty of it was enough to break Leonie's heart. Her six months were up and she would be leaving in the morning. She was driving to the Schembris to say her farewells and not looking forward to it. She would merely tell them, and anyone else who asked, that she was going away for a few weeks and would be back. But they would know differently.

She simply did not want to leave but Creasy had been implacable. 'A deal is a deal,' he had stated flatly, and without a word he had handed her the plastic wallet containing her ticket and the letter from the Notary.

Now, as she drove down the track to the Schembri farmhouse, she just prayed that she wouldn't break down in front of them.

'You're an actress,' she told herself sternly. 'Act your role out to the last.'

The farewells, in fact, went like a scene in a choreographed play, with all the players knowing their parts, but not relishing them. Joey and Maria were also there. She was given a glass of wine and they sat out on the patio, watched the sun set and said the sort of things people say in such a mechanical situation. It was only at the end, when they walked to the car, that the emotions began to show. She held on to Laura for a long time, feeling the strength in the woman and trying to draw some of it to herself.

'I will never forget you,' she said against her cheek. 'I cannot thank you enough.'

Laura squeezed her hard and replied in a low voice:

'You certainly won't forget me. In the new year, I'm going to make Paul take me to London for a holiday. Meanwhile, I'll write. God bless you.'

In the morning, Creasy drove her down to the ferry in the jeep, with Michael and her suitcase on the back seat. They drove in silence. At Mgarr they climbed out of the jeep and Michael carried her suitcase across the ramp and gave it to a deck-hand he knew. Then he came back onto the jetty.

They stood in a silent triangle and Creasy said, 'The taxi will be waiting on the other side.' He looked at his watch. 'You have plenty of time to make your flight. Goodbye and thank you. You did better than anyone could have expected.' He gripped her by the shoulders, bent down and kissed her on both cheeks, then stepped back.

She turned and looked at Michael. He was staring down at the ground, his face a blank mask.

'Goodbye, Michael,' she said softly.

He lifted his head and she saw the pain in his eyes. Quickly she moved forward and put her arms around him.

She fought against her emotions, saying to herself, 'Play your role out to the end . . . to the very end.' She kissed him on the cheek and said, 'Take care of yourself, Michael. Make me proud

205

of you.' Then she pulled away and without looking back, walked across the ramp. She went up the steps to the top deck and stood at the stern rail, looking down at the two men standing by the jeep. She waved and they waved back. The last cars were being loaded.

Michael turned to Creasy and said, 'I'm going with her on the ferry. I'll make sure she gets her taxi all right. Don't wait for me. I'll get a lift back to the house.'

As Michael turned towards the ramp, Creasy said, 'I'll wait for you at Gleneagles.'

At Cirkewwa Michael carried her suitcase to the waiting taxi. During the crossing, he had been very taciturn, simply standing beside her at the rail and looking at the receding island. The driver put her suitcase in the trunk and opened the back door. She turned to Michael. He was about four feet away. He did not come closer. He simply stated flatly, 'I will see you again.'

Then he turned and walked back to the ferry.

FORTY-FOUR

AHMED JIBRIL LEFT his office ten minutes after receiving a phone call from Colonel Jomah. An armed convoy of jeeps was hastily arranged and instructions given to send on clothing, certain files and his Macintosh computer. The convoy consisted of two jeeps in front of his bullet-proof Mercedes and two jeeps behind.

As he left the outskirts of Damascus, Jibril considered the situation. He was one of the world's experts in dispensing terror and of course he knew the possible consequences. During his entire adult life it had been necessary to take extreme precautions. He had learned to live with the nagging physical fear that at any time, a bullet or a bomb could instantly end his life.

But this was different. He could not define how it was different but when Colonel Jomah had given him the brief details on the phone, he had felt his whole body go cold. He had felt akin to a man in a dark, locked room, knowing that there was a deadly snake somewhere close to him. So he had decided to go to the PFLP–GC training camp at Ein Tazur where security would be even tighter than at his headquarters in Damascus.

During the drive, his mind ranged over the tactics for his defence. Of course the best defence is attack, but attack where and how? This man Creasy was supposed to be dead. Very obviously, that wasn't the case. Also very obviously, he was able to call on extremely competent help and direct it brilliantly.

They arrived at the camp in the early evening. Jibril's son Jihad, who commanded it, was waiting inside the gates.

He embraced his father and asked immediately, 'What happened, father?'

Jibril shrugged nonchalantly, patted his son's cheek and said, 'I decided to spend some time with the fighters. After sitting in an office too long, I need to draw some inspiration from them.'

Jihad smiled. 'You will give them inspiration,' he answered. 'You always have . . . how long can you stay?'

'I'm not sure,' his father replied. 'At least three weeks. I'll get involved with the training . . . it will do me good.' He smiled. 'It will make me young again.'

He took his son's arm and they walked together to the large, reinforced concrete blockhouse, which was the camp's nerve centre.

Colonel Jomah arrived the next afternoon. In the privacy of Jihad's office, which Jibril had commandeered, he silently handed over a fat folder. Jibril placed it on the desk, but before opening it, poured a coffee for his guest and chatted about other subjects, which is what every well-mannered Arab should do. Then he opened the folder and pulled out the newspaper clippings and photographs. He studied them carefully. When he came to the photograph of the blackened twisted truck, lying on its back, the Colonel murmured, 'That was an RPG7.'

Jibril looked up at him and asked casually, 'Are there any leads at all on this man Creasy?'

Slowly the Colonel shook his head.

'Nothing. In the old days, we could have asked the KGB for help, but now they're virtually useless.' He stood and picked up his braided cap from the desk. 'You will stay here long, Ahmed?' he asked.

'As long as necessary.'

The Colonel smiled slightly and turned to go, saying, 'I think that's wise.'

FORTY-FIVE

'DUNGA JUSTO BASNE.'

Michael was lying spreadeagled on his stomach beside the swimming pool. He turned his head to look at the small, brown man sitting on a cane chair a few feet away. He was wearing immaculately creased grey flannel trousers, a starched white shirt and highly polished black shoes. His face was round and unlined, with small, black eyes. His short hair was neatly combed. He looked as though he might have been sitting in a leather chair in an army officers' club.

'Dunga Justo Basne,' he repeated. 'Those three words are the Gurkha sniper's bible. They mean "still as stone". Now this is how your training starts. I want you to lie there and not move more than a stone would move for the next half hour. You have to let your brain send the message to every part of your body, even to the tips of every hair on your head.'

Michael settled his cheek against the hard limestone slabs, narrowed his eyes and lay still. The small man watched him. After ten seconds, he said, 'You moved.'

'I did not.'

'You moved the little finger of your left hand and also your right foot. Even such a move could be death for a sniper. Stand up a moment.'

Michael stood up, as did the small Nepalese. He took Michael by the arm and they walked to the edge of the pool deck. They looked down over the green fields and the small man pointed up to the sky and said, 'A hawk can be as high as a thousand feet, but if a mouse moves its tail half an inch, the hawk will see it. A sniper must have in his mind that he's being watched always by a hawk. It makes the difference between living or dying. Today you will lie still as a stone for half an hour. Tomorrow, for an hour. The next day for two hours. You will lie over stones and pieces of wood, in great discomfort. I will be here for thirty days. On the day before I leave, you will lie *Dunga Justo Basne* from dawn to sunset. If you cannot, I will have failed . . . and so will you.'

'Will I get to shoot the rifle?' Michael asked with a trace of sarcasm.

'Yes. After you can lie *Dunga Justo Basne* for more than four hours.'

The small man had arrived the night before. Creasy had picked him up from the ferry. At the house, he had made the introductions.

'This is my son Michael. This is my friend Captain Rambahadur Rai. Late of the 2nd/10th Gurkhas. He will be your teacher.'

During dinner that night Michael had covertly studied the small man. He would have placed him at no more than forty-five. He sat erect in his chair and all his movements while he ate were precise and controlled. Creasy had told him that Rambahadur Rai had been decorated seven times by the British, during the Malayan Communist War in the fifties, and in North

Borneo fighting the Indonesians, in the early sixties. The decorations included the Military Cross with bar.

Now Michael lay again on the limestone paving concentrating his mind and body not to move. He was dressed only in his swimsuit. In Gozo, there is a variety of fly that bites with a sting sharper than that of a mosquito.

One such fly landed on Michael's right ankle and bit him. His leg twitched.

'You moved!'

'The flies sting,' Michael said defiantly.

'Do they sting worse than a bullet?' Rai said. Then he stood up and walked over to a clump of young trees. He tore a long, thin branch from one of them and stripped off the leaves. He pulled his chair up close to Michael, holding the willowy branch in his right hand. Then he sat down and said, *'Dunga,'* thus shortening the 'bible'.

Michael lay still for several minutes and he was bitten again by a fly on his right arm. He twitched involuntarily. A second later he yelped, as the branch thwacked across his buttocks.

'Dunga!'

Unseen, Creasy was standing on the balcony outside his study, looking down at the scene. He was smiling. Twenty years before, he thought he had been an expert sniper, trained both by the Marines and the French Foreign Legion. Then he had met Rambahadur Rai and realised that he was an amateur. He had submitted himself to the same training that Michael was now starting out on.

Over the next ten minutes, the branch thwacked down three more times, until Michael twisted, sat up and said angrily, 'It can't be done!'

Creasy went down the steps, walked past the pool to the garden and picked up three large limestone rocks. He then walked over to the two men and laid the rocks next to Michael, with a gap of about a foot between them. Then from his back pocket he took out a wad of notes, peeled off ten and put them under one of the stones. He nodded at Rambahadur.

The Gurkha stood up and took off his shirt. He folded it

carefully and put it on a wicker table nearby. Then he took off his trousers, made sure that the creases were perfectly aligned and placed them next to the shirt. Then his shoes and socks and set them neatly under the table. He was naked, except for a pair of white boxer shorts. Michael stood up looking puzzled. Rambahadur walked over to the rocks and lay down over them. One was under his chin, another under his solar plexus and a third under his crotch. It looked extremely uncomfortable.

Creasy pointed to the chair and said, 'Sit down, Michael, and watch him closely. If he moves one millimetre during the next two hours, you get the hundred pounds under that rock. You also get to hit him with the stick. If he doesn't move, he gets the money and gets to hit you with the stick. Six times. And believe me, under those circumstances, he hits damn hard.'

The young man grinned, sat down and picked up the stick. He leaned forward and gazed intensely at the prone man in front of him. Creasy went into the kitchen, got a beer from the fridge and went back up to his study. First, he wrote a long letter to Senator James Grainger, and then another one to Corkscrew Two, and finally a third one to Blondie. He addressed three envelopes and put them all together into a larger one which he addressed to a poste restante number in Brussels, from where they would be forwarded. He had just sealed the envelope when he heard a thwack and a yelp from below. He lifted his head and waited. When he heard the second thwack and the second yelp, he started to smile. By the time he heard the sixth thwack, he was grinning broadly. After the second yelp, there had been no more. He looked at his watch. It had been two hours and a few minutes. By the time he got down the steps, Rambahadur was walking to his bedroom, carrying his clothes over one arm and his shoes in the other hand. Michael was standing by the pool, rubbing his backside. Creasy walked over and kicked the middle rock aside. The money was still there.

He looked at Michael who grinned ruefully and said, 'He wouldn't take it. He said to leave it under that rock for thirty days. Then if he's satisfied, it will be mine, but I have to use some of it to take us all out for dinner to the best restaurant.'

Creasy lifted a foot and rolled the rock back over the money. Michael said, 'I wouldn't have believed it. He lay there like one of those rocks.'

'I know,' Creasy said. *'Dunga Justo Basne.'*

Michael looked up in surprise.

'You speak Gurkhali?'

Creasy shook his head. 'No, but I know those three words. They were hammered into my backside about twenty years ago.' He gestured over his shoulder to the house. 'I was trained by Rambahadur in exactly the same way.'

'Is he really sixty?' Michael asked. 'He doesn't look it.'

'Yes, he is,' Creasy answered. 'And I'll tell you a story about him that I heard from an even older British Colonel, who used to command the 2nd/10th Gurkhas during the Malayan war. The Communist insurgents used to raid local farms and villages for food. There was a large, isolated chicken farm, up near the border of Thailand. The British received intelligence that a guerilla group was going to raid it. The position was such that it was impossible to mount an ambush. The guerillas already had the farmhouse under surveillance from nearby hills. The Colonel sent Rambahadur and one other Gurkha into the farm at night. They gave instructions to the Malayan farmer and his family and then they went into the largest chicken shed and set up a machine-gun at the end farthest from the door. Then they waited. After a while the chickens settled down and ignored them, but if they had moved, the chickens would have been disturbed and the guerillas would have heard the disturbance and been warned.'

'How long did they wait?' Michael asked.

'Three days and three nights. And during that time they didn't move a millimetre. In fact, the chickens began to roost on their heads and their shoulders and on the machine-gun barrel. They were *Dunga Justo Basne.'*

'How did they shit and piss?'

'They didn't shit at all. They had fasted two days before the operation and when they pissed, they did it down their trouser legs. And that was only the first day. After that they had nothing left to piss. During the heat of the day the temperature in that chicken shed was over a hundred and ten degrees. The guerillas came on the third night. They tied up the farmer and his family, then they went into the shed to catch the chickens. There were eight of them in the shed when Rambahadur opened up with the machine-gun. He got all eight and a Military Cross.'

Michael was thoughtful for a while, looking towards the house. Then he smiled.

'He must have got a few chickens too.'

'I guess he did,' Creasy answered. 'I bet the officers' mess were eating chicken for the next two months.'

FORTY-SIX

IT SHOULD HAVE BEEN like coming home, but it wasn't. She dropped her suitcase by the door and surveyed the room. All the furniture and objects were familiar, collected over the years. She walked into the bedroom and looked at the bed and felt somehow glad that it had not been necessary to rent out the apartment while she was away. She should have felt gratitude to Creasy for that, but the only thing she felt about him was bitterness. She picked up the phone on the bedside table, called Geraldine at her office and arranged to meet her for dinner that evening. Then she soaked in the bath for half an hour and washed her hair.

Geraldine came into the restaurant fifteen minutes late and sat down apologising.

'A bloody ship sank in the South Atlantic. We're the main

insurers and the whole thing landed on my desk ten minutes before I was due to leave the office. Didn't even have time to go home and change. Sorry about the snotty business clothes.'

She was wearing a severe grey skirt and jacket and a pale green blouse.

'You look great,' Leonie said. 'Very high-powered.'

Geraldine grinned and asked, 'So, the series has finished?'

'It never got started,' Leonie answered and handed her a menu. 'Let's order first and I'll tell you all about it. My God, I need to tell someone about it and you're the only one.'

'But you got paid?' her friend asked anxiously.

'Yes, I got paid,' Leonie said with satisfaction. 'And tomorrow, I send a big and final cheque to the building society. It will be one of the great moments of my life.'

Geraldine studied the menu.

'I'm starving,' she said.

An hour later, Leonie was in tears. She had sworn her friend to secrecy. Explained that she was, in a way, breaking a contract, although that contract had technically expired. She simply had to get it out of her head. Somehow bury it forever, then try to resume a normal life. Not that her life had ever really been normal.

So she poured out the whole story and when she came to the end, to the part where Michael had stood with her next to the taxi and said, 'I will see you again,' and then turned away, she lowered her head and the tears started.

Geraldine leaned over, placed a hand over hers and muttered, 'It sounds like something out of a film. What are you going to do?'

Leonie got herself under control, blew her nose and said angrily, 'There's nothing I can do. The divorce papers were prepared a month ago as stipulated in the contract. It will go through almost automatically. I don't even have to go to court.'

'The man sounds like an animal.'

Leonie shook her head.

'No. He's just a machine created by hate. On the outside, he

214

can be pleasant and in some circumstances even fun. I danced with him once at a wedding, heard him tell jokes ... very funny jokes. But two hours later he was just a machine again.'

Geraldine was intrigued. 'Did you have any feelings for him at all?' she asked.

'No. I never really ...' Leonie started to say and then stopped, looking down for a time in silence at her empty coffee cup. She lifted her head, beckoned a waiter and ordered two more coffees and two Cognacs. She didn't say a word until they had arrived, even though she could tell that Geraldine was seething with impatience.

Finally she said, 'I slept in his bed for several months, but he never touched me.'

'So?'

Leonie shrugged. 'So I don't know. I don't know if it's possible to be in such close proximity to a man without something happening. Something more than indifference.'

'Is he good-looking?'

Leonie smiled.

'No. He's got a face that's been lived in. If anything, it reflects a battered life.'

'And his body?'

'Also battered. It's taken a lot of abuse but he's very fit. As fit as a man twenty years younger.'

Knowing her friend, Geraldine started to probe.

'So, you felt only indifference?' she asked. 'Nothing else at all? Be honest, Leonie.'

After another pause for thought, Leonie said, 'I suppose, within the last two months when he was being kinder to me, I felt something. Maybe it was only a reaction to something.'

'Something like what?'

The older woman took a sip of her Cognac and said, 'Something like affection.' She smiled without humour. 'The sort of affection you might feel for a gorilla caged up in a zoo.'

'Is he caged up?'

'Definitely. At least his emotions are. Caged up by hatred.'

'Were you attracted to him physically?'

Leonie smiled again without humour.

'Yes. I won't deny that. He has something about him. A sort of presence. An aura. Many women would be attracted to him physically. There's a mystery about him and that can bring physical attraction. Also his hardness. He's the hardest man I've ever known in my life.'

'And Michael?'

Leonie had obviously thought all that out.

'Michael is somehow different but somehow the same. He's also hard and has his emotions caged in but I've been inside the cage, been with him when he was totally vulnerable. My feelings for Michael are maternal and I know that his feelings for me are similar. He never had a mother before I came along. There was never a woman in his life. That's why I'm so bitter . . . Michael needs me.'

'But he said he would see you again.'

'Yes.'

'Do you believe it?'

'Yes.'

'How?'

Leonie took another sip of her Cognac, shrugged and said, 'I don't know exactly, but if he says he will see me again, he will. In some ways, Michael is as hard as Creasy.'

FORTY-SEVEN

MICHAEL LAY STILL as stone for four hours. It was a Saturday afternoon, two weeks after the arrival of Rambahadur Rai. For four hours he had been lying up against a mound of rocks in the garden between the palm trees. He did not know where the Gurkha was.

In fact Rambahadur Rai had been sitting cross-legged on the flat roof of the lounge, overlooking the garden. But for the last hour, he had not been watching the young man. He had been gazing out over the sea, his mind far away. Finally he looked at his watch, rose to his feet and went down. Michael did not hear him approach. He just felt a finger on his shoulder and a voice saying, 'The stone can move.'

That night Rambahadur cooked a mutton curry. He had brought some of his ingredients with him, and after the first mouthful Michael thought that his mouth had caught fire.

'Is it good?' the Gurkha asked him.

Michael drew air into his lungs, clamped his teeth together and nodded. Rambahadur smiled.

'I made it mild,' he said. 'I know that some people don't like it too hot. It takes a new British officer at least a year in a Gurkha battalion to eat curry the way we like it.' He grinned, showing yellow teeth. 'It's traditional among them. They are considered soft if they show it. Believe me they go through hell that first year.'

Michael took a gulp of cold lager and then another mouthful of curry. He glanced at Creasy. There was a sheen of sweat on his forehead, but he was munching away unconcerned.

Michael decided that Creasy was suffering. He then decided that if Creasy could suffer and not show it, he could too.

'Now do I get to fire the rifle?' he asked the Gurkha.

Rambahadur shook his head.

'Tomorrow and Monday, you learn how to hold it, how to carry it, how to look after it and maintain it. Have you ever had a lover, Michael?'

The surprise showed on Michael's face. He glanced at Creasy, who was looking at him interestedly and the sweat on his forehead was now more than a sheen. It had begun to run down the sides of his face. He wiped it away with his napkin, still watching the younger man.

217

'Well, yes,' Michael muttered.

'How many?' the Gurkha asked.

Michael squirmed on his chair. 'Well, not many,' he answered.

'How many?'

Michael looked down at the pot of curry in the middle of the table and was silent.

'Answer your teacher,' Creasy said gruffly.

Michael looked up at the Gurkha and said quietly, 'Only two.'

Rambahadur did not smile. Instead, he nodded in satisfaction. 'Good. It means you will not be spoilt for the new lover you will meet tomorrow.'

'New lover!'

'Yes,' the Gurkha answered. 'You will hold her, caress her, and treat her like a ranee . . . a queen. You will even sleep with her.'

Michael began to get the drift. He smiled and asked, 'What is her name?'

'Her name is Heckler and Koch PSG1, the best sniper rifle I ever fired. She is not the newest. They have some fantastic weapons now, specially in America. But she is sturdy and reliable and has never let me down. And I tell you, Michael, she is more beautiful than the two lovers you have had and more beautiful than any you will ever have.'

'So when will I get to fire her?' Michael asked.

'When you have seduced her,' Rambahadur answered.

He reached forward and pushed the pot of curry towards him.

'Have some more, Michael. I think you like curry.'

Michael groaned inwardly and reached for his lager.

He did not seduce her. She seduced him. In the morning Rambahadur came out of his bedroom carrying a long, hand-tooled black leather case. He laid it on the table under the trellis, worked the combination locks and lifted the lid. It was strapped down, recessed into a bed of soft chamois leather. In other recesses were a day scope, a night scope, a wind gauge and four magazines.

Rambahadur undid the leather straps, gestured to Michael and said, 'Meet your lover.'

218

FORTY-EIGHT

CREASY'S EYES ACHED from the strain of the search. He lowered the binoculars, turned to Rambahadur beside him and said, 'You're sure he's within four hundred yards, to the south-east?'

'Yes,' the Gurkha answered.

'Can you see him?'

'Yes. But I know where to look.'

It was late afternoon and the two men were sitting cross-legged on the roof of the house. Michael and Rambahadur had left an hour before dawn. Rambahadur had returned just after dawn and spent the entire day on the roof, watching. Creasy had been in Malta to see George Zammit and had only returned half an hour earlier. He lifted the binoculars again and studied the terrain in front of him. Dry stones, low rubbled walls and limestone rocks. After ten minutes he lowered the glasses.

'You have done well, my friend,' he said. 'When will he make the shot?'

'Five seconds after I show him the target,' Rambahadur answered. He tapped the empty beer bottle on his lap. Creasy looked away to his right at two farmers about five hundred yards away, who were using a small rotavator to plough their field.

'The rifle is silenced?' he said.

'Yes,' the Gurkha answered. 'And as you know, at that distance it makes the shot more difficult.'

'You think he will make it?'

Rambahadur nodded.

'I think he will.' Then he turned to look at Creasy. He said, 'He is good, my friend. Very good.' He smiled to take away any offence. 'He is better than you, Creasy ... and you are very good.'

'I'm grateful to you,' Creasy muttered, searching again with the binoculars.

'I only repay a kindness,' Rambahadur answered. 'And I only repaid a small part of that kindness. Now I'm going to repay some more.'

Noting the tone of his voice, Creasy lowered the binoculars and turned to look at him. The Gurkha lifted his head and pointed with his chin. He said, 'I'm going to tell you something about that young man out there. Something perhaps you know or do not know. It is important that you know.'

Creasy remained silent and the Gurkha continued in a low monotone.

'There is a flaw in him. You selected him well and he has been trained by the best, but there is a flaw.'

Creasy started to say something but the Gurkha held up his hand.

'Hear me, Creasy. Yes, he has lain there all day, *Dunga Justo Basne*. Yes, I believe he will make the shot. I have seen him on the range in Malta with hand-guns and SMGs. He is as good as I have ever seen. Except for you with an SMG.' He smiled slightly at a memory. 'Except for you and Guido, but I tell you honestly, my friend, I would not wish to take Michael on a mission with me, if it was just the two of us.'

Again Creasy started to speak and again the Gurkha held up a hand.

'Be silent, my friend. Listen to a man who is older than you. Listen to a man who has seen as much war as you. Listen to a man who loves you as only a man can love another. The flaw is in his mind. It was created by you, just as you created everything else in his mental and physical state.' He leaned over and touched Creasy lightly on the shoulder. 'My friend, only you can take away the flaw. If you can and if you do, he will be as near perfect a soldier as is humanly possible. He will also be a man I would trust with my life.'

Quietly, Creasy asked, 'What is the flaw?'

220

Equally quietly, Rambahadur Rai answered, 'You created him. He should worship you. But he hates you.'

'He told you this?'

Sadly the Gurkha shook his head. 'He told me nothing.' He reached for the beer bottle, leaned far over to his right and placed it on the very edge of the roof.

Five seconds later, it shattered into shards behind them.

FORTY-NINE

THAT NIGHT RAMBAHADUR got drunk. Michael took them to dinner at Ta Cenc. In the bar before dinner the Gurkha drank six gin and tonics. At the table Michael ordered a bottle of dry, Italian white wine. The day before, he had rung a friend who worked as a waiter in the restaurant. In turn the friend had gone to the kitchen and given the Italian chef a bottle of Chivas Regal whisky. The chef had produced a superb chicken curry, hotter than he had ever made it in his life. Rambahadur was both impressed and grateful. They finished the bottle of wine and Michael ordered another. The Gurkha drank most of it and happily answered Michael's questions about his days in the army. Creasy remained almost silent throughout the meal, listening only with half an ear, eating and drinking sparingly, his mind elsewhere.

Rambahadur drank two large Cognacs with his coffee. After Michael had proudly paid the hefty bill from his roll of ten-pound notes, they stood up to leave. The Gurkha had to hold onto the table. Before Creasy could move, Michael was next to the small man, supporting him with an arm. They staggered out to the car and Michael lifted him, like a baby, into the back seat of the jeep. When they were back at the house, he was fast asleep. Michael climbed out and stood looking at him. He smiled and said, *'Dunga Justo Basne.'*

Creasy stood at the other side of the jeep, unsmiling. He asked, 'What do you think of him, Michael?'

The young man's answer was immediate.

'He is a man,' he said, and reached down to pick him up.

When Michael came out of Rambahadur's bedroom, Creasy was standing by the pool, looking down at the dark water. Michael moved to the wall and flicked a switch. The water lit up, pale blue. The young man walked over and stood next to Creasy and said very quietly, 'Now is the time.'

'The time for what?'

'The time for the race.'

Creasy turned to look at him. He could feel the radiating antagonism and the challenge.

'How many lengths?'

'Fifty.'

'What is the bet? The same bottle of wine?'

Michael shook his head.

'If you win,' he said, 'I will do any single thing you ask . . . any- thing.'

'I will beat you,' Creasy said flatly. His voice was hard and as cold as an arctic wind. 'You think too much of yourself.' His voice became angry. 'You may be a marginally better sniper than me,' he gestured upwards at the roof behind him, 'but the only thing you've ever hit is a target or a beer bottle.' He stabbed a finger at the pale blue water. 'But in there, I'll beat you.'

'And if you don't?' Michael asked.

Creasy started to unbutton his shirt.

'I will return your bet,' he said. 'Any single fucking thing you want.'

For forty-nine lengths they swam shoulder to shoulder. Twice, Creasy tried to break away. Both times Michael quickened his stroke and stayed on his shoulder. At the end of the forty-ninth lap, Michael made the perfect racing turn that Creasy had taught him over the months. Creasy's turn was slower. They started the last length with the younger man three feet ahead. That's how it ended.

They stood in the shallow end with the water up to their waists, both chests heaving. Michael gasped out, 'What was your mistake?'

Creasy drew in a deep breath, exhaled and snarled, 'You tell me!'

'I have a greater motive than you,' Michael answered.

'What was it? Hatred?'

Michael pulled himself out of the pool and sat on the edge. He was still drawing in great gulps of air.

'No, the opposite,' he said. 'It was to do with the bet.'

'What do you want of me?' Creasy asked.

Michael lifted his head, drew a breath and said, 'I want you to go and fetch my mother.'

'Your mother is dead.'

Michael shook his head. 'My mother is a whore in Malta. My mother is a painting on the wall. My mother is in London.' He reached out a hand and pointed. 'For twelve hours today I lay out there like a stone, lizards crawled over me, insects bit me, twice I had cramp in my fingers. I did not move. For twelve hours, I lay there and thought about my mother. In Malta. Hanging on the wall. In London. I thought of the one question I ever asked Rambahadur Rai about you. I asked him if you were a man who kept your word. He answered, "Yes." I beat you, Creasy.'

A long silence and then Creasy muttered, 'You beat me . . . and I honour my bets.'

FIFTY

'HOW DID YOU get to be so wise?' Creasy asked.

They were bumping along the road in the jeep towards the ferry. Rambahadur's suitcase was on the back seat. The Gurkha massaged his aching forehead.

'What do you mean?'

Creasy grinned.

'About Michael and the flaw that I created. You saw something that I did not see.'

Rambahadur grimaced and said, 'The only flaws I know about this morning are in my stomach and in my head.'

Creasy laughed. 'It's traditional, my friend. You always got drunk after a successful mission.'

'What are you going to do about that flaw?' Rambahadur asked.

'I've already done it.'

'Done what?'

'Managed to marginally lose a swimming race.'

'When?'

'Around midnight, when you were snoring in a drunken stupor.'

'So?'

'So I lost a bet.'

Light dawned in the Gurkha's eyes. 'So! That's why Michael asked me that question when I left him on that outcrop of rock at dawn yesterday.'

*

At the ferry the small man and the big man embraced and the small man carried his suitcase across the ramp and started his long journey back to the village in the eastern mountains of Nepal. Creasy went to Gleneagles, drank two ice-cold lagers and phoned his travel agent.

FIFTY-ONE

THEY WERE HALF-WAY through dinner when the doorbell rang. Leonie looked at her watch and said, 'Who can that be? I hope it's not the creep from next door wanting to borrow some sugar or some other excuse to get his foot in the door.'

Geraldine pushed back her seat and stood up.

'I'll go. If it is, I'll remind him that the corner shop stays open till midnight.'

She went down the corridor, out of Leonie's sight. Leonie poured more wine into the two glasses. She heard muttered voices and then Geraldine's cheerful voice calling, 'It's not the creep from next door.'

'Who is it?'

'It's the gorilla from Gozo.'

Leonie spilled wine onto the white table cloth and looked up startled as Creasy came into the room, followed by Michael, who was followed by Geraldine, her eyes aglitter with curiosity. Leonie stood up in confusion. Michael brushed past Creasy and in a moment was holding her in a tight hug. She found herself crying.

Lightly, Geraldine said to Creasy, 'Can I get you a drink?'

It took a few minutes for the situation to settle down.

225

Geraldine poured a whisky and soda for Creasy and a lager for Michael and then deftly took her leave.

'But you haven't finished your meal,' Leonie said, once more composed.

'No matter,' Geraldine answered, putting on her coat. She gave Leonie a look that said, 'Call me later or I'll kill you,' and then she was gone.

Michael lifted the lid off the casserole dish and inhaled the aroma of *coq au vin*.

'The food on the plane was awful,' he said with a grin.

'Sit down and eat,' she said and pulled up another chair for Creasy. She ladled out the food, saying, 'Fortunately I made plenty. I always make enough to reheat a day or so later. Now tell me what you're doing here.'

'We've come to take you home,' Michael said simply.

She looked at Creasy and he nodded. He was looking uncomfortable.

'But why?' she asked.

Creasy had decided not to rehearse anything with Michael. He shrugged and said quietly, 'We miss your cooking.'

She smiled without humour.

'Then go to an agency and hire a cook. They can even send her over here and I'll teach her how to make Yorkshire pudding.'

Creasy smiled, but said nothing. Michael glanced at him and then said to Leonie, 'I beat him last night over fifty lengths of the swimming pool.'

'So?'

Creasy supplied the answer. 'The bet was that the winner could ask the other to do anything he wanted to.'

'That's why we're here,' Michael injected. 'It was close, but I won.'

She looked from one to the other then said to Creasy, 'So you lost a bet and came to fetch me like a sack of potatoes?'

Michael's face had fallen. 'It's not like that,' he said. 'We both want you to come back.'

She was still looking at Creasy. He was looking at his plate. He raised his head and said, 'Yes, we both want you back.'

226

'Why?'

Michael said, 'Because we miss you . . . it's not the same.'

She was still looking at Creasy. She said, 'I know Michael misses me. I've missed him too but there's no way you can convince me you miss me. No way I'll believe you want me to come back.'

He looked up at her again and said, 'I would not be here if I didn't want you back.'

'I believe you,' she answered. 'But the reason is for Michael, not for me.' She turned to look at Michael and said, 'When I saw you come into the room, I knew I loved you like a son, but I cannot live in Gozo like I lived before. I loved Gozo but not the way I lived.' She spoke as though Creasy was not in the room. 'It's been five weeks, now, since I returned here and I know I cannot live with this man. He makes me feel like a piece of furniture or a robot in the kitchen. Yes, he was kind to me in the last weeks, but it was an artificial kindness, perhaps knocked into him by Laura.'

A silence, then Creasy muttered, 'I have an affection for you.'

She laughed derisively.

'If you do, it's like the affection you might have for a pet dog.'

He was looking down at his plate again. His food was untouched. Almost inaudibly, he muttered, 'I have never had a pet dog . . . I never had any pets at all.'

He lifted his head and looked at her. She gazed back at him. She looked into his eyes and somehow they became a cage around him. Slowly, she put her knife and fork on the plate.

'Where are you staying?'

'At the Gore Hotel in Queensgate.'

She stood up and walked into the kitchen. They heard the tinkle of a telephone being lifted, then a few low, inaudible words. She came back, and said to Michael, 'I've called you a taxi. It will be outside the front door in about three minutes. Go to the hotel, I'll talk to you tomorrow.'

Michael looked at her and then glanced at Creasy who said nothing. Michael stood up.

'I understand. I'll see you later.'

*

After he left she cleared the table, brought Creasy a cup of coffee, sat down and asked quietly, 'Tell me. What does affection mean to you?'

He sipped his coffee. It had exactly the right amount of sugar. He said, 'I don't know. I'm not very good at . . . putting it into words.'

She smiled a genuine smile.

'That's an understatement but you're going to have to try.'

'What does it mean to you?' he asked.

She pondered and then said, 'It's something you can only truly feel if it's returned.'

He thought about that and when his reply came it devastated her.

'That means you have absolutely no affection for me.'

'That's my problem,' she answered. 'I can't think why, but I do.'

'Then, by your definition, it must be returned.'

She sighed and said, 'Perhaps, but it's brilliantly disguised.'

He said, 'I don't show much.'

'Have you known many women?' she asked.

His answer was forthright. 'I've known many physically, even lived with some for periods varying from a few days to a few weeks. But I only ever loved one. Maybe that's been the problem these past months. I never understood what love was all about until I met Nadia. I never understood what happiness was all about, it was just a word. I saw my daughter born. I was there. I see my wife and daughter every day. I see them lying on a slab in the morgue. On a cold day. They are what I see when I wake up and when I go to sleep. It's hard to talk about affection when that's all I can see. It's impossible for me to think about loving another woman again. Not like that. I don't know about other people but I know it can never happen twice to this man.'

A silence hung in the small room and then she said, 'Have you slept with any other women since your wife died?'

'Yes.'

'And do you feel anything for them? Apart from the sex?'

228

He drank more of his coffee, then fired the second barrel.

'I like you more than I liked them. I came to like you more and more during the time you spent in Gozo. But I cannot believe I'm capable of loving again. I think that emotion blew up with the bomb on that plane.'

She nodded.

'I understand. Now be honest about one more thing. You are going to kill them, aren't you?'

'Yes.'

'And use Michael?'

'If I have to.'

'So, it's just like the contract you had with me? Just an instrument of revenge?'

His smile was wry. 'That was the original idea. But the fact that I'm sitting here means that original ideas don't always work out. You know very well when I say it's not just Michael that wants you back I mean it. You will not be frozen out. You will be treated with . . . with what perhaps you call affection.'

For a long time there was silence and then she asked, 'Where would I sleep?'

'I hope you will sleep in my bed.'

'Will you touch me?'

'If you wish.'

'What do you wish?'

'To touch you.'

It was morning. She brought him coffee and woke him. She sat on the bed beside him and said, 'I just phoned Michael. I told him we'll pick him up in an hour or so and show him the sights of London.'

He pushed himself up in the bed, reached out, pulled her face to him and kissed her.

'What did he say?' he asked.

She smiled and ran her fingers through his hair.

'He said tomorrow's Saturday and he wants to go and see Tottenham Hotspur play. Apparently the hotel porter can get tickets.'

229

'Is that all?'

She shook her head. 'No, he said a few other things too. But that's between mother and son.'

FIFTY-TWO

BLONDIE APPLIED THE finishing touches to the eyes, using a very fine brush. Then she stood back and critically examined her work. Finally satisfied, she gestured towards a mirror. Leonie stood up and walked over. It was surrounded by bright lights and could have come out of a make-up room of any film or TV studio. Leonie looked at herself and audibly gasped. She was looking at the face of a beautiful woman whose age could be no more than twenty-seven or twenty-eight.

She looked at herself for a long time then turned and said, 'You must have done this professionally.'

Blondie smiled. By comparison, her own make-up was thick and obvious.

'I was in the business,' she said. 'I worked in Rome, just before the war, as a small-time actress making propaganda films for Mussolini.' She arched an eyebrow coyly. 'I once actually slept with him . . . well not really slept. It was over in five minutes. He was like that, did you know? He needed four or five women a day and it was always the same, just five minutes or less. After the war ended, we used to make a joke about it. If the war had only lasted five minutes, he might have won.'

Leonie smiled and asked, 'What happened to you then? Did you stay in the business?'

Blondie shrugged.

'It was a hard time. I left home when I was sixteen and

230

couldn't go back. I was twenty-five when the war ended and no films were being made. I managed to get a job scrubbing floors in an American army mess. Then I got pregnant by one of the officers. He refused to acknowledge it.' She shrugged again. 'Anyway it died at birth . . . it was a girl.'

'I'm sorry,' Leonie said. 'I've also lost a child. What did you do then?'

The old woman looked at her watch and went over to her drinks cabinet.

'Creasy and Michael will be back in about half an hour,' she said. 'Let's have a drink and I'll tell you. What's yours?'

'A whisky and water, please.'

As Blondie mixed the drinks, Leonie looked at herself in the mirror again and wondered if she was dreaming. They had arrived on a late flight from London the night before. At the airport, Creasy had explained about Blondie and the Pappagal.

'You mean we're staying in a brothel?' Leonie asked incredulously.

'Yes, but a very high class one,' he had answered with a smile. 'If it bothers you, I can book you into a hotel.'

'But what about you and Michael?'

'Michael and I will stay at the Pappagal,' he had replied. 'Blondie's a very old friend. She would be upset if she knew I was staying somewhere else in Brussels.'

'And Michael?' she had asked. 'You're taking him to a brothel?'

'Don't worry about Michael. I'll keep a close eye on him. Besides, it's necessary that he gets to know Blondie and a couple of other people there. Don't worry, I'll find you a good hotel close by.'

She had thought about it and then shaken her head.

'No, I'll come with you . . . as long as this Blondie woman doesn't try to put me to work.'

Creasy had said solemnly, 'She won't do that, but she will do something else to you.'

'Like what?'

'Wait and see,' he had answered. 'You'll enjoy it.'

*

231

They had taken a taxi to the Pappagal. As they drove through the streets, Michael's head had constantly swivelled to take in the sights. For him the last few days had been a total revelation. His lifetime on Gozo had not prepared him for big cities. He had been amazed at the traffic, the people and the pace of everything. It was only when they had gone to see the soccer match between Tottenham Hotspur and Chelsea that his confidence had returned. He knew a lot about soccer and, like most young men in Gozo, followed the progress of the English teams avidly. Creasy and Leonie knew very little about it and amidst the uproar of thirty thousand fans he had explained the finer points of the game. That night, Leonie had taken him to see *Starlight Express*. She knew some of the actresses, and during the interval had taken him backstage and showed him around. He had been completely tongue-tied when she had introduced him to a few of the glittering girls in their glittering costumes.

As they drove through the streets of Brussels, she had wondered what was going on in his mind. These few days must have been a kaleidoscope of impressions, ending up with a couple of nights' stay in a fully fledged brothel. In point of fact, her own mind was in similar disarray. At first, Creasy had suggested that she flew straight from London back to Malta, while he and Michael went to Brussels for a couple of days to do some business.

'I will if you insist,' she had answered. 'But I prefer to stay with you. I promise I won't get in the way. Besides, I don't want to return to Gozo on my own this time. Later on, I don't mind, but this time it's important to me that we all return together.'

He had agreed with surprising ease.

So she had found herself being ushered through the door of a plush brothel and introduced to a woman who could have stepped straight out of a macabre movie. But within minutes, she had felt relaxed. She had been introduced to Raoul, the bouncer, and a couple of the girls, who were just leaving for home. It was a bit like arriving late for a party that has just ended.

They had gone into the bar, Raoul had poured them all drinks and then left, taking their bags upstairs.

Creasy's explanation to Blondie had been brief.

'This is Leonie, my wife, and Michael, my son . . . this is Blondie, an old friend . . . she owns the place and Michael if you get out of line she'll give you a clout so hard that you won't wake up till Christmas.'

Michael had smiled but his eyes were rolling around the room, taking in the opulent furniture and fittings.

'We'd like to stay two nights,' Creasy had said to Blondie. 'Tomorrow, Michael and I have to meet Corkscrew Two in the afternoon and then go on somewhere else. We'll be back about six o'clock.' He had gestured at Leonie. 'Can you look after her? I promised that you wouldn't put her to work.'

Blondie smiled.

'Of course not.'

'But there is something I want you to do with her,' Creasy said seriously.

'What's that?'

'Tomorrow, while we're out, make her look ten years younger and if it is possible, even more beautiful.'

Leonie had glanced at him in astonishment, but before she could say anything the old woman had taken her gently by the chin and moved her face slightly in the light. She studied the face carefully and then moved it again. Then Blondie had smiled.

'I can take off the years and I can make her beauty more spectacular, if that's what you want.'

'That's what I want,' Creasy answered.

Now Blondie brought over the drinks. They settled themselves in two comfortable chairs and the old woman resumed her story.

After she had lost the child, she had drifted into prostitution.

But it had been difficult. She was no longer young and even when she was young, she had not been really beautiful. In the Italy of the time, there had been many young and beautiful women. So she had slipped slowly down the ladder. Until one day another prostitute she worked with had told her that they were recruiting girls for the famous Foreign Legion brothel at Sidi-al-Barres, in Algeria. The work would be hard but the money steady.

The work was hard. There were over two hundred girls in that brothel and it was run like a regiment. Each girl had a tiny cubicle and the Legionnaires came and went at clockwork intervals. She described the scene to Leonie, explaining how the girls worked on a shift basis, sometimes up to eight hours a day. It was mindless and sometimes painful.

'Is that where you met Creasy?' Leonie asked softly.

'Not in the brothel,' the old woman answered. 'He never went to brothels. I met him in hospital.'

'Hospital?'

'Yes, he was a sergeant then. A top sergeant. One of the men in his company, a Spaniard, had come to the brothel and was assigned to my cubicle. He was drunk and little better than an animal. We all had buttons in our cubicles, just like I have buttons in all the rooms here, in case there's trouble. There was trouble with that bastard. He pulled a knife on me and I was slow getting to the button. The Legionnaires who acted as guards to protect the girls were slow getting to my cubicle. I was badly wounded in the stomach and breasts and so I ended up in hospital. The Spaniard had been in Creasy's company. He was sentenced to two years in a penal battalion, but not before Creasy had beaten him to within a millimetre of death. But I only found out about that later.'

Meanwhile, Creasy had visited her at the hospital. He had been acutely embarrassed by what one of his men had done. He had brought her flowers and chocolates.

'And so that's how I met Creasy,' she concluded with a smile.

Leonie stood up as the door opened. She smoothed down the blue, full-length, velvet skirt and straightened the heavy, shantung silk, gold blouse. When she looked up they were in the room. Creasy smiled at her in appreciation. Michael was looking stunned.

FIFTY-THREE

THE THREE OF THEM had dinner at Maxie's Bistro. Leonie still wore the long skirt and silk blouse and appeared overdressed among the other clientele. She did not care. She enjoyed the covetous glances coming her way from the single, male customers. Creasy watched her and smiled.

'The answer is no, Leonie. We are not taking Blondie back to Gozo with us.'

She laughed and said, 'It's strange, but I actually feel ten years younger.'

She looked around the small bistro. There were only eight tables, covered with red and white checked table cloths. Seven were occupied. A bar ran the length of the room with twelve leather-topped bar stools. The music coming from the speakers was from the late fifties and early sixties. She studied Maxie behind the bar, his bald head and plump face, and she recalled how Creasy had greeted him when they entered the bistro. It had been a strange ritual. They had each put their hands behind the other's neck and kissed each other on the cheeks, close to the mouth. When Creasy had introduced Michael as his son, Maxie had kissed the young man in the same manner, but when he had introduced Leonie as his wife, she had been kissed on both cheeks in the normal manner. Nicole had come out of the kitchen and thrown her arms around Creasy's neck and hugged him long and hard. She was very beautiful and for a moment, Leonie had felt a twinge of jealousy.

When the two women were introduced, Nicole gave her a

beaming smile and a huge hug and said simply, 'You are always welcome here . . . or at our home, which is upstairs. You don't need to see the menu. When you rang this morning, I decided to make something special.'

Then she had bustled off to the kitchen.

Maxie came over with an unmarked bottle of wine and a large plate of biltong.

'I get the wine from Lamont,' he said. He grinned at Creasy. 'The biltong comes from my nephew's ranch outside Bulawayo.'

Leonie had been out to dinner with Creasy and Michael many times in Gozo and twice over the last few days in London, but tonight was the first time she felt that they were a family unit.

'I have some questions,' she said.

'So have I,' Michael said.

'Go ahead.' Creasy munched contentedly on a piece of biltong. 'By the way, this is not made from beef, it's the real thing. Probably wildebeest.'

'Who are Maxie and Nicole?' Leonie asked.

'Maxie's an old friend,' he answered. 'And a very good one. I fought with him in Rhodesia. If either of you ever has a problem and I'm not around, you call him.'

'And Nicole?' Michael asked.

'She's a newer friend. They've only been together a few weeks . . . but believe me, it's a match made in heaven.'

Michael gestured at the bottle of wine and asked, 'And Lamont?'

'Another old friend . . . an ex-Legionnaire. He has a small vineyard in the Rhône valley. One day when all this is over, we'll go and stay with him.'

'One last question,' Leonie said. 'Why am I elegantly dressed and looking ten years younger?'

Creasy poured the wine, tasted it and nodded in approval.

'It was an exercise,' he said to her. 'Do you remember what you said to me in your apartment in London, after Michael had gone back to the hotel?'

'I told you several things,' she answered.

236

'You told me that you wanted to be part of what we were doing. After you'd gone to sleep I thought about it and I decided that the only way this thing could work is if you were part of it. That's why I called the lawyer the next morning to cancel the divorce. That's why I agreed that you should come to Brussels with us. That's why I wanted you to meet my friends.'

There was a silence and then she reached out and covered his hand with hers.

'But why am I looking like this?'

'Because of a man called Khaled Jibril.' As he said the name, she saw his face harden. She glanced at Michael and from his expression, realised that he knew all about Khaled Jibril.

'Tell me.'

'He is the son of Ahmed Jibril, who is the man who arranged to have the bomb planted on Pan Am 103.'

He gave her a thumbnail sketch of Jibril's organisation and structure. When he finished she asked again, 'But, why am I looking like this?'

'Because Khaled Jibril has a fascination, even an obsession, with beautiful, blonde Scandinavian women. He spent more than two years operating a PFLP–GC cell in Sweden. That's where the fascination began. He lived with a Swedish woman, who was blonde and beautiful but she left him when she discovered that he was a terrorist. It's just possible that I may get to Ahmed Jibril through his son's obsession.'

She digested that and then remarked, 'But I am not beautiful and blonde.'

Creasy looked at Michael, who immediately said, 'You are beautiful, even without Blondie's make-up.'

She smiled at him and then touched her long, straight black hair.

'But I am certainly not blonde.'

'By tomorrow afternoon, you will be,' Creasy answered. 'As blonde as the blondest Scandinavian ever born. After lunch, Nicole will take you to the hairdresser. Incidentally, do not ask what she did before she met Maxie.'

'I won't,' she said. 'Can you tell me?'

He thought for a moment and then said, 'She did similar sort of work to what I used to do.'

'She was a mercenary?' Michael asked in surprise.

'Something like that.'

A young waitress, Nicole's sister, came out of the kitchen carrying a huge black metal pot. She placed it in the centre of their table and took off the lid.

'What is it?' Michael asked inhaling the aroma.

Proudly the girl said, '*Pot-au-feu provençal*. It's my grandmother's recipe. It's been cooking very slowly all afternoon.'

They demolished the food in almost total silence. The *pot-au-feu* was followed by salad, cheese and then *sabayon niçois*.

'Homemade,' the waitress said sternly, as she served.

Creasy smiled and said to Leonie, 'Before they opened this place, I once asked Nicole if she could really cook.'

'She's a genius,' Leonie stated. 'Do you think she'd give me the recipe for the *pot-au-feu*?'

'If she doesn't, I won't pay the bill.'

'She's also very beautiful,' Michael said. 'And so is her sister,' he muttered reverently.

Later, when all the other customers had left, Maxie and Nicole joined them at the table. The two men talked about old friends and current politics, while Nicole wrote out the recipe for *pot-au-feu* and for the *sabayon*. Michael kept silent but his eyes never left the young waitress as she cleared the tables. Finally, she joined them, poured herself a brandy and then asked her sister something in French. Nicole shook her head. The girl started to argue and then Creasy intervened. Turning to Michael he said, 'There's a disco nearby. Lucette wants to go but after midnight sometimes rough types get in there and there's trouble. I told Nicole that you would take her and keep an eye on her. Just make sure she's home before two and since you're looking after her, make sure you don't have more than a couple of drinks.'

Michael grinned and then Creasy spoke a few rapid sentences to him in Arabic. The young man nodded solemnly, took Lucette's arm and they left the restaurant.

'What did you say to him?' Nicole asked curiously.

'I told him not to show off.'

'Why would he do that?'

'Any tough kids in the disco would be no match for Michael. Not even two or three of them together. He's well aware of that. He's also with a beautiful girl. The temptation is obvious.'

FIFTY-FOUR

IT WAS SPRING when Senator James S. Grainger was summoned to the White House late one afternoon.

He was shown into the Oval Office. The President greeted him warmly and personally poured him a whisky and soda. Curtis Bennett was also there, nursing a drink and looking serious but expectant.

When they were all seated, the President said, 'Jim, we have a final conclusive report that the PFLP-GC were responsible for the Lockerbie bombing. Sure they used others: Libyans, Syrians and probably a few freelance. But they were behind it.' The President leaned forward and continued sternly, 'Now, Jim, you know the difficulties executing arrest warrants. You will also remember your promise to me some months ago, when you phoned me and asked that I instruct the Director to pull all security off you. I went along with it. You promised that when I asked you to co-operate with the FBI, then you would do so.'

'Yes, Mr President,' Grainger replied.

'I'm asking you now, Jim.'

Grainger said, 'Of course I will keep my promise.'

'Good.' The President turned to look at Bennett and said,

'Curtis, I don't want to know anything. I don't want to know that the Senator here is involved in any way whatsoever. I don't even want to know that this conversation ever took place. I don't want any Watergates, Irangates, or any fucking gates at all. Are you clear about that?'

Bennett nodded firmly. 'Yes, Mr President.'

'I don't want any internal memos circulating in the CIA which mention myself or the Senator. All I want to get one day is a report telling me that those men have either been arrested or eliminated by third parties unknown.'

'Yes, Mr President.'

The President nodded, turned to Grainger with a grim smile and said softly, 'Now tell me, Jim. How are you going to vote tomorrow on the tax bill?'

Grainger grinned.

'Naturally, in favour, Mr President.'

An hour later, Grainger and Curtis were closeted in an office in the White House basement. For half an hour Grainger studied the final CIA report on the Lockerbie bombing. He made notes on the pad beside him.

When he finished he looked up and asked, 'Are you sure that you're getting a total input from Mossad?'

Bennett shrugged and said, 'I'm sure that we're getting everything that they give to the FBI. But that's all I'm sure about.'

'What about the BND and MI6?'

'The same thing applies, but I'm more confident with MI6. Since the plane came down over Britain and killed some of their citizens, they have a stronger motive. We're working together on it. Now, Senator, tell me about Creasy and what you're up to.'

Grainger closed the report and studied his notes. He said, 'Curtis, over the past months, Creasy has been preparing his team. I don't know what that team is or who it consists of but if it's anything like the team he sent over to look after me, I'd say he has a good chance of exacting justice.'

'I go along with that,' Bennett said. 'Do you know how he's going to go about it?'

240

'I do not,' Grainger answered. 'Or when. I have two functions. One to supply half of the money and the other to pass on any information which comes my way.' He tapped his notes. 'I'm going on that Congressional junket to Europe on Thursday. I'll set up a meeting with Creasy and pass this on. When he makes his play is anyone's guess. According to the report, Ahmed Jibril has moved into his training camp outside Damascus. His son Jihad is also there. The last sighting of Khaled was three weeks ago in Tripoli, Libya. Curtis, I need constant updates as they come in. I don't want Creasy to think he's alone out there.'

'He won't be alone out there,' Curtis answered firmly, collecting up his papers.

FIFTY-FIVE

AHMED JIBRIL WAS by nature a patient man. It is a necessary trait for a terrorist. But after two months in the camp at Ein Tazur, his patience was wearing thin. He missed the cosmopolitan life of Damascus and the occasional company of his two mistresses. None of his soldiers were allowed to have women in the camp and it would have set a bad example for him to do so. He decided that he was over-reacting to the threat and drove back to his headquarters in Damascus with an armed escort. He took his son Jihad with him. His other son, Khaled, had returned from Libya a few days earlier. On arriving at his headquarters, Jibril's first action was to call a meeting. It comprised himself, his two sons and Dalkamouni, his Chief of Staff. For the first time, he outlined the full situation to them and showed them the file supplied by Colonel Jomah.

241

Khaled was dismissive.

'One man,' he said derisively. 'Mossad and half the Western intelligence agencies have been trying to kill you for years without success. What is one man going to do?'

Jihad had nodded in agreement, but Dalkamouni was more concerned. He leafed through the file and studied the photograph.

'He effectively stopped us from getting hold of Senator Grainger,' he said. 'And he was not alone. Obviously the people with him are well trained.'

But Jihad was unconvinced. He waved a hand at the file and said, 'They were up against a bunch of common criminals. You cannot compare a Mafia gang to the PFLP–GC.' He turned to his father and said, half apologetically, 'We should have mounted an operation ourselves, with our own people.'

Jibril shook his head and replied firmly, 'It would have taken too long. Besides our strength lies here in the Middle East and in Europe.' He turned to look at his Chief of Staff. 'I agree with Hafez. The threat has to be taken seriously. We all know that sometimes, one man can do what an army cannot. We have sent our fighters as individuals against the army of the Israelis. They have succeeded and usually die because they have the motive of hatred and patriotism.' He gestured at the file, now back on the desk in front of him. 'This man Creasy has a similar motive and if we are to be honest, he has more experience and training than any of our soldiers. I think that he does not care for his own life, even though he is an Infidel and has no thoughts of eternal paradise.' He looked at the three men in turn and then asked, 'Does anyone have any suggestions?'

Khaled immediately answered.

'Yes. We have to find him first and kill him.'

'And how do we do that?' Jibril asked softly. 'We do not know where his base is, not even on which continent he is. For all we know, he could be in Damascus right now.'

There was a silence then Dalkamouni said thoughtfully, 'But he has to have a base. I doubt if he will work completely alone. We have to look at his background for clues, to find out who his friends and associates were and are. We know something of his past and so we must delve into it to find clues to the present.'

'How do we do that?' Jihad asked.

'With patience and thoroughness,' Dalkamouni replied. To Jibril he said, 'Ahmed, will you leave this with me for a day or two? Let me think on it. I may wish to send someone to Europe. Probably Paris. If so I will send Dajani. He is experienced, intelligent and patient. If we send him, we would need to ask for the co-operation of Colonel Jomah.'

'We will get it,' Jibril stated. To Khaled he said, 'I'm going to do something else . . . I'm going to sacrifice those two Libyans who helped us plant the bomb.'

His son looked startled. 'But why?'

Jibril smiled thinly. 'To lay a false trail. We will leak their names and some evidence to our contacts in the French SDECE. They will pass it straight on to the British police and the FBI. Grainger, with his connections, will get it from the FBI and pass it on to that bastard Creasy, and maybe he will change direction and target Gaddafi instead of me . . . I've never liked that jumped up peacock anyway.'

'But he knew nothing about it,' Khaled protested. 'We bribed his men in Malta directly.'

Jibril shrugged. 'Tough luck.'

Khaled was about to protest but he saw something in his father's eyes that he had never seen before – fear. He stilled his protest and muttered, 'I will arrange it immediately.'

Jibril nodded firmly. To Jihad, he said, 'Return to the camp. I want to bring forward Operation Kumeer, try to launch it before the end of the month. I do not want people to think that we are inactive.' He turned to Khaled. 'I want you to remain here and take personal charge of my bodyguards.' To Dalkamouni he said, 'That will be your task, my friend. To find this man Creasy . . . and to kill him.'

FIFTY-SIX

AS AN AUTHOR OF fiction Georges Laconte was a failure, something he could never bring himself to acknowledge. He constantly waged a war with himself and concurrently with his bank manager, who happened to be an old friend.

'Forget the great novel,' the bank manager would say with stern patience. 'You are one of the best investigative journalists in France. Every serious newspaper and magazine in the country begs to give you assignments, lucrative assignments. And yet you sit out there in the wilds of Brittany for weeks on end, trying to do something which is not going to work.'

But Georges Laconte was fifty-five, and he felt a novel was to him like a cancer which had to be cut out. And so he sat in his tiny farmhouse, pounding away at a battered old Royal typewriter, which had been his constant companion for thirty years.

But writers have to eat and eating costs money, so when his agent rang from Paris summoning him to an urgent meeting, he had no choice but to climb into his battered old Citroën.

'I smell a rat,' was his first reaction. 'They are compiling a book on élite forces around the world, past and present. Why don't they simply stick with military historians and experts and why do they want me?'

'They want you because they are going to include a section on mercenaries,' his agent replied with studied patience. 'You happen to be an expert on mercenaries . . . Your book *Wolves of War* is recognised as being definitive on the subject . . . apart from that, it pays extremely well.'

He sighed and spread his hands and said, 'Fifty thousand francs plus expenses is very good money for what should be no more than a month's work.'

'True enough,' Laconte conceded. 'But it's very fishy, an obscure Jordanian company producing such a book in the first place. Secondly the section on mercenaries is confined to three men: Mad Mike Hoare, John Peters and Creasy. Why not a couple of Frenchmen like Denard or the Rhodesian, Max MacDonald? They're both still alive. It's only rumoured that Creasy is alive and yet they want me to concentrate on him. Furthermore, they want all the information sent on a weekly basis. Why?'

'Who knows?' the agent replied. 'And who cares? You get twenty-five thousand francs up front plus twenty thousand for expenses and the balance on completion. You already have all you need on Peters and Hoare so all you have to do is nail down the rumour about Creasy being alive. If he is, you try to find and interview him. If not, bury the rumour once and for all. Can you afford to turn it down?'

Ruefully, Laconte shook his head. 'You know very well I cannot. I need to make at least a dent in my overdraft.' He looked at his watch and stood up saying, 'I'll send you ten thousand words on Mad Mike Hoare and John Peters by the weekend and then I'll head for Brussels. If Creasy is alive, that's where the trail will start.' He turned towards the door, but his agent's voice stopped him.

'You don't believe the rumour?'

Laconte shrugged. 'I don't disbelieve it, for the simple reason that I never believed anyone could kill that man, outside of an act of God.'

FIFTY-SEVEN

RAMBAHADUR RAI HAD BEEN exactly right in his assessment of Michael. With the flaw removed, his mind and concentration blended into perfect harmony with his born skills and his training.

On his eighteenth birthday Creasy bought him a Suzuki jeep. Leonie bought him a steel Rolex Oyster watch. The Schembri family all came to lunch and bought him an old but very usable shotgun, to use in early summer when the turtle doves migrated across Malta from Africa back to Europe. They also brought a few litres of their homemade wine. It was a good and relaxed afternoon. Creasy barbecued great chunks of steak, lamb chops and a whole Denci fish. Michael cooked the jacket potatoes and made a huge bowl of salad. Leonie was not allowed to do anything except pour the wine. She chatted with Laura and Maria under the trellis, while the men stood around the barbecue telling each other what to do.

After lunch, Creasy set up a clay pigeon trap and the four men took turns. Paul and Joey were very good and hit about seventy per cent of the clays. Creasy and Michael hit one hundred per cent.

'That's unbelievable,' Maria commented in awe. 'My brothers shoot all year. Even out of season. But they could never shoot like that.'

With each resounding echo of the gun Leonie's mood headed downwards to depression. In bed that morning she and Creasy had made love. It had grown better every time and for her the affection had turned to a deepening love. But afterwards Creasy had told her that in a few days he and Michael would be leaving Gozo.

Michael would be going to Tunisia with his Arab teacher for two or three weeks to learn how to live like an Arab. To eat Arabic food, learn how to pray like an Arab and to absorb their customs. Creasy would be going to Europe to have a meeting with Senator Grainger, and then to start the operation rolling. As they lay on the vast bed entwined in each other's limbs she had asked, 'When will you be back?'

He had stroked her shoulder.

'When it's over. It could be many weeks.'

'What can I do?' she had asked.

'You have the hardest part. You have to wait here in case there's any messages. If so, they will always come via Blondie. Later, I may need you.' He had stroked her long newly blonde hair.

'I will be trying to find a way to aim you at Khaled Jibril. It may be very dangerous and physically unpleasant.'

'You mean I may have to go to bed with him?' she asked.

He had looked into her eyes and said softly, 'I hope not, but it may be necessary.'

She had kissed him and answered, 'I will do what is necessary.'

FIFTY-EIGHT

'THE SOLE IS overcooked,' Creasy remarked, 'which is a pity because the Montrachet is perfect.' He picked up his glass and drank half of the amber liquid.

'Send it back,' Senator Grainger suggested.

They were sitting at a window table in the Riverside Restaurant of the Savoy Hotel.

Creasy shook his head and grinned. 'I'll save my appetite for the cheese tray and a couple of glasses of their own port. It's been ten years since I drank it here and by now it should be even better.'

Over the months the two men had drawn close.

The Senator had given Creasy the latest update from the FBI. He told him that a few hours before, he had received a phone call from Curtis Bennett. Apparently the French SDECE was getting information from a Middle East source that two Libyans were involved in the actual planting of the bomb, both Intelligence agents. One, named Fhimah, had been the Libyan Airways station manager in Malta at the time of Lockerbie. He had since returned to Libya. A strong theory was that the bomb had started its journey from Malta.

'It's possible,' Creasy conceded. 'Those bastards will co-operate, but Jibril is the mastermind. He would never have paid Rawlings all that money if Gaddafi or anyone else was behind it. No, Jibril remains my target.'

'I agree,' Grainger said. 'So what are your plans?'

Creasy told him that the operation was now active and that he would make the 'kill' within four to six weeks.

Over the cheese and port the Senator had asked how he was going to do it.

Creasy answered, 'He will die by a bullet. That's all I can tell you, Jim, except that it will be in Damascus.'

'How big is your team?'

'We are three. Myself, an actress and a young man. She is my wife and he is my son.'

The Senator's head jerked up in surprise. Creasy nodded.

'Yes, my wife. I married her to get the son . . . he is adopted.'

Grainger was puzzled.

'But why use them?' he asked. 'Why not Frank and Maxie or Rene? Christ, those men are the best, even the FBI admit that.'

'There are two reasons,' Creasy answered. 'First because this is a very personal matter and my wife and son are very personal to me now. I did not expect that to happen but it did. Secondly this matter is not going to end in a shoot-out. It's going to be a single bullet and it only takes one finger to pull the trigger.' He reached out and tapped the red folder on the table between them. 'According to this Jibril left the camp at Ein Tazur four days ago with an armed convoy and returned to Damascus. He probably got bored out there in the desert. His son Khaled also returned to Damascus from Libya. Over the next three or four weeks, I will be travelling in and out of Syria, confirming my cover. You know the phone number to call as each update comes in to your intelligence services.'

Grainger said, 'You will be kept fully informed. The President has made sure of that. He wants Jibril dead and he doesn't care how. He's been told on good authority that you're the most likely man to succeed. He doesn't want to know any more than that.'

Creasy took a sip of his port and said, 'I can only tell you one more thing, Jim. Ahmed Jibril will die from a single bullet. Harriot, Nadia and Julia died almost instantly when that bomb went off. Some might say a quick death is an easy death. A death without time to dwell on it.' He drained his glass and looked at the Senator and his voice went very cold. 'Ahmed Jibril will not die an easy death. He will die knowing why. His journey to hell will be lit by arc lamps. He will see the flames from far away.'

FIFTY-NINE

THE *MOULES MARINIÈRES* were delicious and so was the *coq au vin* that followed. Later, at the bar, Georges Laconte complimented Maxie MacDonald warmly. In return he got a complimentary Cognac.

'Are you really out of the business, Maxie?' the Frenchman asked.

Maxie nodded firmly.

'Damn right. And glad to be out.'

Laconte glanced around the small, busy bistro, then leaned forward and lowered his voice.

'I've been in town a few days and dropped in on a few of the old places. It's a bit sad to see all those ageing mercs hanging about, waiting for a job that's never going to come. It's the end of an era, Maxie . . . you did well to get out when you did.' He gestured at the room behind him. 'You have a nice place here. The food is good . . . very good, and you have a good woman. Do you ever get any of your old comrades in here?'

Maxie was polishing a glass. He turned and put it on a shelf behind him, shook his head and said, 'No. I discourage them. I leave all that behind me.'

'So, you're completely out of touch?'

'Yes, completely, and as a favour I'd like you not to broadcast it around, where I am and what I'm doing.' He poured more Cognac into the Frenchman's glass.

Laconte nodded in appreciation, took a sip and said, 'It's a promise, Maxie, and perhaps you can do me a favour in return?'

'What's that?'

The Frenchman leaned forward again.

'While I've been in Brussels I've heard a rumour, repeated several times.'

Maxie was polishing another glass. 'What rumour?' he asked.

'That Creasy is alive.'

Maxie stopped polishing. He lifted his head and looked the Frenchman in the eye, then shrugged and said, off-handedly, 'You know how rumours get around. Creasy died five years ago in Italy. You should know that, you're the expert.' He started polishing again.

Laconte smiled.

'I was the expert, but I've been out of touch for a few years.' He drained his glass, slid off his stool and said, 'Well, if anyone would know, it would be you, Maxie. I guess it is just rumours.' He reached for his wallet to pay the bill but Maxie affably waved it away.

'It's on the house, Georges. It's been good to see you again.'

250

Outside in the street Georges Laconte walked slowly back to the hotel, deep in thought. He had noticed that at the mention of Creasy's name, Maxie MacDonald had briefly stopped polishing the glass. It was a sort of confirmation. During the previous two nights he had hung around three bars frequented by mercenaries and ex-mercenaries. The rumour of Creasy being alive had been a talking point. There was a further rumour that Maxie MacDonald had just completed a job with Callard and Miller, the Australian. A very lucrative job. Was it a coincidence that all three men had worked closely with Creasy in the past?

Consequently, the Frenchman had offered a substantial reward to various people in the three bars he had visited, to anyone who could substantiate the rumour. In particular, he had offered it to a South African and an Italian who, if Creasy were alive, would dearly like to see him dead.

Back in the kitchen of the bistro, Maxie was on the telephone to Blondie. He gave her the gist of his conversation with Laconte, listened to her reply and then said, 'No, just pass it on when he comes in. I doubt there's much to it but Laconte could be fronting for somebody.'

He hung up, gave Nicole a kiss and went back to the bar.

SIXTY

OVER A TEN DAY period, Creasy and Corkscrew Two were in and out of Damascus twice. They had checked the holes and the machinery in both Damascus and Lattakia. Creasy had been well satisfied. They also had several meetings with small Syrian import-export companies and instigated some business. Heavily disguised, Creasy had made two recces of Ahmed Jibril's head-quarters and several buildings in the city.

During this period he had made Blondie's his European base but on returning from Syria the second time and getting Maxie's message, he decided to relocate to London. He would use Leonie's flat. Being the kind of man he was, he first called Gozo to ask her permission. She laughingly agreed and suggested he also use her battered Ford Fiesta and save money on taxis. They chatted on easily for ten minutes and after he had cradled the phone, he stood looking down at it for a long time, picturing her in the house on the hill. Then he did something on impulse. He picked up the phone and called her again.

'Why don't you come to London for a few days?' he asked. 'We could take in a couple of shows and sort of have a relaxed time before this thing happens.'

Her answer was immediate.

'When?'

He chuckled and answered, 'Give me four or five days to sort out some business. Try and book a flight for the weekend. I'll be in London tomorrow afternoon. Phone me at the flat in the evening to let me know when you're coming.'

He hung up again and then called the airport to book his own flight.

SIXTY-ONE

MICHAEL WASHED HIS hands and feet, then followed his teacher through the entrance into the crowded mosque. Side by side they laid their prayer mats on the dusty floor and knelt facing Mecca. The teacher listened carefully as Michael intoned his prayers.

An hour later, they sat at a food stall and the teacher watched closely as Michael ate from a dozen dishes.

The teacher was pleased. Within a few more days, Michael would be able to go into any Arab mosque or souk and be taken for nothing less than a full-blooded Arab, albeit one who had spent much of his life within a European culture. The teacher knew the age of his pupil and marvelled at his confidence. He had the bearing and stature of a well-travelled man of thirty.

After they left Tunis, the teacher would not see his pupil again. That was the agreement. The teacher had not grown fond of his pupil but he had built an immense respect for him. Creasy would be pleased.

SIXTY-TWO

FOR TEN YEARS during the sixties and early seventies, Piet de Witt had been an agent of BOSS, the notorious South African Security Service. He had been a field agent operating mainly in Angola and Mozambique and occasionally carrying out assassinations in South Africa itself against ultra-liberals, communists or anybody else his superiors took a dislike to. All that had ended when he was caught running an extortion racket on the side. He had been kicked out of the service and in a natural progression, had become a mercenary, first in West Africa and then South East Asia.

He was ruthless and merciless and liked to hurt people. He also liked money and of late, money was very scarce. Work was scarce. The only offer he had had in the last three months was to join a dubious gang to rob a small bank in Luxembourg. He had not liked the plan or the people and had declined.

He had heard a rumour of a job being set up by Denard in Paris. Something to do with taking over an island in the Indian Ocean. He decided to go to Paris to check it out.

But at Brussels Airport he had diverted. He was about to get out of his taxi at the departure terminal, when the man crossed in front of him. He recognised the figure immediately. Tall and bulky. He also recognised the walk. A curious walk with the outsides of the feet coming onto the ground first. He watched the man walk into the terminal building carrying a canvas bag. He thought about the French journalist, Georges Laconte, and the offer that he had made three nights ago in Blum's Bar.

He entered the terminal building cautiously, his eyes sweeping the hall. He saw the man at the Sabena ticket counter and moved behind a column, dropping his battered leather suitcase at his feet.

As he watched, Piet de Witt's emotions were a mixture. Part indelible hatred. Part fear. Part consuming curiosity. The hatred stemmed from an incident many years before in Vietnam. The man at the ticket counter had physically humiliated him. The fear stemmed from the terrible beating he had received at his hands. The broken bones and the weeks in hospital. The curiosity stemmed from the fact that the rumours were true; Creasy was alive. Where was he going? What was he doing? There was money in the answers.

He waited until Creasy had moved away from the counter towards Immigration. Then he walked up to the same ticket clerk, who was a middle-aged woman. He smiled at her. He was a tall man, sandy-haired and with a bushy, sandy beard. His smile was very charming.

'I think I just saw a friend of mine going through Immigration. Haven't seen him for years. Maybe you can help me. He was coming from this direction. Did he buy a ticket here?' He described Creasy. She nodded and answered, 'Yes, to London on the two forty-five.'

'Economy or Club?'

'Club.'

De Witt looked up at the departure screen. Apart from the

two- forty-five there was another flight to London at four-thirty.

To the woman he said, 'I'm going to London myself but on the four-thirty. Any chance of switching me to the two-forty-five?'

She punched some buttons on her console, studied the screen, then nodded.

'There are a few seats left but only in Economy.'

'That's fine,' he said, reaching for his wallet.

SIXTY-THREE

THE FERRY WAS warped alongside the dock. The ramp clanged down and Michael raced over and into Leonie's arms.

As they drove back to the house, he said with a grin, 'It's good to be home. What's for dinner? I'm fed up with Arab food.'

She laughed.

'I'm taking you out to dinner. To Sammy's. It's a special treat. He's got a fresh lobster and he's keeping it for us.'

'Why a special treat?'

She glanced at him, marvelling at how rapidly he had grown up. 'Because tomorrow afternoon I'm leaving for London,' she said. 'Creasy phoned a few days ago.'

In mock disappointment, he asked, 'And you're not taking me with you?'

She slowed the jeep to let a flock of sheep cross the road. 'Very definitely not,' she answered with a smile. 'I'm only going for three days. It will be a sort of delayed honeymoon.'

'Good,' he said firmly. 'Any other news?'

'Nothing. Creasy will brief me in London and I'll brief you when I get back. He said you should be ready to move in about a week. He wants you to go to Malta for a couple of days and get

255

some time in with the Heckler and Koch on the range. He's fixed it with George.'

Later that night, they sat in the harbour, hardly talking as they enjoyed the lobster. Over coffee, he glanced at his watch. She noticed and said, 'Yes, I know, Michael. It's Friday night and La Grotta will be swinging. But tonight you have to spend another half hour with your mother.'

He grinned, reached forward, covered her hand with his and said with total conviction, 'I'd rather be here with you than anywhere else.' He gestured at the crowded restaurant. 'The people here who don't know us think you're my girlfriend and they're all mad with jealousy . . . I like that.'

She laughed and answered, 'And the women are jealous of me for having such a lovely toy boy.' Her face turned serious and she looked at the young man's face for a long time before shaking her head and saying, 'No, Michael, you are not a toy boy. You are a man. I'm proud of you . . . and frightened for you.'

'Don't be frightened,' he said softly.

'But I am. As I waited for the ferry this afternoon, I realised that for the first time in my life I'm truly happy. Sometimes in the past I thought I was happy, but I didn't understand the word. It has to be matched to contentment.'

Suddenly she looked up again into his face and said, 'I believe that Creasy loves me. I don't know why . . . but I believe it . . . I know he'll never say it because he's not like that . . . but inside I believe it.'

Equally serious, Michael said, 'I believe it too.'

SIXTY-FOUR

HE PICKED HER UP at Heathrow in her battered Ford Fiesta.

As they drove through the heavy evening traffic into London he said, 'I've booked a table at Lou Pescadou. They have excellent seafood. Especially shellfish.'

She laughed and said, 'I had lobster last night with Michael. At Sammy's.'

'You're spoiling him,' he said sternly but with a smile. 'So where would you like to go?'

'How about that Indian place, off the Gloucester Road? I really like a good curry.'

'No problem.' He glanced at his watch. 'Let's go straight there and on to the flat afterwards. I've got a little surprise for you.'

'Like what?'

'Like a surprise.'

She watched his big hands move on the small steering-wheel. She noticed again the mottled scars on the backs of both of them. She reached out and touched his left hand and asked, 'How did you get those, Creasy?'

His reaction was instantaneous. He jerked his hand away. The car swung to its right almost hitting a truck in the next lane.

She pulled herself up in shock, while he corrected.

She looked at his face. At the ice-cold expression. Apprehensively, she asked, 'What did I say? Do?'

'Nothing,' he muttered. 'It's just that . . .'

She glanced again at his face and saw the trouble in it. Saw him struggling to find the right words.

Gently, she said, 'If you don't want to talk about it, I understand.'

He shook his head.

'It's not that. It's just that a few years ago, someone sitting next to me in a car, like you are, touched my hand and asked the same question.'

'A woman?'

'No. A young girl.'

They threaded through the traffic in silence, then she murmured:

'The girl in Italy . . . the one who was killed?'

'Yes.'

She touched his hand again and said, 'I'm so sorry, Creasy.'

He shook his head, lifted his hand from the wheel and looked at the scars. Quietly he told her, 'It was while I was with the Legion, in Vietnam. We had just lost the battle of Dien Bien Phu. With many others in the Legion I was captured. We were marched many miles through the jungle to a prisoner of war camp. Many died on the way. I survived. At the camp, I was questioned by a young, French-educated Viet Minh captain. There were many questions. My hands were strapped down to a table. I refused to answer. The captain smoked a lot. There was no ashtray.'

They drove in silence, then he glanced at her. He felt the same sense of *déjà vu* and heard himself speak the words he had spoken to the girl those years ago.

'Sometimes bad things happen in the world.'

The sense of *déjà vu* increased dramatically as he heard her reply. She smiled warmly, touched his hand again and said, 'Good things happen too.'

At the restaurant their mood lightened. It was small, dark and intimate. They sat at a corner table and held hands between four different curry dishes. They did not talk very much. Somehow it was not necessary. The impending operation was never mentioned. What little conversation took place concerned Gozo.

She wanted to make some changes to the garden and to redecorate the sitting room. She raised the matter tentatively, knowing that the whole house and garden had been planned by Nadia. He was not at all concerned.

'It's your house now,' he said. 'You must put your own character in it. Nadia would have understood.' He paused and smiled slightly. 'Nadia would have liked you.'

Sensing the ease with which he was able to talk about it, she asked, 'Was she like Laura?'

'Yes, in many ways. Also in many ways she was like you.' Abruptly, he changed the subject. 'But the past is the past. What do you want to do tomorrow?'

She thought about that and then answered, 'In the morning, I want a long lie-in. Then I want to go shopping. I want to buy some new furnishing fabrics and curtains, and some things for the kitchen.'

'I'll make a deal with you,' he said. 'You do that on your own because I hate shopping, then in the evening we'll go and see a movie, have a good meal somewhere, go on to a club and do a little dancing.'

She smiled.

'It's a deal.'

He was lucky and found a parking place across the road from the flat.

The surprise in the flat was a bottle of chilled pink champagne.

'Let's drink it in bed,' she said in delight.

So they undressed and kissed and felt each other and climbed into the bed with the two glasses and the champagne in an ice-bucket on the floor.

Between sips of champagne, they made love and it was near perfect. When they fell asleep, the bottle of champagne was half full. Three hours later, she woke him up and the love-making was totally perfect. She spoke some words. When they fell asleep again, the champagne bottle was empty.

259

SIXTY-FIVE

HE WOKE AT DAWN, slipped out of bed and went into the bathroom. He came out fifteen minutes later, freshly showered and changed and wearing a white towelling robe.

He stood at the foot of the bed watching her sleeping face, then he went to the kitchen and made himself a cup of coffee. For the next two hours he sat at the table studying his notes and maps and diagrams; and making more notes in a small, compact notebook.

Once or twice, she murmured in her sleep. Each time he stood up, went over to the bed and looked down at her.

At nine o'clock he went into the kitchen and made her scrambled eggs and a mug of tea. He carried the tray into the bedroom and put it next to her on the side table. Then he bent over and kissed her awake.

She reached an arm around his neck and pulled him close in a tight hug.

'You're sweet,' she said and heard his grunt of amusement.

'No one has ever called me that before.' He pulled himself up and looked down at her. She smiled tentatively and suddenly there were tears in her eyes.

'What's the matter?'

She shook her head and with the back of her hand wiped the tears away.

'It's just that I'm so happy . . . I never believed I could be so happy.'

'Eat your breakfast,' he said gruffly.

She pulled herself up in the bed and the sheet fell to her waist. He surveyed her body and then murmured, 'You are beautiful.'

She reached for the plate, 'You told me that last night . . . you told me other things last night. Did you mean them?'

'I meant everything I said.'

She ate the scrambled eggs in silence, put the plate back on the side table and said, 'Do you know why you love me?'

He shrugged, looking puzzled, and she knew he would never find the words.

'I'll tell you,' she said. 'It is not because you find me beautiful. It is because of Nadia.'

His head jerked up in surprise.

'Nadia!'

'Yes,' she answered firmly. 'You met Nadia when you were in your forties. Did you ever love any woman before that?'

'No.'

'Do you know why you loved her?'

'No.'

She spread her hands and said simply, 'It was Nadia who awakened and nourished in you instincts you never knew you had . . . never expected to have. Once they were awakened, they remained. Those instincts remained even after Nadia and your daughter died. Without those instincts you could never have fallen in love with me. Nadia made it possible.'

He sat looking at her for a long time, then cupped her face with his hands and kissed her.

'Thank you,' he said.

The corners of her mouth turned up in a very small smile.

SIXTY-SIX

SHE RANG HER FRIEND Geraldine and arranged to meet her for lunch and a shopping spree.

Creasy dressed, made several terse overseas telephone calls, then sat back at the table studying his notes and maps.

She came out of the bedroom wearing a silk blouse and navy trousers, and putting her arms into the sleeves of a cream cashmere blazer, looking radiantly lovely. She leaned over and kissed him on the ear and said, 'I'll be back at four and I promise not to spend a fortune.'

He smiled and asked, 'What's that perfume you're wearing?'

'Oscar de la Renta,' she answered. 'Michael bought it for me, duty free, on his trip to Tunisia. Do you like it?'

'If you don't get out of here, I'm going to rip those clothes off you and drag you back to bed.'

She laughed, kissed him on the cheek and walked to the front door. He stood up.

'I deserve a better goodbye kiss than that.'

She turned and smiled and walked back, put her arms around him and kissed him deep and fiercely.

'I'll cancel Geraldine if you like,' she said. 'I'll cancel shopping if you like. Nothing's important any more except being with you.'

He gave her another kiss and then gestured at the papers on the table. His voice was gruff.

'You go ahead. Have a good lunch. And buy a new dress for yourself. Something slinky for tonight.'

She kissed him again. He watched the door close behind her and then moved to the window and pulled aside the white lace curtains. He watched her cross the road, watched her climb into the battered blue Fiesta. It was a clear, bright day. The Fiesta pulled out of its parking space and began to accelerate down the road. He was turning away when he saw the yellow-white flame erupt beneath the car, saw it bulge and lift onto its front end. Instinctively, he ducked below the window, heard the glass shatter above him, felt the pressure in his ears and heard the dull, rolling roar of the explosion.

It took him less than two minutes to pack his canvas bag and leave the apartment. He pushed his way through the crowd, past people, some dazed, some crying, some screaming. He walked

quickly for ten minutes hearing the sirens behind him, then he
went into an underground station and caught the tube train to
Heathrow.

SIXTY-SEVEN

AHMED JIBRIL READ the report and studied the newspaper critically. Yet again he felt a twist of fear deep inside him.

'He was lucky,' he muttered.

'No,' Dalkamouni answered. 'The IRA were at fault. They
should have risked using a line-of-sight radio controlled bomb.
Sooner or later, they would have got him.'

'Who was the woman?' Jibril asked.

'As yet, we don't know,' Dalkamouni answered. 'British security have clamped a silence on the whole matter.'

'British security? You think they are involved?'

Dalkamouni shrugged.

'Who knows. We know that this man is coming at you. It's
likely that the Americans know, and the British. I guess that
they're sitting back and waiting for it to happen. I guess that
they'll give him any passive help they can. After all, why not? The
woman might well be a lead to him but they'll keep a lid on it for
as long as possible.'

Jibril was looking down at the press photographs of the
wrecked car.

'A pity,' he muttered. 'A great pity.'

'There's more,' his aide said. 'The Frenchman Laconte has
cancelled his contract. Wants nothing more to do with it. You
can be sure he's informed the French SDECE, who'll inform the
British.'

'What else can we be sure of?' Jibril asked sarcastically.
Dalkamouni grimaced.

'We can be sure the man Creasy is on his way here.'

'Then he will die here,' Jibril answered harshly.

SIXTY-EIGHT

THE FOLDED WHITE HANDKERCHIEF landed on Michael's lap. The harsh voice said, 'That's enough. Dry your tears.'

The young man looked up. His wet face was a picture of pain.

They were sitting in a room in the Pensione Splendide on the hills above Naples. Michael had followed the brief instructions contained in a phone call from Blondie forty-eight hours earlier. He had packed his bag, locked up the house, taken the overnight ferry to Naples and then a taxi to the Pensione Splendide. He had enjoyed the ferry trip, having met a young female American back-packer, who was going to sleep on deck. Instead she had slept in his cabin. At the pensione he had been met by a taciturn, middle-aged man called Guido who had shown him his room and said, 'Creasy will arrive soon. He said to wait in here until then.'

In fact it had been three hours before Creasy turned up. He had walked stone-faced into the room, tossed his bag onto the bed and said tersely, 'Your mother's dead. Car bomb in London meant for me. Probably the IRA fronting for Jibril.'

He had briefly sketched in the details and then Michael's tears had started.

Now Michael wiped his face with the handkerchief and asked, 'You didn't go back to check? . . . to make sure she was dead?'

'I did not. I saw the explosion. There was no chance.' His voice softened slightly. 'Michael, it was instantaneous. She would have known nothing.'

Michael stared down at the floor, then drew a deep breath, looked up and said, 'The night before she left, we had dinner together at Sammy's. We had lobster.'

'I know.'

'She talked about you. Did you know how much she loved you?'

'I think so.'

'Did you love her?'

'Yes . . . and she knew it before she died.'

Creasy stood up.

'Dry your tears, Michael. Think of who did it . . . think of Jibril.'

They had dinner on the open terrace of the pensione together with Guido at a table set apart from the others.

The lights of Naples dropped away beneath them, the bay beyond. An old waiter served them. Obviously he knew Creasy long and well.

As they sat down Creasy gestured at Guido and said to Michael, 'This man is your friend and the friend of your friends. You can tell him anything you wish. You can talk to him as you talk to me. If you need anything . . . and I mean anything . . . come to Guido.'

The young man was composed now with his confidence fully restored. He glanced at the Italian and then asked Creasy, 'What makes him so special?'

Creasy smiled, as did Guido.

'He's my closest friend,' Creasy answered. 'He was married to Nadia's sister which also makes him my brother-in-law . . . Over the years he has saved my life more times than I can remember.'

Michael glanced at the Italian. He was short and square, the black hair greying at the temples. He had a Roman nose above a wide mouth and eyes that saw everything.

'You were also a mercenary?' Michael asked.

Guido nodded soberly.

'Yes, for most of my life, but after I married I gave it up. Before Julia died I promised her I would never kill or fight again. I've kept that promise.' He smiled and waved a hand at the other tables and guests. 'So now I run a pensione and watch football on television.'

Michael studied the Italian, then turned to Creasy and asked, 'Was he as good as you?'

Creasy nodded. 'Yes. And with a machine-gun he was the best ever.'

'And as a sniper?' Michael asked with a smile.

Creasy shrugged and answered, 'First class.'

'As good as me?'

Slowly Creasy shook his head. 'No, but then he was not trained by Rambahadur Rai.'

Guido's face showed surprise.

'You had this kid trained by Rambahadur Rai?'

The American nodded. 'He was with him for a month and at the end pronounced himself very satisfied.'

Guido looked at the young man with more respect. Michael said tetchily, 'And I'm not a kid.'

Guido smiled and nodded in acceptance of the rebuke.

The old waiter brought three huge plates of baby calamari with rice, salad and red wine in an unlabelled bottle.

'Eat everything,' he said to Creasy, 'or the cook will kill you. She knows it's your favourite and sent out especially for the calamari.'

For the next ten minutes there was silence as the three men ate.

Michael finally broke the silence. He wiped his mouth with a napkin, glanced at Guido and then asked Creasy, 'So what's the next step?'

'On a certain day next week there's a ninety-five per cent chance that Ahmed Jibril will attend a ceremony in Damascus on the anniversary of the establishment of the State of Palestine. It's an open-air ceremony. He'll be heavily guarded but from a distance it will be possible to get a single shot at him.'

'What is the distance?'

266

Creasy sighed. 'About five hundred metres.'

'What time of day?' Michael asked urgently.

'Evening, just before sunset.'

Michael said simply, 'Rambahadur Rai.'

Creasy looked up sharply. 'I would never use him.'

Michael shook his head and said tersely, 'I don't expect you to use him. It is personal. And don't forget it's personal for me too. You don't have a monopoly of vengeance. I mentioned Rambahadur because of his opinion. He said I'm a better sniper than you are.'

Defensively Creasy answered, 'That's debatable. On a firing range maybe. But you have no experience in the field. I've had plenty, as Guido will tell you.'

The Italian nodded and said, 'It makes a difference. A human being is not like a cardboard target. Shooting at flesh and blood can affect the mind and the eye.'

'Jibril is not flesh and blood,' Michael retorted. 'My mind and my eye will be cold and sharp. I will not miss.' He asked Creasy, 'How many rifles do you have in Damascus?'

'Two.'

'Heckler and Kochs?'

'Yes.'

Michael leaned forward and said with great intensity, 'Then I make the hit. You act as backup. Have you got that, Creasy?'

Michael stood up, dropping his napkin on the table. 'I'm going to bed,' he said. 'Creasy, she was my mother.' He turned to Guido and said, 'Thank you for a fine meal. It was a pleasure meeting you. I will obey Creasy. I will look on you as a friend. I hope it will be a two-way street.'

He turned and walked through the tables to the door.

'Where did you find him?' Guido asked with a wry look.

'In an orphanage,' Creasy answered gruffly.

'Is he as good as he thinks he is? Is he really a better sniper than you . . . ? I've seen you take a man between the eyes at six hundred metres.'

Creasy shrugged and said, 'Rambahadur Rai is the greatest sniper I've ever known. He rates Michael his equal. He's got an affinity for it. It's something that you're born with and then trained for. He was born with it and he had the best trainer on earth.'

'What about other weapons?' Guido asked curiously.

'Very, very good,' Creasy answered. 'I turned that kid into a killing machine. And in a way he's right. I don't have a monopoly of vengeance. He loved Leonie and in a way he loved Nadia and Julia. And maybe I'm taking him to his death,' he said. His voice turned very sombre. 'I seem to have the curse of death on me.'

Quietly Guido answered, 'We always had that on us. We were born with it.'

SIXTY-NINE

THE TWO DINNERS took place about a thousand miles apart, but the conversations covered the same topic.

In Damascus, Ahmed Jibril dined at his headquarters with his two sons, Dalkamouni and Colonel Jomah.

On the overnight Rome to Paris train, Creasy dined in the restaurant car with his son, Michael.

'I will not change my routine,' Jibril insisted. 'Tomorrow I will go to the camp and bid farewell to our fighters who go on Operation Kumeer. They go to almost certain death. I will not send men to their deaths and hide away myself.'

'His headquarters are impregnable,' Creasy observed as the train slowed to greet the foothills of the Alps. 'He's only vulnerable when he leaves them.'

'You're sure he will leave?' Michael asked.

The dining car was only half full and the tables behind and in front of them were empty. They had both ordered *steak au poivre* as a main course and after the steward had served it, Creasy answered, 'I'm ninety-five per cent sure he'll attend the ceremony marking the anniversary of the establishment of the State of Palestine at the end of next week.' He looked at the young man and asked, 'What does *Saahat el Chouhaada* mean?'

Michael swallowed a piece of steak and took a gulp of wine.

'It means Martyrs' Square. Is that where the ceremony will take place?'

'Yes.'

'And you have a nest about five hundred metres away?'

'Yes. And it has line-of-sight on the square. Michael, drink the wine slowly. It's a good wine, savour it, don't just glug it down.'

Khaled Jibril remained totally sceptical. He reached forward to the steaming bowl, picked up a piece of mutton and put it in his mouth.

'There is nothing to fear,' he mumbled. 'We are on our own territory. Not even Mossad can infiltrate here.' He looked at his father. 'You have not lived this long to be killed by one man.'

Colonel Jomah drank whisky and water with his meal, the only one of the five to touch alcohol.

He swirled it around in his glass and remarked, 'There is a theory about Mossad. A theory that they never intended to assassinate any of the top Palestinian leaders.'

'It's a crazy theory,' Jihad said angrily. 'They are experts at assassination.'

'That's true,' the Colonel conceded. 'And they have killed many people. German scientists who worked for Nasser in Egypt, when they tried to develop missiles. French and Swiss scientists who worked with Saddam Hussein in Iraq on his nuclear programme. More recently, they killed a Canadian ballistics expert in Brussels. He had convinced Saddam Hussein that he could build him an artillery piece powerful enough to drop chemical shells on any part of Israel. But Mossad has never in the past fifteen years assassinated a Palestinian leader.'

They all thought about that and then Khaled asked, 'Why not?'

The Colonel spread his hands and said, 'The theory is that terrorist activity against innocent third parties creates sympathy for their cause in the West. In essence, they believe that people like your father and Abu Nidal work in a strange way towards the interests of Israel.'

Jibril said, 'Really, Colonel, what you are saying is that our security has never been truly tested.'

'Exactly,' Jomah answered.

Michael looked up at the towering, snow-covered peaks of the Alps. It was the first time he had ever seen snow. Several minutes had passed, then he refocused his attention.

'The nest. Is it in a building?'

'On top,' Creasy answered.

'Then we will be exposed.'

'Only briefly. The point is that within a radius of three hundred metres of Martyrs' Square every building will be totally secured. Every roof-top will have its quota of troops and police.'

The steward brought dessert of profiteroles and fresh cream. Michael tucked in heartily, then remarked, 'So, that's why we have to make the hit from five hundred metres . . . outside the security perimeter?'

'Exactly.'

Khaled had taken out a notebook and pen.

'I will need to know your movements over the coming days,' he said to his father and made his first note, saying, 'Tomorrow you go to the camp at what time?'

'What time do the fighters leave?' Jibril asked Jihad.

'An hour after sunset,' his son replied.

'Then I will arrive at the camp an hour before sunset,' Jibril stated.

Khaled made a note and then looked up again. Jibril waved a

hand at him and said testily, 'I will give you details of my further movements tomorrow.'

Dalkamouni entered the conversation.

'You will attend the ceremony for the State of Palestine next Friday?'

'Of course,' Jibril answered. 'It could not be otherwise.'

Creasy and Michael were back in their sleeping compartment in the Pullman carriage. Michael was in the top bunk. He found it difficult to sleep.

'Are you awake?' he called softly.

Creasy's voice floated up from the bottom bunk.

'Yes. What's the matter?'

'I just can't sleep.'

'You'll get used to it,' Creasy answered. 'As for me, I sleep better on a train than anywhere else.'

They swayed along in silence, then Michael said, 'I guess you've worked out a way to get onto the roof of the building?'

'Of course.'

'And how to get off it? . . . after the hit?'

'One side of the building backs onto a narrow alley. It's not used much. We take ropes with us and after we make the hit we rappel down . . . George Zammit told me you do it well.'

Creasy heard Michael's soft laugh. The young man said, 'There's going to be a zillion security men around. How do we get into Damascus in the first place?'

'I go in by sea. From Cyprus to Lattakia. You go in on a guided package tour from Turkey. You're a student of archaeology. Syria is an archaeologists' paradise. Your tour ends up in Damascus, then you'll leave it and meet me in the hole.'

Another silence, then Michael asked, 'What are we going to be doing in Paris?'

'Meeting up with Corkscrew Two. He'll give us an update on Damascus, passports and papers and some bullets.'

'Bullets?'

'Yes. Very special bullets. Now go to sleep.'

SEVENTY

THEY WERE SITTING in the lounge of a suite in the Hotel Meurice in Paris. Corkscrew Two had given them their passports, tickets and a typed itinerary for both of them. He had also handed Creasy a small wooden box measuring three inches by three. Creasy had opened it. Nestling in the box were four silver-tipped bullets, each with a cross carved into the tip.

As Creasy studied them, Corkscrew Two had said, 'They are more potent the sooner they are used.'

Michael had looked on puzzled.

'What are they?' he had asked.

'They are bullets,' Creasy answered succinctly. 'Special bullets for Jibril. I will explain later.'

'How sure are you about the distance?' Michael asked Creasy.

'It's approximate,' Creasy answered. 'But beforehand I'll pace it out. Also the downside angle. Then we'll calibrate the sights on the rifles.'

Michael turned to look at Creasy and said with a grin, '*Dunga Justo Basne.*'

Creasy grinned back but he was disconcerted. During the discussion Michael had very much asserted himself. He was no longer a junior lieutenant but very much a partner. It continued so.

'Will we have a wind gauge up there?' Michael asked.

Corkscrew Two nodded.

'Yes. A Jasker Three. Extremely accurate.'

272

Michael's head was lowered in thought, his mind encompassing the words of Rambahadur Rai. Finally, he looked up at Creasy and asked, 'The idea is to use silencers?'

'That's the optimum situation,' Creasy answered gruffly.

Michael thought some more and stated, 'If there's a crosswind factor of more than five knots, the silencers have to come off. At five hundred metres the drift will be too much with silencers. The suppression factor is too great.'

Creasy glanced at Corkscrew Two who smiled again and remarked, 'He seems to know it all.'

Creasy smiled back and said, 'He's a smart-ass young prick, but in this case he's right.'

Corkscrew left at eight in the evening with the two laconic words, 'Good luck.'

Michael was to catch a flight to Ankara at midnight.

Creasy took him to the airport and they had a final dinner at the Maxim's branch looking out over the runway and the taxiing aircraft. It was a mostly silent meal, both men lost in their thoughts. They had a dozen oysters each, followed by noisette of lamb. Creasy ordered a bottle of La Croix Pomerol '61. As the sommelier decanted and poured the wine, Creasy said to Michael, 'This wine is a gift from a man called Jim Grainger.'

Michael looked up with a query in his eyes.

'He's a friend,' Creasy explained. 'A very good friend. A very powerful man in America.'

'Why would he buy us such a wine?' Michael asked.

'His wife was on Pan Am 103,' Creasy answered. 'He knows what we are doing. He has supported us all the way through. When it's over, you will meet him.' For a reason he could not understand, Creasy added, 'His wife's name was Harriot. They had no children.'

Creasy did not accompany Michael to the departure lounge. They said goodbye outside the entrance of the restaurant. They hugged each other and then Creasy laid his right hand against Michael's left cheek, kissed him hard on the corner of his mouth and walked away.

SEVENTY-ONE

MICHAEL WOKE EARLY after a restful sleep, despite the humidity and constant buzzing of mosquitoes in the room. He dressed and fixed the linen scarf, essential in the heat, around his head.

The previous afternoon the tour bus had crossed the Turkish border into Syria and arrived a couple of dusty hours later at the Baron Hotel on the outskirts of Aleppo.

The group of young archaeology students from the Sorbonne and various universities around Paris congregated in the foyer of the hotel, and once more Michael caught the gaze of the young French girl on the tour. He had noticed her immediately they had left Paris and determined to get to know her before the end of the tour.

While their Syrian tour guide ran through the itinerary, Michael reflected on his mission. These next few days would be his last to relax and enjoy himself as the possibility of death loomed closer.

The guide issued maps of the city on the bus, as they drove through the tree-lined streets, past the parks and high-class restaurants. They alighted at the Citadel and arranged to meet back in the early afternoon to continue their tour. Until then, they could sightsee at their leisure.

Michael grabbed his chance as the auburn-haired French girl turned to leave the group.

'You know it's not wise for a pretty European girl to walk unaccompanied through these streets.'

She seemed taken aback but Michael knew she was pleased he had approached her. Within minutes they were chatting.

Her name was Natalie.

They wandered off, already at ease in each other's company.

The stalls of the vast covered market were adorned with everything imaginable from food to perfumes and gold and silver jewellery. The aroma of cardamom and cloves swirled around from various spice stalls and pistachio shells crunched under their feet as they walked. The cries of hawkers and barrow pushers filled the morning air.

Michael watched bemused as Natalie swept from one stall to another with perfect grace, her white linen, sleeveless dress flowing behind her. Her laughter echoed around the souk as she admired the beautiful jewellery and colourful silks and cottons. He was drawn in by her flamboyance and his laughter echoed with hers long into the afternoon.

The following day they journeyed to the Crac des Chevaliers, via the coast of Lattakia, through the orchards and high cypress hedges. The eight-hundred-year-old castle of the knights was one of Syria's prime attractions and Michael relished the fact that he knew more about it than their guide.

'You make it so much more interesting, Michael. I'm starting to enjoy this sightseeing,' Natalie remarked.

Three airforce jets zoomed low overhead. A reminder that Lebanon was only a few kilometres away. They walked, hand in hand, to the upper floor of the castle to the Tower of the Daughter of the King, from where they could see the snow-capped peak of Kornet as Saouda in the Lebanon to the south and the valley of Nahr al-Kabir to the east.

Michael was so preoccupied that the impending operation faded temporarily to the back of his mind. All too soon, they were on the bus on their way back to Damascus.

As he lay in his hotel room that night, contemplating the day's events, he hardly heard the door open and close. He saw Natalie coming towards him, two beers in her hand.

'I'm exhausted from all the walking today and since you said you weren't going out, I brought you some refreshment.'

She moved forward and sat on the bed.

Suddenly, Michael was on his guard. He sat up, his mind racing with suspicion. For the first time he felt himself turning away from an almost certain romantic involvement. He was attracted to the girl but could only imagine that she was an agent and might know of his plan. His mind turned to Creasy and the anger and hate and reasons that spurred him on his way. He thought of Leonie and of the last supper they had had at Sammy's. She was the only woman who had ever loved him like a mother and treated him like her own son. Jibril had shattered his dream and now Michael would shatter his life.

He looked at Natalie. No emotion showed in his face or in his eyes.

'You can't stay,' he said coldly. 'My tour has come to an end and you won't see me again. Believe me, I've had a good time but don't ask me any questions.'

He stood, walked to the door and gestured for her to leave.

Her expression turned from puzzlement to anger.

'You're probably gay,' she snarled and stalked out.

SEVENTY-TWO

THE FERRY FROM Cyprus docked in Lattakia in the early afternoon. The Syrian Immigration and Customs officials came aboard with the usual bureaucracy; it was two hours before Creasy carried his canvas bag down the gangway. He had enjoyed his overnight journey. The food had been passable and there had been a small casino on board, run by some young Londoners. Over a couple of hours, he had won three hundred pounds. Before joining the ship, he had disguised himself by dyeing his hair black and adding a moustache.

He took a taxi to the souk and then walked three hundred metres to the hole. It was a one-bedroomed apartment on the third floor of a modern five-storey building. In the small kitchen he opened the cupboard doors above the sink and lifted out tins of food. Then he pulled open the wooden partition at the back of the cupboard. In a recess behind was the machinery. He took the weapons out and checked them carefully, then put them back and replaced the tins of food.

Half an hour later, he was boarding an air-conditioned Karnak bus to Damascus. He arrived just after ten o'clock and before going to the hole, recced the building on El Malek. He stood on the curve of the avenue about two hundred metres from where it joined Souq Saroujah Street. It was a dilapidated ten-storey office building with a large restaurant on the ground floor, which had tables on the pavement. He sat at an empty table and ordered a coffee. He estimated the height of the building. Later he would buy the rope they would use to abseil down it. The restaurant and the street outside were still busy. Pedestrians were interspersed with men in uniform, soldiers and police. Across the street was a row of smart shops selling everything from appliances to clothes. Traffic on the street was heavy.

He finished his coffee and walked the few hundred metres to the hole near the souk.

It was also a one-bedroomed apartment, on the second floor of an old building. First he pulled aside a chest of drawers in the bedroom and checked the machinery in the recess behind.

Satisfied, he went into the kitchen, opened a can of Irish stew, heated it in a saucepan and ate, while his mind ranged over the coming days. If everything had gone to plan, Michael would be ringing the doorbell at nine o'clock the next morning.

SEVENTY-THREE

MICHAEL WAS FIVE minutes late. As instructed he brought eggs, bread and milk, a fresh chicken, potatoes, carrots, half a kilo of sirloin steak and a cabbage. He also had two bottles of Lebanese claret, which were not included in his instructions. Creasy did not complain. After dumping the supplies on the table, the two men embraced, then they put away the food, took out all the machinery and double-checked it. Michael handled the sniper rifle as though it were a woman, holding it and caressing it, snuggling the butt against his shoulder, laying his cheek against the black stock.

Creasy watched him and murmured, 'It's a big distance.'

Slowly, Michael lowered the weapon onto the bed, smiled grimly and said, 'I won't miss . . . believe me, Creasy. I won't miss.'

For lunch, they roasted the chicken and opened one of the bottles of wine.

During the meal, Creasy questioned the young man about his trip. About the other people who were on it. Michael explained about the French girl and how he had turned her out of his room the night before.

Creasy was pleased and it showed in his face. He raised his glass and said, 'Let's leave all that until it's over. If we get out of this country alive, we'll go to Cyprus and have a holiday.'

'How do you rate the chances?' Michael asked soberly.

'Fifty-fifty,' Creasy answered flatly. 'I call those good odds.'

After lunch, they left the apartment separately and went their

278

different ways, Creasy to Martyrs' Square and Michael to take a look at the building on El Malek.

At Martyrs' Square Creasy watched, as workers erected the dais where the review would take place. He stood in line with it and the building on the corner of El Malek. He could see the corner of the roof. It looked a very long way away. Using his forefinger, he roughly calculated the angle from the top of the building to the dais. He estimated between twenty and twenty-five degrees. It would be important when they calibrated the rifle sights.

At that moment, Michael was in the restaurant on the ground floor of the building. He finished his coffee and walked casually into the foyer of the building itself. There was an old wooden desk near the entrance, with an old door-keeper sitting behind it. Corkscrew Two had told them that the door-keeper would leave at six p.m. The front doors would not be locked as it was pointless because there was an entrance to the foyer from the restaurant itself. Opposite the door was a lift and to the right-hand side a stairway. At the top of the building, there was a door to the roof, also unlocked. Michael left the building and walked down the avenue to Martyrs' Square. Creasy had already left to pace out the distance from the dais to the hole. It came to about five hundred and twenty metres. Michael lined himself up between the dais and El Malek. He also surveyed the distance and decided that it was a long way. He retraced his steps down El Malek to the building and then, as instructed, paced out the distance from the building to the hole. He also timed himself. It was just over five hundred metres and at a brisk walk took him six minutes.

Creasy was already back at the apartment. They spent the rest of the afternoon going over the procedures, codewords and contingencies.

That night, Michael cooked dinner, steaks, rice and vegetables. It had taken a long time, but Leonie had finally convinced the young man not to eat over-cooked meat. At the orphanage, everything had been over-cooked and he was used to it that way. Now he cooked the steaks medium-rare and thought about her

279

as he did so. The meal would be their last solid food for the next forty-eight hours. They ate in silence. Michael was hungry, relaxed and confident. Creasy was in a strange mood. The young man kept glancing up at him, wondering at the mood.

Only Guido would have understood Creasy's mood at that moment. It was always the same before he went into combat; always very quiet, thoughtful and introspective. Going back over the past. Thinking about the times of danger. Thinking of the dead . . . the many dead. At this moment he was thinking of Michael, trying not to see him as one of the dead. He knew that the chances of killing Jibril were good, but that the chances of getting away alive themselves were slim. At that moment he also knew that although what he had created was a killing machine, that machine had become part of himself. Nadia was dead, Julia was dead, Leonie was dead. He would do everything in his power to make sure that Michael did not die. He thought briefly about leaving Michael in the hole while he went to do the job himself but he quickly discarded the idea. Michael was right: there was no monopoly on vengeance. And Rambahadur Rai was right: Michael was the better sniper. But if he had to, he would give his life to save his creation.

SEVENTY-FOUR

THEY SPENT ALL the next day in the apartment, eating nothing and drinking only water very sparingly. At seven in the evening they packed the long canvas bag. Everything was first laid out on the beds and checked. The two sniper rifles, with the telescopic sights and silencers, the Jasker wind gauge, the forty-metre lengths of rope, the plastic bottles of water with glucose, the bottle of Dexedrine pills which would keep them awake. The bottle of Pyron which they would take before making the 'hit'. Pills which would calm their nerves and keep their hands steady. The pills that the world's top snooker players and marksmen are not allowed to take but sometimes do. Several black rubber wedges of different sizes. Two thick woollen blankets, a pair of small but powerful binoculars. Two black woollen sweaters, two pairs of fine black cotton gloves, two small torches, eight spare batteries, the twelve-foot-square camouflaged canvas and finally the small wooden box containing the four special bullets. They would be wearing ankle-length Arab robes, under which would be concealed the hand-guns and the coils of rope around their waists. Their only way off the building.

They left separately, shortly after ten o'clock. Creasy went first. Before opening the door, he embraced the younger man and said, 'Whatever happens, Michael, you are truly my son and always will be.'

'And you are my father,' Michael replied against the big man's shoulder.

SEVENTY-FIVE

IT WAS A clear night. Creasy sat drinking coffee in the restaurant on the ground floor of the building. He was close to the door.

Across the street, he glimpsed Michael through the traffic, sitting at a table outside a small café. The canvas bag was at his feet. The restaurant was busy, some of the customers in traditional Arab dress and some in smart business suits. An open truck full of troops passed in front of Creasy. Across the street, a policeman strolled lazily along, a holstered hand-gun on his right hip. Creasy was watching the main entrance of the building. During the next half hour, several people came out. He ordered another coffee and sipped it slowly. For the next fifteen minutes nobody came out of the doorway. Finally, Creasy lifted his left hand and brushed his hair several times. He saw Michael stand and pick up the bag. The young man crossed the road, weaving in and out of the traffic. Without glancing at Creasy, he moved straight through the side entrance of the restaurant.

Five minutes later Creasy climbed the ten floors of the building quietly on rubber-soled shoes. Michael was waiting at the top, next to the door to the roof. The canvas bag was at his feet. A Colt 1911 with silencer was in his right hand. Creasy pulled up his robe and took out his own Colt 1911. He nodded to Michael who reached forward, turned the handle and pushed open the door. Creasy went through in a crouch, the gun held in front of him. Staying in a crouch, he quickly surveyed the roof. To his left was the concrete room housing the lift machinery, and next to that a large round water tank. He glanced quickly around over the roof top. There were no other buildings nearby that were taller. They were not overlooked for at least three hundred metres. He gestured behind him. Michael came to the door also in a crouch, carrying the bag. He closed the door behind him, immediately unzipped the bag and took out the black rubber wedges. The third one fitted. With the heel of his hand he hammered it under the door. It took them three minutes to prepare. First they laid down the black blankets side by side at the edge of the roof, then they unpacked the sniper rifles and the rest of the equipment. They took off their outer robes and unclipped the hand-guns, laying them next to the sniper rifles on the blankets. They uncoiled the ropes from their waists, moved to the back of the building and peered down at the dark alley. There was a thick water pipe at the base of the short wall. They quietly tied one end of the rope to the pipe and carefully coiled up the remainder. Then they moved back to their firing position.

They lay on their stomachs on the blankets and pulled the camouflaged canvas over them. It exactly matched the sand-coloured surface of the roof. Creasy took off his Rolex Oyster and put it in front of his face. It showed ten fifty-five. He picked up his rifle, pulled the canvas back slightly and sighted down the avenue. Through the scope, he could clearly see the reviewing dais. In approximately forty hours, Ahmed Jibril would be standing there.

'Take a quick look,' he whispered to Michael. 'Then we go *Dunga Justo Basne.'*

SEVENTY-SIX

AHMED JIBRIL HAD a penchant for rather flashy Western clothes: Italian suits and brightly coloured sports jackets. But for this occasion he dressed in faded combat uniform. The same clothes that he had worn when he was a young fighter.

He left his headquarters in a jeep, sitting in the back seat with his son Khaled, and a heavily armed fighter next to the driver. His jeep was sandwiched by two others, both full of bodyguards. The streets were lined with soldiers and police and as they neared Martyrs' Square he could see sharp-shooters on the roof of almost every building.

At the square, he was greeted by Colonel Jomah. The two men saluted each other and then embraced, kissing each other on both cheeks. They climbed the steps of the dais, followed by Khaled. There were a dozen men already there, all wearing uniforms and all from various factions of the Palestinian resistance. They all greeted Ahmed Jibril with warmth and respect. Only three days earlier, four fighters from the PFLP–GC had penetrated the Israeli border and killed three Israeli settlers before being killed themselves by Israeli security forces. They made space in the centre of the dais for Jibril, Khaled and Colonel Jomah.

About five hundred and twenty metres away, Creasy's hand moved out from under the camouflaged canvas, holding the Jasker wind gauge. It was three thimble-sized cups on a spindle and a needle gauge. The needle registered nine knots. He pulled the gauge back under the canvas and both he and Michael unscrewed the silencers from the sniper rifles. Both men were stiff from the hours of stillness. Several times during the day helicopters had passed overhead. Especially during the last two hours. On the first day, both men had urinated in their trousers. On the second afternoon, Creasy had gone through the agony of cramp in his leg three times.

'Let's take a look,' he whispered.

The barrels of the rifles edged out from the bottom of the canvas, followed by the scopes. They surveyed the scene on Martyrs' Square. After a few seconds, Creasy whispered, 'He's in the centre. Do you see him?'

'Yes. I have his head in my cross sights.'

'OK,' Creasy said. 'Now we adjust sights, a nine-metre crosswind from the left. Five hundred and twenty metres with, say, a twenty-seven-degree depression . . . Give a fraction more on the depression . . . Better a bit low than over the top.'

They both turned the wheels on their sights, thinking through the calibrations. Creasy said, 'You shoot first, I'll follow right after.'

'Head or heart?' Michael whispered.

'Neither. The way he's positioned, go for his right shoulder . . . Just above his right nipple.'

Michael's head twisted to look at him in astonishment.

'Shoulder? I thought we came here to kill him!'

Creasy's voice came back very low and hard. 'His right shoulder. Do what I tell you.'

'Why?'

'Never mind why. I'll explain later . . . Take him in the right

284

shoulder. Wait until the review starts. He will salute his own unit. At that moment take him in the right shoulder . . . Just do it, Michael.'

The young man grunted and took aim.

SEVENTY-SEVEN

FIFTY YARDS IN FRONT of the dais the Syrian Airforce band played the Palestinian national anthem. Creasy and Michael pulled back their rifles as a helicopter clattered overhead. The barrels re-emerged as the noise receded. In Martyrs' Square columns of fighters began to march past the dais, holding their rifles aloft and shouting slogans.

As the column from the PFLP–GC approached, Ahmed Jibril pulled himself to his full height; pride swelled in his chest. On the roof, Michael reached forward and made a minute adjustment to his sight, and then lined the cross hairs onto Jibril's chest. The clattering sound of a helicopter approached.

'Do it!' Creasy hissed. 'Don't wait! Forget the chopper . . . The right shoulder.'

The helicopter was overhead, its blades thrashing the air.

'It's directly above,' Creasy said loudly over the noise. 'So the crew can't see us . . . The right shoulder.'

Very slowly Michael moved the cross hairs of his sight to Jibril's right shoulder. He took a very deep breath. He could feel the wind from the helicopter in his hair. His mind held nothing. The rifle was part of his body. An arm, a leg, a brain, or a heart.

The PFLP–GC contingent came abreast of the dais. Their eyes

were jubilant as they shouted their loyalty to their leader. He smiled with pride and his right arm lifted in a stiff salute.

Like a caress, Michael's finger stroked the trigger; half a second later, Creasy's finger did the same.

Michael's bullet found its target. Jibril spun sideways and backwards. Creasy's bullet plucked at his sleeve.

For three seconds they both watched through their scopes as pandemonium erupted on the dais. Then Creasy muttered an old Rhodesian hunting expression.

'Dead one. Let's go.'

They left everything in place and ran for the ropes. The helicopter clattered off urgently towards Martyrs' Square.

They came down the side of the wall, the ropes under their armpits, pushing off with their feet. Towards the bottom Michael made his first mistake, in his excitement he let himself go too fast. He hit the concrete lane hard, and only on his left leg. The ankle twisted under him.

Creasy landed easily on both feet. He heard the gasp of pain next to him. He ignored it, first reaching for his pistol and glancing down the alley towards the main road. The helicopter was back overhead. There was no one else in the alley.

He bent over Michael.

'Is it broken?'

'I don't think so . . . just sprained.'

'Can you walk?'

Michael pushed himself up and tested his foot.

'Yes, but slowly.'

Creasy took a decision.

'You go first. Stay on the main road moving towards the square . . . Follow the crowds out of curiosity, then break away down a side street to your left and make your way back to the hole. I'll follow about fifty metres behind . . . if you run into trouble turn back towards me.' His voice went low and hard. 'They won't take us alive. If it looks like that I'll shoot you . . . And then myself . . . Go.'

Without a word Michael hobbled down the alley.

He reached the main road as a column of police cars with

286

sirens and lights all alive swept past. Crowds of people were streaming towards Martyrs' Square. He mingled among them. Creasy followed, trying to keep him in sight. His pistol was tucked under his left armpit, enfolded in his robe, butt forward.

He saw Michael limp to his left towards a side street. Creasy pushed through the crowd and turned into the same street.

Michael was face to face with three paramilitary policemen. One of them was shouting at him. All three had pistols in their hands.

Creasy watched as Michael dropped to his right knee, pulling his gun from under his robes. He shot the man in front of him and then the one to his left. As they both jerked backwards onto the street the man on the right shot Michael.

As a woman screamed behind him Creasy pulled the gun from his armpit and put a bullet into the face of the man on the right.

Michael was lying on his side. He was moving, trying to push himself up. Across the street an old man was half-way out of the door of a green Fiat. Creasy ran across and held his gun at the man's head.

'The keys!' he hissed in Arabic. Terrified, the old man gestured at the dashboard. Creasy pulled him out of the car and snarled, 'Run, or you're dead.'

The old man scuttled away.

Creasy turned, Michael was on his feet. His left arm was clutching his right shoulder. One of the policemen was on his knees. Creasy shot him in the chest. He rolled back and lay still. Sirens were wailing like tom-cats. Michael was hobbling towards the car. Creasy opened the passenger door, then ran forward, literally picked him up and bundled him onto the seat. Five seconds later the Fiat was accelerating down the street.

'Where?' Creasy asked, narrowly avoiding an oncoming truck.

'My right shoulder . . . Or just under it.'

Creasy turned left, then right. He slowed down. It seemed that all the traffic was going in the opposite direction.

'It's very simple,' he said. 'I drop you about a hundred metres from the hole. You have to get yourself back there. I've got to dump this vehicle at least a mile away. It will be some time

287

before I get back, if at all. If you make it, keep a wad of cloth against the wound. If I don't make it in an hour . . . shoot yourself. It's better than a hell's death in a Syrian torture chamber.'

It was dark now. Creasy stopped the car on a corner. There were only a few pedestrians. The street lighting was dim. He pointed through the windscreen.

'Down there on the left.' He reached across and opened the door. 'Go for it,' he muttered.

With a grunt of pain, Michael lurched out of the car. Creasy pulled the door shut and accelerated away.

SEVENTY-EIGHT

IT TOOK CREASY forty-five minutes to get back to the hole. He let himself into the entrance of the building and noticed the dark stains of blood on the wooden floor, and on the steps. He pulled out a handkerchief and wiped them up as best he could.

There were more drops of blood inside the apartment, leading to the bedroom. The bedroom door was open. A weak voice called, 'Creasy?'

'Yeah, it's me.'

Creasy walked to the bedroom door and looked in. Michael was lying on the bed. His pistol was in his left hand. Slowly he lowered it to the bed, then moved the hand to the wadded-up towel on his right shoulder. Creasy could see the pain in his eyes. Harshly he asked, 'Did anyone see you come in?'

'I don't think so.'

'Wait.'

Creasy went into the kitchen. He filled a saucepan with water, lit the gas ring, then he opened a drawer and took out a pair of kitchen scissors.

Back in the bedroom he sat on the bed next to Michael and cut away the top of the robe and the inner shirt.

Carefully he examined the wound, which was small; blood seeped from it. It was just below the collar-bone. Creasy pressed his thumb against the bone. Michael drew in a sharp breath but made no other sound. Creasy grunted in thought and then said, 'I'm going to pull you up a little. It's gonna hurt.'

He put his left hand under Michael's neck and pulled him forward. Another hissing of breath. With his right hand Creasy probed beneath Michael's right shoulder-blade, then he muttered something to himself and eased the young man's head back onto the pillow.

'It's good and bad,' he said. 'The bullet didn't hit an artery and it didn't hit a main bone . . . But it didn't exit. It's lodged in the muscle of the shoulder . . . And it's got to come out . . . Let's see what we've got.'

He stood up and went back to the kitchen. The water in the saucepan was boiling. He left it there. From a cupboard he took out the medicine box, opened it and examined the contents. Then he opened a drawer and examined the various knives. He selected one with a point, felt the blade with his thumb, and grimaced. He dropped it into the saucepan of boiling water, then carried the medicine box into the bedroom.

Michael looked at him with pain and apprehension.

'It could be worse,' Creasy said, putting the box on the bed. 'We've got novocaine and morphine and God knows what else kind of drugs and dressings. But we ain't got no scalpel.'

'Which means?' Michael asked.

'Which means I've got to cut you open with a kitchen knife . . . The novocaine will help, but it's still going to hurt like hell.'

'Can't it wait until we get out of here?' Michael asked. 'Can't you bandage it up until we get to a doctor?'

Creasy sat on the bed and shook his head.

'We have to stay here at least a week until the dust settles . . . It can't wait that long. It has to come out.'

289

'Have you done this sort of thing before?'

'Sure, several times,' Creasy answered cheerfully. 'And I've watched good doctors do it. I had medic training in the Legion . . . It's not difficult but it's going to be painful . . . even with the novocaine.'

It was pure agony. Creasy administered novocaine and morphine injections and after waiting for them to take effect he used the kitchen knife to widen the wound, cutting horizontally to do minimal damage to the muscles. Michael lay there with part of the sheet rolled up and clenched between his teeth, his body jerking spasmodically as Creasy's fingers probed into his flesh, seeking the bullet. Blood covered the bed; and both of them.

After fifteen minutes Creasy found it. He held it between thumb and forefinger saying, 'Lucky it was only 7mm. Anything bigger and you'd have had no shoulder left.'

More pain when he stitched the wound and bound on a dressing. Then he fetched a bowl of warm water, washed Michael, lifted him to the adjacent bed, gave him another mild dose of morphine and sat beside him until he drifted into sleep.

He watched over him all night, wiping his face with a damp cloth and praying to a God he did not know and did not understand.

SEVENTY-NINE

THE QUESTION CAME two days later. Michael was sitting up in bed drinking a mug of vegetable soup.

'So I shot Jibril in the shoulder and then got shot in the same shoulder. What's the difference?'

'I'll tell you later. But there is a difference.'

'How long is later?'

'When we get the hell out of here.'

'Where are we going?'

'First Lattakia and then by ferry to Cyprus where a good doctor will check you out . . . Then to the States to see Jim Grainger . . . another friend to add to your fingers.'

EIGHTY

THE DOBERMANN lay at Creasy's feet, contentedly asleep in the warm sunshine. They were sitting by the pool, drinking mint juleps.

'A damn fine effort,' Grainger said. 'At least the bastard got the fright of his life. At least he knows he's not immune from threat.'

He was sitting opposite Creasy. Michael was sitting between them.

'It was more than a fine effort,' Creasy said, reaching down to scratch the Dobermann's ear. 'It succeeded one hundred per cent.'

The Senator looked puzzled.

'But I've seen the CIA report. Sure he was hit, but he's alive, even though he'll never use his right arm again.'

Creasy glanced at Michael whose own right arm was strapped tightly to his chest.

'It's not just Jibril's arm,' he said in a low voice. 'It's his brain.'

'His brain?'

Creasy leaned forward. 'His brain,' he repeated. 'It was no

ordinary bullet that Michael put into Jibril. I told you before that the bastard would not die easy.'

'What was it?' Grainger asked.

'First it was a dumdum,' Creasy answered. 'That means it explodes on impact, which is why his arm is ruined. Second, inside it was a poison with a name too complicated to remember. It's known by its initials TTK. Right now that poison is in Jibril's bloodstream.'

There was a silence while Creasy continued to scratch the Dobermann's ear. Then Grainger asked quietly, 'What does it do?'

'It's a bit like getting a very severe case of cerebral malaria,' Creasy answered. 'The blood carries it to the brain. It turns the victim into a vegetable. Later it causes death but that could be months or even years. But the brain damage is rapid. Within a couple of weeks from now Jibril will be incapable of planning any more terrorist attacks.'

A woman brought out a fresh jug of iced mint julep. She was short, blonde, plump and cheerful.

'That's the last one,' she admonished the Senator. 'And lunch will be on the table in half an hour.'

He smiled at her absently and as she walked away he asked Creasy, 'Does Jibril know?'

Michael answered.

'Yes, just in case his doctors missed it we sent him a post-card from Cyprus telling him to have a very thorough blood test.'

Grainger studied the young man's face. His gaze was steadily returned. Grainger turned his head to look at Creasy. He looked into his eyes. They held the same chill as that contained in the young man's eyes. He remembered Curtis Bennett's comment, made so many months ago.

'Death on a cold night.'

The Dobermann had rolled over onto her back. Creasy scratched her stomach.

He said, 'We signed the postcard: "Pan Am 103".'

Grainger looked silently across the pool.

Quietly Creasy asked, 'Does vengeance give you a conscience, Jim?'

The Senator shook his head.

'No. I was thinking of Harriot . . . Maybe it would have given her a conscience.'

He shrugged and shook his head again.

'No. He had it coming . . . So what are you guys gonna do now?'

'Head back to Europe,' Creasy answered. 'Michael's going straight home to Gozo. I have to stay on in England for a couple of days.'

'And then?'

Creasy thought for a moment and then answered, 'We've decided to kind of go into business.'

'Doing what?'

'Doing what we know best.'

A silence while the Senator studied them. Obviously they looked different but they had the same stillness. The same indefinable aura. The same unstated menace.

'You're going to be a mercenary again?' he asked Creasy.

'Not exactly. But if somebody needs something done, or put right, then we're available . . . for a fee.'

'A big fee, I guess.'

Creasy shrugged.

'It depends on who they are . . . And what their means are. We won't work for crooks; or governments.'

Grainger smiled. 'Much the same thing, I guess . . . Well, if I know anyone who needs a Panzer Division I'll tell them I can get one at cut price.'

They all laughed as the Senator poured more mint julep.

Then Creasy said, 'Jim, I have a favour to ask.'

'Ask.'

'In a couple of months I'd like to send Michael here to the States for some time – maybe months. Gozo's a small place and he needs to widen his mind – and learn how to behave socially.'

'I know how to behave,' Michael said indignantly.

Creasy turned to him.

293

'Do you know how to behave at a formal dinner for a hundred people? Which knife and fork to use? When to talk and when to be silent?'

Now Michael was silent. Grainger smiled.

'No problem,' he said. 'Michael can stay here with me. I'll take him under my wing. Introduce him around – both here and in Washington. He'll travel with me as a kind of aide. Even overseas. He'll meet important people. Go to good concerts and good theatre.'

'Girls?' Michael asked.

'Girls?'

'Yes . . . do I get to meet any girls?'

The Senator grinned.

'Sure. The day after you arrive I'll throw a party here in the house.' Wistfully he muttered, 'It's been a long time since this house saw a party.' His face brightened. 'I'll hire a jazz band . . . and don't worry, there'll be scores of our beautiful Colorado girls.' He turned to Creasy. 'I'll enjoy having him with me. What did you say here all those months ago? Grief is loneliness.'

Creasy nodded and then smiled. He said, 'Jim, after hearing about parties, jazz bands and scores of beautiful girls . . . I might leave Michael at home and come myself.'

He scratched the Dobermann again on her belly.

EPILOGUE

IT WAS THE lambing season. Foster Dodd lay asleep in the warmth of his bed, next to his wife. He was bone tired.

It was just before dawn when the sheep-dogs started barking outside. Foster Dodd woke up, as did his wife. He moved his cramped limbs and cursed softly.

'Don't worry,' his wife murmured sleepily. 'It's probably just a fox. The dogs will chase it away.'

The noise of the barking dogs was receding into the distance. The farmer rolled over, pounded his pillow and tried to go back to sleep. But sleep eluded him. It was always so during the lambing season. Finally he got up, pulled on his clothes and boots and went out.

The dogs had stopped barking but he walked across the fields in the direction from where he had last heard them. The sun was just rising red, over the low hill. There was a fine, white mist in the undulations and crevasses. Several sheep were already grazing on the dew-covered grass, lambs nudging up under their mothers' bellies seeking milk. His three dogs ran towards him, tails wagging. One of them, a wise old bitch called Lisa, stopped about fifty yards away, crouched and watched him. He recognised the posture and walked towards her. She turned and walked on and he followed.

They came to a clump of bushes and Lisa stood beside it. He walked up and peered over the nearest bushes and saw them.

A large bunch of white and red long-stemmed roses, lying on

the grass. He recognised the place. The flowers lay exactly where he had found the little girl in the bright red jumpsuit.

He looked around. There was no one in sight. Just the sheep and the lambs and his three dogs watching him.

He remembered the little girl and he remembered the man who had come and who had told him he was sorry about the sheep he had lost.